THE WAR
MOUNTAINS

THE WAR MOUNTAINS

John McKinna
writing as John Mannock

SPEAKING VOLUMES, LLC
NAPLES, FLORIDA
2019

The War Mountains

Thank you, Kurt Mueller and the whole Speaking Volumes staff for keeping John's books alive. We know he would be as pleased as we are with your representation of his work.
The McKinna family.

ISBN 978-1-64540-126-1

The War Mountains is dedicated to my father, A. J. McKinna, of Alida, Saskatchewan—professional baseball player, World War II combat flier, renowned neuro-ophthalmologist and surgeon, professor emeritus of medicine, Fellow of the Wilmer Institute at Johns Hopkins—who passed on suddenly in January of 2003. In addition to his many professional accomplishments, he was a beloved husband, father, brother, teacher, and friend.

I know you're not gone, Dad—just gone on ahead. Leading the way for the rest of us, as usual.

—J. M.

Author's Note

This novel is set aginst the backdrop of World War II and is based upon historical fact. Utmost care has been taken in executing the necessary research regarding the weapons, vehicles, and field equipment of sixty-plus years ago, but alas, nobody's perfect. Therefore, as usual, for any and all technical inaccuracies, intentional or otherwise, I claim Sanctuary in the Cathedral of Fiction.

—J. M.

Acknowledgments

Many thanks to my longstanding literary agent,
and one of the best in the business,
Jimmy Vines,

and

my excellent editor at NAL,
Mark Chait.

Also

special thanks to my father-in-law,
Master Sergeant Richard E. Durrance, USMC (ret.),
for editorial advice on military content.

And of course

all my love and gratitude to my wife,
Teresa, for whom all my books are written.

Part One

"The enemy of my enemy is my friend."

—Arab proverb

"What's past is prologue."

—William Shakespeare

Prescript

I put my youngest grandson on the bus this morning. He trembled slightly as he mounted the boarding steps and my hand slipped from his shoulder, but he was a brave boy and gave no other indication of his trepidation. At the tender age of eleven, who would not tremble at the prospect of embarking upon an unfamiliar journey? He smiled at me through the window as the bus pulled away, and to give him courage I smiled back.

I sit now beneath the awning of a streetside café, in the shade where the sun cannot leach away what little strength remains in my eighty-six-year-old body. It is burden enough to carry the permanent pain of old wounds. The coffee is good; hot, black, and sweet. Likewise the tobacco in my cigarette. It is Turkish and roughly cut. Out of long habit I have rolled the cigarette myself. The smoke is dark, heavy, and with each inhalation produces the customary pleasing ache deep in my chest.

The bus is long gone, and the street is full of people. People hurrying here and there to complete their business before the morning sun reaches its full, burning height. No one notices an old man sitting alone at a shaded table in a streetside café, sipping coffee and smoking.

Waiting.

Prologue

There had always been tales of unholy things that lurked in the dark alpine forests of central Yugoslavia. Tales of werewolves and trolls, of vampires and witches, of goblins and dwarves and strange forest people with eyes in their shoulders that let them peer at you sideways. Ancient things that were aligned with the old gods and the devil, and were kept at bay after nightfall by locked doors and well-stoked fireplaces and the power of the Eastern Orthodox priest in his church in the center of the village.

The girl was fifteen years old and long past believing in spooks and spirits and monsters, as did young children and many of the old people. The great forest of the Majevica Mountains had always been a place of solace and refuge to her, not a wilderness to be feared. Most country folk were superstitious and silly, she had long since decided, and she did not wish to be either of those things. When she was older, she would live in one of the grand cities like Belgrade or Bucharest, where people were educated and notions of fell creatures never entered their heads.

That was why she was so completely unprepared, as she carried a pail of milk from the barn to her grandfather's house one cold autumn afternoon, to see monsters burst from the forest edge, down the slope from the village, and begin to charge up the incline.

They were huge and black and hideous and they climbed the steep slope between the trees and the first houses with terrifying speed, churning up clods of dirt and shale and grass and snow. They roared and snarled as they came loping upward, belching black fumes. The girl screamed and dropped the milk and ran for the house.

The small band of Partisans—perhaps thirty—had been using the village as a temporary base for nearly a week; an out-of-the-way sanctuary from which to scout the common border areas between Serbia, Bosnia, and Croatia. Experienced guerillas, they were accustomed to having enemies all around. But this time, despite all their precautions, they were taken completely off guard.

The Partisan commander was the first man to throw open a window in one of the exposed houses and prop a captured machine gun up on its sill. His eyes grew wide as he focused on the two gigantic German tanks that were literally *speeding* up a forty-degree incline toward him, the long barrels of their main turret cannons bouncing like obscene antennae as they lunged over the rough terrain.

"Impossible," he whispered. Then, at the top of his voice: *"Fire, comrades, fire!"*

As if by way of contradiction, the cannon of the nearest tank belched smoke and flame. The huge shell crashed into the house occupied by the Partisan commander and exploded, obliterating the tiny dwelling and its occupants. In the house next door, huddled with her grandmother and grandfather, the girl who had dropped the milk pail screamed. The three Partisans firing submachine guns from the corner window pulled back with shouts of panic and scrambled toward the front door. At the opposite end of the room, the girl and her grandmother and grandfather held each other more tightly and prayed.

The massive black hull of the second Nazi tank smashed through the side of the house at high speed. There was an awful, shattering impact; a horrendous cacophony of bursting masonry, splintering timber, and roaring machinery; a blur of churning, crushing steel treads. And glaring out from the side of the tank's immense turret, the black war cross and diabolical death's-head emblem of the SS. The three Partisans shrieked as, just beyond the ruined house, the tank ran them down.

The two tanks thundered down the little village's single road, veering left and right in order to smash through house after house, firing their cannons and machine guns indiscriminately. The population of the village, terrorized, driven from their homes, fled before the tanks like sheep before wolves. Some dashed for the forest, but most followed the remaining Partisan soldiers to the village square and into the Eastern Orthodox church—a white-painted wooden structure with a single steeple—that stood at its center. The few who tried to flee through the square and down the westward road leading out the far side of the village encountered six German half-tracks loaded with SS troops. The troopers disembarked and began to advance in a tight skirmish line, firing relentlessly into frantic men, women, and children.

The giant tanks wheeled in tandem, crushing dead and half-dead bodies, and clanked to a halt side by side, facing the front door of the church. The SS troops continued their sweep through the village from its western end, killing every living thing in their path. Several dozen SS gathered behind the tanks, eyeing the church and waiting.

The fifteen-year-old milkmaid, whose name was Magda, had fled, at the urging of her grandmother and grandfather, down the same slope the tanks had ascended only minutes before. She reached the cover of the trees just as SS troops entered the ruined house where her grandmother and grandfather still crouched, holding each other. There was a long burst of machine-gun fire. Magda shrieked, pressing her hands to her ears, and half blinded by tears and terror, fled deeper into the gloom-filled alpine forest.

Three of the surviving Partisans were in the belfry of the steeple with sniper rifles. They knew they were about to die, had long expected to, and so were resigned rather than afraid. There was fear only where there was hope.

"Those are Tiger tanks of some kind," one of the Partisans muttered as he changed clips in his rifle. He gazed down into the square below. "How did they charge up the slope like that? Any other tank would have toppled over backward or skidded out."

"Yes, it would be nice to know exactly what new type of infernal German machine is killing us," one of his companions—an educated, acerbic type—said. He glanced down past the stock of his rifle, which was trained on the SS troops crouching behind the tanks. "Oh, perfect. Now here's the damned priest."

The doors of the church opened and the priest came out. He was gray haired, with a long beard, and wore a white cassock trimmed with gold. A short gold cape was draped over his shoulders, and he held a Bible clutched to his chest with one hand. The other hand he raised slowly, palm out, as he stared from beneath fierce, bushy eyebrows at the tanks and soldiers.

"This is a holy place!" he shouted in Serbo-Croatian. His voice was the deep, commanding instrument of an experienced orator. "A house of God. Those within its walls are granted sanctuary, protected by Almighty God!"

A tall SS officer in a peaked cap stepped out from behind one of the idling tanks, leveled a rifle borrowed from one of his men, and shot the priest through the chest. As the cleric pitched forward down the steps of his church, the officer returned the rifle and picked up an intercom phone handset from a metal box on the side of the tank.

"Destroy the church," he said into the mouthpiece. He hung the phone back on its cradle, closed the door of the box, and turned to face his men. "Kill everyone left alive once the tanks are done, and burn the wreckage. Remember: you are *Handschar* of the SS! These are Serbs—Christian infidels who have murdered your kinsmen by the thousands! Hiding with them are atheistic Communist Partisans who would kill you for believing in any god at all! Now is your chance to be rid of an entire nest of these murderous brigands for good!"

A ragged cheer went up from the SS troops; some brandished their weapons overhead. The officer grinned and turned back to the church.

"Good-bye, Herr Sturmbannfuehrer," the acerbic Partisan in the church steeple said, and squeezed the trigger. His rifle cracked.

The bullet hit the death's-head insignia on the front of the grinning Nazi major's peaked cap and blew off the back of his head in a red mist. In the same instant, the cannons of both Tiger tanks blasted point-blank at the church. The hulking war machines bucked on their chassis with the recoil. The church disintegrated in a whirl of shattered planking and timber. The steeple collapsed on itself in a cloud of smoke, dust, and flying detritus.

The tanks kept pouring cannon shells and machine-gun fire into the ruins of the church for a full five minutes. When they were done, the SS troops moved in and with torches and gasoline set fire to the heaps of wood, rubble, and bodies.

The afternoon wore on, and as evening drew near, two of the troopers wandered out to the half-demolished house where the milkmaid Magda and her grandmother and grandfather had lived. The brutal work of soldiering done for the day, the two SS men took a few minutes for personal concerns. Setting down their weapons and removing the field-gray fezzes they wore, both extracted small mats from their packs and unrolled them on patches of clean, dry ground.

Then, like the good Muslims they were, the two troopers of the SS Division Handschar knelt on their mats and began to pray toward the east.

Chapter One

"Permit me to quote from your letter of January 20, 1941," Adolph Hitler remarked, his dark gaze fixed on the face of the Muslim cleric occupying the fine leather armchair on the opposite side of his office desk. "Written a mere three years ago. Addressed to me personally."

Haj Amin al-Husseini, the exiled Grand Mufti of Jerusalem, recrossed his legs beneath his black robe and nodded pleasantly, meeting the Fuehrer's stare with the neutral calm of the seasoned politician. "Please," he said, motioning gracefully with his right hand.

On either side of him, seated in matching armchairs like the remaining two opposing points of a four-direction compass, SS chief Heinrich Himmler and Abwehr head Wilhelm Canaris stirred slightly. Rivals in the Nazi hierarchy, the two men detested each other. In the presence of the Fuehrer, neither showed it.

Hitler cleared his throat, held up a single page, and began to read:

" 'Your Excellence! England, that bitter and cunning enemy to the true freedom of the Arab nation, has never ceased to forge fetters in which to enslave and subjugate the Arab peoples—either in the name of a deceitful League of Nations or by the expression of perfidious and hypocritical humanitarian feelings, but with the actual aim of effecting her imperialist machinations, which are camouflaged by so-called principles of democracy and of deceitful internationalism.

" 'With regard to Palestine: His Excellence is well aware of the problem faced by this country, which has suffered greatly from the deceitful actions of the English. They have attempted to place an additional obstacle before the unity and independence of the Arab states by abandoning Palestine to world Jewry, this dangerous enemy whose secrèt weapons—finance, corruption, and intrigue—have traditionally been aligned with British bayonets. For twenty years, we have confronted these various forces face-to-face. Full of unvanquished faith, the Arabs of Palestine fought with the most elementary means. The Palestinian problem united all of the Arab states in a mutual hatred of the English and Jews. If mutual hatred is a prerequisite for national unity, it can be said that the problem of Palestine hastened this unity. From an international point of view the Jews owe allegiance to England in the hope that after her victory she will be disposed to help them realize their dreams in Palestine and in the neighboring Arab countries. Any aid to be extended by the Axis to the Arabs in their war against Zionist aspirations will, therefore, cause the Jews to lose heart. The Jews of America especially, seeing their dream of a Zionist homeland in Palestine shattered to pieces, will be so discouraged that they will cease to support Britain with such enthusiasm and will reconsider their position before the catastrophe.' "

Hitler paused to sip from a glass of water, eyeing the mufti as he did so, and continued:

" 'Your Excellence, the warm sympathy felt by the Arab peoples toward Nazi Germany and the Axis is an established fact. No propaganda can refute this truth. The Arab peoples are ready to serve our common enemies their just deserts, and to take their place enthusiastically alongside the Axis in order to fulfill their part in bringing about the well-deserved defeat of the Anglo-Jewish coalition.

" 'Your Excellence! Arab nationalism is greatly indebted to you for raising the Palestinian question in your impressive speeches on a number of occasions. I wish to reiterate my gratefulness to His Excellence and to assure him that the Arab peoples feel friendship, sympathy, and a great admiration for His Excellence, the great Fuehrer, and the courageous German people.

" 'I close with wishes for long life and happiness for His Excellence, and for a shining victory and prosperity for the great German people and for the Axis in the near future.' "[1]

Hitler laid the paper down on the desktop. "Most eloquent," he said, gazing at al-Husseini again. "Not to mention verbose. I take it you still stand by these lofty sentiments, Haj Amin."

The white-turbaned cleric responded with a placid nod. "Of course, Your Excellence. One does not abandon the righteous course simply because the path temporarily becomes rocky. Difficult or not, the road of virtue is still the correct road."

Odd, Canaris thought, that an Arab-Muslim leader from Palestine, born in Jerusalem, would have such a Caucasian—even Aryan—appearance. Haj Amin al-Husseini's eyes were a pale gray-green, his neatly trimmed beard reddish blond. His complexion was not particularly dark. His nose was large and straight, dominating his face, but his chin was weak, receding, and his mouth had no set to it—only a pulpy softness that suggested either intellectual smugness or a surfeit of inner tranquility.

Or maybe both. Canaris's shrewd eyes flickered over the mufti from head to toe once more. Haj Amin al-Husseini, although he was certainly no fool, had at least one tedious mannerism that seemed to be congenital in political leaders whose authority was religion based: when answering straightforward questions he tended toward the cryptic, decorating his replies with theological platitudes or mundane parables. Canaris had observed the same affectation in a rogues' gallery of popes, cardinals, archbishops, abbots, ministers, rabbis, imams, and other assorted denominational riffraff, and it bored him to no end. Not because he had anything against so-called spiritual leaders, particularly—they had their place in the food chain—but because on a personal level it smacked of one-upmanship; the spiking of a reply with a mini lecture that inferred the respondent had special access to higher knowledge.

"Indeed, my Fuehrer," Himmler contributed, "Haj Amin has been instrumental not just in the formation of the SS Division Handschar, but in numerous other mobilization projects involving Muslim peoples in the disputed territories of the Third Reich—"

"All of which have come to naught," Canaris cut in dryly. He waved a hand as the bald, pudgy Reichsfuehrer-SS turned to stare, buglike, at him through his pince-nez. Very few people dared interrupt Heinrich Himmler in the middle of a sentence. "The proposal that Arab-Muslim intelligence and army units under Haj Amin be created and deployed to help secure Italian and German conquests in North Africa—abandoned in early 1943. Attempts by Haj Amin to inspire the Muslim leaders of Tunisia, Morocco, and Libya to join the fight against the—what was the phrase? 'American-Jewish-English aggression'—completely without result."

"My Fuehrer," Himmler countered, displaying the

chilling absence of emotion that was his trademark, "no one could have foreseen that the Italians—with whom the mufti was working at the time—would give up the ghost so easily, first in Africa, and then in their own homeland.[2] Admiral Canaris is conveniently forgetting Haj Amin's many successful contributions to the sacred goals of the Third Reich. As I have just stated, he was responsible for inspiring numerous Bosnians, Croatians, and even Palestinians to join our exclusively Muslim SS Division Handschar—which even as we speak is achieving considerable success in Yugoslavia against the communist Tito's Partisan vermin."

Canaris rubbed his upper lip. The mufti was sitting with his eyes on the wall just above Hitler's head, the very picture of placid benevolence, listening to Himmler further laud his efforts on behalf of the Handschar division. Haj Amin looked very pleased with himself. But pudgy Heinrich the malignant superbureaucrat, the admiral knew, was in reality not singing the mufti's praises as much as his own. The all-Muslim SS Division Handschar—"Scimitar"—was a pet project of Himmler's, a logical extension of his bizarre racial theories and ongoing fascination with supposed historical Aryan connections to the Islamic peoples of Yugoslavia, Turkey, Persia, and Arabia.

In early 1941, with the state of Yugoslavia distintegrating into a snake pit of internecine rivalries even as the SS and Wehrmacht armored divisions of the Third Reich smashed southward to overrun the country, the Muslims of the newly repartitioned territories of Croatia, Serbia, Montenegro, and Bosnia and Herzegovina had found themselves subjected to genocidal attacks from militant Roman Catholic and Eastern Orthodox forces—their former Yugoslav countrymen exacting a blood toll for ancient ethnic and religious hatreds. Murdered by the thousands, Yugoslavia's Muslims had seen less of a threat in the invading Germans than in their own erstwhile fellow citizens.

Recognizing in their desperate situation an opportunity, Himmler had proposed the formation of the SS Division Handschar—conveniently loosening his rigid Teutonic racial qualifications for entry into the SS—and with the help of Haj Amin al-Husseini's recruitment efforts had filled its ranks with twenty thousand Muslim volunteers and willing conscripts, primarily from war-torn Bosnia. The premise was that after fighting under German command to destroy the threatening elements within the former Yugoslavia—Serbian patriots, Croatian rebels, and Tito's Partisans, among others—the Muslims would be permitted to live in safety and stability in their own state within the Greater German Reich. As a side benefit, the complete elimination of Yugoslavia's Jews, whom no one—Serb, Croat, Catholic, Byzantine, Muslim, or modern atheist—wanted anything to do with, could be accomplished.

Canaris's subtle gaze drifted to Hitler. The great Fuehrer, savior of Germany, was not looking well these days. After the debacle of Operation Barbarossa—the failed invasion of Russia—the Nazi regime's string of exhilarating conquests had turned into a series of costly defeats, and the war situation at present was deteriorating on nearly every front. Hitler's face was deeply lined, troubled, and he had developed a nervous tic in the muscle of his right cheek. In earlier days, he had been engaging, spontaneous, positive. Now he was paranoid and borderline delusional, given to fits of rage and bouts of black depression. And yet he still held power, still operated with a megalomaniacal cunning and personal omniscience that kept his best generals, despite their better judgment, subservient to his will. An amateur tactician at best, Hitler's impractical strategies routinely took precedence over the carefully considered plans of the most competent military professionals in the Third Reich. It was an unworkable situation that would lead Germany to disaster. *God help us,* Canaris thought, *if our sins are not so great already that whatever god may be listening has decided to wash his hands of us altogether.*

Himmler was still talking. "Just recently, my Fuehrer, Haj Amin played a key role in preventing the emigration—by that I mean *escape*—to Palestine of over four thousand dangerous Bulgarian Jews. He did so by counseling our good soldier Eichmann, in charge of their disposition, to ship them to concentration camps instead. In so doing, he provided direct support for our goal of a Final Solution to the Jewish problem in Europe."

That was more than Canaris could bear. "The dangerous Bulgarian Jews you speak of," he stated coldly, "were four thousand children, most of them orphans, who were about to vacate Europe permanently by fleeing to Palestine via Turkey and Syria. It would have made good operational sense for Eichmann simply to let this particular crop of noncombatant Jews remove themselves from Reich-controlled territory— he is all but overwhelmed by the sheer enormity of the task of eliminating every Jew in Europe—but Haj Amin, who as we all know can be very convincing, had other priorities."

The Grand Mufti turned his head slowly to look at Canaris for the first time, then blinked and smiled. "SS Obersturmbannfuehrer Adolph Eichmann is a personal friend," he said mildly. "I am more than pleased to be able to offer him my humble advice on issues of mutual interest."

"The Jewish children and their adult handlers were about to cut and run," Canaris persisted. "Not having to transport them to the camps would have freed up several trains for more pressing military uses. But Haj Amin convinced Eichmann to keep the Jews in Europe, not simply let them remove themselves from the picture. Why? Because he is more concerned with keeping fleeing Jews out of Palestine, where they could one day outnumber the Arabs and compete for political dominance, than he is with truly aiding the Third Reich in its difficult task of cleansing Europe of its Jewish infestation. To the extent that he helps us, he does so out of self-interest."

Hitler actually smiled. "Self-interest is the engine that drives politics," he said, waving a dismissive hand. "I don't have to remind an intriguer as experienced as yourself, Admiral, of that fact."

The elegant Canaris came close to scowling. "It is also the engine that drives treachery, my Fuehrer. And there is a very fine line between the two."

You should know, Himmler thought in silent retort. *No one walks it more brazenly than you.* But the Reichsfuehrer-SS said nothing and kept his expression impassive. As wily as Canaris—the aging master spy and head of Abwehr, or German military intelligence[3]— was, he seemed unconscious of the fact he was fast losing favor with Hitler, a consequence of both his own questionable intrigues and the Fuehrer's increasing suspicion of those who did not treat him with absolute deference. The halcyon days when the white-haired fox of the Abwehr could spar with the Fuehrer in conference were long gone. Now the admiral's familiarity and directness of speech were driving a wedge between him and his supreme leader, and he could not see it. All he, Himmler, head of the Black Order of the SS, had to do was stand quietly by, the embodiment of Nazi loyalty, and let Canaris dig his own grave, word by word. His inevitable downfall would leave the Abwehr rudderless, and the SD and Gestapo—the intelligence and security entities of the SS—perfectly positioned to fill the power vaccuum.

"You seem inordinately concerned with the fate of a few thousand Jews," Himmler observed, his steel-blue eyes narrowing behind his pince-nez.

"I am concerned when vital military assets such as trains are not utilized to optimum advantage!" Canaris retorted, letting an edge creep into his measured tones. He glanced at the mufti. "I am concerned when a 'friend' of the Reich, who draws substantial pay from both the German Foreign Office and the SS, *and* enjoys state-provided luxury accommodation and personal security here in Berlin, uses his influence to advance his own agenda to the detriment of his host nation."

Al-Husseini held up his hand again, patiently shaking his head. "I really must protest, Admiral Canaris."

"One would almost think you'd developed a soft spot for that particular swarm of Jewish brats," Himmler commented. "Good heavens, considering how many we've already managed to eliminate, why bother?"

Canaris's smile was steely. "I am far too old to let you put your words in my mouth, Herr Reichsfuehrer. And I stand by my analysis: these particular Jews should have been allowed to emigrate out of Europe, in order to reduce the load on our severely overtaxed supply lines and infrastructure."

Himmler snorted. "Preposterous."

Hitler's fist slammed into his desktop, bringing the exchange to an abrupt halt.

"Shall we dispense with this bickering?" he growled. His dark, sunken eyes shifted from man to man, finally coming to rest on the Grand Mufti. "Haj Amin: you are not here to answer to any charges. You are a representative of the Arab people as a whole, a valued ally, and an honored guest of the Third Reich."

Al-Husseini smiled and nodded, spreading his hands. "Thank you, Your Excellence."

"You will excuse the momentarily lively debate between Reichsfuehrer Himmler and Admiral Canaris," Hitler went on. "As heads of coexisting but separate intelligence organizations, they are understandably occasional competitors. A healthy thing—as long as both are striving for the same goal: the ultimate triumph of National Socialist Germany over its enemies." His gaze shifted and lingered on Canaris for a long moment.

"As an ally and admirer, I could not agree more, Your Excellence," Haj Amin responded. "I—"

"Good," Hitler continued, "because a problem has developed that you are in a unique position to remedy. In prior conference, Admiral Canaris has raised the issue of a decline in the morale of Reichsfuehrer Himmler's much-vaunted Handschar division. If you would elaborate, please, Admiral."

The white-haired Abwehr chief smoothly picked up the narrative. "Reliable intelligence coming to me from front-line Wehrmacht infantry and armored units in Yugoslavia, fighting alongside the SS Division Handschar, indicates a slow but steady stream of desertions by the Muslim rank and file. Some are joining Tito's Partisans—occasionally switching sides in the middle of a battle!—while others are simply forming independent bandit groups and making for the mountains of their Bosnian homeland. Apparently they have forgotten the oath of allegiance they swore to the Fuehrer and to Germany upon completion of their training."

Himmler shifted irritably in his chair. "It is essential to point out that overall the performance of the Muslim SS Division Handschar has been and continues to be outstanding. In less than a month, the division has driven the Partisans southward back across the Sava River and into the foothills of the Majevica Mountains."

"Nevertheless," Canaris continued, "the steady stream of desertions is indicative of serious internal problems within Handschar. A cancer of unreliability—"

"A slight morale issue," Himmler interrupted, "which can be addressed most effectively by—"

"Unreliability that cannot be considered acceptable in any German unit," the admiral reinterrupted, "much less a front-line combat division!"

"This is absolutely intolerable—" Himmler fumed, adjusting his pince-nez.

"*Verdammt,* enough!" Hitler's outburst was punctuated by a second crash of his fist on the desktop. There was a long pause, during which the Fuehrer drew breath and stretched his arms out at full length, palms down on the expanse of polished marble in front of him. When he spoke again, his voice had regained a measure of its familiar composure. "Come now, gentlemen, you must get along. I really cannot do without either of you." He turned to the mufti. "You can see, Haj Amin, the pressures that times such as these force upon even the oldest of colleagues. Reichsfuehrer Himmler is quite rightly protective of the reputation of his new SS Division Handschar, and is justified in his assertion that it deserves full credit for its recent— and ongoing—victories against the Partisans in Yugoslavia. Admiral Canaris, on the other hand, is quite rightly concerned with the problem of potentially traitorous or subversive elements that may linger within this otherwise effective combat division."

Hitler raised a conciliatory hand and gestured first at Himmler, then at Canaris. "Both the Reichsfuehrer and the admiral want the same thing, although they are pursuing it from different angles: the consolidation of morale within SS Division Handschar in order to guarantee the unit's continued effective deployment in Yugoslavia. This, my dear Haj Amin, is where you come in."

Al-Husseini smiled beneficently. "Of course I would be honored by the opportunity to assist the Reich in any way I can."

"Yes," Hitler said, "of course you would. Particularly since you were instrumental in organizing Handschar's internal officer corps of imams charged with the spiritual leadership of the Muslim rank and file. I need not remind you that an SS division which permits the incorporation of company-grade religious authority alongside its standard military command structure represents a considerable concession to our Muslim allies. A considerable sensitivity on the part of the Third Reich to the spiritual needs of the Muslim soldier."

Oh yes, Canaris thought fleetingly, *if there's one thing we're known for in the Third Reich, it's our sensitivity.* He shot a glance at Himmler. The Reichsfuehrer-SS was sitting in silence with his hands folded in his lap, regarding Hitler with the diffident attentiveness of a grade-school math teacher. It was truly remarkable, Canaris reflected for the thousandth time, that a man so plain, so banal in appearance, could be the repository of so much dark, sociopathic power. Heinrich Himmler would happily murder the world if in so doing he could realize his vision of absolute Aryan racial supremacy. A vision of blond Teutonic warriors and maidens frolicking in a Wagnerian paradise—a paradise free of squat, dark, inferior races such as Jews, Slavs, and Mongols.

And there he sat: squat, plump, balding, with a chin that receded even more than al-Husseini's. Like Hitler, the antithesis of the Aryan superman he so adored.

For a split second, Canaris was overwhelmed by desperation. Such moments of internal panic, unfortunately, were becoming increasingly frequent. *How did things come to this?* he anguished in silent turmoil. *Why did we who should have known better follow these malevolent fanatics so far down the road to ruin?*

Haj Amin al-Husseini spoke carefully, addressing Hitler: "The SS Division Handschar is indeed a magnificent testament to the Third Reich's willingness to partner itself with brethren races. The Muslims of Yugoslavia, in return, are at this very moment proving their fealty by shedding their blood under the banners of the swastika and death's-head. The soldiers of the Islamic world are honored by the opportunity to serve in the great Nazi war machine—a machine which will ultimately be victorious in the global conflict currently underway.

"Of course," the mufti went on, "it bears mentioning that the combat utilization of twenty thousand Muslims by the Waffen-SS in Yugoslavia *relieves*, to a not-inconsiderable degree, the military recruitment pressure on the German male population. The Third Reich can no longer fight a multifront war using only its purely Teutonic native sons; the manpower requirements are too great. In this regard, Germany truly needs the continued cooperation of the Muslim peoples, if it wants to keep its armies fighting at full strength."

Ah, Canaris thought, *there it is.* The thinly veiled threat. The allusion to withdrawal of support.

"With regard to the morale of the Muslim rank and file within Handschar: is it not true that the morale of soldiers is largely dependent upon the quality of their leadership? While the bulk of the division is made up of Muslims, including the imam officer corps, the ranking officers are all German. Is it not possible that a certain amount of miscommunication between German officers and their Muslim soldiers is responsible for the alienation of some individuals? After all, as we have found in the past, there are some barriers of language and culture that can be difficult to overcome completely." A faint smile developed on al-Husseini's thin lips. "Perhaps the entire division should be placed under the command of Muslim officers, to avoid . . . misunderstandings."

You went too far there, my friend, Canaris thought.

Hitler's face twisted into a dark scowl. "The SS Division Handschar," he stated, "will remain exclusively under the authority of German SS officers. This is the only way the Reich can maintain the integrity of its military command structure. The imams within Handschar are charged with the duty of maintaining the spiritual health and morale of the Muslim recruits. If there is a problem of communication between the German officers and their men, that is the responsibility of the imams. That is what they are there for." He paused and leveled on al-Husseini the penetrating stare that had transfixed millions the world over. "My conclusion is that the imams have lost focus, and are neglecting to minister adequately to the unique spiritual and motivational needs of the troops under their care. The German SS officers in command of Handschar are making sound operational decisions according to German military doctrine. The division is winning in Yugoslavia. Therefore, this hemorrhaging of personnel cannot be due to disenchantment with Handschar's leadership. Rather the imams—your imams, Haj Amin—have permitted the concentration of the men upon their sworn duty to fight for the Third Reich to wander. You must put this right." Hitler glanced at Himmler. "Herr Reichsfuehrer?"

Himmler looked down fussily at his hands, which he was twisting together in his lap. "It has been decided that you, Haj Amin, should undertake a tour of SS Division Handschar in the field in Yugoslavia, for the twin purposes of inspiring the rank and file and conducting a series of lectures directed at the imam corps."

"In these lectures," Hitler said, "you will use all of your spiritual and political authority, all of your famed powers of persuasion and inspiration, to revitalize the imams' approach to maintaining the combat morale of the Muslim troops—by which I mean a prompt and aggressive reaffirmation of these soldiers' sworn commitment to fight loyally for the Third Reich until its operational goals are achieved."

The Grand Mufti's placid smile was somewhat tighter. "In the field? Your Excellency, while I have every confidence in the combat capabilities of SS Division Handschar, I respectfully remind you that the situation in Yugoslavia is rather . . . fluid. The Partisans are guerillas, and guerilla warfare is by its very nature unconventional—not to mention unpredictable. No field position can be considered entirely secure. Were I to undertake a front-line tour, I would be placing myself at considerable risk. I am nearly fifty years of age, and while I served as an officer in the Turkish Ottoman Army during the Great War, my capacity for dodging bullets has long since deserted me." Al-Husseini licked his lips briefly. "Not that I am concerned for my own safety on a personal level," he continued, "but I must think of my position, my responsibilities as the premier international representative of the Arab-Muslim world. It is my duty to consider my own security—for who will speak for my people if something should happen to me?"

"I have a feeling someone would step up," Canaris commented, deadpan. "And as for dodging bullets during the last war, I doubt if you often found it necessary while serving as a supply officer with the Forty-seventh Turkish Brigade in the Black Sea area, stationed as you were many miles from the front."

Al-Husseini glanced at the head of Abwehr in barely concealed annoyance, at the same time chiding himself internally. It was dangerous to embellish the truth about one's personal history in the presence of Admiral Wilhelm Canaris. The wily old intelligence chief had files on everyone.

"Your security, of course, will be the responsibility of the SS," Himmler declared. "In addition to your own personal bodyguard, you will have a hand-picked escort drawn from the ranks of both the Waffen-SS and the Gestapo. True professionals, whom I myself will select."

"As to the risk involved," Hitler said, sitting back in his chair and folding his arms across his chest, "I remind you that you are under considerable risk right here in Berlin. The British Secret Service and the Jewish Agency in Cairo have each had several cracks at you during the past two years, and they are unlikely to stop trying. It is entirely due to the vigilance of the intelligence and security services of Third Reich that you have not been assassinated already." The Fuehrer paused. "Of course, we are only too glad to be able to extend such protection to our valued allies. . . . Those who continue to cooperate and work with us as we strive toward our ultimate victory."

Al-Husseini, Canaris noted, was not slow to take Hitler's unspoken meaning. But the Palestinian was reluctant to appear unsettled by the inference that his protection might be removed. Straightening in his armchair, he adopted an air of affronted dignity.

"Your Excellency," the mufti said, speaking with deliberate precision, "I reiterate: I must consider the risks involved in venturing into the contested regions of Yugoslavia, for my life is not my own but an instrument to be used—and preserved—for the benefit of my people. I am not at liberty to leave the Arab-Muslim world, at this pivotal point in history, suddenly bereft of its most capable advocate."

"That would be you," Canaris remarked.

Al-Husseini shifted in his seat. "Of course. It is a fact. And therefore, while I would be willing to evaluate the possibility of conducting a series of lectures for the imams of SS Division Handschar in some secure, occupied location such as Prague, for example, or Budapest, I must reject the notion of traveling into the front-line areas of Yugoslavia. Particularly since there *are* no front lines to speak of—only a generalized and continually shifting combat zone characterized by interminable hit-and-run engagements and the occasional large-scale battle."

The mufti folded his hands in his lap and looked at Hitler looking at him. The Fuehrer's eyes seemed to have sunk even farther into their dark sockets.

"Perhaps," Himmler said uneasily, "an accommodation could be reached. The Serbian city of Belgrade is currently under occupation, and is quite secure. It is much closer to Handschar's area of operations. It would be a simple matter to arrange for the division imams to rotate into Belgrade to meet with Haj Amin—"

"Belgrade is a suitable place from which to *start* a motivational tour," Hitler stated, "but all personnel of SS Division Handschar will remain on duty in the field. Their uninterrupted presence in the foothills and higher elevations of the Majevica Mountains, in pursuit of Tito and his Partisans, is absolutely critical to the success of our military initiative to secure Greater Yugoslavia, once and for all, for the Reich." He glowered at the mufti again, then glanced at a small wooden clock on the corner of his desk. "It is late, gentlemen. We will adjourn for the evening. Haj Amin: I am certain that, upon reflection, you will see the vital necessity of this proposed tour of SS Division Handschar. I am confident that you will reconsider your position."

"I do not think so, Your Excellence," al-Husseini replied. "As I have pointed out, my life does not belong to me but to—"

"Your people," Hitler finished. "Yes, I know." He rose to his feet behind his desk. "And as *I* have just pointed out, I am confident that over the next several days you will reflect and reconsider." The Fuehrer clasped his hands behind his back and gave both Himmler and Canaris a cursory nod. "Gentlemen."

He turned on his heel, and as he stalked across the room toward a side door, Himmler got hurriedly to his feet, came to attention, and snapped off a straight-arm Nazi salute. "Heil Hitler!"

Canaris, moving more slowly, merely stood up. He did not salute or speak. When the oaken door closed behind the exiting Fuehrer, he collected his briefcase, donned his old naval cap, and turned to al-Husseini, who was still sitting languidly in his armchair, swathed in his cleric's robes.

"Good evening," he said. He raised his eyes and caught Himmler glaring impotently at him. "Herr Reichsfuehrer."

Without waiting for or even expecting a reply, Admiral Wilhelm Canaris wheeled and departed Adolph Hitler's Reichs Chancellery office through its double main doors.

*   *   *

John McKinna

The old master spy walked briskly through the magnificent main gallery of the Chancellery building, his heels clicking on its polished marble flooring. Designed by Nazi architect Albert Speer, the long hall, like its parent edifice, was a study in strength and elegance—vaultlike spaciousness defined by marble, gilt, and stone. Berlin's high temple of National Socialism. For all Canaris noticed its splendor, he might have been walking through an abandoned coal mine.

As usual in the wake of an important meeting, his mind was awhirl with fresh data: new orders, technical details, personal impressions. And his razor-sharp intellect, out of lifelong habit, was automatically replaying, sorting, analyzing, and evaluating this new material. Storing it in a vast mental archive of potentially useful information—information that was his greatest weapon.

The trouble was, since about 1940—or quite possibly much earlier—Admiral Wilhelm Canaris's conflicts with his own conscience, starting with a deep-seated moral despair about his current position and that of the German nation as a whole, inevitably intruded upon the straightforward intellectual exercise of getting his facts organized. Simple facts no longer, they were nuggets of ever more discouraging information tainted by the dark phantoms of his own worsening depression. He was acutely aware of the problem but could do nothing about it. Objective analysis and subjective worry had become inseparable.

Himmler: a ghoul. A soulless *bourgeois* with a pathological need to elevate himself at any cost; to define for himself a place in history based upon race supremacy and murder. A *chicken farmer*, for the love of God. And one currently simmering with outrage at Canaris's meddling in the affairs of the SS Division Handschar, at his manuevering of Haj Amin al-Husseini into conflict with Hitler.

As usual, the Reichsfuehrer-SS, arguably the second most powerful man in Nazi Germany and a lethal adversary, would bear watching. Even the head of Ab-

28

wehr could not assume total immunity from Himmler's vindictive orchestrations. Fortunately—and despite his worry Canaris came close to smiling at the thought— he had a rather damning file on Pudgy Heinrich the Chicken Farmer. Just as he'd had on SS Obergruppen- fuehrer Reinhard Heydrich, the one-time SD intelli- gence chief, race supremacist, and murderer of Jews whose dirty little secret was that he himself had Jewish blood—not to mention homosexual predilections. That had been a useful file. But useful no longer, however. In May 1942, Heydrich had been assassinated near Prague by Czech resistance fighters.

Canaris paused beneath a huge red wall tapestry bearing the Nazi swastika, and lit a cigarette to calm his nerves. The habit provided little comfort these days, but it was better than nothing. Smoke drifted up through the still air of the great hall, lingering in front of the crooked cross. The admiral drew deeply, trying to relax even as his mind continued to work.

Haj Amin al-Husseini was a garden-variety political opportunist. While he enjoyed a certain undeniable stature in the Arab-Muslim world, his position as spokesman was by no means as official or exclusive as he liked to claim. Canaris had looked into it. The product of a well-positioned Palestinian family that could demonstrate verifiable blood ties to the Prophet Muhammed, al-Husseini had, through astute political handling by powerful Arab friends and relatives, been appointed Grand Mufti—or religious leader—of Jeru- salem in 1921 by the High Commissioner of British Palestine, at the tender age of twenty-six. Since that heady day nearly a quarter of a century ago, he had added many layers to his public persona: rabid Arab- Palestinian nationalist, equally rabid anti-Zionist and anti-Semite, fomenter of abortive revolts against Brit- ish rule in both Palestine and Iraq—for which the Brit- ish had summarily exiled him from his homeland—and now aider and abetter, for his own ulterior purposes, of the marauding Nazi regime. He was on record as saying that when the Germans finally reached the Middle East, they should allow the Arabs to "solve the Jewish problem in Palestine and the other Arab states in accordance with the interests of the Arabs, by the same methods which were used to solve this problem in the Axis countries."[4]

Canaris exhaled smoke, confident that he had re-called the quote exactly. This Amin al-Husseini, spiri-tual leader though he might be, was really nothing more than a classic, wandering agent provocateur—a political orphan combing the international landscape for allies. A manipulator in search of an advantage that would return him to power.

What made him so dangerous, and what had not been lost on Reichsfuehrer-SS Heinrich Himmler when he had first enlisted al-Husseini's help in form-ing the SS Division Handschar, was that the high-profile mufti was the most likely conduit through which the world's 350 million Muslims could be brought into the Nazi fold as cocombatants against the British, Americans, and other Allied nations. The success or failure of Handschar as a fighting unit was the test case by which the Islamic world would judge the expedience of throwing in its lot, militarily, with Nazi Germany. Not to mention the prudence of con-tinuing to follow the lead of Haj Amin al-Husseini.

A massive influx of Muslim manpower into the Wehrmacht and Waffen-SS would mean a perpetua-tion of the Nazi regime. An indefinite extension of the Nazi Party's stranglehold on political and military power in Germany and throughout Europe. And a prolonging of the most destructive war in history.

Canaris crushed the smoldering butt of the cigarette beneath his shoe and drew a long breath. God, the things he had to do, to say, in order to maintain his position within the glorious Third Reich—to keep the gangsters at bay and the wolves from his throat. Sprin-kle his conversation with appalling phrases like "Jew-ish infestation." Show no concern for untold masses of murdered men, women, and children—only for the logistical problems associated with their transport and handling. Take occasional food and drink with creatures like Heinrich Himmler, Joseph Goebbels, Martin Bormann, and that fat, discredited ass Hermann Göring without becoming nauseous and throwing up on the spot.

The worst of it was that he couldn't stay and he couldn't go. As head of Abwehr he was forced to issue atrocious, immoral orders on a regular basis—but at the same time he was in a position to frustrate some of the worst excesses of the Nazi regime. How many Jews had he saved from the concentration camps by sending them on supposed spying missions to Allied countries, knowing full well they would never return? He'd lost count. How much vital information had he disseminated to the Allies, taking on for himself—at dreadful risk—the role of double, triple, *quadruple* agent? Enough to fill a small library.

Canaris walked toward the main doors of the Reichs Chancellery, continuing to brood. As he approached, a black-uniformed SS trooper, resplendent in silver gorget, polished black helmet, and bright red swastika armband, gave the straight-arm salute and opened the door.

Absently the admiral flipped his hand up as he walked out into the light evening rain that was wetting down the cobblestones and pavement of the Willemstrasse. As the door closed behind him, he could not suppress a short, bitter laugh. How innately hypocritical, he mused, that out of reflex he would return the signature Nazi salute in kind. Despite his high position within Hitler's regime, he had never even joined the Nazi Party.

No, he could not stay and he could not go. The pressure of trying to dismantle the Nazi power base from within—before his beloved Germany was subjected to total ruin—was slowly killing him; he often felt less than one short breath away from a fatal heart

31

attack. But he could not simply abandon his powerful position and disappear. As cold and ruthless as he often had to be in order to fulfill his role as Germany's greatest spymaster, whoever came after him would certainly be a diehard Nazi—and a hundred times worse.

He put another cigarette between his lips and lit it, shielding the flame from the misty rain with cupped hands. *You are a walking contradiction, Canaris,* he told himself. *A damned enigma. And quite possibly damned to hell.*

But at least, he thought as he began to make his way along the Willemstrasse, *you're going to have plenty of company.*

Exactly one hour later, in a dilapidated apartment on one of central Berlin's seediest side streets, an old man with an unkempt mop of shaggy gray hair and an equally unkempt handlebar mustache sat hunched in a simple wooden chair, an ancient woolen overcoat pulled around him, listening intently to the muted sounds—broken phrases in English, French, and German—that seemed to be coming from a large radiator beneath the room's single window. Heavy blackout curtains covered the window's narrow panes of grimy glass, permitting not even the meager light from the lone candle perched on the sill to escape into the street. Britain's Royal Air Force had not yet turned its devastating night-bombing capability against Berlin—the high-flying Lancasters were concentrating on industrial centers like Hamburg and Dresden—but it would not be long now.

The old man leaned forward, his head almost on his knees, and reached in between the pipes of the radiator with two fingers, adjusting something. The droning, monotone sounds became imperceptibly louder. German technology had not yet come up with a way to jam the BBC's continuous flooding of the European airwaves with Allied radio programming—including the hourly recitation of encoded messages intended for the resistance fighters and special agents who were operating everywhere on the embattled continent.

"And now"—the dulcet tones of the British announcer seemed incongruous with the desperate wartime atmosphere into which they were being broadcast—"a message for our friends within Germany itself: *Mary had a little lamb, its fleece was white as snow. Mary had a little lamb, its fleece was white as snow.*"

Pause.

"Jack has a brand new car. Jack has a brand new car."

Pause.

"The black lyre plays a solo nocturne. The black lyre plays a solo nocturne."

The old man started violently, nearly losing his seat on the chair.

"Next messages to come in one hour. And now let's listen to the swinging sounds of Benny Goodman and his orchestra as they perform their marvelous number 'Stompin' at the Savoy'. . . ."

The old man reached between the pipes of the radiator and turned off the hidden radio. Then he heaved himself up out of the wooden chair, gathering his bulky, threadbare overcoat around him, and headed for the door of the apartment.

From the spacious rear seat of the Daimler touring car, Haj Amin al-Husseini took a moment to examine the partial reflection of the driver's face in the windshield rearview mirror. The helmeted SS trooper behind the wheel did not once look away from the road, though an increased stillness in his already rigid expression suggested that he was well aware of the mufti's perusal. The Daimler cruised around a sharp turn, rocking gently on its soft suspension, and the driver's youthful Teutonic features—immaculately pale and hard planed—disappeared from the mirror.

Al-Husseini looked briefly out through the rain-slicked bulletproof glass of the left rear side window, then glanced at the two Germans sitting opposite him in the luxury passenger compartment. His plainclothes Gestapo bodyguards—a young Hauptsturmfuehrer named Julius Neurath and a lesser rank identified only as Grohl—continued to study the upholstery of the car's floor and roof liner, respectively, looking humorless, professional, and bored.

Neurath was a stereotype: a slender, blond mixture of effeminacy, toughness, and arrogance that was the very definition of the Nazi *Übermensch*, or superman. Grohl, on the other hand, was a neckless, swarthy beast of a man who was wider across the shoulders than three Neuraths put together. The backs of his huge hands were covered in black hair, and his lower jaw was immense—a massive, squared-off mandible that made the rest of his features appear far too small for his face. Both Gestapo men wore suits, knee-length overcoats, and wide-brimmed fedoras, the hats soaked with rain and pulled low over the brow.

Al-Husseini shifted uncomfortably. You never knew with Europeans. He had seen many Englishmen and Jews who looked just like these two. Plants and traitors were everywhere—even, he did not doubt for a moment, within the ranks of the dreaded Gestapo. That was why he never traveled anywhere without being accompanied by Mustapha Snagi.

He looked sidelong at the fourth man in the passenger compartment, who was sitting next to him on the forward-facing bench seat. Mustapha Snagi appeared to be dozing, arms crossed and chin on his chest. Haj Amin al-Husseini knew otherwise.

His personal manservant and bodyguard never seemed to sleep at all—only slip into a kind of conscious trance that apparently sufficed to refresh and rejuvenate him. Snagi—a Macedonian Muslim with numerous relatives in Palestine—was al-Husseini's constant shadow, sworn to protect him with his life. Jowly and black bearded, of middle height and medium build, the twenty-five-year-old manservant was altogether unremarkable in appearance—an effect that was amplified by his ill-fitting gray suit and the water-stained brown rain cape that he wore around his shoulders like a large, dirty blanket. The grubby ensemble was topped off by a purple fez, tassel dangling, that was nestled on top of his generous head of dark curls.

Mustapha Snagi smacked his lips in his apparent doze, and al-Husseini saw Neurath's pale eyes shift onto the rival bodyguard in distaste. Grohl did likewise, looking like a bad-tempered ogre. The mufti smiled faintly. The two Gestapo men had little use for Snagi, who never spoke to them, and who exhibited behavior they did not understand—such as bedding down on the outer doorstep of any room in which his master happened to be quartered for the evening. It was quite clear that they regarded him as some kind of subhuman, dismissable curiosity—a misperception arising from the fact that they had never seen Mustapha Snagi in action.

The front and rear seats of the touring car were separated by a sliding glass partition, which was open. Neurath twisted his head sideways and spoke over his shoulder impatiently to the driver: "What's taking so long tonight, Beckmann? Road repair?"

The SS trooper's helmet bobbed in response. "*Jawohl*, Herr Hauptsturmfuehrer. Crews are out replacing damaged cobbles. Several of the streets along our usual route are blocked off. I've had to take two detours already."

Agitated, Neurath tapped nicotine-stained fingers on the sleeve of his coat. "How much farther to the hotel?" Al-Husseini did not permit smoking in the close confines of the Daimler, and it had been nearly half an hour since Neurath's last cigarette.

"If I can take the next left, only two more miles, Herr Hauptsturmfuehrer," Beckmann replied. "Perhaps five minutes."

"Hurry it up, man."

"*Jawohl,* Herr Hauptsturmfuehrer."

Mustapha Snagi raised his swarthy head and opened his eyes as the touring car swayed through a left-hand turn and accelerated. He and Grohl stared at each other across the passenger compartment for a long moment. Snagi finally terminated the pointless confrontation by setting his chin back on his chest and closing his eyes again.

The Daimler bounced elegantly over a set of streetcar rails and began a wide turn to the right. A large black edifice, seven stories tall, appeared in the rain-streaked windshield. The building's numerous windows emitted no light, but the main entrance was illuminated by the soft glow of two curbside pedestal lamps. A canopy-style awning extended from the entrance to the street, providing some rain protection for anyone arriving or departing by car.

"The Hotel Jürgenplatz, Herr Hauptsturmfuehrer," Beckmann said.

"About time," Neurath muttered. He sat up and began to peer intently out the windows of the Daimler, examining the darkened street. "All clear on your side, Grohl?"

The oversized Gestapo agent took a moment to answer. *"Ja,"* he grunted.

Neurath nodded. "All right, then." He leaned forward, opened the rear door, and stepped out onto the curb. Even as he reached for his cigarette case, his eyes were automatically scanning the immediate surroundings. In the arch of the hotel's main entrance, at the top of a short flight of marble steps, a liveried doorman was standing. Neurath caught his eye, recognized him. It was the usual weeknight attendant—one who correctly knew not to approach a guarded dignitary's car without first being beckoned.

Neurath bent his head to light his cigarette as Grohl began to exit the Daimler. As a result the wide brim of his fedora prevented him from seeing the silent bicyclist come gliding down the street out of the darkness. By the time Neurath straightened, inhaling deeply, the rider was beside the car's front bumper.

Several things happened simultaneously. Mustapha Snagi threw himself on top of al-Husseini, forcing him down onto the rear seat and covering his master's body with his own. Hauptsturmfuehrer Julius Neurath bit his cigarette in two and clawed inside his left lapel for his shoulder-holstered Walther P-38 automatic pistol. Agent Grohl, moving with uncanny speed for so large a man, twisted out of the Daimler, banged his head on the door frame, and dropped to one knee on the curb. And the old man on the bicycle, shaggy gray hair and bulky overcoat flying, bent low and with one hand bowled a spherical object about the size of a grapefruit under the car.

"*Get—*" Neurath screamed. It was as far as he got.

A fiery explosion kicked the rear end of the Daimler four feet into the air. All of the vehicle's tires and bulletproof windows blew out in the same instant. The curbside pedestal lamps flanking the hotel entrance shattered like twin prisms of ice.

Only the two inches of steel armor plate lining the underside of the specially built limousine saved Snagi and al-Husseini from being cremated or killed by concussion. That same armor plate redirected the main force of the blast out laterally from beneath the Daimler, catching the kneeling Grohl and throwing him back into Neurath. Grohl's misfortune was Neurath's salvation. The slender Hauptsturmfuehrer landed hard on his back on the lower stairs of the hotel entrance, the shrapnel-riddled body of his much larger companion on top of him. Incredibly, Neurath was unhit.

But he was winded and dazed, his vision blurred and his ears ringing. Gasping for breath, he shoved

Grohl's limp, torn body to one side and staggered to his feet. Off balance, disoriented, he steadied himself against the stone railing of the hotel stairs and got his Walther out of its shoulder holster just as Snagi and al-Husseini lurched out of the twisted, burning Daimler. Snagi had one arm around his master, supporting him, as the pair stumbled toward the hotel entrance. A second or two later, Beckmann forced open his jammed front door and reeled out onto the sidewalk, minus his helmet. His close-cropped blond hair was smoking, and the right side of his face was black.

"Inside!" Neurath yelled, waving the mufti and his bodyguard past with his pistol. A sudden billow of acrid smoke stung his eyes, and when it cleared, he saw the old man approaching at the run. . . . Pulling something from beneath his flapping overcoat . . .

Neurath jerked up his Walther. The old man raised his own pistol, aiming at al-Husseini from less than fifteen feet away. Neurath pulled the trigger of his weapon. The usually reliable P-38 jammed.

The old man fired four times in rapid succession—*crackcrackcrackcrack!* On the top step of the hotel stairs, Mustapha Snagi interposed his body between al-Husseini and the would-be assassin. One slug went wide. The other three hit Snagi in the back as he drove his master forward through the glass doors of the entrance and into the Hotel Jürgenplatz's main lobby.

Cursing, Neurath dropped the jammed Walther and dove on top of Grohl, groping for the dead agent's weapon. As he did so, Beckmann opened fire with his own sidearm, from a kneeling position beside the wrecked Daimler. One of his flurry of shots struck the old man high in the right shoulder, spinning him around.

Deftly the old man switched his pistol to his left hand, snapped off two quick rounds at Beckmann—

which missed but sent the driver sprawling—and
sprinted off down the darkened street.

"Get him!" Neurath shrieked, apoplectic. *"With
me, Beckmann!"*

Jerking up Grohl's Walther, he fired several shots
at the dodging, ducking assailant and took off in hot
pursuit, with Beckmann on his heels.

Neurath was young and fast on his feet, so it came
as something of a surprise to him that he did not
appear to be closing the distance on the old man after
nearly a full minute of flat-out running. Beckmann, fit
and approximately the same age as he, was twenty
yards behind and laboring to keep up. But the old
man was able—somehow—to match Neurath's best
pace.

The Gestapo agent cursed, frustration and fury
boosting his already soaring adrenaline level, and
willed his legs to move faster. Three sets of rapidly
pounding footfalls, interspersed by ragged gasps,
echoed through the empty, blacked-out streets. The
crack of a pistol split the night as Beckmann tried
another shot. But no lights flickered on in darkened
windows, no doors opened to reveal the curious. In
Berlin, as in all of the Third Reich, no one dared draw
attention to themselves when the Gestapo were on
the hunt.

The old man, some forty yards ahead, was approaching another intersection. Instinct told Neurath
that his quarry was about to make a sharp right
around the corner of an upcoming bank and continue
on down the crossing street. Halting abruptly, he
raised his Walther in both hands, took steady aim,
paused his breathing, and fired.

He thought he saw the old man stagger slightly as
he cut around the corner of the bank and out of sight.
A hit! Neurath felt a surge of vicious jubilation. He
half turned as Beckmann caught up and passed him
on his left shoulder.

"I got him!" Neurath panted, breaking into a run again. "The swine won't be able to move so fast with a bullet in his—"

The old man reappeared suddenly around the corner of the building, firing rapidly from a distance of less than twenty feet. Beckmann, slightly in the lead, went down with a cry. Neurath dove into the gutter behind a parked Volkswagen truck. Several slugs punched into the vehicle's side panel. Neurath rolled away, getting a face full of backed-up sewer water. As he scrambled around the street side of the truck, he could hear Beckmann yelling incoherently and returning fire.

He reached the driver's door, threw his arm up on the hood of the truck, and emptied his Walther at the corner of the bank. Granite chips and dust flew. But when the percussive echoes of his rapid-fire volley faded away, the old man was nowhere to be seen.

Beckmann staggered to his feet, grimacing, and leaned heavily on the hood of the truck, changing clips in his pistol. Blood was soaking the left shoulder of his uniform where a bullet had clipped the top of his trapezius muscle.

Neurath ejected the spent clip from his Walther and slapped home another. "Come on, man!" he shouted, vaulting past the trunk's front bumper and onto the sidewalk. "Get after the bastard!" He did not bother to inquire whether or not Beckmann could.

The Gestapo agent skirted wide around the corner, pistol raised, in case the old man was still there. He was not. He was at the far end of the block, running diagonally through the center of the next intersection. He was moving less quickly than before, and there was an odd jink in his stride.

You're mine, Neurath thought exultantly. He glanced at the wet sidewalk in front of him as he dashed toward the end of the block. There it was. A sporadic trail of blood, mixing with the rainwater and running in slow, dark rivulets off the edge of the curb. A *lot* of blood.

The animal was badly wounded. Very soon now, it would go to ground. Neurath's mouth flattened into a sliver of a smile. This was his favorite part of the hunt—overtaking and cornering the game—because it was the most dangerous. The thrill was almost sexual.

The old man was running down the right sidewalk of the next street, skirting garbage cans and trying to keep low. Neurath sprinted off the curb and out into the intersection, keeping his eyes fixed on the fugitive. There were many narrow alleys on this street, and instinct again told him that the old man, no longer able to escape his pursuers by flight, would try to duck into one of them and hide.

As he reached the center of the intersection he heard a shout. Glancing over his shoulder, he saw a knot of black-uniformed SS troopers—security guards from the small contingent stationed inside the Hotel Jürgenplatz—advancing down the crossing street from the opposite direction. The trooper in the lead brought up a Schmeisser machine pistol and yelled at Neurath to halt.

"*Nicht schiessen!*" the agent bellowed, slowing and throwing up his arms. "Don't shoot! I'm Gestapo, idiot!" He gestured frantically over his shoulder. "The terrorist is getting away, damn you!"

The SS Rottenfuehrer at the head of the security squad heard *Don't shoot, idiot,* and *Damn you,* and was about to cut down the suspect in the trench coat— who was still moving away at a half-run in defiance of the order to halt—with a burst from his machine pistol when the SS-uniformed Beckmann stumbled into view. At the last second, the Rottenfuehrer reconsidered and held his fire. Then as the two figures in the intersection turned and sprinted off down the street together, he barked a command for his three comrades to follow, and broke into a run himself.

In the exchange with the Rottenfuehrer, Neurath had lost sight of the old man. Cursing, he dodged between two parked cars and up onto the sidewalk. Beckmann stayed on the street, running parallel to him. Desperately Neurath scanned the doorways and closed-up shop fronts as they flashed by, searching for some sign of where the old man had gone.

"Watch the alleys!" he shouted to Beckmann. "He might have gone down—"

The crash of an overturning garbage can reverberated out of the alley they were just passing. Neurath leaped to the side of the nearest building and flattened himself against its rough brick, his Walther up and ready. On the sidewalk at the front of the alley, a large smear of blood glistened darkly.

Beckmann took up position on the opposite wall, breathing hard. Neurath caught his eye, held up his open palm, then leaned forward and peered cautiously into the alley.

A flurry of shots exploded out of the black void, chipping brick next to Neurath's face and sending him recoiling back. Beckmann swore aloud and without exposing his head shoved his pistol around the corner of the building and emptied it blindly into the darkness. Recovering, Neurath did the same. More crashing of garbage cans.

At that moment, the SS Rottenfuehrer and his three troopers arrived on the scene. Without needing Neurath's shouted prompting, the four soldiers spread across the entrance to the alley and opened up with their machine pistols, saturating the narrow passageway with fire. The shattering volley lasted nearly fifteen seconds, until each of the four automatic weapons had exhausted its magazine. Then there was silence.

Reloading hurriedly, the SS guards looked into the empty blackness of the alley, then at each other. At the walls flanking the entrance, Neurath and Beckmann crouched, waiting. Still no one spoke.

There was a sound like a piece of pipe rolling across the floor of a garage.

A smooth gray sphere, about the size of a grapefruit, rolled slowly out of the alley and onto the sidewalk. The Rottenfuehrer stared quizzically at the benign-looking object.

"*Vas ist?*" he muttered.

Neurath and Beckmann threw themselves back, clawing for cover, just before the custom-made rolling bomb exploded. The blast knocked the SS security guards off their feet—killing the Rottenfuehrer, mangling the arm of a second man, and stunning the remaining two.

In the aftermath of the explosion, the old man burst out of the alley—a staggering, stumbling apparition wreathed in swirls of dirty smoke. He was doubled over, one arm clamped across his stomach, his right leg dragging. His gun hand was up, swinging, as he tried desperately to fire in every direction at once.

Neurath rolled into the partial shelter of a shop doorway as several of the old man's wild shots ricocheted off the sidewalk near his feet. Beckmann was on his hands and knees, groping for his dropped pistol, when a random slug drilled through his jackboot and smashed his right ankle. He belly flopped onto the pavement with a howl.

The old man made it nearly halfway across the street when the two unscathed SS troopers opened up on him simultaneously with their burp guns. The crossfire caught him in the upper body, hammered him upright, and for a moment seemed to hold him there—a shaking, demoniac figure with flying hair and disintegrating overcoat—before propelling him backward and depositing him in crumpled heap in the gutter on the far side of the street.

Neurath rose to his feet and ran toward the downed assassin, brandishing his Walther at arm's length. He slowed as he approached the body, keeping his pistol aimed at the shaggy gray head, and gave it a vicious kick. There was no reaction.

"Ach!" Neurath spat. "Dead." He lowered the pistol in disgust and looked at one of the two SS troopers. "What can a dead man tell me? Eh?" He looked back at the corpse. "Not a damn thing." On impulse, he jerked up his Walther and fired three quick shots into the body. The two SS troopers glanced uncertainly at each other.

On the far sidewalk, Beckmann had ceased to howl and was now merely groaning, rolling from side to side on his back and clutching his shattered ankle with both hands. Neurath regarded him dispassionately for a few seconds.

"Go help my driver," he told the nearest trooper, his tone making it clear that Beckmann's agony was little more than an irritant to him, and turned back to the bullet-riddled body in the gutter.

The dead assassin was lying with his torso twisted sideways, his face turned into the curb and partly concealed. Neurath stooped down, seized the tangle of gray hair, and yanked. The body flopped over and the mop of hair came away in his hand.

Neurath blinked. But for its gray handlebar mustache, the face staring up at the starless night sky bore no marks of age. Neurath tossed the blood-soaked gray wig aside, took hold of the mustache, and pulled. It too came away easily.

The old man was not old but young—younger than he. His short hair was very dark, as were his sightless eyes and the sparse patches of stubble on his chin. He would have had trouble growing a full beard. His features were square and clean, ruggedly handsome, but with a hint of scar tissue around the brows and a slight flattening of the bridge of the nose, suggesting that at one time he might have been a boxer.

"Of course," Neurath muttered. "Of course . . ." He reached into his trench coat, withdrew a black-ivory pocket knife, and pressed a button on the handle. A five-inch stilletto blade snicked into view.

Squatting on his haunches, the Gestapo Hauptsturmfuehrer jerked open the dead man's bullet-torn overcoat, slid the knife blade under the thin leather belt securing his cheap, baggy trousers, and slashed upward. The belt parted. Another slash, and the trouser material was opened from waist to crotch.

Roughly, Neurath yanked down the corpse's trousers and undershorts, exposing the genitals. Then he sat back on his heels and nodded with grim satisfaction.

"Ah, there, you see?" he declared triumphantly, without glancing back at the SS trooper hovering near his shoulder. "Circumcised. A filthy Jew." In a sudden fit of viciousness he slashed a few times at the dead man's groin, got to his feet, snapped shut the switchblade, and put it back into his pocket. "No matter how many of these brutes we manage to exterminate, there are always a few more running around, stirring up trouble." Neurath paused to withdraw a cigarette from his case and light it. "But we'll weed them all out eventually. Do you know why?"

"No, sir," the SS trooper said quickly.

"Because we can always readily identify them," Neurath said, sounding both amused and disgusted. "Their own repulsive traditions betray them. They all cut their cocks like that." He glanced down at the desecrated body of the young man as if regarding roadkill. "Can you imagine? What a barbaric culture."

He let out a short, harsh laugh, turned on his heel, and walked away, trailing cigarette smoke. Headlights began to cast moving shadows over the walls of the surrounding buildings as several armored personnel carriers converged on the scene, engines roaring. A military ambulance pulled up beside Beckmann, who was still lying on the sidewalk. The first personnel carrier shuddered to a halt in the middle of the street,

disgorging helmeted SS troops like a cascade of black-
carapaced beetles.

The soldier to whom Neurath had spoken was still
standing beside the assassin's body when his comrade,
who had been aiding Beckmann, rejoined him two
minutes later.

"What about the driver?" the first trooper asked.

The second trooper shrugged. "Hit in the ankle.
Smashed to bits, it looks like. And damned painful,
too. But the meat wagon boys have him now." He
looked down at the dead man in the gutter. "So. A
Jew. Well, we really took care of him, didn't we?"
He patted the machine pistol slung around his neck
and grinned.

The first trooper swallowed. "I suppose."

"What's the matter with you?" his comrade demanded. "You look pale."

Other soldiers were beginning to mill around the
body. The first trooper glanced furtively over his
shoulder and rubbed his fingers across his upper lip.

"You know, Horst," he muttered, his voice very
low, "I'm circumcised myself. The doctor my mother
took me to when I was a baby thought it was a good
thing. A matter of medical hygiene."

The second trooper looked shocked. "Really?"

"Yes, really."

The second trooper stared at the first for a long
moment. "How did you pass the physical to get into
the SS?"

"I lied. I said it was corrective surgery for an infec-
tion. The way the doctor did it, you see, it's not that
obvious. And my Aryan heritage is indisputable. The
SS medical officers believed me."

The trooper named Horst shook his head. Ten feet
away, several other SS soldiers began to drag off the
assassin's limp body. Beside the nearest personnel carrier, Gestapo Hauptsturmfuehrer Julius Neurath was
watching the proceedings with a baleful eye, smoking.

"Well, for God's sake, Willi," Horst whispered to his friend, "keep your mouth shut about it."

The orderly tiptoed up to the huge four-poster bed, laid a hand on the hunched shoulder beneath the satin coverlet, and shook gently. It was just after four thirty a.m.

"My Fuehrer," the orderly said, keeping his voice low. "My Fuehrer."

"Mmphnng . . ." Adolph Hitler came groggily out of his drug-induced slumber. The orderly waited. The insomnia that had plagued the Fuehrer for decades could now only be overcome by a nightly injection of sedative.

Hitler sat up, looking bedraggled and dyspeptic, and leaned back on the pillows that his orderly hurriedly rearranged against the headboard. "What is it?" he demanded, smoothing his lank forelock sideways with one hand. His toothbrush mustache twitched in irritation.

The orderly produced a telephone, cord trailing. "Admiral Canaris, my Fuehrer. He insisted it was most urgent."

Hitler smacked his dry lips and grunted. "Isn't it always, Kirchbaum?" He held out his hand. "Give it to me."

Kirchbaum relinquished the phone and departed, pulling the bedchamber doors closed behind him. Hitler rubbed his swollen, black-circled eyes.

"Obviously you have something pressing to tell me, my dear Canaris," he grumbled into the receiver.

"Good morning, my Fuehrer," Canaris replied, his voice sounding tinny and far-off. "My apologies for disturbing you this early, but there has been an interesting development, and I thought that you should be informed of it without delay."

"Go on."

"Last night," Canaris said, "the Grand Mufti was

the target of another assassination attempt. It took place at approximately eleven o'clock, outside the main entrance of the Hotel Jürgenplatz."

"Good heavens."

"Indeed, my Fuehrer. A lone operative—Jewish, apparently—who rolled a small bomb under the mufti's car and then pressed the attack with a handgun."

"How shocking," Hitler remarked. "In the very heart of Berlin. Was the mufti injured?"

"No," Canaris replied. "Through the courageous actions of his security detail he was able to escape into the lobby of the hotel. But his personal bodyguard—the Macedonian named Snagi—took three bullets in the back."

"Dead?"

"No, my Fuehrer," the admiral continued. "Oddly enough, the man was wearing a very fine vest of chain mail under his clothing—a virtual museum piece. The kind of lightweight body armor Saladin's horsemen would have worn into battle against the Crusaders a thousand years ago in the Holy Land." Canaris paused. "The bullets penetrated, but only superficially. He'll recover."

Hitler grunted. "How interesting. Any other casualties?"

"One of the mufti's Gestapo bodyguards, Grohl, was killed by the explosion of the bomb. The assassin fled. In the ensuing chase, the SS driver, Beckmann, was shot in the shoulder and ankle. An SS Rottenfuehrer who had been assigned to the hotel was killed by a second bomb, and one of his squad injured. But the assassin was eventually dispatched by Gestapo Hauptsturmfuehrer Neurath, agent in charge of the mufti's security detail—according to his own oral report on the incident."

"Mmm."

"Interestingly enough, preliminary investigation indicates that the bombs used by this Jewish operative were of the same compact, rolling design utilized by

Czech resistance fighters to assassinate Obergruppen-fuehrer Heydrich back in 1942."

"You mean Czech terrorists," Hitler said.

"Of course, my Fuehrer."

"In other words," Hitler went on, "the bombs were of British origin."

"Exactly," Canaris confirmed. "Built by the British Secret Service. Supplied by the British Secret Service. For all we know, the British Secret Service parachuted the Jewish agent into Germany, just as they parachuted the Czech resistance commandos—er, *terrorists*—into the outskirts of Prague to ambush Heydrich."

"The British, the British," Hitler muttered. "They are the great bogeymen of the civilized world, are they not? Working their intrigues everywhere, always, with their confounded fingers in every pie. A nation of warrior-pirates. If only they would join us, instead of fighting against us. United—true Anglo and true Saxon—we would be unstoppable."

"Unlikely, my Fuehrer," Canaris said. "But, as you say, they are the great bogeymen—particularly as far as our friend Haj Amin al-Husseini is concerned."

Hitler sat up straighter in bed. "Ah. He is aware that it was a Jew, backed by the British, that nearly got him last night?"

Canaris did not chuckle, but his tone lightened. "Yes, my Fuehrer. I myself made him acutely aware of that fact when I debriefed him only two hours ago."

"Elaborate please, my dear Canaris."

"He was somewhat . . . distraught, shall we say. Shaken. While I sympathized, I took the opportunity to point out to him that here was a brutal reminder of the fact that he is a prime target of one of the most relentless secret service organizations in the world—and that it would be tragic indeed if by his own refusal to work in harmony with his host nation, that nation were forced to deem it impractical to continue to provide him with the personal security he so obviously requires."

There was a long pause.

"And what was his response?" Hitler inquired.

Canaris let a beat pass for effect.

"He informs me that he has had a change of heart, and that he would be only too glad to undertake the proposed inspirational tour of the SS Division Handschar in the field in Yugoslavia—at the Fuehrer's earliest convenience."

Chapter Two

"They missed him," the British general said. "The Jewish Agency. Their operative botched it. And got himself killed into the bargain."

The broad bulldog face behind the immense Victorian desk worked for a moment, producing reams of smoke from a foot-long Havana cigar. It took several seconds for the slowly rotating ceiling fan to clear the fog. The eyes that met the general's were small and quick, leprechaun sharp and diamond bright.

"What happened?" Winston Churchill demanded.

General Sir Stewart Graham Menzies—chief of Britain's primary secret service, MI-6—shook his head. "Our information—very spur-of-the-moment, mind you—was that the mufti would be entering his new residence at the Hotel Jürgenplatz last night, accompanied by only his personal bodyguard—no Gestapo." Menzies paused. "That did not turn out to be the case. The usual contingent was with him: two agents and an SS driver."

"Damnation," Churchill growled. He plucked the

cigar out of his mouth and exhaled a long cloud of smoke. "The JA's operative didn't think to back off and wait for another opportunity once he saw that al-Husseini was sporting full security?"

"Unfortunately not, Prime Minister," Menzies replied. "You know how these Jewish agents are—just like the Poles and the Czechs. Their enthusiasm for mixing it up with the Nazis knows no bounds. I imagine the poor devil just couldn't restrain himself."

Churchill harrumphed, shifting in his chair and crossing his legs beneath the red satin day robe he preferred to wear before noon. "Not to split hairs," he grumbled, bringing the cigar to his lips again, "but the mufti isn't a Nazi. Not strictly speaking, anyway."

A grim smile creased the general's face. "A distinction which is lost upon our Hebrew friends, I'm afraid. Association is as good as affiliation, to their way of thinking. And who can blame them?"

"Certainly not I," the prime minister said. He puffed thoughtfully on his cigar. "It's just a damned shame to lose an agent who was so well placed. The follow-up information out of Berlin is interesting, but good Lord, his handlers in Cairo had him living within a stone's throw of the Reichs Chancellery."

"Yes, well," Menzies sighed, "*c'est la vie*, as de Gaulle would say."

Churchill scowled. "Please don't put me in mind of that pompous bloody *crapaud* right now, Sir Stewart." Cigar smoke billowed furiously. "Constantly maneuvering at cross purposes under our very noses to ensure that he, and only he, will run France when this is all over. Creating conflicts at every turn."

"Mmm," Menzies replied, nodding in agreement. "He's pursuing his own agenda; there's no doubt about that."

Churchill stalked around his desk and poured a splash of brandy from a crystal decanter into a large snifter. "I was speaking to Roosevelt just yesterday," he growled. "Do you know he actually recommended that I have British troops place de Gaulle under arrest and hold him in exile?"

Menzies's canny eyes widened momentarily and he smiled. "What did you tell him?"

Churchill swirled his brandy and took a sip. "I told Franklin we call de Gaulle Joan of Arc, and we're looking for some bishops to burn him."

A brief guffaw escaped the general's lips. "My word," he chuckled.

"Frustration manifesting itself in my renowned wit," Churchill went on acidly. "Obviously we can't arrest him without alienating all the Free French, and we're not about to do away with him on the sly. So we'll just have to put up with the bugger."

"Rest assured, Prime Minister," Menzies said, "for the immediate future, we'll be able to keep him at least partly under our thumb."

"Fine, fine." Churchill drained the snifter and set it down on the desk. "Now, look: have you talked to Gubbins over at SOE about this latest Yugoslavian project?"

"I have," Menzies said. "I spoke to Sir Colin yesterday. Special Operations Executive[1] confirms that Operation Handschar is a go. Personnel selected, trained, and equipped. Schedule set. The Yanks anted up with a couple of OSS agents who have been fully integrated into the team. Former Jedburgh candidates—very tough fellows."[2]

"Good," Churchill said. "With the SOE and the OSS both operating in Yugoslavia, we can't afford to risk putting Uncle Sam's nose out of joint by executing a dazzler like this without inviting the Americans in on it. Not when we're finally starting to work together effectively in the Balkans. Of course," he added ruefully, "if the whole bloody undertaking turns into a royal cock-up, they might be glad if we'd left them out of it."

"Too late," Menzies said. "They're in."

"Hmph." Churchill chewed on his cigar, circumnavigated the desk once in silence, and sat down in the leather armchair behind it. When he looked up at the chief of MI-6 again, his eyes had the enthusiastic glint of the thoroughly stimulated gamester. "All right," he said. "Now to our concept of killing two birds with one stone. You're certain the standard protocol of not informing the majority of the team of the mission's true objective has been maintained?"

"According to General Gubbins," Menzies replied, "absolutely. Only the team leader and the other necessary principal know the real goal. The other team members have been purposely kept in the dark so that if they are captured, they cannot be forced to give up information crucial to the success of the mission."

"Excellent," Churchill said, rubbing his palms together. He was enjoying himself—the supreme strategist in love with strategizing. "Two birds with one stone . . . and now maybe even three." He gazed off into the distance for a moment, then refocused on Menzies. "In light of the information that's just come out of Berlin regarding this particular deceased Jewish Agency operative *and* the newly stated intentions of the glorious Grand Mufti of Jerusalem, I want you, Sir Stewart, to take the following instructions to General Gubbins at SOE. . . ."

The young man was of medium height and athletic build, with dark, close-cropped hair, tan complexion, and a belligerent set to his jaw. Not unlike several million other highly motivated, highly trained, highly aggressive twenty-something-year-old males presently roaming England and Europe, General Sir Colin McVean Gubbins thought. He continued to watch as the young soldier in the khaki uniform and black beret strode to within the regulation three paces of his superior's desk, came to attention, and saluted smartly.

"Sergeant David Weiss reporting as ordered, sir!" he rapped out.

Gubbins touched his brow. "At ease, Sergeant." He

sat back in his swivel chair as Weiss widened his stance and clasped his hands behind his back. The warm sunlight of an uncharacteristically clear London day flooded into the office through the single large window, the blackout curtains of which had been drawn back.

The SOE chief gazed down at the personnel profile on his desk, stroking his neatly trimmed mustache, and then up at the young NCO before him. Jerusalem born, American educated, combat experience with the British Expeditionary Force in France all the way up to the Dunkirk evacuation, currently a member of the Jewish Brigade, on tap for special operations duty. The general continued to look him over, head to toe. Weiss's eyes dropped to meet his briefly, then resettled on the hand-painted portrait of an Elizabethan noble on the wall above Gubbins's head.

"Do you know who that is?" Gubbins asked mildly.

Weiss hesitated, then cleared his throat. "I'll guess Drake, sir."

"Not a bad guess." Gubbins smiled. "You have the correct era. That is Sir Francis Walsingham, the spymaster of Queen Elizabeth the First. He founded the British intelligence service—what is now MI-6—in order to deal with the threat of the Spanish Armada."

Weiss nodded slowly, trying to think of something appropriate to say. "Er . . . did it work, sir?"

Gubbins continued to stroke his mustache and appraise Weiss. "You might say that. Most of the invading armada ended up burning to ashes in the middle of the English Channel, thanks to Walsingham's advance warning and a subsequent encounter with a fleet of British fireships." He pointed a finger to the right. "Perhaps you recognize that other gentleman."

Weiss looked at the wall to his left. Another portrait hung above a set of steel-gray filing cabinets. "That's Benjamin Franklin, sir," he said. "The famous American diplomat and scientist."

"Correct," Gubbins responded. "Now, Walsingham

decorates my office because even though he is the
founder of what is essentially a rival secret service as
well as an allied branch of government, I admire his
skill and effectiveness. But what about Franklin?"

Weiss shifted his weight from foot to foot, unsure
of where all this was going. "Well, from what I understand, he was a very admirable and capable person,
sir." He paused to lick his lips. "Uh . . . an
inventor . . . a—a publisher . . . the discoverer of
electricity . . ."

Gubbins let him struggle on to the point of failure,
as if Weiss were a schoolboy singled out to recite a
lesson for which he hadn't prepared. It was a tactic
the general used often—the immediate maneuvering
of a person into an exchange in which they were
forced to play catch-up with him. Rank notwithstanding, it conditioned that person to accept the role of
He Who Would Be Told, rather than He Who Would
Do The Telling. Gubbins, like most effective leaders,
believed in the establishment of authority on an unconscious as well as a conscious level—particularly
when dealing with the independent, often headstrong
young individuals who staffed his cadre of field agents.

"You are correct, Weiss," Gubbins remarked, gazing across the room at the portrait of the cherub-faced
older man with the long white hair, bemused expression, and wise, fathomless eyes. "Franklin was all of
those things. A scientist, inventor, publisher, adminis-
trator, celebrity diplomat—one of the most famous
men of his age." The general looked at Weiss again.
"He was also one of the greatest spies who ever lived.
Before he ever got around to being one of the Found-
ing Fathers of the United States of America, he was
a founder of the Secret Committee of Correspondence—
the secret service of the original Thirteen Colonies.
He helped to run guns, influence and bribe world leaders, establish a spy network in Europe, and originate
codes and cyphers—all the while hiding in plain sight

as one of the most visible guest celebrities in France. Truly remarkable."

Weiss shook his head. "I had no idea Benjamin Franklin was a spy, sir," he said.

"Which, of course, is definitive proof of how good he was at it," Gubbins remarked. "Great spies are never known as such. At least not in their lifetimes. Franklin's been dead for one hundred and fifty years, and people still think of him as the charmingly rustic colonial physicist out flying his kite in a thunderstorm—not as America's first spymaster."

"Yes, sir," Weiss said. He waited, fixing his gaze on Walsingham again.

"We all have role models in life," Gubbins went on. "These two men from the past are a couple of mine." He paused, studying the young sergeant from beneath salt-and-pepper brows. "You see, Weiss, in addition to being brilliant and idealistic, they were also cunning and realistic. They wished for a perfect world—as they defined it—but in the absence of that were quite capable of doing what was necessary for the greater good of their respective countries—capable, in other words, of doing the dirty work."

Weiss looked down from Walsingham's portrait. "Ruthless, sir?"

Gubbins smiled. "Yes. That would be another way of putting it. The fact is, Weiss, in their business—our business—the willingness to indulge in lies, deception, manipulation, duplicity, and betrayal in the name of the greater good is a heroic quality. Frankly, not everyone is capable of it. You understand that, don't you?"

"Yes, sir," Weiss answered. "The end justifies the means."

Gubbins lifted an eyebrow. "Precisely. And of course, anyone—*anyone*—in our business can find himself in the position of having to use lies or manipulation, even with respect to allies, to achieve an immediate goal. To serve the higher motive. Some people object to this, Weiss. What's your personal opinion? Could you do it if you had to?"

Conversely, the general thought, *anyone in our business can also find himself in the position of having been lied to or manipulated.*

"I could, General," Weiss replied. "I believe that if it's necessary to deceive someone—even an ally—in order to accomplish a mission, then it has to be done."

"Excellent," Gubbins said. Then he added almost casually, "Could you respect the higher motive, even if it was done to you?"

The general watched as instantly Weiss's guard went up. The young sergeant hesitated, then cleared his throat before answering. "If it was a higher motive I believed in, sir, then yes. If I could see the necessity." He met Gubbins's gaze directly and held it. "I beg your pardon, General, but are you trying to give me a warning?"

The head of SOE chuckled and rocked back in his chair. "Oh, heavens, no, Weiss. Nothing like that. This is merely a theoretical discussion. You see, my boy, we have to flesh out a special operations team scheduled to drop into Yugoslavia four days from now—a key member has suddenly taken ill—and I'm thinking of replacing him with you. You have the necessary qualifications, which we'll go into in a minute, but my primary concern is that you understand that in taking part in a mission in Yugoslavia, you will be entering one of the most confusing, internally divided, treachery-filled combat theaters of this entire global war. In order to accomplish its mission, your team will not only have to liaison with Tito's Partisans, but navigate safely past a host of rival groups—Chetniks, Ustashe, and the like—who are all battling each other for future control of the country even as they fight, and in some cases collaborate with, the occupying Nazis.

"There is essentially a vicious civil war going on in

Yugoslavia," Gubbins continued, "in tandem with an equally vicious war against the Nazi invaders. A more dangerous, backstabbing situation you will not find anywhere." He smiled. "Hence my fatherly little lecture about the need to nurture an appreciation for the tactics of duplicity and manipulation. You're about to jump into a place where you can trust no one—not even if he presents himself as a friend. Do you follow?"

Weiss nodded, relaxing somewhat. "Yes, sir. I do."

Gubbins stroked his mustache. "Good. And of course, I could simply order you to report to the team. But like all SOE endeavors, this is exceptionally hazardous duty. On key missions, I prefer to offer my men the courtesy of declaring themselves." The general paused, his shrewd gaze very steady. "So, Sergeant Weiss, knowing no more than the little I've already told you: are you up to this?"

Weiss blinked at the portrait of Walsingham, then spoke: "May I ask one question, sir?"

"Go ahead."

"Will I have the opportunity to kill Germans on this mission?"

Gubbins smiled again slowly. "Most definitely, Sergeant."

Weiss smiled in return. "Then yes, sir. I am up to it. . . . Most definitely."

"Good," Gubbins said. "By the way, have you ever hunted gamecock?"

"Sir?"

"Gamecock," the general repeated. "The wild fowl of the moors. Have you ever had an opportunity to hunt them in the field?"

Weiss cleared his throat, taken off guard again. "Well, yes sir, I have, actually. With an officer acquaintance of mine whose family owns a country estate up near the Scottish border."

"Wily little buggers, aren't they? Evasive."

"Yes, sir."

"Did you enjoy hunting them?"

"Yes, sir. Very much."

"And how did you do?"

"I believe we knocked down several dozen between the two of us in one afternoon, sir." Weiss's brow furrowed and he looked directly at his superior. "I beg your pardon, sir, but why are you asking me this? It seems an odd question."

Gubbins waved a hand. "Oh, it's just something Prime Minister Churchill mentioned. He saw you on the SOE range the other day, was impressed with your marksmanship and said you had the look of a hunter." The general smiled enigmatically. "He just wondered in passing if you'd ever tried your hand at gamecock."

Later that day, precisely at tea time, SOE head General Sir Colin McVean Gubbins was sitting comfortably in a velvet-and-mahogany armchair in the parlor of the prime minister's official residence at 10 Downing Street. To his right was MI-6 head General Sir Stewart Graham Menzies, on his second residence visit of the day, studiously adding milk to his bone china cup of Darjeeling. To his left, in front of the parlor's tall bay window, Winston Churchill was pacing quietly back and forth, hands clasped behind his back, smoking. Gubbins was reminded of an old, restless lion.

On the richly upholstered davenport next to Menzies sat two American officers. One was Gubbins's U.S. counterpart—Colonel Joseph Haskell, head of SO, or Special Operations. The other was a handsome, silver-haired man in his midfifties who exuded the confident, aggressive air of the successful Wall Street lawyer he was. General William "Wild Bill" Donovan had been many other things in his spectacularly active life: thrice-wounded World War I veteran, Medal of Honor winner, international businessman and gatherer of intelligence, New York State gubernatorial candidate, confidante of presidents from Wilson through

Roosevelt, and now, by executive order, founder and head of the Office of Strategic Services—the OSS, parent organization of Haskell's SO.

There was a sixth man in the room—a tall, slender civilian in his early sixties with a full head of snow-white hair, an immaculately tailored suit, and the distinguished air of a retired bank director. He sat somewhat apart from the others, legs crossed with his intertwined fingers resting on one knee. He appeared to be examining the weave of the expensive Persian rug that covered the parlor floor.

"Where the hell are they?" Churchill grumbled. He pulled a pocket watch from his waistcoat and consulted it. "I'm five minutes fast, but they should have been at the front door by now."

As if on cue, a dull chime sounded through the residence, followed by a low muttering of voices from the entrance foyer. Shortly thereafter a uniformed aide entered the parlor and came to attention.

"Major Merritt and Captain Throckmorton are here, Mr. Prime Minister," he said.

"Ah, good." Churchill slipped the watch back into his waistcoat and beckoned with his cigar. "Thank you, Hopkins. Send them right in."

"Sir."

As the aide departed, Churchill sat down in the thronelike armchair that dominated the room, and recut the dead end of his cigar. "A faulty roll, this," he growled to no one in particular. "Poor draw. You'd think at the price of these things the bloody Cuban who made it would have taken a little pride in his work."

Donovan smiled. "How often do you get a bad Cohiba, Mr. Prime Minister?" he asked.

Churchill chuckled as he stuck a wooden match and put it to the cigar's newly trimmed end. "Well, General," he replied, "admittedly not often." His sharp eyes, amused, flicked up to meet Donovan's. "Not so long ago I was grateful when a Cohiba of any description made it past the Atlantic U-boat packs and into England. I must be a bit testy today. Perhaps I'm feeling my age."

Donovan's smooth attorney's manners slipped effortlessly into gear. "Not so, Mr. Prime Minister," he said. "You remain your usual charming and imperturbable self, I assure you."

Churchill grinned past his cigar. "It's easy to see why you did so well on Wall Street, General."

Donovan shrugged good-naturedly.

The aide returned and ushered two officers in British uniform into the room. The first, who wore the rank insignia of major, was a well-proportioned six-footer with the lean look of an athlete. He removed his peaked cap and tucked it under his arm in one motion, revealing close-cropped auburn hair. His clean-shaven face seemed permanently tanned and windburned, as if he had spent his entire life out of doors in harsh weather, and exhibited that quality peculiar to the seasoned combat soldier of looking both young and old at the same time—a physical age of approximately thirty in combination with a much greater age of experience.

He locked his heels together and saluted. "Major Walter Merritt and Captain Duncan Throckmorton reporting as ordered, sir."

The second man, a rather weedy-looking individual of perhaps thirty-five with a gaunt, deeply lined face, limp blond hair, and an air of upper-class dissipation about him, also came to attention and saluted, much more casually. To Donovan, the contrast in personal styles between the two officers was striking. Merritt exuded the quiet, controlled lethality of the trained commando—a kind of stillness that suggested great physical competence. Throckmorton, on the other hand, seemed an absolute HQ attaché/Officers Club type—one of the species of high-born, aging rich kids that tended to cruise through the war kowtowing to, shuffling paper for, and occasionally dining out with rear-echelon brass, courtesy of parental connections. The command centers of Washington and London were choked with them: the sons of senators, of Members of Parliament, of judges and millionaires and dukes and lords, most of them using the war as an opportunity for career advancement even as they sidestepped the brutal reality of having to face enemy fire. Donovan felt nothing but disdain for them.

But even though Throckmorton's carriage and demeanor had put him in mind of such creatures, Donovan had learned to reserve judgement until a man had revealed his character unequivocally. So he filed away his first impression and waited to find out more.

Churchill nodded in response to Merritt's salute and address, settled back in his chair, and looked over at Gubbins. Sir Colin rose to his feet, returned the salute, and pointed toward a vacant couch.

"Please sit down, gentlemen," he said. He resumed his seat, as Merritt and Throckmorton complied.

"The reason you are here," Gubbins continued, "is to provide our American allies General Donovan and Colonel Haskell an opportunity to have a look at the officers who will be leading Operation Handschar—the least we can do, considering they have supplied two top-quality U.S. combat specialists to flesh out the team."

Throckmorton crossed his legs elegantly and made a languid gesture with his hand. "Actually, sir," he said, "the mission leader is Major Merritt here. I'm simply along for the ride. . . . More or less."

Once again, Donovan was irritated. There was an effete ennui in the way Throckmorton spoke, in the way he crossed his legs and moved his hand. And the first words out of his mouth were an unsolicited contradiction of his commanding officer. But to Gubbins it appeared to be water off a duck's back. He did not seem perturbed in the slightest. In fact, when the SOE head spoke again, Donovan found his tone surprisingly gentle, almost paternalistic.

"Now, now, Duncan—it's not necessary to sell yourself short. It's true that Walt is the tactical leader, but you know how crucial you are to the success of this operation."

Throckmorton regarded the ceiling idly. "I suppose. Mind if I smoke?"

Donovan glanced sidelong at Haskell. The color was rising to the SO colonel's cheeks. Donovan felt an indignant flush begin to sting his own face. But the two American commanders remained silent.

Gubbins nodded good-naturedly and waved his hand. "Absolutely, Duncan, go ahead. You too, Walt."

Merritt shifted his weight on the couch. "Thank you, sir. I don't smoke."

"Ah, that's right. Of course you don't."

Donovan continued to regard Throckmorton with distaste as the slender captain extracted a cigarette from a gold case and lit it with a jeweled Dunhill lighter.

"Major Merritt does not indulge in tobacco," General Gubbins remarked, "a legacy from his days as an Olympic athlete."

"Indeed?" A former athlete himself, Donovan was immediately interested. "Which Olympics, Major Merritt?"

"Munich, back in 'thirty-six, sir."

"What event?"

"The hundred-yard dash, General." Merritt gave a wry smile. "I didn't win. I was beaten in the semifinals by several other sprinters—most notably an American Negro named Jesse Owens."

"Ah yes," Donovan said. "the famous Mr. Owens. What an embarassment he turned out to be for the so-called Master Race, eh?"

Merritt looked at Haskell, then back at Donovan. "Not just for the Germans, sir." The wry smile again. "He made me look like I was standing still."

"Major Merritt has since gone on to even greater

things," Gubbins interjected, "such as organizing a last-minute counterattack to cover the evacuation of the British Expeditionary Force at Dunkirk back in 'forty. After that little escapade, we at SOE, who occasionally manage to recognize a good thing when we see it, plucked the major for special operations duty. In the past three and a half years, he has led various commando raids in Norway, France, and Italy. But his true area of expertise is Yugoslavia. So far, we have parachuted Major Merritt and his supporting personnel into that country . . . how many times is it now, Walt?"

"Six, sir," Merritt answered. "Five by parachute into the mountains, once by gunboat to the coast of Montenegro." He looked at Donovan. "Short-term operations, General, with specific targets: bridges, dams, railways. My great advantage in Yugoslavia is that I speak Serbo-Croatian fluently, along with several related dialects. My mother's maiden name is Petrović. She was born in Sarajevo."

Donovan nodded. "Useful, Major, without a doubt." His piercing blue eyes shifted to Throckmorton, who was lounging and smoking. "And you, Captain. Are you also fluent in Serbo-Croatian?"

Throckmorton picked his cigarette from between his lips with a bored flourish. "I'd say competent rather than fluent. Unlike Major Merritt, I didn't learn the language at my mother's knee." He paused to draw on his cigarette again, and took his time about it.

Donovan felt his molars set together, the heat rise to his cheeks. Throckmorton had a rare gift for getting on a man's nerves. . . . *His* nerves, anyway. He cleared his throat. "And so? How did you learn it?"

"I picked up Serbo-Croatian while yachting in the twenties and thirties with various and sundry uncles who kept boats in Trieste and enjoyed cruising the Dalmatian Coast."

The bored, petulant way Throckmorton drew out the word "yaww-ting" nearly caused Donovan to blow a main fuse. But with the possible exception of Haskell, no one in the parlor was aware of it.

"I would imagine that yachting in the Adriatic these days is somewhat limited," Donovan commented tightly.

"Yaas," Throckmorton responded. "Quite."

"As a matter of fact," Menzies put in, "Sir Colin and I had discussed the option of inserting Major Merritt's team into Yugoslavia by submarine, possibly in the vicinity of the Croatian port city of Zara. But that would have required too much overland travel through hostile territory to reach the mission target, which is in the Majevica Mountains of the interior. So no yachting, so to speak. We're going with parachute insertion."

"Another railway bridge, I understand?" Haskell said.

"Not just any railway bridge," Gubbins replied. He handed the American colonel two identical eight-by-ten photographs. Haskell passed one to Donovan, who put on a pair of steel-rimmed glasses to study it.

"This is the Zpoda Skyway Bridge," Gubbins continued, "one of the highest multiarch, brick-and-steel constructions in the world. And high in this case does not refer just to the bridge itself, but where it is located: at an altitude of nearly seven thousand feet on the upper rim of the Zpoda Gorge.

"The Germans—notably the SS Division Handschar—have pushed Tito's Partisans far back into the Majevica Mountains and are managing to maintain a more or less consistent line of advance that runs from gorge to peak to gorge across the northern third of this range. There is one rail line supplying the advance, and it runs across the Zpoda Skyway.

"Now then, most of this railway lies in the flat country of the Sava River plain. As it ascends through the foothills of the Majevicas and up to the Zpoda Gorge, it runs through numerous tunnels connected by narrow, well-supported rock beds and embankments. Naturally Marshall Tito and his Partisans, who are at present in a rather hellish mountain-warfare situation, would very much like to have this rail line cut. . . . Permanently, if possible."

Donovan grunted and removed his glasses. "The obvious solution," he said, "is to send bombers to destroy it."

"We tried that," Menzies responded, "twice. Lancasters and then Halifaxes out of Bari, in southern Italy. It didn't work."

"Why not?" Haskell demanded. "Did they miss the mark both times?"

Menzies glanced at Gubbins, who cleared his throat and answered. "No. They hit the line in several places. But there are some problems. First of all, we've learned that if we bomb the railway in the flatland area of the Sava River plain, the Germans have the capacity to repair it virtually overnight. On such accessible terrain, they can reconstruct five miles of blown track in ten hours.

"The higher a rail line climbs up into a mountain range, the more difficult it is to repair—normally. But the abundance of tunnels in the Majevicas provides shelter from aerial attack over much of the train route. In addition, the Germans have stationed heavy-duty plow engines and repair cars inside the tunnels at regular intervals, so that if a bomb blast brings down rubble on an exposed section of line, it can be cleared—and if necessary reconstructed—in short order.

"But the Zpoda Skyway Bridge . . . that's another story. It's such an inaccessible and complex structure that if we were able to destroy it, there would be no way the Germans could replace it. The mountain supply route would be dead-ended at its highest, most inconvenient point—directly behind the main line of advance. The German thrust would begin to starve."

"Once again," Donovan said, "why not bombers?"

Gubbins stroked his mustache and shook his head.

"Take another look at that photograph, General. The bridge links two tunnel entrances that face each other on opposite sides of the gorge. It sweeps around in a quarter-mile-long curve, hugging the sheer cliff just beneath the gorge's uppermost rim. Do you see that thick, shelflike cap of rock that overhangs the bridge along its entire length between the two tunnels? That's the problem.

"The Royal Air Force can't get its bombs on the bridge because they keep hitting the overhang, which our engineers inform us is no less than one hundred and fifty feet of solid granite. We can't get a vertically falling bomb to travel horizontally enough to slip under the overhang and hit the bases of the support arches where they tie into the cliff, much less the track itself."

Donovan scratched his chin. "How about using Mosquito fighter-bombers to fly straight up the gorge from north to south? Pull up hard at the last minute and try to lob their bombs under that rock shelf?"

"The Germans have installed antiaircraft gun positions on the ridgetops along the entire length of the gorge. In addition, there are antiaircraft gun cars located on side tracks in nearly every tunnel. These too can be rolled out in the event of an aerial attack. Pilots flying up the gorge in the manner you suggest to try to bomb or rocket the supports would be running a suicide gauntlet." Gubbins gave a grim smile. "Not that we wouldn't try it if we thought such an approach had a ghost of a chance of succeeding. We've used similar tactics in fjords in Norway. But in this instance our best planners put the likelihood of success at nil, and the projected losses at one hundred percent."

"Rather unpromising," Donovan remarked.

"Yes, rather."

There was a long pause as Gubbins poured himself a cup of tea from the silver service on the tray next to his chair. He glanced at Churchill as he set the teapot down; the prime minister shook his head silently and continued to puff on his cigar. Donovan and Haskell reexamined the photographs they had been given.

"So that's why you requested a couple of specialists from the Tenth Mountain Division," Donovan said finally. "You need skilled climbers, men who know rope work, to help place charges on the supporting arches of that bridge."

"Correct," Gubbins replied. "Men who can keep up with Walt Merritt here, who also happens to be an expert mountaineer." He sipped tea. "But this operation has not one but two interesting elements—both of which we feel you and Colonel Haskell should be made aware of."

"Elements of an extremely . . . *delicate* nature," Churchill grunted. It was the first time he had said anything since Merritt and Throckmorton had entered the parlor.

Gubbins looked at the prime minister and nodded. "Extremely delicate," he reiterated.

He set his teacup down on the service tray, glanced at Churchill again, then gestured across the room in the direction of the elegant, white-haired gentleman who had been sitting in complete silence off to the side throughout the meeting. "General Donovan, Colonel Haskell, allow me to introduce an old and dear friend of the prime minister's, Mr. Martin Judson. Mr. Judson is a renowned British industrialist and economic expert with a large number of prewar ties to the European continent. Some of these ties have proven to be . . . useful.

"Mr. Judson, with Major Merritt's assistance, would you please elucidate for our esteemed American colleagues on the 'elements of a delicate nature' to which the prime minister has just referred?"

It was well after dark by the time Donovan and Haskell exited 10 Downing Street and climbed into their waiting military staff car. As the vehicle pulled away from the prime minister's residence, Haskell puffed his cheeks and blew out a long breath.

"What do you think, General?" he asked.

Donovan shook his head. "Damnedest multiobjective operation I've ever heard of. Churchill was right: two birds with one stone."

"If they can pull it off," Haskell said dubiously.

The general was silent for a moment. Then he rubbed his chin and folded his arms. "Look," he said, "the whole thing's a high-wire stunt—literally. But if they can succeed in executing even half of it, it'll be worth it. Either one of those two objectives is worth achieving."

Haskell grunted. "Even if they all get killed in the process?"

Donovan turned and looked at his Special Operations chief in feigned surprise. "Well, of course, Joe. Even if they all get killed. Business as usual. As you're so fond of pointing out, this is war, not checkers."

Chapter Three

Every rivet in the shuddering fuselage of the Halifax seemed on the verge of vibrating loose. *Not unlike my teeth,* Merritt thought, shifting his weight on his small metal seat and rebracing his feet. The Royal Air Force heavy bomber continued to batter its way through the turbulent night air above the coastal mountains of Montenegro, its four Rolls-Royce Merlin engines driving it onward to the northeast. . . . Ever deeper into the rugged interior of war-torn Yugoslavia.

Not for the first time, Merritt found himself longing for a window, a port of some kind—anything through which he could catch a glimpse of the sky, the stars, the moon, or the horizon. Every one of his five previous jumps into Yugoslavia had been from a Halifax bomber, and this particular design of warplane afforded viewing capability only to aircrew for whom it was essential—pilot and copilot, nose and turret gunners. Parachutists huddled amidships in the darkened fuselage above the empty bomb bay did not need to see where they were going. Or what might be coming at them.

The Halifax heaved upward in a sudden vortex of turbulence. Merritt felt his stomach bottom out, his spine compress. In the floor of the modified bomb bay, the four-foot circular wooden hatch that covered the joe hole rattled violently against its retaining clips, buffeted by the irregular slipstream.

"Jeezus H. Christ!" a voice shouted from the opposite side of the fuselage. "Think that sky jockey's tryin' to hit every patch of bad air in the goddamn Balkan Peninsula?" It was Bristow, one of the two Americans plucked by OSS from the Tenth Mountain Division. He was a big, brawny Texan with a wide Scots-Irish face, a ready smile, and a dry, laconic wit. Beside him, dwarfed by comparison and all but smothered by the equipment he was wearing, sat the other American, a feisty little New Yorker of Italian extraction named D'Amato. The two—sergeants both—were best friends, and for their own amusement kept up a habitual banter consisting largely of routine back-and-forth insults interspersed with disgusted observations about military life and the war in general. It would have been easy, upon first listen, to dismiss them as frivolous or negative, but Merritt had observed them carefully during SOE mission training in Scotland, while en route to Allied-controlled southern Italy via North Africa, and in the few days before the team's final departure from the Adriatic port of Bari, and concluded that Bristow and D'Amato, despite their irreverent mannerisms, were indeed professional soldiers, highly competent and disciplined. Disciplined enough, in fact, to have picked up basic Serbo-Croatian language skills in a matter of weeks. Merritt—well traveled, down-to-earth, and personally devoid of the Anglocentric puffery that characterized much of the British officer class—had found that he liked them both immensely.

The Halifax heaved and bucked again, then settled

down. Merritt's eyes shifted to the two bulky, helmeted figures sitting just aft of Bristow and D'Amato. Sergeants Hurst and Stirling were British Regular Army—experienced commandos with demolition and mountaineering training. Each of them had accompanied Merritt on one previous mission: Hurst to Norway; Stirling to France. They were good men, resourceful and reliable.

Next to Stirling sat the late addition to the team, Weiss. He appeared to be asleep, his helmet tipped forward over his eyes, his arms folded on top of his reserve chute. He was something of an unknown quantity to the other men. Merritt watched him for a moment.

A wet cough sounded in Merritt's ear above the roar of the engines. He glanced to his left as Throckmorton, sitting beside him, wiped his lips with a handkerchief. The slender captain was calmly reading a Serbo-Croatian grammar book, a pencil flashlight stuck in the webbing of his jump helmet. The two men's eyes met.

Merritt leaned in close. "How are you, Duncan?" he called.

Throckmorton nodded. "Just ducky, thanks. You?"

"All right." Merritt glanced at the illuminated dial of his wristwatch. "Should be only another few minutes to the drop zone."

Throckmorton shrugged and smiled. "Fine. Have the butler notify me when it's time to go." He went back to reading his grammar text.

Merritt gave a short laugh and sat back. He noted without concern that, as expected, his mouth had become quite dry. The tension was building now, as it always did just before a night jump. So many things could go wrong. Parachutes could fail to open or get hung up on the rear undercarriage of the plane. Even with deployed canopies, jumpers could be swept into cliffs or gorges, or killed on impact with the ground— particularly in rough terrain in the dark. And as mission commander he worried not just about himself, but about every man on his team.

And as usual he countered the looming worry by reminding himself that every member of the team was a skilled, experienced combat parachutist equipped with the best British and American gear available, that everything from static lines to reserve chutes to boot soles had been checked and rechecked a half-dozen times, and that if by some chance anything crucial had been overlooked, it was too damned late to fret about it now.

An RAF flight sergeant waddled past in the darkness, clad against the bitter chill in heavy insulated coveralls and trailing a long safety tether from a full-body harness. He grinned at Merritt, stepped down into the bomb bay, and bent over a large aluminum canister the approximate size and shape of three fifty-gallon oil drums laid end to end. Working quickly, he shucked his heavy gloves and ran his hands over the elongate parachute pack strapped to the canister's midpoint. Then he pulled out a length of the cargo chute's static line, leaned over, and hooked the end to a heavy steel ring bolted to the port side of the fuselage.[1] As he did so, a small red light mounted on the forward bulkhead of the bomb bay compartment came on, bathing the six jumpers and the flight sergeant in a dull crimson glow.

The sergeant turned to Merritt, on the starboard side of the aircraft, redonning his fleece-lined gloves, and stepped partly up out of the bomb bay.

"Got signal fires up ahead, Major. Pilot's going to overfly the drop zone once, confirm that it's the Partisans down there and not the bleedin' Nazis by exchanging the correct series of identification flashes." The sergeant's cockney accent was all but indecipherable over the roar of the engines. "Once that's done, we'll come around for another pass, and I'll slide your gear canister out the bleedin' joe hole. Third time around, it's your turn." He grinned again. "All seven o' you, quick like."

Merritt nodded. "I'll lead off, followed by Captain Throckmorton here."

"Yes, sir," the sergeant said, touching his eyebrow.

The bomber began to bank steeply. The RAF sergeant braced a leg against the side of the bomb bay and waited. The aircraft canted to nearly forty-five degrees, maintained that attitude for the better part of a minute, then eased back down onto level flight. As Merritt and his team members resettled themselves, the sergeant bent down and released the clips on the joe hole cover. He pulled the circular wooden lid aside, revealing the open mouth of a four-foot-diameter metal tube, three feet deep, that extended below the belly of the Halifax. Merritt leaned forward and peered down, on the off chance that he might catch a glimpse of a signal fire. There was nothing at the lower end of the tube but a frigid black void of rushing air.

The sergeant heaved one end of the big cargo canister over the joe hole, then stepped around to its opposite end and waited, looking up at the red light in the forward bulkhead. The plane's engines throttled back, changing in pitch. Merritt felt his ears pop as the Halifax sank through the air, losing altitude. The red light winked off and was instantly replaced by a flashing green. The sergeant seized the canister, tilted it up against his shoulder with a curse, and slid the eight-foot-long package out through the joe hole in one practiced motion. There was a faint *whap* beneath the bomber as the cargo chute opened, and then a light battering sound as the deployed static line, now detached from the parachute, began to beat a tattoo on the underside of the fuselage in the slipstream.

"Clear and gone!" The sergeant grinned and gave Merritt the thumbs-up. "Your turn now, sir," he called. "Come on down and have a seat. The captain, too." On the forward bulkhead, the flashing green light switched back to red.

Merritt and Throckmorton clambered down into the bomb bay and sat next to each other on the forward edge of the joe hole, legs dangling, facing aft. The RAF sergeant motioned for Bristow and D'Amato to sit in similar fashion on either side of the two British officers. As they moved into position he tended to all four static lines, ensuring that they were lying fair and there would be no risk of entanglement.

Along the port side of the fuselage, Hurst, Stirling, and Weiss shuffled forward until they were occupying the metal seats nearest the joe hole. As Bristow and then D'Amato followed Merritt and Throckmorton out, the last three would step down into the bomb bay in sequence, as per their training, and make their respective exits.

The Halifax began to bank again. Once more, the RAF sergeant turned sideways and braced a leg. Merritt, Throckmorton, Bristow, and D'Amato leaned back from the gaping joe hole and found secure handholds. The bomber rose steeply onto its port wingtip, repeating the pattern of its first circuit. The four big Merlin engines roared in angry chorus as they powered the heavy warplane around.

Another gale of turbulence rattled the fuselage. The aircraft settled back down to level. Again, the engines dropped in pitch as the pilot throttled back. Merritt felt the seat of his pants nearly leave the floor of the bomb bay as the Halifax lost altitude.

The RAF sergeant half turned and knelt on one knee on the opposite side of the joe hole, facing forward. His broad Cockney face, serious now, was bathed in the eerie glow of the red light directly behind Merritt.

"When I point at you, you go," he shouted to everyone. "In sequence. Got it?"

"We've got it," Merritt confirmed. He placed his gloved palms on the floor of the bomb bay, fingers and thumbs over the edge of the joe hole, eyeing the sergeant. Just below his dangling boots, the black slipstream shrieked and howled past the underbelly of the plane. Unconsciously he licked his lips. His mouth was very dry.

The seconds dragged by. Merritt stared at the red-tinged flight sergeant. The sergeant stared at the red light behind Merritt's head.

The color of the sergeant's face changed from red to green. As the fleece-lined glove came down to point at him, Major Walter Merritt leaned forward and for the sixth time in his life dropped through the joe hole of a Halifax bomber into the night skies over Yugoslavia.

"I can hear it coming around again," Haak said, his breath condensing into frosty plumes. "A Halifax, for certain."

"No lights, of course, sir," Langwolt muttered at his side.

"Of course."

Haak stopped searching the sky long enough to glance across the open, semiwooded slope where four evenly spaced signal fires were casting faint orange glimmers across the new-fallen snow. The silhouettes of his men moved back and forth in front of the leaping flames.

"I want those fires kept bright," Haak said, tipping his head back and resuming his upward gaze.

The windblast hit Merritt with such freezing force that it literally snatched the breath from his lungs. Gasping, he tumbled downward in pitch-blackness, buffeted by invisible fists of air, straining to maintain the proper compact body position.

WHAP.

The opening of the parachute canopy jarred him from neck to tailbone, the straps of his body harness momentarily cinching garotte tight. He felt himself bounce in the chute risers and swing wildly, a cork-screwing human pendulum. . . .

And then the chaotic motion subsided and he was swaying gently in his harness, suspended like a life-sized marionette at the end of twenty-eight invisible strings, drifting through a vast black void of bone-chilling cold. The throaty roar of the Halifax's engines seemed very far off now. He looked up. Just below the lower edge of his deployed canopy he could see four faint blue dots set close in a horizontal line—heat glow from the bomber's engine exhausts—receding in the darkness.

He looked down. The mountainous terrain below his dangling boots was broken, gloomy, and forbidding. There appeared to be no level ground, only a jigsaw puzzle of crooked, twisting shadows, snow-covered slopes, and dense clusters of spirelike ever-green trees. Every other shadow looked like a jagged ridge or bottomless crevasse. A sudden gust of wind hit him, taking his breath away and rocking him in the parachute risers. The whirl of frigid air felt like a white-hot blade against his cheek.

He twisted in his harness, looking over his left shoulder and down. *There.* Two signal fires, flickering like tiny oases of orange warmth in the desolate land-scape. The only visible orientation points. Merritt tugged on his risers, trying to slip the chute sideways to the left.

The humped outlines of ridges, arêtes, and peaks, looming snow blanketed and tree bearded like the sleeping winter giants of Norse myth, rose dramatically around him as he sank out of the night sky. He craned his neck and looked upward, trying to catch a glimpse of his comrades' parachutes, but could see nothing. He looked down again.

He was heading for a dense black tangle of trees, and it was coming up very quickly. To the right, a pale expanse of snow gleamed dully in the ambient starlight. Merritt yanked on his risers, got his boots together, flexed his knees. . . .

He brushed past the drooping branches of an evergreen, slipping sideways fast, and hit the slope in an explosion of snow. The chute dragged him through the drifts like an unwilling plow for another fifteen feet before finally collapsing. He was down.

Rolling over, he hit the release buckle of his parachute harness and shucked it. Then he scrambled to his knees, blinking snow out of his eyes, and freed up the Sten submachine gun strapped across his chest. Several dark figures were running toward him, laboring across the slope through thigh-deep drifts. Behind them, through the trees, flickered the orange flames of a signal fire.

Merritt swung the Sten up and fell forward onto his stomach. The nearest figure was less than twenty yards away, floundering toward him through the snow with greatcoat flapping and rifle at high port. Identifying details were impossible to make out. Merritt leveled his weapon at the charging form and shouted, *"Živio Tito!"*

"Long live Tito." The prearranged challenge, spoken in Serbo-Croatian. Second by elapsing second, Merritt waited for the correct reply. His finger tightened on the trigger of the Sten.

The greatcoated figure stopped thrashing toward him and raised the rifle above its head with both hands. *"Smrt Fašismu!"* came the hoarse cry. *"Smrt Fašismu!"*

"Death to Fascists." Correct. Merritt let out a long breath and eased his grip on the submachine gun. As he rose to his knees and sat back on his haunches, the man in the greatcoat lowered his arms and bulled forward through the deep snow. Beneath an immense fur hat, Merritt could make out the pale curve of a broad grin.

"Hello, British, hello!" The man stopped about a

yard in front of Merritt, beaming downward through a bushy black beard that would have done justice to a Cossack. He had to be at least six and a half feet tall. . . . Perhaps more. "Jolly good to see you, comrade! Eh, wot?" He nodded at his own fractured English and bent over to clap Merritt on the shoulder. It was like being hit by a ten-pound maul.

"Greetings to you, comrade," Merritt replied, opting for Serbo-Croatian. He got to his feet and brushed snow off his heavy battle jacket. "I take it you're with Cernović."

"If I wasn't," the giant answered happily, "you'd be dead."

"Look out below, goddamit!"

The yell was in West Texas American twang, and a heartbeat later Bristow came swinging by, narrowly missing the big Partisan. He hit the snow with a muffled curse about ten feet behind Merritt and was dragged downslope another fifty by a gust of wind that kept his parachute inflated at an oblique angle. Two other Partisans floundered after him, shouting encouragement.

Merritt watched with concern, then broke into an unconscious smile as the big Texan somersaulted to his feet, still swearing, and collapsed the canopy with a powerful yank on one of the risers. A hundred yards away, near the stand of trees through which the closest signal fire could be seen, D'Amato's compact form hit the snow, feet together, under a quietly descending parachute. It was a perfect landing, without wind interference, but the little sergeant had touched down on a particularly deep drift. He plunged through the clean white surface and disappeared completely. His camouflage-patterned canopy settled over over the entry hole like a shroud.

Merritt began to stride through the snow toward D'Amato, sinking thigh deep with every step. He paused as the collapsed canopy began to heave and billow. A few seconds later, the long blade of a jump knife poked through the camo silk and slashed length-wise. D'Amato emerged from the slit, shedding snow, and began to cut away the suspension lines of his chute, which had become tangled around his head and shoulders.

Merritt turned back to Bristow. The big Texan was wading through the snow toward him, flanked by the two Partisans who had pursued him down the slope. Being considerably shorter than the American, both were struggling to keep up, even as they maintained a constant stream of congratulations in some obscure Serbo-Croatian dialect.

Merritt looked skyward, checking for more para-chutes.

Throckmorton, second through the joe hole, after Merritt, had been blown by a random gust of wind past the drop zone demarcated by the obvious signal fires and along a precipitous ridge of ice-covered rock. At first he'd thought he would be able to land in the snow at the far end of the clearing before being car-ried into the cliff face, but the same icy zephyr that had pushed him past the DZ had updrafted at the last minute, briefly interrupting his descent. The short delay had been enough to waft him like a helpless kite into the jagged wall of black rock.

He'd hit hard about eighty feet above the snowdrifts at the base of the cliff—an impact violent enough to knock the wind out of him. His canopy had collapsed, snagged, torn, snagged again, and then hung fast on an outcropping of rock approximately twenty-five feet above his head.

Currently Captain Duncan Throckmorton was try-ing to keep very still in his harness, even as he searched for a way out of his predicament. Every few seconds the overstrained silk of the parachute would give way a little more with an ominous tearing sound.

Most unpleasant.

*　　*　　*

John McKinna

Sergeants Hurst and Stirling had exited the Halifax almost on top of one another. Hard-earned experience had taught them that the best way to avoid wide dispersal on a combat drop was to leave the plane simultaneously. Now they were descending under deployed canopies barely fifty feet apart, Stirling perhaps ten feet higher than Hurst. The close jump grouping would put them on the ground together, at the same time, where each could watch the other's back. For the professional British soldier, the fighting war had started in 1939. They'd been watching each other's backs for a long time now.

"There, Hurstie!" Stirling called out, his voice hoarse in the freezing air. "Two signal fires, just over that bleedin' ridge. Slip left, mate!"

"Left it is," Hurst shouted back, pulling on his risers. Facing the wrong direction, he could just barely see one of the fires, glimmering through the black trees below, out of the corner of his eye.

A gust of wind hit the two commandos, lofting them over the knife-edged ridge. Now Hurst could see not one but three signal fires, spaced several hundred yards apart in a series of small, snow-covered clearings that interrupted the dark mat of evergreen trees. Close to the nearest fire, the silhouettes of men were clearly visible against the pale luminosity of open ground. They were moving in a ragged group to meet the two parachutists at their likely landing point in the middle of the clearing.

The same gust that had lifted Hurst and Stirling past the ridge had also moved them farther apart. Hurst was the first to touch down, sinking to his hips in deep snow. Just overhead, he caught a glimpse of Stirling being wafted sideways toward the trees at the edge of the clearing. Then his parachute canopy came down over his head and the view was lost.

Swinging his arms, he swept the camouflage-patterned silk off his head and shoulders, kicked free of the clinging snow, and struggled to a kneeling posi-

82

tion. He looked up the gentle slope of the clearing toward the signal fire. Coming toward him, spread out in a skirmish line and plunging forward through the snow, were at least twelve to fifteen dark figures, all armed. There were more behind.

At least the bloody Partisans were where they were supposed to be. Hurst brushed snow off the back of his neck and put a hand on the reassuring grip of his Sten. Force of habit.

"Živio Tito!" he shouted. Again, just to be sure they'd heard: *"Živio Tito!"*

The dark figures continued to advance, but no one gave the countersign. Hurst felt the well-conditioned hackles at the back of his neck begin to rise. . . . Or maybe it was just the confounded snow melting under his collar. The pilot of the Halifax had exchanged the proper flash signals with the Partisans on the ground, or the team wouldn't have gotten the green light to jump. Wouldn't do to start off the mission by machine-gunning a baker's dozen of the friendly resistance for want of a short verbal response.

Bloody foreigners. Hurst raised his free hand and tried again. *"Živio* perishin' *Tito*, damn your eyes! What the hell d'you lot think a countersign's for?"

The lead figure—a tall man in bulky winter mountain gear—halted, raised his arm, and leveled a pistol at Hurst. The others pressed forward, beginning to fan out around the British commando.

"Get your hands above your head, tommie!" SS-Obersturmfuehrer Rolf Langwolt barked in perfect English. "*Schnell!* You have no chance—"

Hurst's was the instinctive reaction of a true warrior. He threw himself sideways in the snow, jerking up his Sten gun, and opened fire.

Langwolt staggered back, firing his Luger as Hurst's first two rounds slammed into his shoulder and collarbone. Desperately the British sergeant fanned the compact machine gun to the left, across the line of ducking soldiers less than thirty feet away, twisting his body in the snow as he did so. The enemy troopers were so taken off guard by the reaction of the out-flanked man they'd expected to capture without a fight that for a brief moment they couldn't return fire. Hurst continued to swing the long, continuous burst through the infantrymen to his left. . . . Hitting some, driving the others onto their faces.

But there were half a dozen more on his right. . . .

Stirling was on his belly in the snow at the edge of the clearing, squinting through the rear battle sight of a No. 4 Mark 1 Enfield sniper rifle. The weapon was minus its telescopic sight, which was stowed deep in the commando sergeant's jump duffel to protect it from landing shock. Stirling had little need of it now—the squad of enemy soldiers virtually on top of Hurst was less than fifty yards away. A second skirmish line was bypassing Hurst's position and advancing toward him, barely a hundred yards distant.

Stirling blinked icy sweat out of his eyes, settled the battle sight on a dark hump just beyond Hurst, and fired. The .303 slug found its mark; the hump jerked and sagged into the snow. It took the veteran commando sniper less than a second to work the Enfield's bolt, eject the spent shell, chamber a fresh round, locate another target, and fire again. And again. And again.

The dark figures ringing Hurst had finally opened up, some with machine pistols. Little slivery lines of fire were converging on the half-surrounded sergeant like spokes to the hub of some hellish wheel. Stirling realized with a sudden numb rush that his old friend was no longer moving.

"Hurstie!" he yelled once, then rolled over and over in the deep snow, gained his feet, and plunged head-long into the black trees at the edge of the clearing, bullets hissing and snapping through the pine needles all around him.

*   *   *

THE WAR MOUNTAINS

SS-Hauptsturmfuehrer Ulrich Haak was standing beside the prostrate body of the bleeding, grimacing Langwolt, gesturing in angry frustration with his drawn Luger. He took a quick step to the side as a medic ran up and dropped to one knee to tend to the wounded Obersturmfuehrer.

"Alive, you idiots!" he bellowed at his scattered men, who were in hot pursuit of Stirling. He glanced over in annoyance at the huddled, bullet-riddled corpse of Sergeant Hurst. *"I want at least one of these cursed jumpers alive, do you understand?"*

"They'll . . . they'll get him, sir," Langwolt grunted. He winced as the medic applied pressure bandages to the twin wounds in his right shoulder. "The snow's too deep for him to move fast."

"Maybe they will—the Muslim turds. Unless he makes it over the ridge and finds the Partisans first. And he might; paratroopers are always elite soldiers—look at this one." He gestured again at Hurst's body. "A brave death, eh? It's enough to make me wish I hadn't transferred out of the airborne infantry myself. I'm getting particular about the company I keep." Haak peered down at his second-in-command. "How bad, Rolf?"

Langwolt grunted again. "Bad enough, sir. But I think I can walk in a few minutes."

Haak pulled a silver cigarette case from his pocket, opened it, and offered it to his wounded second-in-command. "Take a couple, Rolf, to calm your nerves. The last of my custom hoard from Munich."

Langwolt accepted with a grateful nod. "Thank you, sir."

"The wound in the top of the shoulder is just a graze," the medic offered, "but the other bullet went right through near the collarbone front to back. The clavicle may be broken, sir." He looked up askance at Haak, the commander's offhand remarks about Muslims—of which he was one—burning in his ears.

Haak repositioned his forage cap on his close-cropped blond head, pulling the brim down over his brows almost to the bridge of his aquiline nose. "Get back to the half-tracks," he ordered. "Try to follow along the base of this ridge; see if you can find a way through. We'll rendezvous in that vicinity in forty minutes." He started forward. "After we kill or capture the jumper, we may be able to intercept some of the Partisans he and his companion were trying to coordinate with."

"There may have been other jumpers," Langwolt said, struggling to his feet with the aid of the medic. "They may have hit the Partisans' landing zone instead of our decoy."

"Possible," Haak commented over his shoulder, "or maybe they're just wandering around in the woods, lost." He began to high-step through the snow in the tracks of his infantrymen, toward the trees through which Stirling had fled. "With any luck we'll run into a few of them, too."

"I am Anton Cernović," the goateed, huskily built Partisan commander had said to Merritt in accented English, extending his hand as he approached. The words were barely out of his mouth when the muted rattle of Hurst's Sten gun echoed out of the woods to the left. Instinctively the little knot of parachutists and Partisans had dropped into a collective crouch, eyes scanning the darkness for signs of attackers.

"Major Walter Merritt, Commander Cernovć," Merritt reciprocated in a low voice. "British Special Operations Executive." He shifted his own Sten gun to one knee, continuing to search the tree line. "These are Sergeants Cole Bristow and Frank D'Amato, American mountain warfare specialists on loan to SOE for this mission."

The din of machine gun fire increased, punctuated by the flat crack of rifle shots. Reverberating through the snowy crags and sentinel trees along with the clamor of the furious firefight were the sounds of men yelling.

"I'm short four of my men, Commander," Merritt stated tersely, his breath rolling out in clouds of condensation. "And obviously one or more of them has run into a German patrol, from the sound of those Schmeisser machine pistols."

Cernović didn't hesitate. Standing up, he waved a gloved hand at the Partisans scattered across the slope on either side of him. "Lost parachutists!" he shouted in Serbo-Croatian. "Move out and engage the Fascists! *Try not to kill any parachutists, comrades!*"

Bristow glanced at D'Amato, then Merritt. "Try?"

Cernović heard him, gave a rueful smile and a shrug. "The best we can do, my friend," he said, switching back to English, "under the circumstances."

"Jeezus," Bristow growled, hefting the .45-caliber Thompson submachine gun that was his weapon of choice.

The Partisan infantry was disappearing into the woods in a ragged skirmish line, led by the black-bearded giant who had first made contact with Merritt. The sounds of an ongoing firefight had stopped now, replaced with those of men shouting to each other and the occasional lone rifle shot. Each rifle report was answered with a brief clattering of fire from multiple Schmeisser machine pistols.

Merritt cocked his head, listening. "Enfield sniper rifle," he said. "That's Stirling. He's on the run, and they're hunting him." He rose to his feet and started forward. "Let's go."

Cernović grunted an order over his shoulder to the three Partisans who'd remained with him, and moved up alongside Merritt. Bristow and D'Amato spread out on the British major's opposite side, cradling their weapons and trudging through the thigh-deep snow.

Again, a lone rifle shot cracked through the trees above the mournful whine of the alpine wind.

*   *   *

Sergeant Colin Stirling was running for his life. *Fire and evade. Fire and evade.* The familiar phrase pulsed through his brain like a mantra. But it was hard to evade when you were plowing through snow up to your belt and leaving a trail as plain as a drainage ditch for your pursuers to follow.

Stirling floundered up a forty-five-degree slope toward the base of an immense black crag that jutted out of the mountainside like the bow of a ship. He might be able to move faster among the rocks beneath the overhang, where the snow was not as deep. His breath was coming in agonizing gasps, the thin, frigid air lancing his lungs like a chestful of razor blades.

His head was spinning from lack of oxygen. He had to stop—get his wind back. With a final effort he plowed upward through the crest of a snowdrift and staggered behind a massive boulder at the base of the cliff. Vision blurring, steam rising off his sweat-slick face, he sagged to his haunches with his back to the rock, momentarily done in.

The shouts of his pursuers resonated off the black crag that towered into the night sky above him. They were very close, working their way up the slope. Following his trail.

Stirling gathered his strength, pushed himself erect, and brought his rifle to bear around the back side of the boulder. There were five dark figures laboring up the slope toward him, machine pistols slung across chests. They were less than thirty yards away. Stirling centered the Enfield's battle sight on the middle figure and fired.

It was an easy shot for a marksman of Stirling's caliber, despite his dizziness and blurred vision. The slug hit the enemy soldier square in the chest and knocked him backward down the snowy slope. The other four dove left and right and opened up with their Schmeissers.

The barrage of bullets drove Stirling back down behind the rock in a flurry of granite splinters. Desperately he rolled to the opposite side of the boulder and swung his rifle around, preparing to shoot from a prone position. Unrelenting machine-gun fire continued to hammer into the rock all around him. Stirling knew what the Germans had in mind: two of them would keep him pinned down with a base of fire, while the remaining two would rush his position. He had to return fire. There was nowhere to run.

Abruptly the machine-gun fire ceased. Stirling rolled out on his elbows, trying to expose himself as little as possible. Over the barrel of his rifle he was just in time to see the dark shape of an enemy soldier, legs pumping, burst through the snowdrift directly in front of him. He was so close that Stirling could make out the pale gleam of gritted teeth in a swarthy face beneath a death's-head fez.

The British sergeant fired. The enemy soldier stopped as if he'd run into a wall and fell backward with a strangled cry, dropping his machine pistol. Stirling rolled toward the opposite side of the boulder, working the Enfield's bolt as he did so. Just above him, there came the scraping sound of boot soles on rock. . . .

With the speed born of desperation, Stirling rammed the bolt home and swung the rifle around, adrenaline pumping through his body like an electric charge. . . .

It was too late. The second enemy soldier had made it around the boulder and was standing over him, his Schmeisser already brought to bear.

Everything went into slow motion.

Stirling locked eyes with the SS trooper through the Schmeisser's ring sight.

Damn, he thought, waiting for the burst.

The enemy soldier's head snapped over onto his right shoulder. At the same time, Stirling heard an odd, sharp *pop*.

Like a marionette with its strings suddenly cut, the

SS trooper folded up and crumpled facedown into the snow.

The death's-head fez he wore somehow remained on his head. In the top of it, near the tassel attachment, was a small hole. Stirling blinked. Blood began to spread out around the enemy soldier's head, a dark stain on the pristine pallor of the snow.

Bewildered, Stirling glanced around. Then, his eye catching nothing, he rolled to one knee and shouldered his rifle once again. There were at least two more enemy soldiers on the slope, and they'd be coming next.

Stirling raised his head and shoulders above the boulder, sighting down the Enfield. The two remaining SS troopers were standing thigh deep in the snow, aiming their machine pistols . . . *straight upward.*

Stirling fired. The .303 slug smacked into the forehead of the soldier on the left, sending his fez flying end over end and his limp body toppling backward down the slope. The last enemy soldier jerked down his Schmeisser and trained it on the British sergeant.

Stirling hunched back down behind the boulder, working the Enfield's bolt. In his haste, his boot slipped on a patch of ice. He lost his balance and fell onto one arm, partially exposing himself beyond the edge of the covering rock.

As the SS trooper squeezed the trigger of his machine pistol, Sergeant David Weiss stepped out from behind a pine tree some twenty feet farther along the slope and killed him on his feet with a two-second burst from his Sten gun. The Schmeisser slugs hammered harmlessly into the snow as the dead man fell.

Stirling regained his balance and, crouching behind the boulder, waved at Weiss. The younger sergeant waved back and began to climb rapidly across the snow-packed slope toward him. As Weiss neared the base of the crag, Stirling spotted first one dim human form, then another and another, appearing through the trees from around the contour of the incline. Alarmed, he threw up his rifle and sighted on the lead figure.

"Quick, Weiss!" he hissed. "Get in here!"

Weiss lunged through the top of the snowdrift that abutted Stirling's boulder and ducked down beside him. "What is it?" he asked, breathing hard.

"Don't know. Maybe more Huns." Stirling's brow furrowed as he concentrated on the new arrivals. "But they're coming from the opposite direction, and they're not all wearing the same winter gear. Mismatched clothing, no real uniforms. Mismatched weapons, too."

Weiss peered cautiously over the top of the boulder. "Sounds like Partisans."

Stirling watched in silence for another few seconds, then lowered his rifle. "It is."

The two British commandos stood up as the skirmish line of Partisans advanced across the slope like a sparse, ragged wave. The lead figures had only just disappeared into the dark trees through which Stirling had fled when there was an outbreak of machine-gun and rifle fire, accompanied by frantic shouts in both German and Serbo-Croatian. Instinctively Stirling and Weiss hunched back behind the boulder.

"I guess they found more of the Nazis who were chasing you," Weiss said. He glanced over at the body of the dead enemy soldier with the hole in the top of his fez. The pool of dark blood around the man's head was a yard in diameter and already frozen solid. "Looks like SS, by that death's-head symbol on the fez. . . . But I don't see any SS runes on the collar or anywhere else. Strange."

"The man is a Muslim trooper of the SS Division Handschar," said Anton Cernović, approaching with practiced stealth along the base of the crag. Following him were Merritt, Bristow, D'Amato, and three very tough-looking Partisan infantrymen. Startled, Weiss and Stirling spun around and brought their weapons up, but upon recognizing Merritt lowered them immediately.

Cernović halted and regarded the body with casual disinterest. "As a non-Aryan," he continued, "he is not permitted to wear the actual runic symbol of the SS. Only German officers within Handschar may do so, on the left pocket of their battle tunics." He pointed. "You see the insignia on the collar? The arm holding a scimitar in combination with a Nazi swastika? That is the official emblem of the Handschar division."

The Partisan commander glanced up as another heavy outburst of small-arms fire echoed through the dark trees below and to the right. Then he shrugged, fished beneath his coat, withdrew a crumpled hand-rolled cigarette, and stuck it between his lips. One of the Partisans stepped forward with a match, and Cernović turned his head sideways to take the light.

"This man was a dangerous fighter," he remarked, exhaling smoke. "You did well to kill him and his companions. They are members of a Jagdkommando unit within Handschar."

Weiss shifted his Sten in his arms. "What exactly is a Jagdkommando unit?"

"A hunter-killer group," Cernović replied, "varying from platoon to company strength. The Jagdkommando are sent out into the hills on tracked vehicles and on foot, heavily armed, with orders to hunt down and kill every Partisan they can find. So naturally"— he smiled swarthily around his cigarette like an evil gypsy—"when we get an opportunity to kill *them*, we do so with considerable relish."

"Commander Cernović has just told me that the Jagdkommando have recently taken up the habit of stalking Partisan drop zones and then quietly setting up duplicate signal fires nearby—perhaps just over the next ridge," Merritt said. "Jumpers can get confused, head for the wrong lights. Apparently that's what just happened to some of us. By the way," he added, "good to see you alive, Weiss. And you, too, Stirling."

"Thank you, sir," the two sergeants replied in unison.

Merritt turned to Cernović as yet another burst of gunfire chattered through the trees, none too distant. "What's your assessment of the situation, Commander? Is there a whole company of SS Jagdkommando out there? If so, you're badly outnumbered."

The Partisan commander shook his head, exhaling smoke. "We had reports of only two platoon-strength hunter-killer groups operating in this area in the past three days. No other deployments from the main forces of Handschar. Even if the two groups have linked up, that's still only eighty or so men and perhaps four or five half-tracks. I have ninety-two men, Major." The swarthy smile again. "Even odds, more or less."

Merritt nodded and looked at Stirling. "Where's Hurst?"

The commando sergeant cleared his throat before replying. "Dead, sir. Shot it out with the buggers when they tried to take him alive."

"I'm sorry, Stirling. He was a good man."

"Yes, sir. That he was. And a good friend."

Merritt blew out a long, frosty breath. "So that leaves Throckmorton. Have either of you seen him?"

Stirling and Weiss shook their heads. "Afraid not, sir," Stirling said. "Frankly, I haven't had time to look. Been running for my life since I touched down. And if it weren't for Weiss here taking out these two troopers for me"—he pointed down at the corpses on the slope and at the body of the enemy soldier with the holed fez—"I'd have been as dead as poor Hurstie." He paused, then glanced at Weiss. "Can't think how you managed to shoot *up* and still hit this one bastard in the top of the head, though. . . ."

Weiss blinked. "The only man I killed was lower down on the slope," he said. "I never shot up in this direction."

"You didn't?" Stirling looked confused. "Then who—"

"I say, there." The voice, clear but at the same time strangely distant, seemed to come out of the rock face itself. "Perhaps you chaps would care to lend a gentleman a hand, now that the excitement's died down somewhat."

The little knot of men glanced around, momentarily baffled. Then Merritt looked up. Eighty feet overhead, suspended against the cliff in the torn remnants of his parachute, was Throckmorton. As the rest of the party stepped back and stared upward, the slender British captain waved the Webley pistol he held in his right hand and gave a wry smile.

"Tallyho," he remarked, his tone as dry as the alpine air.

Abruptly Merritt grinned. "What the hell are you doing up there, Duncan?" he called.

"Just hanging about," came the reply. "Taking in the scenery."

Stirling cleared his throat. "You mean to say you've been up there the whole time? Watching the SS hunt me to the base of this cliff?"

"Well, I couldn't see you until you actually got here, Sergeant," Throckmorton said. "And since you brought company with you, I thought it might be wiser just to hang here like a wallflower and not attract any attention. That is," he added, "until it became expedient— for *your* sake—to drop a round into the top of that fellow's head." He waved the pistol again and smiled. "Unfortunately his remaining two comrades then noticed me. A bad moment, that—looking down into those machine pistols. But you and Weiss took care of them, so all's well that ends well, eh?"

"You might have said something a little sooner, Duncan," Merritt said. "Let us know you were up there."

"Well, you were having such a pleasant conversation," Throckmorton replied, managing somehow to look mildly bored with it all despite his precarious position, "I didn't want to interrupt."

"Jeezus," Bristow muttered to D'Amato under his breath. "What a pisscutter this guy is."

Merritt put a hand on Cernović's shoulder. "Commander. We need the mountaineering gear in the equipment cylinder that was dropped before we jumped—at least one rucksack with a full length of rope. Did you receive it?"

"Yes," Cernović answered. "That was one supply container that did not end up in the hands of the Germans." He clapped his gloved hands together and pointed back along the cliff base. "Vlado! Boris! The equipment, back up in the clearing! One rucksack and a long rope, quickly!"

Two of the three Partisans took off through the rocks at a fast trot. Cernović grunted, inhaled the dregs of his cigarette, and flicked the butt into the snow. "They'll be back in ten minutes," he mused. "Now if we only had—"

"People coming through the trees down there, Major," D'Amato said, swinging up his Thompson. "Heading up the slope."

Merritt peered down over the snowdrift. A dozen or so armed guerillas were plodding up the incline toward the base of the crag. In the lead was the giant Partisan with the black beard.

"Friendlies, Sergeant," Merritt said. "Easy, now."

"That big bastard in front don't look so friendly," D'Amato muttered, lowering his machine gun. "Didn't I see him back on the drop zone?"

Cernović let out a short, guttural laugh and raised a hand to the oncoming Partisans. "That is Bozidar Yagovac," he said. "Known to all simply as Bozi. One of my senior lieutenants, and my best combat leader. A force of nature, you might say."

"Damn, I believe it," Bristow commented. "He's a big 'un, alright."

"He is . . . useful," Cernović said.

Merritt watched for a moment as the Partisans—most of them a full head shorter than Yagovac and one much shorter than that—continued to trudge up the slope. Then he looked back up at Throckmorton.

"How are you, Duncan?" he called.

"A trifle chilled, thanks," Throckmorton answered. "I can't really move, you see. When I do, the chute I'm hanging from has a nasty habit of ripping."

"Right, stay still," Merritt said. "We're coming up with a rope in just a few minutes."

"Ah, splendid. I'll just relax here, then."

There was a sudden sound of fabric tearing, clearly audible to everyone at the base of the cliff.

"Oops," Throckmorton said.

Merritt's mouth tightened into a hard line as he stared up. "Where the devil is that climbing gear, Commander? My man's about to fall."

"Christ, it'll take another fifteen minutes to get up to him once we have it," Bristow growled, "driving pitons all the way. This cliff's sheer and damn near smooth."

Merritt continued to stare up helplessly. "Bloody hell."

Cernović, standing off to one side, turned to Yago-vac as the giant Partisan clambered over the top of the snowdrift, followed by his ragtag soldiers. "Report, Bozi," the commander said, digging in his coat for another cigarette.

"One large platoon of Jagdkommando, Comrade Commander," Yagovac rumbled, brushing snow off his greatcoat. "About fifty men total. Plus two half-tracks with MG-42 machine guns mounted. But they couldn't use them." The giant grinned through his beard. "They couldn't maneuver. The terrain was too uneven and the snow too deep. We kept to the slopes, swept around both flanks and killed maybe a third of them as they retreated toward their vehicles." He chortled happily, rubbed his hands together, and looked back at the little band of ragged, grimy fighters behind him. "Maybe half of them, eh?" There was a general cackling of satisfied agreement from the soldiers, along with the metallic clanking of weapons being adjusted. The steamy vapors of evaporating sweat and condensing breath rose into the night air.

"Is that Comrade Kozo back there?" Cernović demanded, squinting as he lit his cigarette.

"Yes, Comrade Commander," Yagovac said. "With three fresh kills tonight, no less."

"Excellent, excellent," Cernović declared. "Come here, Kozo. I have a job for you."

A Partisan fighter who barely came up to Yagovac's greatcoat lapel appeared from the rear of the motley pack and shuffled forward, carrying—like many of the men—a captured Schmeisser machine pistol. The soldier's head was covered with an immense fur hat, earflaps tied down. A scarf protected his face, leaving only a small slit for the eyes. Layers of bulky winter clothing, all of it dirty and threadbare, provided insulation from neck to knees. The soldier's lower legs and boots were wrapped with long strips of cloth, making his feet appear huge. He waddled to a halt in front of Cernović, exhaling condensation through his frost-rimed face scarf.

"Ah, here comes a rope," Cernović said, glancing back along the cliff trail. Vlado and Boris had reappeared and were hurrying through the rocks toward the group. "Kozo, I want you to climb up there and secure a line to the parachutist so we can lower him to the ground. Quickly, I think. His parachute seems to be on the verge of giving way."

The small Partisan nodded, unslung and handed off his machine pistol, and began to undo the buttons of his thick combat jacket.

Merritt looked up at Throckmorton dangling on the sheer cliff, over at the undressing Partisan, and finally at Cernović. "Ah, Commander," he said, "you don't need to put one of your people at risk. We're quite capable of handling this ourselves."

Cernović chuckled and drew on his cigarette. "Of course you are, Major. But not as quickly as Comrade Kozo, I promise you."

Merritt was about to reply when the harsh sound of tearing silk came from above once more.

"Blast," Throckmorton said.

"Stay still, Duncan!" Merritt shouted. "Someone's coming up with a rope right now!" He stepped back and regarded Cernović. "All right, Commander. If your man's as fast as you say, the job's his."

"I'm sure Comrade Kozo appreciates your confidence," Cernović said, looking amused.

Merritt frowned slightly, puzzled at the Partisan commander's odd, secretive grin.

"Ah. Ready now, Sylvia?" Cernović inquired, looking past Merritt's shoulder.

The furrow in Merritt's brow deepened, and he turned around.

The short, stocky Partisan in the thick layers of winter clothing was gone. In his place was a lithe, pale-skinned young woman of perhaps twenty-two. She was clad in tight, high-cut shorts, a snug-fitting man's sleeveless undershirt, and the immense fur hat the Partisan soldier had worn. On her feet were what appeared to be black ballet slippers.

Merritt gaped. So did Bristow, D'Amato, Stirling, and Weiss. The loitering Partisans chuckled among themselves.

The young woman stood with her shoulders back, firm breasts pressing against the grimy fabric of the undershirt, her arms loose by her sides. Her legs were slender but well muscled—dancer's legs—and she stood with the unconscious poise of a ballerina. Her face was fine featured, pixieish, with sharp, high cheekbones and slanted, vaguely oriental eyes. Her mouth was small and full lipped, slightly downturned at the corners, and her pointed chin jutted forward aggressively—a function of her high-held head and what seemed to be a permanently set jaw. The biting cold appeared to have no effect on her whatsoever.

Cobra-eyed was the phrase that leapt to Merritt's mind. The young woman's eyes were hooded, the lids heavy and half closed. They lent her a dangerous rather than doeish aspect.

"Allow me to introduce you to Comrade Sylvia Kozo, Major Merritt," Cernović said. "Our climbing specialist."

Merritt nodded, still somewhat dumbfounded. "Charmed, Miss."

Unsmiling, the young woman ignored him, stepped forward, and extended a hand toward the Partisan named Vlado. "Rope," she said.

The soldier tossed her the end of a long, finely braided mountaineering line. Working quickly, she knotted a bowline into it, slipped the loop diagonally over her shoulder, and walked to the base of the cliff.

"Slack," she said to Vlado. With that, she kicked snow off her black slippers, reached up, found all-but-invisible fingerholds in the sheer rock face, and began to climb.

Chapter Four

"G*oddamn*," Bristow muttered. "What's holdin' her on there? That little gal must have suction cups for fingers."

"Or magnets," D'Amato said. He craned his neck farther back and scratched the stubble on his chin. "Or maybe claws, from the look on her face. Hell, Cole—think she ever *smiles*?"

"Don't look like it," the Texan concluded.

The young woman named Sylvia Kozo was already forty feet off the ground and moving steadily upward with the agility of a spider monkey. It was mesmerizing to watch her climb; her movements had a rhythmic economy, in combination with tremendous flexibility and considerable strength, and resembled nothing so much as a vertical, slow-motion dance. It would have been an impressive display of skill on a warm summer's day on dry, clean rock, never mind in the dead of a Balkan winter, *at night*, on a cliff face booby-trapped with innumerable ice patches.

"That's quite incredible," Merritt said, standing beside Cernović and gazing upward. "She's an amazing athlete."

"Yes, she is," Cernović replied. "In fact, she's one of the best professional athletes in Eastern Europe. A circus acrobat of considerable renown."

Merritt raised an eyebrow. "Really?"

"Oh yes. From a family of acrobats. The Flying Kozos. A star act in the Moscow, Vienna, Budapest, and Berlin circuses. Surely you've heard of them?"

"Unfortunately not. Perhaps they didn't get the attention they deserved in Britain."

"No doubt." Cernović puffed on his ubiquitous cigarette. "Anyway, Sylvia was the eldest daughter, and the family's star flier. The first woman to execute a triple aerial somersault to a catch without a net."

Merritt whistled through his teeth. "I'm impressed."

"All the more impressive when you consider she did it in 1937, when she was only fifteen. As she got older and more . . . fully formed, shall we say . . . she found it more difficult to execute high-speed aerials—to improve on what she'd already accomplished. Plus she wanted to develop her own identity separate from that of her famous family—Sylvia is a very independent-minded young woman, you see. So she began to promote herself as the Great Sylvia, Conqueror of Buildings. There was no man-made structure she could not climb using only her hands and feet, she claimed. And then she proceeded to prove it, climbing cathedrals, castles, and towers all over Europe—at least until this war unpleasantness developed."

"A remarkable story," Merritt said. "And now she fights with the Partisans."

Cernović exhaled smoke into the night air, watching idly as the young woman maneuvered to within fifteen feet of the dangling Throckmorton. "Yes, she does," he said. "Her entire family, with the exception of one younger brother, was killed by Stuka dive bombers in the German attack on Belgrade back in 'forty-one. It changed her dramatically, as similar experiences have changed so many of us over the past several years."

Merritt nodded. "Tragic. And her brother?"

"Murdered by SS troops a month later. Shot in a ditch along with fifteen other civilians because someone threw red paint at an SS commander in a passing tank."

"Not that it matters," Merritt said bitterly, "but he probably didn't even have anything to do with it."

"A fairly accurate assumption, I'd say. He was only eight years old."

Merritt looked at Cernović, met his eyes. The Partisan commander's mouth tightened into a grim smile. "Sylvia enjoys killing SS," he said.

Eighty feet up the cliff, Sylvia Kozo was just drawing abreast of Throckmorton. "Hello, my dear," he said in English, intrigued.

Sylvia glanced sideways at him through her hooded lids and climbed on past, trailing the long mountaineering rope behind her.

"Nice to have met you," Throckmorton called, as a slender ankle and black slipper moved upward past his head. The icy granite jutting into his back was considerably warmer than the pale sprite that had just manifested itself on the rock, he decided.

Carefully he craned his neck and looked up. The young woman was already at the small horn of rock that had snagged his chute. One black-slippered toe was balanced on some indiscernable irregularity in the cliff face; the opposite leg was drawn up so that the knee was hooked over the rock horn. The woman was leaning back, hips in, holding herself in place with only her legs. With both hands thus freed she was rapidly sorting through the tangle of loose parachute lines.

In less than a minute she had knotted two of the lines into a double loop around the rock horn and passed her trailing rope through it. Tying the end loosely around her waist, she then down-climbed to within arm's length of Throckmorton, pulling the rope with her.

"Hello again, my dear," Throckmorton said pleasantly. "Captain Duncan Throckmorton at your service."

Sprawled against the rock face, hanging on by two toes and one hand, Sylvia responded by pulling the rope from around her own waist and jamming the end roughly through Throckmorton's harness belt above his groin, making him flinch.

"I *say*!" he wheezed.

One-handed, the young woman threw a locking hitch into the mountaineering rope, yanked it tight, then leaned away from Throckmorton to take the strain off her toes and supporting hand.

"Well, I'll try once more," Throckmorton said, this time in Serbo-Croatian. "Captain Duncan Throckmorton, madam, at your service."

Sylvia turned her head slowly and regarded him without expression from beneath her heavy lids. "I understood you the first time, Captain," she said in accented but fluent English. Repositioning her hands and feet on the rock, she leaned down and withdrew Throckmorton's jump knife from its leg sheath.

"Did you, now?" Throckmorton replied, arching an eyebrow. "I would have thought a courteous hello would have warranted a courteous acknowledgement."

Sylvia's hooded eyes closed a fraction farther. "Perhaps you haven't noticed. I've been busy saving your life."

"Actually I had, my dear—"

"Of course, you couldn't possibly know how weary I am of being subjected to smug English aristocrats with greasy manners and ulterior motives, who routinely drop into my country to play at war for a few weeks at a time—as if war were nothing more than an exotic sporting event to be rehashed over brandy and cigars at some posh, private London club upon their heroic return."

Throckmorton was silent for a moment, his expression pleasant but immobile. "And here was me," he said, "thinking that you were merely rude."

Sylvia reached out and with one swipe of the jump knife slashed through both parachute risers supporting Throckmorton. The British captain dropped like a stone for twenty feet before bouncing painfully to a halt in his harness as, far below, Vlado and Boris threw their combined weight against the lower end of the mountaineering rope.

It took the better part of three hours to reach the Partisan encampment, trudging down a series of steep, snow-clogged switchback trails in single file beneath silent, snow-laden evergreen trees, coaxing along the dozen or so cranky, obstinate mules that carried most of the field supplies and ammunition. The succession of gullies and small gorges that had to be traversed, in particular, seemed endless—down one side and up the other, again and again, to the point of exhaustion. Only two-thirds of the original Partisan force was returning; Cernović had sent the giant Yagovac and thirty men to harass the shot-up Jagdkommando unit all the way back to the main body of Handschar.

"Home, for the moment," Cernović said, stepping off the trail to a small overlook between two immense slabs of rock. "Such as it is."

Merritt moved up beside him. The dim light of pre-dawn was just beginning to filter through the trees. One hundred and fifty feet below was yet another heavily forested, snow-blanketed gorge, its sides so steep that a man could not descend into it without local trail knowledge or the aid of a rope. It was not unlike the last ten gorges the small guerilla column had negotiated, but scattered on the floor of this one were several dozen log lean-tos, their roofs covered with snow and certainly all but invisible from the air.

Here and there in front of these rudimentary shelters, a small pennant of smoke from a carefully concealed fire twisted up into the still air of early morning, dissipating before clearing the tops of the trees.

"The Soujak Mine," Cernović said, pointing. Through the still haze Merritt could make out a dark opening in the far side of the gorge, a fracture in the rock. "An abandoned copper dig." The Partisan commander smiled thinly. "Now one of many Majevica Mountain bolt-holes used by the underfed but undaunted Second Proletarian Brigade of the glorious Partisan Army of Yugoslavia."

Merritt matched Cernović's rueful smile with one of his own. "Do I detect a touch of cynicism, Commander?"

"What you detect, Major Merritt," Cernović answered, "is *weariness*."

The two men turned away from the overlook and stepped back onto the trail. Stirling was just passing by, trudging along in the single-file track behind a mangy, uncooperative pack mule that was practically being dragged through the snow by a cursing Partisan. The veteran commando sergeant appeared very tired—heavy footed and with head down—and his lean face had a haunted look to it. He was whistling tunelessly under his breath.

Merritt touched his shoulder. "All right, Sergeant?"

Stirling glanced up and nodded. "Yes, sir. Never better."

"Good. Not far now."

"Yes, sir."

Stirling resumed both his slogging pace and quiet, unmelodic whistling. Merritt watched him for a moment, then looked back up the trail at the thin, ragged parade of exhausted Partisans. About fifty yards back he caught sight of Throckmorton.

"Coming, Major?" Cernović inquired, falling in behind a soldier bearing a captured MG-42 machine gun across his shoulders.

"I'll be right along, Commander," Merritt replied. "I want to speak with Captain Throckmorton."

"Certainly. Watch your step as you make your way down."

"We will."

Merritt leaned back against a tree trunk as the soldiers, looking like a procession of tattered specters in the wan gray light of early morning, continued to file past at a slow shuffle. Throckmorton was clearly having difficulty, staggering through the snow with his breath coming in great billows of condensation. Merritt stepped in beside him as he drew abreast, and got an arm under his.

"Steady, Duncan," he muttered. "We're there. No need to hurry."

"Blood . . . bloody good . . . thing," Throckmorton gasped. "Bloody air's . . . too . . . bloody thin . . . up here." He coughed violently, turned his head, and spat into the snow.

The Partisan just ahead of them turned and peered back at Throckmorton, then at the dark spot where the phlegm had landed. Merritt gave him a hard look. The soldier shook his head slightly, turned back around, and continued on down the trail.

Merritt pulled Throckmorton off to one side. "Let's just rest here for a minute," he said.

"Bloody . . . fine with . . . me," Throckmorton wheezed, bending over and bracing his hands on his knees.

The ragtag soldiers continued to trudge past, the dry snow crunching and squeaking under their boots. No one spoke, and very few of them even bothered to glance up at the two Englishmen. All those who did wore the same expression: a hollow-cheeked, sunken-eyed mask of strain, resolve, and bone-deep fatigue.

A Partisan wearing a filthy greatcoat and an immense fur Cossack-style hat, his Mauser rifle slung across his back with a piece of rope, staggered past, panting. The next man in line was Weiss. He nodded to Merritt and stepped off the trail.

"Hard going, sir," he said, wiping a glove across his frost-rimed nose and mouth. "Need help?" He looked pointedly at Throckmorton, who was still bent over with his back heaving.

"We'll be all right in a minute," Merritt said.

Weiss pulled off his gloves and blew into his cupped hands. "God, it's cold up here." Merritt nodded silently, his eyes roving through the trees. Weiss blew into his hands again, then cleared his throat. "You know, Captain Throckmorton," he said, "that was a fairly spectacular shot—putting a pistol round into the top of that SS trooper's head while you were dangling eighty feet in the air."

Throckmorton nodded from his bent-over position. "At night, too, don't forget." His wind seemed to be returning.

"Of course. At night."

Merritt stopped scanning the trees and turned to Weiss. "Captain Throckmorton is a former Olympian, like myself. In fact, that's how we first met back in 1936. British Olympic team."

Weiss smiled and began to put his gloves back on. "Ah. That explains a lot. Don't tell me: target pistol shooter."

"Silver medalist," Merritt confirmed, "and second only by a hair."

"Quite an accomplishment," Weiss said. "Who won the gold?"

Throckmorton stood up, put his hands on his hips, and tipped his head back, concentrating on his breathing. "Some Nazi sod," he remarked. "One of those damnable Von-something-or-others. Personally I think he was using doctored ammunition—flatter shooting, you see. Of course, I couldn't prove it, and the German judges buried my protest, curse them."

Merritt smiled faintly behind Throckmorton's left shoulder. His old friend was feeling better.

"But I got my own back that evening at a reception at the British ambassador's residence. Von Whatsit showed up in SS evening tails, with his gold medal draped around his neck and some slinky baroness clinging to his arm—her upper works spilling half out of her gown beneath her fox stole, I might add."

Sensing Throckmorton's rhythm, Weiss filled in dutifully, "And what did you do, Captain?"

Throckmorton's fine right nostril curved upward. "I cut the bugger dead on the entrance carpet in front of everyone, impugned his honor to the upscale riffraff for the next two hours, then concluded the evening by spiriting away his jiggly Junker harlot and rogering her red in the face until dawn. A quite deliciously nasty piece she was, too."

Weiss burst out laughing. "You have a poet's turn of phrase, Captain."

"He's famous for it," Merritt said. He clapped a gloved hand onto Throckmorton's shoulder. "Shall we go now, Duncan? We want to be down in that encampment before it gets too light."

The slender captain nodded. "Might as well," he said, stepping onto the trail. "There's no sign of the bloody limousine I ordered."

Bozidar Yagovac and his thirty Partisan guerillas had dogged and harassed the retreating Jagdkommando unit for nearly six miles through the rugged alpine forest when the three Fieseler Storches floated in over the trees in the cold silver gleam of dawn. Light, low-level reconnaissance aircraft with fabric skins and small single engines, they would have appeared as innocuous as the American Piper Cub they resembled were it not for the pair of MG-42 machine guns each had clamped to either side of the fuselage just ahead of the wing struts—vertically mounted, muzzles pointing straight down. They drifted ahead like great dark-green bats, side by side, heading directly into the wind with engines throttled back so that their forward motion was almost impossibly slow. But not too slow to overtake tired men floundering in deep snow.

"Disperse, comrades!" Yagovac bellowed right and left into the trees. *"Hunter-Storches! Disperse and find cover! And fire at the bastards when you can!"*

He threw up his Schmeisser and let loose a long burst at the nearest Storch as it hovered toward him at treetop level. Then he turned and began to struggle through the snow toward the trunk of a huge pine tree. Crouching behind it was Vlado, the Partisan infantryman who, along with Boris, had manned the rope Sylvia had taken up the cliff to the snagged British officer Throckmorton. He was gazing up at the black-crossed Storch like a rat caught in the paralyzing stare of a viper.

"Fire if you're going to stay there!" Yagovac shouted, churning his way forward. *"Try to knock the bastards down before they open up on us!"*

Vlado started as if stung, looked uncertainly at Yagovac, then sprang to his feet and floundered off beneath the overhanging pine boughs. The giant Partisan cursed eloquently in four dialects and made it to the base of the tree just as the trio of Storches moved directly overhead and opened up.

The vertically mounted machine guns on each plane spat twin cones of fire downward at fifteen hundred rounds per minute, chopping the forest below into a maelstrom of pine needles, wood splinters, and exploding snow. The chaotic line of death advanced steadily through the trees as the planes came on, maintaining their high volume of fire.

Partisan fighters were flushed from their places of concealment as the moveable killing zone swept toward them; vertical tree trunks provided cover from horizontal fire, not a continuous barrage coming straight down out of the sky. As the first panicked soldiers tried to flee clumsily through the deep drifts, the advancing wall of fire overtook them. Screams echoed through the trees above the relentless mechanical snarling of the aerial machine guns, floundering men became contorting silhouettes within a blizzard of whipped-up snow, and then the wall passed, leaving ruined foliage and dead shapes in its wake.

"Crūmgržkt!" gnashed Yagovac, which was a curse so ancient, pagan, and blasphemous that any person who dared utter it in the presence of an Eastern Orthodox priest was sure to receive a week's hard penance on the spot. He stared in helpless fury at the dozen or so slaughtered men who lay like torn scarecrows in the stained snow.

Abruptly the Storches stopped firing. Having overflown the main concentration of Partisans, they revved their engines and banked off in opposite directions, two to the north and one to the south.

Yagovac staggered to his feet. *"Move, comrades!"* he roared. *"They're coming around for another pass! Everyone split up, disperse! Make your own way back to the mine, and make sure the planes don't follow you! Disperse, curse you, disperse!"*

He turned, and there was Vlado again, behind the next tree, staring at him with the same erratic look in his eyes.

"Well, don't just stand there, idiot!" Yagovac growled, striding past. "Follow me!"

The interior of the Soujak Mine was cold and damp, but palpably less frigid than the little hidden valley outside. Kerosene lanterns hung here and there on rough walls hacked long ago by pickax and hammer from the ore-rich rock of the mountain, providing a flickering orange light. Oily smoke hovered in the stagnant air, which was also permeated by the reek of human sweat; the aroma of horse meat, paprika, and garlic stewing in cook pots; the tang of fresh blood; and the sickening stench of putrefying flesh. The severely wounded were lying shoulder to shoulder along the walls of the main passageway, some of them with advanced gas gangrene.

Merritt, Throckmorton, Bristow, D'Amato, and Weiss were sitting in a shallow, lantern-lit alcove in the rock—alternately smoking, eating bowls of horse-meat stew, and checking through the containers of explosives and mountaineering equipment piled around them. Stirling sat slightly apart from the rest, on the floor of the alcove with his back against the rock wall, head down, slowly sipping from a tin mug of broth that he held in both hands.

"What's wrong with him?"

Merritt looked up from the detonator he was inspecting to see Sylvia Kozo, clad now in shapeless wool trousers and a moth-eaten, too-large British Army turtleneck sweater, standing over him with a bucket of stew in one hand and the other on her cocked hip. She was looking down her small nose at him from beneath her heavy lids, fairly exuding aggression, challenge, and no small measure of calculated hostility. A reasonable defensive posture for a beautiful twenty-three-year-old woman accustomed to acclaim and privilege who now found herself the sole survivor of a murdered family and an active combatant in a world gone mad, Merritt decided.

He smiled carefully and looked back down at the detonator in his hand. "Sergeant Stirling lost a friend last night," he said.

Sylvia frowned across the alcove at Stirling, considered a moment, then gave a brief snort and shifted her weight to her opposite hip. "Losing friends is an occupational hazard around here," she remarked, scowling. "It hardly makes him unique." As Merritt sat in silence, reflecting that her comment merited no response, she plucked the ladle from her bucket and slopped a fresh serving of stew into the bowl by his side with a wet, messy sound—*flotch*.

"There," she declared, lifting her chin and turning

on her heel, "have some gourmet Serbian horse." She glared down at Throckmorton as she stalked past. "You won't find any Savoy Grill crown roast in the Soujak Mine."

"My, you're a sour one," Throckmorton drawled, recrossing his legs atop a munitions crate as he lounged back against the cave wall. He contemplated his fingernails for a moment. "Tell me, my little Gorgon: has any man ever gazed into your lovely eyes *without* being turned to stone?"

Sylvia rounded on him. "Listen, you English bast—"

"That's enough, Comrade Kozo!" The barked command came from farther down the passageway. A stocky figure in an unbuttoned officer's coat, misshapen peaked cap, jodhpurs, and battered black riding boots emerged from the lantern-lit dimness. Beneath the cap, a striking, highly chiseled Slavic face smiled wearily. "Go to your bed, Sylvia. Don't terrorize our English and American friends any more tonight. You might make them leave, and they've only just arrived."

"Huh!" Sylvia looked like a pouting twelve-year-old for a second or two, then lowered her head slightly and stepped out of the alcove. "Yes, Comrade Marshall Tito," she muttered, and moved off down the passageway.

All the men got hurriedly to their feet. *Marshall Tito*. Aka Josip Broz, leader of the Yugoslav Communist Partisans. The warlord who along with his hardscrabble army was the one wild card in the Balkans that kept the Nazis from subduing the entire region. Winston Churchill's favorite thorn in the side of the Third Reich, whose relentless hit-and-run military operations forced the ongoing commitment of German manpower, machinery, and munitions that could otherwise have been utilized on the Eastern and Western Fronts.

Tito was not particularly tall, but broad shouldered

and strong looking along peasant lines. His tanned, seamed face supported a square, set jaw and a pair of startlingly pale blue eyes that had the quality, as such eyes often do, of seeming to look right through whomever they fixed upon. Then, once again, he smiled, and it was an engaging, charismatic smile.

"Please come this way, Major Merritt," he said, beckoning. "Your men, too."

Chapter Five

"What happened to your former partner? Grohl, wasn't it?"

Gestapo Hauptsturmfuehrer Julius Neurath continued to gaze out the window of the luxury train car as the lights of Zagreb flickered past. His arrogantly handsome features pinched as he drew on his cigarette. Then he plucked it from his lips and blew a thin stream of smoke at the plate glass.

"He was killed by a terrorist a short time ago in Berlin," he said. "A Jew who was trying to assassinate the Grand Mufti with a hand bomb." Neurath raised the cigarette to his mouth again with a black-gloved hand. "Grohl was too slow and clumsy. The fool didn't get out of the way in time and caught the full force of the blast." As usual, his brief recounting of the incident omitted the fact that Grohl's body had stopped the shrapnel that almost certainly would have resulted in his own demise.

The black-uniformed SS Hauptsturmfuehrer who had posed the question settled back in his coach seat

and swirled the red wine in his glass. "Unfortunate.
You were nearby?"

"We had arrived at the Hotel Jürgenplatz in the
same staff car."

"And yet you emerged unscathed, while the other
two bodyguards with you—your partner and the SS
driver—were killed and quite severely wounded, respectively." The SS man, a rugged-looking Bavarian
with dark hair and complexion named Matthias Juttner, smiled thinly and sipped his wine, leaving a silence that resounded with innuendo.

Neurath turned slowly and regarded him with a pale
stare. The armored train—engine, coal car, SS bunk
car, antiaircraft-gun car, private coach, and caboose—
clattered and shook over a level crossing. Juttner
raised his glass carefully to prevent the wine from
being spilled by vibration.

"If you know about Grohl and Beckmann," Neurath said, "then obviously you've been briefed on the
assassination attempt or read my official report. You
know I was there in the thick of it, so what the devil
are you implying?"

Juttner smiled again and held his glass up to the
dim light of the overhead chandelier, examining the
wine's color. "I'm inquiring, not implying," he replied.
"I merely find it interesting that the two men with
whom you were formerly partnered both found themselves either suddenly dead or mangled beyond repair,
while you sustained not a single scratch." He blinked
pleasantly up at Neurath. "After all, *I'm* your new
partner in this al-Husseini security assignment."

Neurath stared down—unpleasantly. "I was
knocked flat on my back by the bomb blast," he said.
"The device went off beneath the car and Grohl was
in the wrong place at the wrong time. Beckmann was
protected from the major force of the explosion by
the car's armor plate, and was only singed. He assisted
me in running down the assassin, but in so doing lost
his composure and became hysterical, indulging in a

series of ill-advised heroics. This resulted in his being shot several times. His own fault."

Juttner finished his wine and set the glass down on the coach-seat service table. "You won't find me so obligingly eager to step into the path of every bullet that comes our way, Hauptsturmfuehrer Neurath," he said.

"I think I've absorbed enough of your insulting ruminations for one night, Juttner," Neurath declared. "I'm retiring to my berth. And by the way, you'd do well to remember that *I'm* the senior man on this security detail."

"By virtue of duration only," Juttner riposted seamlessly. "Not by rank."

Neurath turned a shade paler than his usual bone white. "Good night, Hauptsturmfuehrer."

"Good night, Hauptsturmfuehrer."

As Neurath stalked, simmering, down the length of the passenger compartment toward the door of his berth, Juttner lit a thin black cigar with a gold lighter, propped one gleaming jackboot up on the service table, and gazed contentedly out at the thinning lights of the outskirts of Zagreb. Why the city would not be under blackout, what with Allied planes flying random bombing and reconnaissance sorties over northern Croatia, he could not imagine. At the other end of the coach, Neurath's door closed with a notable bang.

Juttner chuckled and blew a smoke ring at Zagreb. Never before had he found himself on assignment with a fellow officer of equivalent rank who had proven to be so instantly contemptible. The man was, without a doubt, a borderline sociopath.

There was a sustained thumping from within Neurath's quarters.

Juttner drew again on his cigar. The train trip from Berlin to Belgrade was a long one. It was mildly diverting—if too easy by half—to push his new counterpart's buttons, and if Neurath woke the Grand

Mufti with his exhibition of temper and caught hell for it, the evening would be complete.

In a side chamber of the Soujak Mine, Tito, Cernović, Merritt, and Throckmorton, with occasional input from Stirling, Bristow, D'Amato, and Weiss, were still working out the final details of the proposed assault on the Zpoda Skyway Bridge. They had been talking and poring over topographic maps by lantern light for nearly three hours. Tito, in particular, seemed tireless—completely absorbed by the minutest of details, concerned about the most improbable chance of failure.

Periodically this or that Partisan lieutenant would appear at the chamber entrance and interrupt briefly to inform Tito and Cernović that several more members of Bozidar Yagovac's guerilla unit had returned. Tito would nod, exchange glances with Cernović, and ask to be kept up to date until all the men were accounted for.

Finally Tito pushed his battered peaked cap back on his head—an oddly American gesture, Merritt thought—and stepped back from the wooden table that held the last topo map.

"That's it," he said. "I can think of nothing else." He rubbed his eye with a knuckle, looking quite tired for the first time. "A daring plan, Major Merritt. And very, very risky."

"Name me one thing that isn't these days, sir," Merritt returned.

Tito gave rueful smile. "I can't."

"With this bridge gone," Merritt continued, "the German advance through the Majevica Mountains will starve. The Partisans will be able to roam these passes at will; fight, fall back, regroup, and redeploy. You'll have breathing room, Marshall."

"Lebensraum," Cernović put in, quoting the infamous Hitlerian term that meant "living room." He smiled slyly and lit another cigarette.

"Ha," Throckmorton said, nodding. "*Lebensraum*—I like that. Back at the bastards, eh?"

Cernović grinned openly and exhaled smoke. "Back at the bastards, Captain."

"So all that is left to do," Tito said, "is assign you your guides and supporting infantry."

"The smaller the group, the better," Merritt said, "as we discussed. This is not an operation that will succeed by force of numbers. The fewer men involved, the greater the chance of remaining undetected."

"In that case," Tito replied, "you'll be delighted to hear that I've decided I can spare only two of my remaining people to participate in this admirable fool's errand with you—both of them guides."

Merritt looked at Throckmorton. "Only two?"

"And only one is a man."

Throckmorton rolled his eyes and turned away. Merritt hesitated, then cleared his throat. "You don't mean—"

Tito raised a hand, and suddenly the ruthless commander, the iron man of Yugoslavia, was very much in evidence. "Yes, I do. Comrade Kusić—you know him as Vlado—will lead you through the German lines and to the base of the Zpoda precipice via a rarely used hunter's footpath known as Zlostup. Of all my people, he is the most familiar with this part of the mountains. He confirmed only three days ago that Zlostup remains open and useable, despite rock slides and heavy snowfall."

"What's Zlostup mean?" Bristow interjected on impulse.

Tito's expression relaxed slightly. " 'Bad Step' "

"Sounds great," Bristow grumbled.

"Don't it, though?" This from D'Amato, at Bristow's shoulder.

"It's called Zlostup," Cernović filled in, "because if you take a bad step, you fall somewhere around three thousand feet, give or take a bounce or two. The trail is about two feet wide, sheer drop on one side, sheer rock wall on the other. It's a thousand years old—probably more—and not well-known. Certainly not by the Nazis."

Merritt looked at Tito. "You were saying something about a second guide."

"That will be Comrade Kozo. I have decided that she will lead you up the cliff face to the bridge supports in the final climb."

"Oh, for Christ's sake," Throckmorton drawled, folding his arms.

"Duncan," Merritt said, his voice hard. He turned back to Tito. "It's not necessary for the girl to be put at risk, Marshall. We have mountaineering specialists on hand to do this: myself, Sergeants Bristow and D'Amato, Sergeant Stirling—"

"She will go," Tito declared, straightening his cap. "The venture has a far greater chance of success with a climber of her skills picking the best way up the rock for you." He gave Merritt a steady look. "There are not many things I can do to improve your odds, Major, but insisting that you use Sylvia is one."

Merritt clamped his lips together in exasperation. "Marshall—"

"I said, I insist. The discussion is closed."

Merritt glanced over at Throckmorton, who was slowly shaking his head, and at that moment the ratty blanket that served as the door to the conference chamber was pushed aside and one of the Partisan lieutenants appeared. "Comrade Marshall. Vlado has returned. He insists on reporting to you personally."

Tito waved a hand. "Send him in. I have a job for him, anyway."

"Immediately, Comrade Marshall."

The man withdrew, letting the blanket fall back into place. Tito silently accepted a cigarette and a light from Cernović, reexamined the topo map briefly, and sat down in the collapsible wooden armchair behind the table. His gaze—stony rather than warm now—roved over the Allied soldiers parked against the walls of the little chamber. Merritt had been warned that Tito, like many a great leader, could be mercurial, moody. Here, he reflected, was hard evidence of the fact. *Proceed carefully.*

There was a stirring out in the main passageway; voices raised, some of them in apparent dismay. The men took notice, shifting in place as they smoked and waited. . . . And then the blanket-curtain was pulled back and the Partisan named Vlado stepped into the chamber. He was disheveled and bareheaded, his lank black hair and scraggly beard moist and steaming with perspiration. His olive drab forage coat and pants—British military cast-offs—were still caked with damp snow, as were his cloth-wrapped winter boots. A Mauser rifle hung from a sling over his left shoulder. His expression was that of a man stricken.

"Ah, Vlado," Tito said. "You turn up at last."

"Any more with you?" Cernović inquired quickly.

Vlado settled his weight back on his heels, let out a sigh of sheer exhaustion, and shook his lank head. "No," he muttered. "No more. No . . . more."

Bristow held out a lit Camel. "Here you go, friend."

Vlado half turned, accepted the smoke with a grateful nod. "Thank you. I haven't had a decent cigarette for months."

Cernović glanced at Tito. "Vlado. Where's—"

"Lieutenant Yagovac is dead," Vlado blurted. He put the cigarette to his lips with a shaking hand. "Bozi is dead." He exhaled a long stream of smoke at the floor.

Cernović blinked, the cynical good humor that usually dominated his face replaced for once by an expression of blank shock. "What? Bozi dead? You're sure?" When Vlado didn't respond, merely kept staring at the floor and smoking, Cernović cursed fluently and added, "How?"

Vlado looked up, his eyes red and wet. "Hunter-Storches, three of them. They caught us in deep snow as we were maneuvering for one more attack on the

Jagdkommando unit. We didn't hear them coming because they flew up out of the next valley and came in low over the nearest ridge at treetop level."

"I heard about the Storches from some of the others who got back before you," Cernović said. "I know at least a dozen were killed before you could disperse. What happened to Bozi?"

"He was killed in the Storches' first pass, Comrade Commander," Vlado said through gritted teeth. "Damn them to hell. He was trying to get the men to take cover, and took none himself."

"That sounds like Bozi," Cernović muttered. "Downward-firing machine guns?"

"Yes, Comrade Commander. The usual."

Cernović said something incredibly foul under his breath, reached out a hand, and put it on Vlado's shoulder. "All right, Vlado, all right. No point in dwelling on it. Take a seat and rest for a moment."

As the exhausted Partisan shuffled over to an unoccupied chair and slumped down into it, Cernović turned to Tito. "A bitter loss, Comrade Marshall. I cannot replace a combat leader like Bozidar Yagovac. He was one of a kind."

Tito nodded, gazing at Vlado sitting in his chair with head bowed. The marshall's expression was a curious blend of sympathy and pragmatic fatalism. "How many irreplaceable men have we lost to date, Comrade Commander? And yet we go on. Those who remain step into the breach, become irreplaceable themselves." Cernović nodded silently, and Tito directed his next comment at Vlado: "You must eat, Comrade. Eat and then sleep. I have another task for you. . . . For you and Sylvia." He turned toward the blanket-curtain. "Marko!" he called. "Come here!" The blanket swung aside and a youthful Partisan stuck his head into the chamber. "Send Comrade Kozo to me," Tito ordered, "and tell her to bring a bowl of stew when she comes."

*　　*　　*

John McKinna

A veritable pall of cigar smoke hung in the air of the prime minister's study at Number 10 Downing Street. Generals Sir Stewart Graham Menzies and Sir Colin McVean Gubbins stood by silently, waiting. Churchill puffed on his Montecristo with the steady rhythm of an automated bellows, examining the document on the desk before him through a pair of half-lenses perched on the end of his pug nose. He was reading the material for the third time. Finally the prime minister sat back with a grunt in his leather chair, plucked off his reading glasses, and tossed them onto the desk.

"Are we sure about this?" he asked Menzies. "King Tigers?"

"Not just King Tiger tanks, Mr. Prime Minister," Menzies replied swiftly, "but a specially modified version. The Black Lyre was most specific."

"Modified how?" The cigar tip glowed red. Smoke billowed like fumes from Vulcan's forge.

"Heavy-duty transmissions," Menzies said. "More reliable steering hydraulics. Fuel capacity and travel range increased at least twenty-five percent. Even larger diesel engines. Special extra-wide treads with multiple steel teeth on every section to improve traction. Maximum elevation angle on the eighty-eight-millimeter main gun increased by more than forty percent."

"The Black Lyre claims that a small unit of these special King Tigers was field-tested recently on the Croatian-Serbian border by the SS, and performed well beyond expectations," Gubbins went on. "Supposedly the tank can climb a rock-strewn forty-five-degree slope at fifteen miles per hour. Trees up to eighteen inches in diameter don't stop it; it just pushes them over."

"The Huns have customized a Tiger tank for mountain fighting," Churchill said.

"There's no other logical conclusion, Mr. Prime Minister, given this vehicle's capabilities." Gubbins

122

looked briefly at Menzies, who nodded in confirmation. "The increased elevation arc of the main gun is to allow the tank to fire upward at a steep angle—say, from the bottom of a deep, narrow gorge to the high ridges on either side."

"I see," Churchill growled around his cigar. "The Tigers are deployed into the valleys of the Majevicas, sweeping them clean as high up the slopes as possible. Tito's Partisans are forced up onto the ridges and mountaintops, where there's little shelter or water, and plenty of extreme cold. There the Tigers can pound them with their high-elevating eighty-eights and the Luftwaffe can bomb them from the air."

"That seems to be the intent, Mr. Prime Minister." Menzies unfolded a small map and placed it on Churchill's desk. "The train—it's huge—left Germany seven days ago. Eight engines pulling it. It's less than thirty-six hours from the deployment point in Yugoslavia as we speak."

Churchill, in the act of redonning his reading glasses, lowered them and peered up at the MI-6 chief. "How many King Tigers are on those flatcars again?"

Menzies cleared his throat. "Forty-eight, according to the Black Lyre."

"Good God. An SS tank force of that size could knock Tito and his Partisans out of the war permanently. Can we scramble our available Mosquitos or B-26s to bomb that train? Perhaps a flight of Typhoons or Thunderbolts to rocket it?"

"Several problems there, Mr. Prime Minister, including availability of aircraft on such short notice for a mission of this range, the time factor—we're already out of it, basically—and the precision required to make such a mission a success. We're dealing with a moving target. In addition, the Black Lyre informs us that the Luftwaffe has committed to a staggered series of covering flights by fighter aircraft all along the route, for the purpose of engaging any Allied aircraft intent on attacking the train."

123

"Bloody hell," Churchill muttered. "We'll try a last-minute interception mission, anyway. Typhoons or Thunderbolts, like I said. Something that can deal with Luftwaffe fighter cover as well as hit the train."

"I doubt if there's time, Mr. Prime Minister," Menzies said, "but we'll have a go at it."

"A second train behind this one carries supporting vehicles—fuel-hauling half-tracks and trucks," Gubbins added. "That sort of thing."

Churchill bent over the map. "And what, according to the Black Lyre, is the tank train's destination? The deployment point?"

Menzies set a finger on a red X in the map's center. "Right here, sir. Mount Zpoda, at the far end of the Zpoda Skyway Bridge."

Chapter Six

The young Partisan named Marko was one of four skilled radio operators attached to Tito's immediate support staff, fluent in Morse and a variety of complex code ciphers. He was also adept at disassembling and tinkering with the bulky, temperamental military field sets provided to the Partisans by the British and Americans. After sleeping through most of the daylight hours since the last of Bozi Yagovac's guerillas had returned to the Soujak Mine, it was now his turn on radio watch—generally a long, boring shift of six hours or more—and he intended to pass the time by rewiring one of the British backpack radios, a battered, aging beast of a unit he'd nicknamed The Ogre.

Working on The Ogre also helped take his mind off the knowledge that one of the gas-gangrene cases lying against the wall of the mine's main passage, just a few yards down from his radio alcove, had died an hour earlier—and that the gas-gangrene case had been Georgi, his best friend from childhood. Georgi, young and crazy-brave, had been machine-gunned in the hips during an ambush several weeks back, and had suffered greatly—and in silence—since then. Mercifully he had slipped into unconsciousness two days ago, and now the gangrene had finally taken him.

Marko set the blade of his screwdriver into the slot of the radio cowl's first retaining screw and began to twist. It was best not to think about Georgi.

Abruptly a rapid-fire series of nonsensical Morse dits erupted from the speaker of the primary headquarters radio set, signaling the imminent arrival of a coherent message. Marko dropped the screwdriver, slid over behind the big radio, clapped a pair of headphones over his ears, and seized a pencil and notepad. The flurry of meaningless tones gave way, after a brief pause, to a smooth flow of sequenced dits and dahs, urgent but controlled. His brow furrowed in concentration, Marko began to write rapidly on the pad.

When the transmission was completed he ripped the page off the notepad, ditched his headphones, and hurried out of the radio alcove into the main passageway. The rocky floor of the mine was littered with sleeping bodies, and he inadvertently kicked a few as he hastened along, drawing muffled curses and threats. He scarcely heard them. His heart was pounding in his ears much too loudly for that.

Tito was lying on his cot, reading, when Marko pushed aside the blanket-curtain and entered the commanders' alcove. On the far side of the little recess, Cernović was stretched out on a second cot, snoring. Marko nodded respectfully as he approached, then held out the notepaper as Tito pulled off his reading glasses and looked up.

"Intelligence communication from the British, Comrade Marshall," the young Partisan said. "Extremely urgent."

Tito hoisted himself up against his pillow and took the paper. "Thank you, Marko. I'll call if I need you."

The boy nodded again and backed out of the alcove, letting the blanket-curtain fall to behind him.

Tito replaced his glasses and scanned the message. His expression began to darken. He swept the rough blanket off and swung his legs to the floor. "King Tigers," he muttered under his breath. "Forty-eight specially modified King Tigers."

Abruptly he got to his feet and crossed the alcove in two quick strides. "Anton," he said, touching Cernović on the shoulder. "Wake up."

The Partisan commander jerked in midsnore and rolled to a sitting position before he was even half awake, the Luger he always slept with brandished in his right hand. Tito quickly stepped sideways; Cernović blinked the sleep out of his eyes, got his bearings, and let his gun hand sag between his legs.

"One day, Anton," Tito remarked, "you're going to come up shooting, and that will be the end of Josip Broz."

Cernović smiled wearily and rubbed the side of his face. "But not this day, Comrade Marshall."

Tito stepped over to the table and consulted the map spread out on top of it. "We've just received some extremely alarming news from British intelligence. A train loaded with King Tiger tanks specially modified for mountain warfare is barely two days away from the Zpoda Skyway Bridge. If those tanks make it across the divide at Mount Zpoda and are deployed into the rest of the Majevicas against us, we could be decimated."

"Wha-what?" Cernović hoisted himself to his feet and stumbled over to the table. "Damn it, I'm so tired I can hardly think. King Tigers, you say? But Comrade Marshall, aren't those open-country tanks? The Nazis use them out on the steppes where they have plenty of running room."

"Specially modified for mountain warfare," Tito repeated. "Here, I'll show you approximately where the train carrying them is right now." He set a finger on the map. "This is the best guess. You see? We have very little time."

Cernović blinked some more, focusing. "But this is perfect. Merritt is on his way to blow that bridge as we speak."

"The plan was for him to take all the time he needed to mine the bridge without being discovered," Tito said. "Since he doesn't realize time is suddenly of the essence, he may take up to three or four days to set his explosives. He has no radio, so he can't know about the approach of the train."

"It could steam across the bridge and offload its Tigers on the crest of Mount Zpoda while Merritt and his people stood there watching it," Cernović mused, "powerless to do anything to prevent it because their charges weren't yet placed or wired." He straightened and looked at Tito. "We have to send a messenger after them; tell Merritt that the bridge must be blown before the train arrives."

"No," Tito said. "We must go one better. If Merritt blows the bridge before the train arrives, the Nazis still have their forty-eight King Tigers." He smiled suddenly, and it was a hard, ruthless smile. "We have an opportunity not just to destroy the Zpoda Skyway Bridge as a primary supply route, but to deny the enemy the use of nearly fifty battle tanks.

"We must tell Merritt to blow the bridge while the train is on it, and send the King Tigers to the bottom of the Zpoda Gorge."

Cernović nodded. "I'll choose someone to send after Merritt and his people. They only have a four-hour head start. If these estimated times for the train's arrival are accurate—"

The blanket-curtain suddenly whipped back, revealing Marko's flushed, tense face. "Comrade Marshall," he hissed. *"Fallschirmjager!"*

The late-afternoon sun was drawing long shadows through the snowbound alpine forest when Merritt paused at the crest of the steep ravine that his team—

complete with three fully laden pack mules—had just traversed. About ten paces ahead of him, Vlado, in the lead, forged onward through the knee-deep snow, looking like a tireless, tattered mummy in his threadbare military coat, dirty scarves, and ragged leggings. Merritt scanned the nearby trees and terrain, then held up a hand as Bristow and D'Amato, next in file behind him, approached, leading one of the mules.

"Hold up a minute," he said quietly. He turned back toward Vlado, who was still slogging his way along the ravine crest. "Vlado! Wait." The Partisan guide halted, turned, and looked back, exhaling condensation. Merritt pointed. "These trees are freshly scarred by heavy gunfire. And there are two bodies in the snow over there. Partisan bodies."

Vlado shrugged and looked out across the gully. The wind had stopped blowing and the forest was quite still now, almost cathedral-like. In the utter silence and bone-chilling cold, Vlado's voice, a husky murmur, carried with stark clarity to the ears of every team member. "This is where the Hunter-Storches caught us as we were about to launch our final attack on the Jagdkommando unit, Major. This is where we took our casualties."

Merritt nodded. "And this is the quickest way to Zlostup?"

"Yes, Major," Vlado replied. "It happens to be. A coincidence."

"All right." Merritt looked back down the way they had come. Throckmorton was struggling up the route next. Behind him were Stirling and Sylvia, each with a hand on opposite sides of the second pack mule's halter. Weiss was bringing up the rear, leading the third mule. "Everyone keep following Vlado. I'm going to move out on our flank for a few minutes."

"What for, Major?" Vlado asked. "They're all dead, and the Germans are gone."

"Just taking a look," Merritt replied. "Maybe I'll

find Yagovac's body. And as a matter of fact, I think I'll take Sergeant Bristow and Sergeant D'Amato with me."

"What for?" Vlado repeated. There was an edge of exasperation in his voice.

"Security," Merritt replied curtly. "Lead on, Comrade." He nodded to Bristow and D'Amato, stepped sideways out of Vlado's tracks, and began to move at a divergent angle toward the bodies under the trees.

"Major, you could easily get lost in here," Vlado persisted, and in his tone Merritt heard the same quality of deceit that had struck him wrong when Vlado reported the death of Bozidar Yagovac to Tito and Cernović in the Soujak Mine.

He shifted his Sten gun from his shoulder to the crook of his arm and continued across the ravine crest, Bristow and D'Amato pacing him to either side. "We'll be fine," he called out to Vlado. "We'll sweep back in and rejoin you in about twenty minutes."

"But—"

"Lead on, Comrade. That's an order."

Vlado stared for a moment, looked back helplessly at Throckmorton, then shook his head and began to slog forward again. As the rest of the team and the small mule train resumed their pace, Merritt and the two American sergeants waded off through the snow and began to push their way through the sagging lower limbs of the evergreen trees.

It was several minutes before they arrived at the two corpses Merritt had spotted from the trail. Both bodies were facedown and badly shredded. Bristow knelt down, resting his Thompson submachine gun on one knee, and pulled the rigid body of the first dead Partisan over.

All three men, battle hardened though they were, felt a jolt of revulsion at the sight of the corpse's face. The young Partisan—not more than seventeen, although it was hard to tell—had been shot multiple times in the shoulders and head. The frontal part of the skull, the forehead and temples, was gone back to the crown. In the void above the brows was a nauseating mass of black-red blood, white bone splinters, and brain tissue. Slugs traveling down from directly above had blown away the boy's lower jaw and exploded one eye out of its socket. The other stared up horrifically like a dull white marble, the pupil and iris occluded. The upper lip was peeled back from the remaining teeth in an an awful grimace, frozen in place by the subzero temperatures.

"Ugh, Jeezus," Bristow grunted, averting his eyes momentarily. "Just a damn kid, too."

"Ain't they all these days?" D'Amato remarked. He surveyed the nearby trees and hefted his Thompson. "Fuckin' Krauts."

Merritt studied the two corpses. "Both literally hammered from directly overhead by heavy machine-gun fire. Ugly and effective."

"I'll say," D'Amato commented.

Merritt nodded at Bristow. "Turn him back over, Sergeant."

As Bristow rolled the dead boy facedown again, Merritt peered through the trees to the left, which were the most heavily bullet scarred. "Do you both have a fair recollection of what Bozidar Yagovac looked like? The big man with the black beard. We all met him on the drop zone and again at the base of the cliff."

Bristow and D'Amato exchanged glances. "Hell, yeah, Major," Bristow said. "Would we forget runnin' into an upright grizzly bear?"

"Right." Merritt let a smile flicker across his face. "I want his body found. Fan out about thirty feet on either side of me. We'll sweep across this little ridge, following the shot-up trees. As big a man as he was, he shouldn't be hard to pick out."

"Got somethin' on your mind, Major?" Bristow asked, moving off.

Merritt began to stride forward. "Just checking a hunch," he replied, "as you Americans say."

131

D'Amato started to move out to Merritt's right, then halted, cocking his head. Bristow glanced back at him, saw him standing there, and paused himself. "Major."

At the big sergeant's word Merritt looked back and halted. Bristow watched D'Amato for several seconds, then said quietly, "Frank. What's up, *amigo?*"

D'Amato cocked his head the other way, listening. "You hear 'em?"

"No, what?" Bristow lifted the earflap of the head muffler he was wearing. Merritt did the same with the lower edge of his wool balaclava.

There was a faint mechanical drone, just barely audible, humming through the sentinel trees.

"Planes," D'Amato said. "More than one, I think. A long way off."

"Flying high enough for the sound to carry," Merritt added. "If they were moving through the valleys below the peaks and ridges, doing search-and-destroy missions like those Storches, we wouldn't hear them."

"Bombers, maybe?" Bristow suggested. "Kraut reconnaissance . . . or maybe our own?"

Merritt listened a moment longer, then pulled the edge of his balaclava back down over his ear. "Maybe," he said, and set off through the snow once more. "Let's go."

SS Hauptsturmfuehrer Ulrich Haak had been the first man out the door of the lead plane as the big Junkers 52 trimotor transport, loaded with seventeen heavily armed Muslim Fallschirmjager,[1] led twenty of its kind over the hidden gorge concealing the Soujak Mine. Now, dangling in his parachute with the frigid air stinging his face and the ragged black tops of snow-laden evergreen trees jutting up toward him, looming ever nearer as he descended, he took a few seconds to look up and note with satisfaction the multiple sticks of jumpers trailing out of the remaining transport aircraft, the white blots of their canopies blooming like sudden flowers in the late-afternoon sky. It had taken an unbelievable amount of paperwork and petitioning of superiors over the past several months to gain both permission and means to parachute-train nearly two hundred volunteers from the Jagdkommando units of the SS Division Handschar, but now here they were, descending upon the abhorred Partisan foe with the element of surprise completely in their favor. It wasn't like Crete,[2] Haak lamented fleetingly, but it was a bona fide airborne assault. *Today,* he thought, *we get results. We make some real progress against these damned subhuman Slavic Communists.*

The drop was going perfectly. He was coming down onto the very edge of the southern ridge overlooking the gorge. Time to get ready.

One of his most recent acquisitions had been a marvelous new personal weapon called a Sturmgewehr.[3] Basically a submachine gun like the more common Schmeisser, it was elongated, more accurate, and had a curved, high-capacity ammunition clip. It fired well on the range, and Haak had seen to it that every one of his new Muslim Fallschirmjager was equipped with a Sturmgewehr of his own.

Haak was low enough now to make out a lone Partisan running awkwardly through the snow along the top of the ridge. As he watched, the figure fell, losing its hat. Long, dark hair spilled out over the shoulders of a tattered, olive drab winter coat.

The Partisan rolled, staring up at Haak with an expression of hatred and terror. It was a woman. She scrambled to one knee, her mouth working in what the Hauptsturmfuehrer supposed were curses or prayers or both, and swung up her rifle, taking aim.

Haak cut her down with a long burst from his Sturmgewehr. She screamed as she died, shuddering under the impact of the bullets, which he found oddly satisfying. Then, with the delicacy of a descending angel, he made a perfect landing in the thigh-deep snow between two immense evergreens.

All around him, his Muslim Fallschirmjager began to drift down through the trees, seeding the southern rim of the Soujak Gorge and half enveloping the Partisan forces bivouacked near the mine entrance.

On the opposite rim of the gorge, Fallschirmjager precision dropped slightly farther to the north were descending under a long row of swaying canopies to close the trap.

Cernović was at the entrance of the mine, gesturing furiously to those nearby and eyeing the numerous parachutes floating down on either rim of the gorge, while behind him men and women fled out across the snow and into the trees, some supporting staggering wounded. The stutter of automatic weapons fire began, and several hundred yards off to Cernović's right, to the south, a grenade flung from the gorge rim exploded with an upheaval of powdery whiteness and a muffled *whumpff.*

"Head down the valley, comrades!" the Partisan commander bellowed. *"Don't let them link up and cut us off! Shoot your way out!"*

A pair of Partisans bearing a stretcher between them stumbled past. Cernović took one look at the ashen face of the blanket-wrapped casualty lying upon the crude bier and seized the trailing soldier by the arm. "Leave him!" he shouted. "He's a dead man. Save yourselves!"

"He's our brother, Comrade Commander," the older of the two Partisans panted, lank black hair falling across his swarthy face. "We are the last three of our mother's nine sons."

"I don't need to lose two more men on top of this one!" Cernović barked. He waved his Luger at the man on the stretcher. "He won't last the night. You know that. And there's no time to argue!"

The two stretcher bearers set their burden down in the snow and looked at each other with anguished faces. "Go, Jakob," the older brother muttered. "I'll do it." The younger man hesitated, then stumbled toward the trees as his brother drew his sidearm.

The older brother pulled off his scarf, knelt down, whispered something in the dying man's ear, and kissed him on the forehead. Cernović looked away.

The pistol cracked.

When Cernović looked back, the older brother was gone. His scarf was draped over the face of the man on the stretcher. The last few Partisans were disappearing into the trees and snowdrifts, firing upward to either side as they fled pell-mell down the gorge to the east.

The angry chatter of a Sturmgewehr on the southern rim, much closer to the mine entrance now, sent snow skiffing up between Cernović and the corpse on the stretcher. Out of sheer defiance, the Partisan commander stood his ground, raised his pistol, and emptied it at the white-clad figures now moving rapidly toward him along the upper lip of the gorge. Then he hunched low and dashed back into the mouth of the Soujak Mine.

The main passageway was nearly empty. Along the walls were crumpled blankets and bedding where the wounded had lain. Here and there a few of them still lay, their bodies covered head to toe by the lice-ridden blankets that were their death shrouds. Too badly injured to be moved, they had been killed by friends or relatives. All knew the kind of mercy Partisan wounded would receive from the SS if captured.

Cernović ran past alcoves and recesses still flickering with the eerie light of cooking fires, the perpetual haze of smoke in the poorly ventilated mine stinging his eyes. In the dimness ahead, Tito was just emerging from the commanders' alcove, a leather document satchel under one arm and a Walther pistol in his free hand. Clustered around and ushering him along the passageway were a half-dozen soldiers of his bodyguard and support staff, including the young radio operator, Marko. Two of the Partisans carried guttering oil lanterns.

"Is everyone out?" Tito shouted to Cernović as he approached.

"All but the dead," Cernović responded. "The main body is attempting to break out through the eastern end of the gorge under subcommanders Lesković and Ribar." He paused, panting heavily. "There are paratroopers above the mine on both sides, starting to work their way down." He glanced at Marko. "Everything ready?"

"Yes, Comrade Commander," the young Partisan replied, bent under the weight of the large field radio strapped to his back.

"Good," Cernović said. "We—"

Two sharp, cracking explosions shook the rock walls and foul air of the passageway. Dust sifted down from overhead shoring timbers and boiled into the mine from the direction of the entrance. Several of the men instinctively clapped their hands over their ears as the double concussion hit them.

"Grenades!" Cernović shouted. "They're coming! Deeper into the mine, quickly!"

The little knot of men, propelling Tito along in their midst, retreated several dozen yards to where the passageway took a sudden turn to the left. Cernović paused, hissed at the two trailing bodyguards, and took cover behind the edge of the rock wall, glaring back the way he had come, with the barrel of his pistol pressed up against his cheekbone. The two Partisans, each armed with a Schmeisser, found shallow firing niches on opposite sides of the passageway.

The first thing German to appear at the far end of the dim corridor was a brace of potato-masher hand grenades, tumbling end over end along the rocky floor. Cernović and his two men shrank back and opened their mouths to protect their ears. The grenades went off simultaneously with a single tremendous bang that nearly knocked the Partisans to their knees. Shrapnel chipped shards of rock from the walls from ceiling to floor.

Hard on the heels of the blast, two Fallschirmjager clad in white winter camouflage smocks and gray field fezzes leapt into view, Sturmgewehrs trained ahead. Cernović and his two comrades opened fire. One of the paratroopers was hammered back against the mine wall and slumped down dead. The other was hit but managed to lurch back behind the curve of the passageway and out of the line of fire.

"Fall back!" Cernović whispered hoarsely, and waited until the two Partisan submachine gunners had taken a few running steps after Tito and the rest of the bodyguard before pulling back himself and following.

"I told you we would trap a few in this rat hole!" Haak declared triumphantly, kneeling on the floor of the passageway with one of his Scharfuehrers as white-clad Fallschirmjager streamed past him deeper into the mine. He grinned, his breath forming clouds of condensation. "We may have some commanders backed up into a corner. Perhaps even Tito himself!"

"*Jawohl,* Herr Haupsturmfuehrer," the Scharfuehrer replied. "We'll root them out."

Haak got to his feet, still grinning, and shifted his assault rifle in his arms. "Just kill them," he said. "These are Slavs, Schmidt—human rats—and this is extermination duty. Leave one or two pests alive out of a nest and the next thing you know they've multiplied back up to plague proportions all over again. Don't complicate my day with prisoners."

The Scharfuehrer nodded but lifted an eyebrow. "Not even Tito sir, if he's here?"

Haak spat on the floor of the passageway. "Especially not Tito. He's the head rat."

Chapter Seven

"Over here, Major!" Merritt paused his steady trudge through the snowdrifts and peered under an overhanging pine bough in Bristow's direction. The big American sergeant was standing between an angled slab of rock and the trunk of an immense evergreen tree, waving. There was a large black shape in the snow at his feet. Merritt and D'Amato moved to join him.

Bristow gestured with a cigarette and then stuck it between his lips. "I believe that's him, sir. Yagovich-or-whatever." There was a metallic *snick* as he thumbed open his Zippo lighter.

"Yago*vac*." Merritt stooped down. Bozidar Yagovac was lying flat on his back, his sightless eyes staring up at the sky between the treetops. Frost had rimed his bushy beard so that it appeared as gray-white as his skin. The giant Partisan's overcoat was unbuttoned and open, as was his threadbare woolen underjacket. Merritt probed Yagovac's pockets gently, gazed at the corpse for a moment or two, then sat back on his haunches and began to survey the surrounding area.

"Some more bodies down in that hollow and along that rise," Bristow said matter-of-factly. He blew a stream of smoke. "Most of 'em partly covered up by new snow. Tracks are still visible, but gettin' filled in, too." He shook his head. "I counted fourteen dead just in that area. Them Storches really tore these boys up. They've all got the same head-and-shoulders wounds."

"The trees are really shot to shit over there, too, Major," D'Amato added. "Chopped into splinters. Not like right here."

Merritt nodded slowly and got to his feet. "That's absolutely correct, Sergeant," he said. "Not like right here." He gazed down at Yagovac's body again, then off into the woods. "Interesting. You can still see three sets of tracks in the snow. Yagovac's, obviously, plus those of two others."

"Vlado and another Partisan, I guess," D'Amato muttered, "probably checking on Bozo here when he got hit—although I'm damned if I can see where. There ain't a mark on him."

Merritt's wry smile reappeared. "*Bozi*, Sergeant."

"Yeah, right, Bozi."

"There are foot tracks all over the place, Major," Bristow said. "They were runnin' every which way, tryin' to lose the planes and get back to the mine."

"Right," Merritt replied. "That's why it's rather strange that one set of tracks takes off to the east, in the direction of the Soujak Mine, with long, running strides, while this set"—he pointed with a gloved finger—"approaches at what looks like a slow, careful walking pace from the direction of the German forces at Mount Zpoda. . . . And returns the same way."

D'Amato frowned. "Kraut? Maybe a scout from a reconnaissance patrol. You know, checking up on the Storches' handiwork."

"Mmm." Merritt's eyes flickered over the tracks,

the blue-white snow, the evergreen boughs drooping nearby. All at once, he took a step to one side and plucked out something caught in the needles of a waist-high pine branch.

"Whatcha got there, Major?" Bristow asked.

Merritt held the item up between his thumb and forefinger. "Cigarette butt. Black paper, small gold-colored filter with the name Richterhaus imprinted on it."

"Filter?" Bristow remarked, looking incredulous. "Who smokes cigarettes with filters? A broad, maybe." He drew heavily on his unfiltered Camel.

"Richter-*who*?" D'Amato inquired.

"Richterhaus," Merritt repeated. He rolled the butt in his fingers. "Translation: 'House of Richter.' A very high-end tobacconist from Munich. That's gold foil around the filter. This is a custom-made cigarette, and very expensive."

"No shit," D'Amato commented. "Some Kraut tossed it for sure, I guess."

"Probably an officer," Merritt said, "and since he had time to smoke, he was in no hurry, evidently." He put the butt in his pocket and gestured at Yagovac's body. "Would you mind turning him over, Sergeant?"

"Yessir." Bristow bent over, his Camel clamped between his lips, and with D'Amato's aid rolled the heavy corpse over. The entire back of Yagovac's coat was encrusted with frozen blood, as was the snow beneath his body. There was a single small hole in the center of the dead man's back, directly between the shoulder blades.

Merritt considered the mortal remains of Bozidar Yagovac for another long moment. Then his mouth tightened and he nodded to Bristow and D'Amato.

"All right," he said. "Let's go."

"Fire!" Cernović yelled.

The pursuing Fallschirmjager flung themselves left

and right as the two Yugoslav infantrymen covering Tito's retreat opened up with their burp guns. Slugs whined and caromed off the passageway walls in a flurry of rock chips and dust. The chattering of Partisan Schmeissers and SS Sturmgewehrs was earsplitting in the close confines of the mine.

The German officers and their Muslim shock troops were finding the pursuit more difficult. They had long since penetrated past the existing light sources— cooking fires and random lanterns—near the mine entrance, and were now probing down the passageway with battery-powered flashlights and lamps. The Partisans, who had the twin advantages of knowing the mine's primary and secondary tunnels *and* being able to stop and wait for their oncoming enemy, lost no opportunity to shield their lanterns and set a mini ambush at every appropriate turn in the passageway. They simply waited for the enemy lights to appear.

"Fall back!" Cernović hissed as the firing died away. Farther up the passageway, a Partisan kneeling with a lantern unmuffled it slightly to illuminate the rear guard's withdrawal. From the direction of the Fallschirmjager came the sound of moans and shouting.

"We're nearly to the fork!" Tito exclaimed. "Left or right?"

"Left to the cascade, Comrade Marshall," Marko said quickly. "The right branch is a dead end after another hundred yards."

"Are the ropes still in place?" Tito asked as the little band of men hustled along the barely lit tunnel. There was a nervous quaver in his voice, Marko thought—probably more due to the unavoidable gymnastics ahead than the killers behind. It was common knowledge that Tito did not like heights.

"The ropes are there, Comrade Marshall," Cernović panted, catching up with the rear guard. "Marko, the box is ready?"

"Yes, Comrade Commander," the young Partisan replied. He shifted the radio pack on his back. "This damned thing is heavy—I call it The Ogre, it's so ugly and awkward. And I'd like to ditch it."

"No." Cernović put a hand on his shoulder as they hurried along. "We have a critical use for it beyond establishing contact with the main body of our forces again. We must get a message to Major Merritt and his team within the next half-day, and with all these cursed SS on top of us we aren't going to be able to send a runner after him."

There was a mind-numbing *BANG* as a grenade went off in the tunnel behind them, barely two turns back. The Partisans clapped their hands to their ears, grimacing in pain.

"Bu . . . but, Comrade Commander," Marko said, as the ringing in his ears died away, "the British major doesn't have a radio."

"Correct," Cernović said. "But Quisp does. We'll radio a message to him, request that he rendezvous with Merritt somewhere on Zlostup. He knows the territory and how to avoid the Germans."

Marko shook his head in the dim light. "Very well, Comrade Commander. But—Theobald Quisp? Begging your pardon, but isn't he somewhat—ah—unpredictable, sir? I mean . . . the one time I saw him . . ."

Cernović coughed forcefully and spat a wad of plegm into the darkness as he trotted along. "Unpredictable, yes. Unreliable, no. There's a difference, Comrade." He glanced over his shoulder at the sound of more shouting from the pursuing SS. "Quisp is a classic English eccentric, but he will get our message to Merritt if asked. Anyway, he's our only option right now. And any later will be *too* late."

"Yes, Comrade Commander," Marko said.

"Alright. I'll give you the message after we make the cascade descent. Go on ahead with Marshall Tito and the others. Hurry."

As the young radioman nodded and trotted on at the rear of Tito's bodyguard, Cernović dropped back behind an outcropping of rock. Just for a moment, there in the darkness where no one could see, his face took on a look of utter exhaustion and all but unbearable sadness. Then, as quickly as it had come, the haunted expression ebbed away, replaced by the familiar rogue-Gypsy grin.

"*Hsst!* Stefan! Boris! Take cover there and there! We'll bloody these damned SS noses one more time before we shut the door for good, eh? Get ready. . . ."

Stirling let go of the pack mule's halter and turned to Sylvia. "Can you handle this animal alone for a few minutes, ma'am?"

Sylvia shot him a hooded-eyed glance that said *Probably better than you*, refocused on the terrain ahead, and kept walking. Stirling grunted, shrugged, and set off at a trot to catch up to Throckmorton, who was struggling along in deep snow with the mule Bristow and D'Amato had turned over to him. Heavily laden and with an uncertain hand on its halter, the mule was becoming uncooperative.

"Miserable beast," Throckmorton grumbled, tugging on the animal's halter as Stirling approached. "Will you move, you stinking nag?"

"Having a little trouble, sir?" Stirling inquired, puffing out condensation. He shifted his Enfield rifle by its shoulder strap and took hold of the opposite side of the mule's halter.

"A battle of wills, Sergeant," Throckmorton said, looking pale and depleted. He coughed hard, turned, and spat wetly. "Damnation."

Stirling watched him, his brows furrowing slightly. "You don't look well, sir. Perhaps you should ride for a while. Save your strength."

"What?" Throckmorton looked aghast. "You're not actually suggesting I should climb up and *straddle* one of these greasy pseudoequines, are you?"

Stirling couldn't help smiling. Sick though he was, Throckmorton's sardonic humor and dry delivery were

143

as incisive as ever. The man was the walking embodiment of the legendary Stiff Upper Lip. "Well, I guess
not, sir," Stirling said.

"Good," Throckmorton rejoined, "because there
isn't enough bug powder in the Allied arsenal to de-
louse me if I *was* to mount one of the foul creatures."
He leaned back, tugging on the mule's halter, while
the animal sat farther back on its haunches and dug
in its forehooves. "Come on, *come on*, curse you!"

Sylvia plodded up, leading her mule without difficulty. She went past Stirling and Throckmorton about
fifteen feet, then tied off her animal's short lead to a
hanging branch and retraced her steps.

"Come to help, have you?" Throckmorton observed. "Or perhaps to gloat?"

"Gloating at the incompetent is a sign of low character," Sylvia told him, "a vicious amusement most
often indulged in by members of the English gentry,
in my experience." She moved past Stirling to the
stubborn pack mule's hindquarters.

"By God, you are a pleasant female," Throckmorton drawled. "Do I really offend you that much?"

Sylvia glanced sideways at him as she rummaged in
one of the pouches attached to her ammunition belt.
"You bore me," she said. "English aristocrats look
down their long noses at everyone else in the world
simply because they're not English. They also feel free
to make denigrating remarks about people who don't
share their peculiar pomposities. Get this through your
head, Englishman: you won't find me a willing target
of your so-called wit."

Throckmorton blinked languidly. "I'm just trying to
get along, my dear. . . . Not make enemies."

Sylvia held up a small metal stick about the size of
a threepenny nail. "This is a pencil flare," she said.
"Phosphorus."

With a quick jerk she broke it in half. There was a
sharp *snap*, and a white-hot ball of light began to sizzle
in her gloved hand. The uncooperative mule jerked

its head around, eyes wide with alarm. Sylvia touched the flare to the back of the animal's rump, just beneath the tail.

With a squalling bray, the mule lunged forward, sending Stirling and Throckmorton stumbling back. Throckmorton lost his balance and sat down heavily in the snow. The smell of burned hair mixed with the tang of phosphorus smoke in the still alpine air.

Sylvia stalked after the mule, holding the hissing flare by her side. "Instead of trying to get along," she remarked as she bypassed Throckmorton, "try getting out of the way."

Stirling crossed the churned snow of the mule track and extended a hand to Throckmorton. "Here, sir," he said.

Throckmorton clasped the hand and got to his feet, brushing snow off the seat of his pants. "Thank you, Sergeant." He gazed after Sylvia Kozo as she prodded the suddenly energetic mule up the trail. "I guess we should take the animal she tied off to the tree," he commented.

Stirling smiled. "Bit of a harpy, isn't she?"

Throckmorton extracted a cigarette from inside his coat. "I like her," he said, "even if she doesn't particularly care for me. She has *verve*." He offered a second cigarette to Stirling. "Let's have a smoke and wait for Weiss to catch up, eh? He's dropped a little too far behind, I think."

He nodded down the slope of the ridge they'd been following. Several hundred yards back, the young Jewish sergeant was coaxing his mule through a series of deep drifts. It was slow going; the heavily laden animal had developed a noticeable limp.

"Is that mule going to bear up, Weiss?" Stirling called.

Weiss looked up as he and the mule floundered out of the last drift. "We may have to spread some of its load between the other two animals," he shouted back, breathless. "It gashed its left rear leg on a chunk of ice about half a mile back. It was bleeding a fair bit until I wrapped it." He patted the mule, which was steaming with sweat and exhaling twin torrents of vapor out its nostrils. "The leg's still giving it a lot of trouble."

"Fetch the brute up here," Throckmorton called, smoking idly. "We'll rearrange the ordnance and co-mestibles more to its liking. Maybe give it a lovely warm Epsom salts bath, too, don't you know."

Stirling chuckled again. "You're a card, sir, beggin' your pardon for sayin' so. Is there anything you don't see the humor in?"

"No, Sergeant," Throckmorton declared, exhaling smoke, "because in my opinion, life itself is one great protracted farce—and I don't wish to be the sort of dullard who isn't in on the joke."

A sharp whistle cut the late-afternoon air. Throck-morton and Stirling looked up to see Merritt, Bristow, and D'Amato emerging from the dense forest on the left-hand side of the upper ridge, some three hundred yards ahead. Vlado, far in the lead on the main trail, raised a hand as they approached.

Merritt and the two American sergeants stalked across the sloping, snow-covered clearing that lay be-tween them and the trail, working their way down. Vlado waited, watching them, his face devoid of ex-pression. Snow disturbed by their passage slid in mini avalanches off to the right, into the deep ravine that bordered the main trail; some of the snow formed balls and ran down the incline with ever increasing speed, leaving little bluish tracks across the clean white expanse before tumbling out into empty space.

"Did you find him?" Vlado asked as Merritt drew near.

Merritt regarded the gaunt Partisan with a level gaze. "No," he said. "We found a few more corpses, but they were partially covered with new snow. Yago-vac's body must be completely covered." He paused as Bristow and D'Amato moved up on either side of him, submachine guns casually at the ready. Bristow dug inside his combat jacket for a cigarette and lit it; D'Amato was chewing gum. Both men were silent, and both of them were looking steadily at Vlado.

Merritt shook his head and let air whistle out between his teeth. "Those Storches made a real mess in there. Shot the poor devils to hell." He half glanced over his shoulder at Bristow. "Didn't they, Cole?"

Slowly, Bristow removed the cigarette from his mouth. The even, unsmiling gaze he had locked on Vlado never flickered. "A real mess, sir."

"Wouldn't you say so, Frank?" Merritt added.

The tough little Italian-American sergeant nodded, working on his gum. "Yessir. A real mess." He, too, continued to look at Vlado, his expression neutral, ambiguous.

"It must have been bad for you," Merritt said to Vlado, his tone leavened with a note of sympathy.

The Partisan's eyes shifted from Merritt to Bristow to D'Amato and back to Merritt again. "It was. It was terrible. A bloodbath. As you saw."

Merritt nodded. "Yes, well, we did see. You're lucky you made it out, Vlado." He reached over and clapped the Partisan gently on the upper arm. "A little farther, and we'll bivouac for the night. Get a few hours' sleep, eh?"

Vlado looked uncertain for a split second, then indicated the trail behind him with a slight jerk of the head. "It looks like we have a lame mule to tend to, Major."

"Ah yes. Weiss's. I see it limping down there. We may have to redistribute its load."

"I think so," Vlado agreed. "Well, I'll lend a hand." He started off through the snow as Sylvia trudged up, leading her own mule.

"Oh, by the way," Merritt said, "before you go— are you absolutely sure that Yagovac was killed in the

Storch attack? I mean, there's no chance the Germans captured him, is there? Not a hope that he may still be alive?"

Vlado shook his head absently. "No. The Storches machine-gunned him from overhead, just like all the others. I saw it happen."

"Ah." Merritt paused, examining the snow at his feet. "Hit in the head and upper body, I suppose. Fatal wounds."

"That's right," Vlado said. "His head was nearly blown from his shoulders. It was terrible, Major. I'll never forget it."

He turned away and continued back down the trail toward Throckmorton, Stirling, Weiss, and the two remaining mules, unaware of the cold stares being directed at him by Merritt, Bristow, and D'Amato.

The extreme end of the Soujak Mine's main passageway terminated at a natural fault in the rock of the copper mountain's heart—a huge subterranean flaw in the form of a yawning vertical fissure some twenty feet wide and several hundred feet from top to bottom. Beside the small ledge onto which the passageway led, a large horizontal crack in the sheer rock face functioned as a natural outlet for alpine groundwater—a cascade that tumbled into the lightless void in summer and froze solid in winter. It was out onto this motionless waterfall of ice, poorly illuminated by weak oil lamps, that Tito now swung, rappelling awkwardly down into the darkness on a single thin rope with two younger, more agile Partisans on either side of him, on ropes of their own, to steady him.

"The rest of you hook up to the other ropes!" Cernović barked to the half-dozen men still lingering on the edge of the precipice. "Get going after the Comrade Marshall, assist and cover him at the bottom! *Go!*"

He turned back to the mouth of the passageway as

the gunfire reverberating out of it doubled in ferocity. Fifty feet in, at the last turn, his four best close-combat submachine gunners were holding the oncoming Fallschirmjager at bay—barely. Just inside the passageway, Marko was bent over a small black box about half the size of a carton of cigarettes, tightening wire ends onto its two brass terminals.

Yet another German grenade exploded with a bone-rattling *BANG*. The concussion hurt Cernović's eyes and sinuses. A scream shrilled out of the darkness above the cacophony of small-arms fire, to be followed by a cry of despair in Serbo-Croatian.

"Hurry up!" Cernović shouted to Marko, and ran into the passageway with his Luger held out in front of him. He was nearly to the rear guard's position when a second explosion—this one filling the mine with white-hot light—threw him against the rock wall, all but blinded. *Flash grenade*, he thought frantically. . . .

The Fallschirmjager came around the corner hard on the heels of the blast, firing, while the defenders' vision was momentarily compromised. Cernović threw his pistol up and fired back, blinking and rubbing his tearing eyes. He could see the silhouettes of his men, backlit by a wall of dancing German flashlights, staggering and falling as they were driven from cover and shot down.

The Luger clicked on an empty chamber and he spun and dashed back down the passageway toward the cascade ledge, still half blinded. Marko was waiting, crouched on the right just outside the exit. Cernović lunged out of the passageway and off to the left side of the ledge as a fusillade of Sturmgewehr fire sprayed out of the darkness behind him.

"Blow it!" he screamed, collapsing against the fissure wall.

Marko twisted the trigger of the electric detonation box. For an interminable second, nothing happened. . . .

Then, with a roar that shook the very bones of the mountain, the twenty-five twelve-pound bricks of high-grade plastic explosive that the Partisans had planted along the ceiling of the final two hundred yards of the Soujak Mine exploded, directly over the heads of the lead Fallschirmjager.

A tremendous gout of dust and shattered rock blasted out of the passageway and into the empty air of the vertical cavern. Cernović was certain he caught a blurred glimpse of a disembodied leg and boot wind-milling past as he huddled against the fissure wall with his hands clasped over his ears.

Then the paltry ledge on which he and Marko were crouching broke in two. The right-hand side support-ing the younger Partisan sagged but stayed in place. The left-hand side under Cernović crumbled and fell into the abyss.

As the rock beneath his feet dropped away, Cer-nović twisted his body and made a desperate lunge for the half-dozen ropes dangling beside the frozen waterfall. He managed to wrap his fingers around two of them. As he slammed backward into the column of ice, the crude steel spike anchoring one of the ropes to the rock pulled out.

The other rope held. Gasping, the wind knocked out of him, the Partisan commander summoned his last reserves of strength and, kicking, managed to get the rope half wound around one leg. It was enough to brake him as he slid downward, the coarse fibers of the rope burning between his trembling fingers.

Still, Cernović had the presence of mind to think of Marko. He stared up at the remains of the ledge as he descended, half out of control, into the gloom. The underpinnings of the little shelf of rock were crum-bling, disintegrating, even as he watched. . . .

"Marko!" he yelled. *"The ropes, boy! Jump! Jump!"*

The young Partisan took two running steps and leapt. He would have made it if not for the bulky pack radio on his back. The extra weight of The Ogre was simply too much. Cernović saw Marko soar, spread-eagled, through the air above him, saw him get a hand on one of the ropes, and for an elated second thought he would hang on. . . .

Then the rope slipped from his grasp and his body came hurtling down, inverting with the weight of the radio as it fell.

"Nooooooooo!" Cernović heard himself scream. He made a frantic grab for Marko as he tumbled past, but it was futile. The cold metal of the radio scraped his clutching fingers—and then the boy was gone. Gone without uttering a sound.

Two seconds later there was an awful, muted *splat* from the darkness below.

Cernović let out an anguished groan and pressed his face to the rope, teeth clenched and eyes tightly shut. For a moment he hung there, dangling in space, squeezing the rope as if by so doing he could embed his helpless grief and fury in its strands.

Then the brief surge of strength left him and his hands relaxed once more, and he resumed his perilous slide down the rope to the bottom of the frozen waterfall.

Twenty minutes later, SS Hauptsturmfuehrer Ulrich Haak and the handful of Muslim Fallschirmjager who had survived the blast staggered out of the mouth of the Soujak Mine and into the white purity of the snowbound gorge, blackened from head to toe by rock dust, and coughing as if to spew up their lungs piecemeal.

Haak and Scharfuehrer Schmidt collapsed to their knees, clutched up handfuls of snow, and pressed them to their stinging eyes and faces. All around them men were doing the same, spitting and hacking as they tried to soothe their streaming eyes.

"I . . . I never thought . . . we'd find our way . . . out of there, Herr Hauptsturmfuehrer," Schmidt croaked, wheezing. He looked slowly over his shoulder. "*Mein Gott.* Only seven . . . maybe eight . . . made it out . . . besides us."

Haak blew his nose between his thumb and forefinger and wiped the sleeve of his combat jacket across his upper lip. With his red, puffy eyes, sweaty, dirt-caked face, and phlegm-covered chin, he looked like the survivor of a poison-gas attack, Schmidt thought. The Scharfuehrer had no doubt that he looked as bad himself.

"We went in . . . with an assault team . . . of twenty-five," Haak panted, his condensing breath wreathing his head. "If it cost eighteen dead . . . to be rid of Tito . . . then it was worth the price."

"You're . . . you're sure . . . he was there, Herr Haupsturmfuehrer?" Schmidt asked.

"I caught . . . a glimpse of him . . . just after we stormed the mine entrance," Haak replied. "The light was on his face . . . as he looked back at us." His wind was returning. "I know it was him; that face is unmistakeable. The head rat of the Slavic Communists, damn him."

Schmidt looked back at the mine entrance, which was still discharging a thin haze of dust and smoke. "So . . . you feel he's dead, sir?"

Haak nodded. "Dead or soon to be. Either way, he's not coming out of that hole again, that's for certain."

"Perhaps there is another way out," Schmidt said. "A back door?"

"No." Haak shook his head. "That miserable mine penetrated right into the heart of the mountain. The far side of it is a solid vertical rock face overlooking yet another cursed gorge, complete with waterfall—we reconnoitred it as we flew in for the drop. The miners wouldn't have dug the main shaft clear to the opposite side of the mountain only to have it open out onto an unusable cliff. Too much work for no reason."

Schmidt got painfully to his feet. "Suppose there

are side tunnels leading back to this opening," he suggested. "Maybe the Partisans knew there was a way to collapse the main passageway on top of us and then bypass the blockage—get back to the main entrance and escape."

"Possible," Haak said, "although I think the bastards committed suicide when they saw we had them trapped—tried to take us with them. But we're not going to take any chances. We're going to set charges in the mine entrance and bring the whole thing down on itself. If any Slavs *do* happen to be alive in there, they can wander around in the dark until they go mad and kill each other or simply starve to death." He removed his cigarette case from inside his jacket, opened it, and extracted a black paper cigarette with a gold foil filter. "Either or," he said, "it doesn't matter to me."

A nearby object caught Haak's eye. It was a dead body on a stretcher with a hand-knit scarf draped over its face. The Hauptsturmfuehrer scowled, cleared his throat, and spat forcefully on the corpse. Then he licked his lips.

Schmidt held out a wooden match, popped it into flame with his thumbnail.

"Ah, thank you, Schmidt," Haak said, bending to the light and drawing. He offered the open case. "Here. Have one yourself."

"Thank *you*, Herr Haupsturmfuehrer," the Scharfuehrer replied. "Richterhaus, eh? Very fine, sir."

Haak smiled and gazed into the empty black entrance of the Soujak Mine. "Nothing but the best," he said.

"Smashed to pieces," Cernović muttered angrily, throwing down a fragment of the radio that had plummeted along with Marko to the bottom of the waterfall chasm. He and the other Partisans, including Tito, were sitting on boulders about twenty feet back from a narrow cleft in the rock through which a cold, ebbing daylight penetrated. He blinked and turned to look at the wrapped-up body lying among the rocks at the foot of the frozen cascade, then put his head in his hands and stared at the ground between his feet. *I'm the one who told him he had to carry that damned beast of a radio. . . .*

"Since the Nazis can no longer pursue us through the mine," Tito said, "we'll wait here for nightfall before making our exit. We should be able to rejoin our main force by dawn. Commanders Lesković and Ribar have certainly broken out by now and will make for the Ugljevik Pass to regain a terrain advantage over any pursuing Fallschirmjager or Jagdkommando units." The marshall paused and looked over at Cernović. "Anton."

Cernović did not answer.

"Anton," Tito said again.

Wearily the Partisan commander raised his head from his hands. "What?"

Tito's handsome face hardened, but he restrained himself, and when he spoke it was without anger. "Anton. The boy is dead. He was a good soldier and died well. And that's the end of it."

Cernović turned his head and regarded the shrouded body lying among the rocks again. Then he looked the other way, toward the daylight filtering in through the cleft in the rock, and cleared his throat. "I know, Comrade Marshall," he said quietly.

"Of course you do," Tito returned. He folded his arms. "We have no radio, Anton. We must get our message regarding the King Tiger train to Merritt before tomorrow is done, or he will not know to accelerate his schedule for mining the Zpoda Skyway Bridge." He gestured at the handful of Partisans sitting nearby. "None of these men know the way to Zlostup. They are from Slovenia in the north, and are not familiar with the hidden pathways of the Majevicas."

Cernović passed a hand over his brow, pushing aside his unruly black hair.

"That leaves you," Tito said.

There was a long silence. Then Cernović sat up, looked about him, and sighed. Slowly the rakish Gypsy grin, albeit subdued, spread across his face once more.

"I'll move out of the cavern ahead of the rest of you," he said, "just after the sun drops behind the mountain."

Chapter Eight

"Keep it tight, Sid. You, too, Peter."

RAF squadron leader Alan Stuart adjusted his throat mike and glanced back past his port and starboard wingtips to check the proximity of the other two Typhoons. The big fighters, heavy with underwing rockets and drop tanks, were spaced perfectly in the close triangle formation, as Stuart had known they would be. Flight Officers Cox and MacLeish were two of his best, if a bit young. He continued to scan the ground rushing by barely three hundred feet below, praying all the while that he wouldn't lead the small attack flight into some barely visible radio tower the Germans had erected. The dim light of evening was fading rapidly into darkness, he didn't know the terrain of north-central Yugoslavia all that well, and there was no telling what the damned Nazis might have stuck in their path. In addition, if they didn't encounter the tank-carrying train in question pretty soon, it would be too dark to maintain visual contact with the railway tracks and the mission would be a scrub.

"Are we even sure this is the right train line?" Cox asked, his voice crackling in Stuart's earphones.

"My drop tanks are nearly empty," MacLeish chimed in. "Are we good for fuel, sir? I don't fancy ditching in the Adriatic and swimming the last fifty miles back to Bari."

Stuart chewed his lip in irritation. "No, I'm not sure this is the right bloody train line," he growled. "And yes, we're good for bloody fuel. For another ten minutes, that is—at which time we'll have to break off and head for home, anyway, because it'll be too dark to see the bloody ground." He paused momentarily. "Anyone have any more bloody questions?"

"No, sir," Cox radioed.

"No, sir," MacLeish echoed.

"Bloody good, then. Keep it quiet and keep it tight."

The two flying officers let out deep breaths and glanced across the intervening fifty feet of airspace at each other. They could still make out each other's faces through the Plexiglas of their fighters' cockpit canopies, although daylight was waning to a fiery golden glow as the sun began to sink behind the purple hills to the west.

Stuart was about to give up and order the flight homeward when he saw first the black, billowing smoke and then the engine of a train coming around a low hill some six miles ahead. He checked his fuel. His drop tanks were empty, like MacLeish's and probably Cox's, and this far into Yugoslavia the Typhoons' regular tankage would get them back across the Adriatic Sea to southern Italy only if their big Napier Sabre engines were mechanically benevolent enough to run on dregs and fumes. It was a toss-up, yea or nay.

"Right," Stuart said, holding his throat mike against his larynx, "let go drop tanks and attack the train coming into view ahead of us. Two passes, line formation. Behind me, Sid, then you, Peter. Two rockets

157

only on the first pass. Then one strafing run and head for home. Everyone clear?"

"Clear, sir," Cox replied. He throttled back slightly to move his Typhoon in behind Stuart's.

"Clear," MacLeish said, letting his aircraft drop back several hundred yards. "Sir, do you think that's the right train?"

"Lis—" Stuart began.

"It doesn't look like the right train to me. It's too short."

"MacLe—"

"And where's the Luftwaffe air cover that's supposed to be following the tank train? We haven't seen a Hun fighter all day."

Suddenly Squadron Leader Alan Stuart—frustrated, tired, scared, and heartily sick of war—became very annoyed with Flying Officer Peter MacLeish. Racing in at four hundred miles an hour barely a stone's throw from the ground to attack a heavily armored military train with inadequate daylight and scant fuel to get home was hardly the appropriate moment for petulance.

"Listen," Stuart barked, "it's a bloody train. We're out of time and we're out of daylight, and it's *here*, so it's the one we're bloody attacking. Otherwise this whole bloody exercise is a wasted trip."

"Yes, sir," MacLeish radioed.

He still sounds petulant, Stuart thought irritably, as he steadied his Typhoon on the onrushing locomotive and thumbed the launch triggers of his rockets.

"More tea, Your Excellency?" Matthias Juttner inquired, lifting the silver-and-glass flask off the white linen cloth that covered the luxury coach's main dining table. The ice cubes in the crystal water glasses rattled slightly as the train swayed around a gradual bend in the track.

"Yes, I believe I will," Amin al-Husseini replied. "A pleasant finish to a rather superb rack of lamb."

THE WAR MOUNTAINS

Juttner smiled as he leaned forward in his chair and refilled the grand mufti's tea glass. "It was quite adequate, wasn't it? For a train meal, anyway." He continued to smile as he turned to Julius Neurath, who was the third diner at the table. "Hauptsturmfuehrer Neurath? Tea?"

The pale Gestapo officer directed a flat stare at Juttner. "No, thank you."

Juttner shrugged, imperturbable, and topped up his own glass. "I hope you're not off your food, Hauptsturmfuehrer. You look somewhat moribund. Perhaps the garlic, eh?"

"I'm fine," Neurath said.

"I'm so glad," Juttner responded. "I was becoming concerned about your rather alarming . . . *translucency* of complexion."

Neurath paled even more, the muscles along his jaw working in suppressed rage, as al-Husseini snapped his fingers in the air. "Snagi! My tonic, please." The mufti always concluded dinner with a cocktail of natural digestive aids—juices, herbs, and spices.

Mustapha Snagi, moving carefully due to the pain of his recent gunshot wounds, appeared at the door of the private car's small galley. "At once, Your Excellency."

He turned to go, and at that instant two tremendous explosions went off on either side of the train, rocking it on the tracks. The panes of several windows on both sides of the coach blew inward, spraying the luxurious interior with glass.

"*Aaaagh!*" al-Husseini cried, throwing his arms up in front of his face.

Juttner and Neurath staggered up off their chairs and made for the front of the car. Snagi came through the door of the galley, followed by a terrorized chef and his assistant, and lunged for al-Husseini. The Macedonian bodyguard collected the mufti in his arms and swept him to the floor next to a large purple velvet divan, partially covering him with his own body.

159

Juttner and Neurath burst through the coach's front door and onto the small forward-end platform. They were just in time to see the smoke trails of two rockets suddenly streak the sky mere yards overhead, accompanied by a whining *whoosh*, and hear the dual impacts as the projectiles struck somewhere just behind the train. Two seconds later there came the deafening roar of a powerful engine as an RAF Typhoon, the distinctive air scoop beneath its propeller hub gaping like the black mouth of some airborne shark, overflew the train, heading in the opposite direction.

"Why don't those fools on the antiaircraft car open fire?" Neurath yelled, craning his neck to watch as the two Typhoons began to bank around over the undulating countryside, setting up for another pass.

Juttner, holding on to the handrail of the shaking, swaying end platform, opened his mouth to reply—and two more rockets shrieked in. One exploded on the hillside to the left of the train. The other hit the cab of the locomotive, just behind the boiler. There was a blast that made all five cars in tow—coal car, bunk car for the bodyguard detachment of SS, armored antiaircraft gun car, al-Husseini's private coach, and caboose—dance on their metal wheels. Scorching clouds of fire, smoke, and steam began to stream back along the entire length of the train. Incredibly the locomotive did not derail, nor did it lose power. Juttner leapt to the left side of the end platform, where he could look up the inside of the curve they were negotiating and see the whole train from the engine back.

The cab of the locomotive was a twisted tangle of blackened steel, with orange flame, black smoke, and white steam gusting out of it. The coal car had caught fire, adding to the smoke and flame licking back over the SS bunk car and the antiaircraft gun car immediately behind it. Juttner grimaced and coughed as oily fumes whipped into his face—and then there was another earsplitting din as a third Typhoon roared down the length of the train less than seventy-five feet overhead.

"The engine's had it!" Juttner shouted to Neurath. "It's only a matter of time before it dies or blows up! And the coal car's burning!" He watched as whipping sheets of flame from the coaler drove back SS troopers who had appeared on the forward-end platform of the bunk car, trying to beat out hot spots with jackets and blankets. "The bunk car's catching fire, too!"

The SS gunners on the two rotating 40-millimeter antiaircraft cannon finally opened up, sending red streams of tracer shells scudding after the three British fighters that were banking low and fast across the purple-and-gold evening sky. The guns fired with a rapid, distinctive sound of their own, their multiple barrels punching in and out with every recoil:

Pom pom pom pom pom . . .

"I don't bloody believe it!" Squadron Leader Stuart fumed over the radio. "Six rockets fired and only *one* hit?" Possibly the worst of it was that his own two rockets had been the first to miss. "Forget strafing. Fire the rest of your rockets on this next pass, and, gentlemen, I want that bloody train *knocked off the bloody track! Clear?*"

"Roger that, Squadron Leader," Cox acknowledged.

"Maybe you'll get a hit yourself this time, sir," MacLeish remarked dryly. He had to say it; it was impossible for him not to. Flying Officer Peter MacLeish was nineteen years old, a tank-busting Typhoon ace three times over, flushed with his own power and apparent immortality, and had not lived long enough to learn that there are many occasions in life when a man, regardless of what he thinks, should resist the urge to sound clever, and keep his mouth shut.

"You're bloody going on report for that, MacLeish!" Stuart shouted, enraged that the young flier's insolence was consuming even a fraction of his mental energy in the middle of an attack. By God, he'd never heard of such a thing. He refocused out the port side of his cockpit canopy on the damaged train as his fighter swept ahead. . . . Around . . .

To starboard, the Messerschmitt 109s came corkscrewing in out of the fiery glare of the setting sun, wing guns blazing. The three Typhoon pilots were caught off guard by the German fighters, concentrating as they were on the ground target to their left.

Cox never had a chance. The first 20-millimeter cannon shells from the lead Messerschmitt tore through the exposed underbelly of his banking fighter and into its primary fuel tanks. Seconds later, the Typhoon exploded in a ball of flame.

Cannon shells from the second Messerschmitt shattered the cockpit canopy of the lead Typhoon, decapitating Squadron Leader Alan Stuart. His relatively undamaged aircraft rolled over, dove straight into the ground, and blew up.

Peter MacLeish's nineteen-year-old reflexes saved him. As German cannon shells hammered into the fuselage of his fighter, puncturing the cockpit wall and shredding the thigh muscles of his right leg, he yanked back on the stick, throttled up, and stood his Typhoon on its tail. Rolling over and through the attacking 109s, missing a midair collision by inches and pure luck, he muscled the plane upright, dove for the deck, and fled at maximum speed into what was left of the setting sun. The Messerschmitts buzzed around in his wake like angry hornets, and four of the attacking flight of eight broke off to give chase.

One of the peculiarities of the Typhoon—and what made it such an effective ground-attack aircraft—was that despite its limitations as a dogfighter and high-altitude interceptor, it was extremely fast at low altitudes, even with its heavy armament. To the surprise of many wartime designers, including its own, the Hawker Typhoon had proven to be faster at ground level than the highly revered Supermarine Spitfire. Faster than the much-vaunted Focke-Wulf 190. And considerably faster than the Messerschmitt 109.

Flying Officer Peter MacLeish would nurse his shot-up Typhoon all the way back across the Adriatic Sea to Bari in southern Italy, racked with the pain of his mangled thigh and dizzy from loss of blood—the sole survivor of the rushed, ill-fated ground-attack mission against the King Tiger train. He would crash-land and live to grow older, wiser, and humbler . . . at the cost of his right leg.

The rail line just over a mile past the bend where the Typhoons had rocketed the Grand Mufti's private train was a beehive of activity. Night had fallen, the temperature had dropped even farther below freezing, and all around the critically damaged locomotive—now sitting motionless on the tracks, with its crumpled superstructure smoking and ruptured boiler steaming—German troops were coming and going, waving lanterns and flashlights, shouting orders and directions to each other. The scene had a surreal, Dantesque quality to it: all shadows and angles and harsh light, interspersed with hissing vapors and the clanking throb of heavy machinery. A hundred yards behind the ruined locomotive, crawling forward along the sloped side of the rail bed like a giant bug, was a King Tiger tank.

The King Tiger train, its numerous tank-bearing flatcars, gun cars, and engines stretching well back around the hillside bend where several of the Typhoon rockets had struck, was stopped dead behind the mufti's damaged and now immoveable train. A slender, middle-aged SS officer in a peaked cap and greatcoat was stalking along the gravel bed beside the mufti's shrapnel-pocked private car, the lantern light glinting off his steel-rimmed glasses. Walking with him were two of his own aides, Haj Amin al-Husseini, Gestapo

Hauptsturmfuehrer Julius Neurath, and SS Hauptsturmfuehrer Matthias Juttner. Snagi trailed along several
paces behind his master.

"But Standartenfuehrer Kronstadt," Neurath was
saying, "one of your train's eight locomotives *must* be
reassigned to the Grand Mufti's train. It is absolutely
imperative that a dignitary of his stature be provided
safe conduct to Belgrade without delay."

"No," the SS colonel replied, "it is absolutely imperative that my forty-eight King Tigers be transported to their deployment point in the Majevica
Mountains without delay. And this heap of scrap
metal"—he waved a black-gloved hand at the steaming hulk that had been the mufti's locomotive—"is
preventing that from happening."

Amin al-Husseini, looking cold and annoyed in his
expensive town coat, stepped aside and reboarded his
private car. As usual, Mustapha Snagi followed him.

"The Grand Mufti is a special guest of the Reich,"
Neurath pressed on, "a key associate and ally of the
Fuehrer himself. If he was to become a fatality due
to your—"

Standartenfuehrer Kronstadt stopped in his tracks
and turned to face Neurath directly. "It was only by
the merest of chances that the British Typhoons attacked your train instead of mine; I was barely twenty
miles behind you. And if my preassigned fighter cover
had not spotted the attack on your train and inter-
vened so effectively, you and your companions, including His Excellency the Grand Mufti of Jerusalem,
would in all likelihood be dead. Now, having saved
your lives once tonight, I have no intention of lingering here, shuffling engines back and forth, while the
British and Americans send out more search-and-
destroy missions. And I will not decrease the hauling
capacity of my train, which must negotiate a number
of steep inclines in the Majevicas, by sacrificing one
of my locomotives just so the mufti can branch off
this line and head directly to Belgrade for his own

convenience. There is a military priority here, Hauptsturmfuehrer Neurath, and the delivery of my Tiger tanks to the battle front takes precedence over the chauffeuring of your temporarily marooned dignitary to his next luxury hotel."

Kronstadt, a supremely no-nonsense individual, had leaned in until his hard, seamed face was now less than six inches from Neurath's. The intelligent eyes behind the steel-rimmed lenses were as cold and steady as chips of ice. "We will proceed thusly: the King Tiger now approaching will topple your damaged locomotive off the track. My train will then move forward to couple to your caboose and remaining cars, and push them ahead of us all the way to the Zpoda Skyway Bridge. I will not stop and expose myself to further air or saboteur attack. The mufti and you can then disembark at the fortified bridge chalet, which is garrisoned by soldiers of the very SS Division Handschar he has come to Yugoslavia to speak to—according to you—prior to my train's final transit across the bridge itself to the crest of Mount Zpoda.

"Frankly, I don't see why His Excellency is so adamant that he be routed to Belgrade when he must then promptly travel on to the very location to which we are now headed. From his standpoint it's six of one, half a dozen of the other.

"And that is how it will be, Hauptsturmfuehrer Neurath. I suggest you inform your distinguished guest of the unavoidable change in itinerary."

Neurath's thin mouth twitched. "I will put a detailed account of your unwillingness to accommodate the grand mufti into my report to Reichsfuehrer Himmler," he said.

"Do that," Standartenfuehrer Kronstadt replied, turning on his boot heel. "I'm a combat officer, not a travel agent." He waved a gloved hand in the air, ignoring Neurath entirely. "Move that Tiger into position, Obersturmfuehrer!"

Behind Neurath, Hauptsturmfuehrer Matthias Jutt-ner smiled to himself, placed a thin black cigar be-tween his lips, and stepped farther down the gravel embankment as the crawling King Tiger approached.

Chapter Nine

Cernović had been alternating between a fast walk and a double-time trot all night. Now dawn's silver light was bringing the cold gleam of a new day to the silent trees and black crags and snow-packed slopes of the high mountain country just east of the Zpoda Gorge. Fortunately after ducking out of the Soujak Mine's hidden rear exit the previous evening, he had been able to evade the Fallschirmjager still patrolling the forests above the mine and pick up Merritt's trail without difficulty. Following along in the trodden-down snow of the mule track had been relatively easy, and he'd been able to make good time.

Now his beard and mustache were caked with ice from the freezing condensation of his own breath, his fingers and toes were numb, his thighs and calves ached, his lungs were raw from panting in the dry, bitter air, and he desperately wanted a cigarette. Even more desperately he wanted to stop and rest. But Merritt and his companions were still somewhere ahead, so he hugged the Mauser carbine he had borrowed from one of his men more tightly between his folded arms, put his head down, and soldiered on.

The terrain had become incredibly rugged and dramatic. The ridgelines he was following were knife edged with steep inclines on both sides—one wrong step could send him tumbling down a snow-covered seventy-degree slope with no hope of stopping beyond crashing into the trees hundreds of feet below. And yet, as hazardous as the ridge trail was, he knew it was nothing compared to the real "Bad Step"—Zlostup—which lay only a few miles ahead.

Cernović quickened his pace to a trot as the trail sloped gently downward for a few hundred yards before resuming its upward course, winding through one of the small thickets of stunted evergreens that were becoming less frequent as he gained altitude. Moving into the trees always gave him a sense of comfort; he did not like being so exposed on the open ridges. The towering peaks and chasms of the high mountains were spectacular, awe-inspiring—but a man could be spotted from a long way off in such country.

The sun shot its first pale rays over the crags to the east just as he reached the center of the copse, illuminating a perfect little sheltered hollow in the trees through which the trail passed. As tired as he was, the temptation to stop was overwhelming. Plus, Cernović realized, he was becoming badly dehydrated, which was dangerous. He had been trying to eat snow while traveling through the night, but it was not enough to compensate for the moisture loss of sweating under his winter clothes and panting in the arid mountain atmosphere. He needed to stop, make a small, smokeless fire, melt snow in the rusty tin can he kept as a field cup, have a real drink of perhaps a quart or more of warm water, eat some of the sugar cubes he carried in his shirt pocket, smoke one of his two remaining cigarettes, and rest for ten or fifteen minutes. Then he could catch up to Merritt.

He sighed, leaned his Mauser carbine up against a convenient boulder, and began to gather low deadwood from the nearby trees. There was plenty available, and it was dry. Obviously no mountain travelers had camped in this particular copse for some time.

He had just gotten the fire going and was filling up his tin can with snow when a stick broke behind him with a sharp *crack*.

He dropped the can and spun, clawing in his coat pocket for his Luger.

"Yoo-hoo, Cerny!" cooed the gaunt, red-bearded man squatting on the boulder against which Cernović had propped his carbine. His eyes, vividly blue in the clear morning light, fixed on the Partisan commander's with the intensity of electromagnets. He grinned, showing a mouthful of long, yellow teeth, and tossed the two halves of the stick he had just broken onto the snow. "A touch jumpy are we, my boy? Yes, a touch jumpy I think."

Cernović lowered his pistol with an exasperated sigh and rubbed his eyes with his thumb and forefinger. "Quisp."

"The very same, I do confess it!" the piratical apparition on the boulder exclaimed, bouncing on his heels. "Do I not? Yes, I do!"

God, Cernović thought. He turned back to the fire and retrieved his dropped meltwater can. "You took me off guard, Professor," he said, refilling the tin with snow.

"And that is a worrisome thing, old bean. Shouldn't happen."

Quisp hopped down off the boulder, walked across the intervening ten feet, and squatted on his haunches on the opposite side of the fire, facing Cernović. The Partisan commander hadn't seen the Englishman for nearly two months, and so examined him with some interest as he held his can of snow over the flames by its wire bail.

Theobald Fenton Quisp, PhD, was one of those

scrawny, red-haired Scots-Irish hybrids who, by virtue of their jittery temperament and unnaturally bright eyes, tend to look perpetually crazed. He could not keep still even when squatting in one place: his hands, eyes, mouth, facial muscles—all the muscles in his body, in fact—were in constant motion, shifting, flexing, wandering. It made Cernović tired just to look at him, not to mention slightly irritable; Quisp's congenital restlessness had a catching quality.

The Englishman was starting to look more than a little worn, Cernović decided, as if advancing middle age and the strain of living alone in the mountains, constantly hunted by the SS and their collaborators, were catching up to him. There wasn't an ounce of fat on his stringy body, but the lines in his face had multiplied and deepened and there was a considerable amount of gray in his unkempt red beard. Cernović wondered how much longer he would be able to keep up his self-declared one-man war of surveillance, sabotage, and general harassment against the Nazi occupiers. His presence and activities in Yugoslavia were not sanctioned by the British military—or any military, for that matter. He was a complete independent; a lone wolf. Or perhaps a lone lunatic. Everyone fighting the Nazi war machine was glad to have Theobald Quisp running around the mountains, gathering intelligence and occasionally blowing something up, but no one was quite sure what he was apt to do from one moment to the next. He would cooperate with requests from the British and Partisan militaries, but he would not take orders and he would not agree to being evacuated from Yugoslavia, although the British had offered to extract him several times.

An improbable person, this eccentric Englishman, this professor of archaeology who had written several prewar textbooks on the ancient Greeks, Macedonians, and Thracians, Cernović thought as he warmed the meltwater in his tin can. This foreign-born guerilla adventurer who was both strangely reliable—loyal, even—undeniably brave, and disconcertingly unpredictable all at the same time.

The Partisan commander lifted the can from the tiny fire and gingerly sipped the steaming water. It was not the last time, he was certain, he would think so about Theobald Quisp.

"Are you thirsty, Professor?" he asked, holding out the can. "We can melt all the snow we need."

"No, thankee," Quisp replied, bouncing. He unslung the Schmeisser machine pistol he was carrying from his shoulder and set it across his knees. Then he pulled off his tattered gloves, cupped his hands in front of his mouth, and blew into them. "Rather balmy up here today, my boy, don't you think? Yes, balmy. Balmy's the word."

Cernović sipped more hot water and crunched one of his sugar cubes between his teeth. "I think it's damned cold. I'm half frozen to death."

Quisp clucked his tongue and slapped his knee. "Circulation, my lad. Circulation is the key. The blood must rush—*rush*, I tell you—around the body, building up and maintaining heat through friction as well as metabolic combustion. One must develop this capacity with a program of internal cleansing, vigorous exercise, and brisk massage. Absolutely essential to good health, what?"

Cernović smiled involuntarily behind the rim of his meltwater can, remembering the disbelief and consternation on Marko's face the day Cernović and the young radio operator had rendezvoused with Quisp at one of his temporary camps, at his request, to change out a faulty transmitter in a field set. The Englishman had been striding in circles around his lean-to, stark naked but for his combat boots, raking his fish-belly-white skin from neck to ankle with two stiff-bristled brushes, one in each hand. His scrawny torso, buttocks, and thighs were livid with red splotches from the vicious self-flagellation, and he was singing some appalling Gaelic folk song in a lusty baritone as he whaled away at himself. He did not so much as blink when Cernović and Marko walked up, and, in fact, asked if they would care to join him in his daily routine. Marko, Cernović recalled, had looked ready to flee for his life.

"I don't doubt it works for you, Professor," Cernović said, "but I think I'll stick to long walks and staying clear of stray bullets to keep myself healthy." He coughed, finished his water, and put a battered cigarette between his lips.

Quisp watched him intently as he lit the smoke with a twig from the fire. "And that is another thing, my boy: the abomination of habitually ingesting toxic gases through one of the body's most vital organs, the lungs. Far be it from me to lecture you on how best to maintain the temple of your material being—yes, far be it." He looked off to one side and up, raising a finger. "However, the harmful effects of this habit have long been recognized, and to support the point I shall now quote from the famous essay 'A Counterblaste to Tobacco.' To wit: it is 'a custom loathesome to the eye, hateful to the nose, harmful to the brain, dangerous to the lungs, and in the black, stinking fume thereof, nearest resembling the horrible Stygian smoke of the Pit that is bottomless.' End quote."

"You're ruining my cigarette, Professor," Cernović said, exhaling. "And how do I know you didn't just make that up?"

Quisp jumped to his feet. "You don't, my lad, you don't! Not unless you are familiar with the insightful writings of the worthy King James the First of England, who penned those trenchant words in the year 1604! By the Leaping Lord Harry, didn't he just? Yes, he did!" Quisp executed a bizarre theatrical flourish with one hand and, bowing, squatted back down.

"Good for him," Cernović grunted, inhaling contentedly.

Quisp clucked his tongue again and wagged a finger.

"I see what you're thinking, old fellow. You're thinking, *Quisp considers me a lost cause, a fellow human
condemned to the slow degradation of health and vital-
ity by means of autotoxification!* But you are wrong—
wrong, I tell you! I shall never give up on you, Cerny.
I shall save you from your own compulsive indul-
gences in the long run, have no doubt!"

Cernović blew out another long stream of smoke.
"I'd much rather you saved me from the Nazis, the
Ustashe, the Chetniks, and the Handschar Muslims, if
it's all the same to you."

"Speaking of the Nazis," Quisp said, changing gears,
"aren't you wondering why I've dropped in on you
here atop this godforsaken rock pile?"

"Yes. It had crossed my mind." Cernović knew
from long experience that one had to allow the loqua-
cious Englishman all the time he needed to get to the
point. Prodding him for specific information before he
was ready to give it only prolonged the waiting
process.

Quisp grinned conspiratorially. "Tito asked me to.
I received a radio communication from him just before
midnight last night. The witching hour—oooooh!" He
bugged his eyes and waggled his fingers at Cernović.

The Partisan commander smiled again. "You're
quite insane, you know, Professor," he remarked. "Of
course, you're well aware of that fact, aren't you?"
The question was rhetorical.

"Naturally," Quisp replied. "Attempting to remain
sane in an insane situation such as total global war
would quickly make one crazy. Far better to adopt a
complementary approach to said situation and truly
accept it, thereby sacrificing one's sanity but retaining
one's wits."

Cernović nodded patiently. "That makes perfect
sense to me. Now, there was a radio communication
from Comrade Marshall Tito?"

Quisp fluttered his hand. "You forced me into a
digression, there, Cerny—shame on you. Yes, as I said,

I did receive a message from the Tito's camp. Some new information has come to light since you departed the Soujak Mine, and I was asked to pass it on to you and this countryman of mine—Merritt, isn't it?—who is even now stealing his way along Zlostup toward the Zpoda Skyway Bridge."

"How far ahead are they?" Cernović asked.

"Approximately seven miles," Quisp told him. "I spotted them from across the gorge early this morning as I was hastening to meet you. We'll soon catch up to them—Zlostup is badly iced and snowed in. They won't be moving very quickly with three mules, will they? No they won't, my boy!"

"And the specifics of the Comrade Marshall's message?" Cernović continued.

"There is, apparently, a military train bearing a large cargo of King Tiger tanks headed in this direction. That you know, and that is what you must relate to Major Merritt. What you do not know is that yesterday afternoon a small private train immediately in front of it was rocketed by British Typhoons, blocking the tracks. It took most of the night to clear away the wreckage, repair some sprung rails, and get the tank train underway again. That amounted to a twelve-hour delay. Merritt and his demolition team have gained half a day's grace to get the Zpoda Skyway Bridge mined."

Cernović nodded. "That's good news. That extra twelve hours may make all the difference."

Quisp bounced on his haunches. "Indeed, indeed. But there is more. Marshall Tito additionally relates that the Soujak Mine units of the Second Proletarian Brigade have broken through encircling Nazi Fallschirmjager and Jagdkommando forces and successfully executed a strategic redeployment into the Ugljevik Plateau region via the Ugljevik Pass."

"Strategic redeployment?" Cernović echoed, raising an eyebrow. "That sounds suspiciously like retreat."

Quisp tsk-tsked. "My boy, as a high-ranking officer

in the Partisan Army of Yugoslavia, you should be quite inured by now to the blatant euphemisms of the Communist ethos. Of course it means retreat. They ran for their lives, shooting wildly, and barely escaped annihilation, from what I can gather. Commander Ribar was killed. Only Lesković and, of course, Tito himself remain."

Cernović cast his eyes down at the ground for a moment, then flicked his cigarette butt into the dying fire. "I am sorry to hear about Comrade Ribar," he said. "He was a good man. His father, one of the party's founders, will be heartbroken."

"Yes, it is unfortunate," Quisp agreed. "But Dr. Ribar is a strong individual. I happen to know him. He will persevere."[1] The Englishman got to his feet. "Perhaps we should do the same and press on, Cerny, my lad, and talk further as we go. Shouldn't we? Yes, I think we should."

Cernović, still dwelling on the thought that yet another close friend had been killed, looked up at Quisp. "Professor," he said with a tired smile, "why is it that you always finish your statements with a question which you then immediately answer yourself?"

Quisp looked incredulous as he slung his Schmeisser over his shoulder. "Good heavens," he replied, "I'm quite sure I don't know what you're talking about. I don't do that, do I? Of course I don't!

"Now, come along, my boy. Up and at 'em, eh? There is more to tell and miles in which to tell it, ha-ha! The good marshall spoke of a possible diversionary attack on the far side of Mount Zpoda just prior to the arrival of the tank train, and of a certain gamecock—of all things—an individual whose updated movements may be of particular interest to Major Merritt, for some reason. . . ."

Chapter Ten

Merritt walked carefully to the break in the narrow footpath, knelt in the snow with his Sten gun in the crook of his arm, and peered down. Veteran mountaineer and parachutist though he was, the vast empty space that yawned beneath him took his breath away. The drop to the bottom of this section of the Zpoda Gorge had to be every bit of two thousand feet—give or take a bounce or two, as Cernović had so colorfully put it.

He stood up, stepped back, and surveyed the towering cliff face that formed the left-hand side of the ancient trail known as Zlostup. The rock was mostly bare, with few cracks, crevices, or protrusions. Not much ice, which was good, but not much to hold on to or drive a piton into, either. Forty horizontal feet away, the narrow trail resumed its snaking, precarious route up and along the southern wall of the gorge. In between was a complete void—a gap where the footpath had once been but now simply did not exist. It was as if a giant ax had hacked out a ten-meter section of solid rock with one swipe.

"Avalanche," Merritt said to his seven companions, who were gathering behind him. "It swept away the trail cleanly for forty feet or more. There's not so much as a toehold left of it." He looked at Vlado. "I thought you told Tito and Cernović that Zlostup was still passable."

The lean Partisan brushed a stray lock of dark hair out of his eyes and avoided Merritt's gaze. "It was, Major, but that was nearly five days ago. The avalanche must have happened since then."

"It doesn't look that recent to me," Merritt said. "And I've seen a few."

Vlado shrugged. "Rock slides are a daily occurrence in these mountains, Comrade Major. I tell you this must have happened only a day or two ago, because the path was intact when I used it during an intelligence-gathering patrol just before your parachute drop."

Merritt turned to face him. "You go out alone on reconnaissance patrols, Vlado? Close to the German positions?"

"Close enough," the Partisan said. "We need a constant flow of information in order to stay one step ahead of the enemy. I and some of the others scout alone because we've learned that one man has less chance of being discovered than two or three."

"I'd say the enemy was one step ahead of you the other day," Bristow commented, leaning against the rock wall with his arms folded on top of his Thompson, gazing at Vlado. "Yagovac and his boys walked right into a shootin' gallery."

"And the Krauts had our drop zone staked out pretty good the other night, too," D'Amato added. "Decoy fires and SS troops layin' low right next to the DZ, all set for us to come floatin' down outta the sky like a flock of dumb pigeons."

Vlado swallowed, feeling the hard eyes of the

American sergeants on him. "The Germans and their Muslim collaborators in the Handschar division are very effective opponents," he said. "They routinely try to interrupt Allied air drops with decoy fires and Jagdkommando patrols. Sometimes they are in the right place at the right time. It's a matter of chance." He looked directly at Bristow. "And *I* was fighting alongside Bozidar Yagovac the morning he and many of my other comrades were killed, Sergeant."

"Yeah, sure," Bristow growled. "I forgot."

There was an awkward silence. Vlado hung his head and put his hands in his pockets and sling his rifle over one shoulder, looking sullen. Merritt looked him up and down, then turned and examined the rock face immediately above the missing section of trail. Most of it was featureless, but there were a few finger-width cracks, and about fifty feet above the opposite trunca- tion of the path, a wedge-shaped chunk of granite that stood out about five feet from the cliff proper like a giant knuckle.

Merritt stood there for a few minutes, considering. The day was clear and fairly still, but high on the stark crags above Zlostup, the wind coursed through clefts and crevices with an eerie, rising moan. Finally he turned and faced his companions.

"Obviously we can climb and piton our way across the gap," he said, "and set up a Tyrolean traverse[1] to get all the equipment across. The problem is the mules. We can't mine the bridge without all the climb- ing gear and explosives, and we can't carry it all with- out the mules."

Vlado shuffled his rag-wrapped boots in the snow. "We're turning back then, Major?"

"Not just yet." Merritt pointed up at the knuckle of granite sticking out of the sheer wall above the far end of the trail. "We have ropes and blocks. If we can secure a block-and-tackle arrangement to that out- cropping, we can rig slings for the mules, support their weight, and pull them across the gap with tag lines after we unload and transfer the equipment. Then we load the animals up again and proceed to the objective."

"You'll never get a mule to step off the edge of that cliff," Vlado said immediately. "When it sees the drop and decides it doesn't want to go, all eight of us won't be able to push it off, either."

"That's why we'll blindfold them," Merritt responded. "Three or four of us on the other side will hoist them off their hooves one at a time and they'll be across before they know what's happening." He looked pointedly at Vlado. The Partisan guide opened his mouth as if to argue, but then thought better of it.

Throckmorton sauntered up. "More aerobatics?" he asked.

"A little climbing and rigging," Merritt replied, "and a lot of unloading and hauling, I'm afraid." He smiled. "It's the only way, Duncan, as you can see."

The slender British captain stepped past his friend and cast a languid glance down into the gorge. "Yaas," he drawled, "it appears to be. Bloody substantial drop, that."

"Substantial's the word," Merritt said. "Where's Sylvia?"

"Loitering in the rear of the procession with her mule—whose company she seems to prefer to ours."

Merritt nodded and walked back down the trail, sidestepping between the rock wall and the first two mules, followed by Bristow. D'Amato, with Stirling and Weiss by his side, continued his casual observation of Vlado.

Sylvia Kozo was seated on a small boulder, smoking, beside the third mule. She looked up as Merritt drew near, regarding him from under her heavy lids.

"Miss Kozo," Merritt said, "perhaps I could prevail upon you to undertake a little climbing for us."

Sylvia nodded silently, the smoke from the cigarette cupped in her hand trickling up through her fingers.

"I need you to establish a line across that gap, then

climb to that protruding rock up there and secure a block and tackle to it," Merritt went on. He glanced over his shoulder as Bristow moved up behind him. "Do you think you can do it?"

Sylvia blinked slowly at him. "I know I can do it." She drew on the cigarette, holding it shielded in her palm between her thumb and forefinger.

Merritt nodded. "It'd save us time and effort. Any one of my men with mountaineering skills can pound a line of pitons across to the far side—and up to the overhead rock, as well—but you can certainly cover the same distance much faster. . . . If you're sure that face is climbable."

"Anything is climbable," Sylvia said, getting to her feet. "It just depends upon who's doing the climbing." She drew once more on the cigarette, flicked it aside, and slipped past Merritt and Bristow, heading for the front of the little column. "Get your ropes and blocks ready, Major."

Merritt did not reply. He and Bristow were looking at the same thing: the black paper cigarette with the gold filter that lay smoldering on the hard crust of the snowpack. The British major and American sergeant met each other's eyes, and then Merritt took two paces forward and crushed the butt down into the snow with the sole of his boot.

"Watch her," he said quietly to Bristow as he moved past the second mule, following Sylvia Kozo back toward the head of the column.

Cernović and Quisp had been walking for nearly two hours and had just moved onto the lowest stretch of Zlostup. Quisp had been doing most of the talking, and had covered everything from the disasterous military consequences of having four dozen King Tigers deployed into the valleys of the Majevicas to the geology of the rock in the surrounding cliff faces. Cernović had listened patiently as he walked, at times lapsing deeply into thoughts of his own. Now, with the empty chasm of the Zpoda Gorge dropping away on the right side of the ever narrowing trail, he interrupted Quisp's latest irrelevant digression—a stream-of-consciousness lecture on the dietary benefits of wild garlic—with a more pertinent concern.

"Something's been bothering me," he said. "How did the German command in the Majevicas know exactly where to drop their Fallschirmjager? How did they know to ring the gorge and to storm the Soujak Mine itself? It was as if they were certain Tito and his staff would be inside."

Quisp, striding along at Cernović's shoulder, shrugged his shoulders. "Intelligence, my boy. The Germans are sticklers for up-to-date intelligence. God knows there are enough low-level reconnaissance flights buzzing the peaks and gorges these days."

"They should not have known about the Soujak Mine," Cernović insisted. "Weather has been too poor for effective air-to-ground surveillance, the mine and its gorge are well concealed and located well back from the main German line of advance, and we have been meticulous about security."

"Not meticulous enough, apparently," Quisp said, "unless, of course, they simply got very, very lucky. Followed a random trail in the snow, perhaps . . . or caught sight of the smoke from a cooking fire."

"No," Cernović said. "We have been too careful about those things. And the weather has almost continuously covered for us."

Quisp looked over at him. "Well, then, Cerny, perchance you have a rat in the hold. A rotten apple in the barrel. A Judas amongst the disciples, eh? Yes. Yes, I think that metaphor is the most apropos. A Judas, my boy—a Judas with a fist full of silver."

Cernović frowned but did not reply immediately. "I've been thinking the same thing," he said finally. "We have Yugoslavs of every stripe in the Partisan Army: Serbians, Croatians, Montenegrins, Bosnians, and Slovenians. We have Roman Catholics, Eastern

Othodox, Muslims, Jews, and Gypsys. All that is required for entry into the Proletarian Brigades is the willingness to discard old nationalistic and religious loyalties and to swear to fight for a united Yugoslavia under the even hand of the Communist authority as personified by Comrade Marshall Tito.

"It is equally easy to leave. Fighters join all the time, and a certain percentage of them promptly desert. We usually shoot the few we catch, just to guard our backs, but obviously a significant number evade us and make their way to our enemies. The thing is, only inner-circle commanders and their trusted lieutenants know specific details about parachute drops, unit maneuvers in force, and command-post locations. We have been encountering improbably well-positioned SS Handschar patrols again and again for more than six weeks now, and taking significant casualties. It is starting to look as though it is not by accident."

"Well, Cerny," Quisp stated, "the easiest thing for a man to do is change his mind."

"It is," Cernović acknowledged. He stepped over a snow-covered tree trunk that lay across the trail. "The question is: which man?"

"Or woman," Quisp said. "Tito and the lesser pashas in the Central Committee keep plenty of those loitering around, too, don't they? Oh yes they do, my lad. Yes they do."

Cernović looked at the Englishman, perplexed. It was a possibility he hadn't considered.

"There are many women in the Partisan Army," he said quietly. "Nearly all of them fight and die as bravely as any man."

"But the women who tend to circulate near Tito and his inner circle," Quisp persisted, "are they not for the most part a gaggle of vicious harridans? You yourself have seen it—not so much out here in the front-line command posts, but in the safer environs of vanguard headquarters locations. The predatory fe-

males gather. Each hates the other; all are manuevering for influence and position. And someone always
has to lose. How many competitors for Tito's af-
fections has that vile-tempered wife of his—Zdenka—
attacked, harangued, humiliated, and ultimately driven
off? Eh? Do you think it possible that some of these
defeated sirens harbor resentment toward Tito, his
wife, his other loves, or the Partisan Army in
general?"

Quisp rolled his eyes and addressed the heavens.
"Oh, it is possible, my boy, it is possible! Remember:
'Hell hath no fury like a woman scorned!' William
Congreve, as I recall."

Cernović's mind was racing now as he trudged
through the snow, rife with images of the women he'd
seen hovering near the great, charismatic Marshall
Tito—flirting, laughing, fawning, sparring, testing,
questioning. There had been so many, starting with
the ferocious Zdenka. . . .

" 'Frailty, thy name is woman!' " Quisp recited in
full theatrical voice, his boots crunching through the
new snow. "The Bard himself—William Shakespeare."

Cernović barely heard him, immersed as he was in
his own thoughts. There had been Tanya, the former
opera singer with the raven hair and the slow, sidelong glance. . . .

" 'All wickedness is but little to the wickedness of
a woman!' Ecclesiastes, that one, my dear boy."

There had been Mileva, the gushing, full-bodied
blond farm girl who was also a superb personal secre-
tary and therefore a major threat and irritant to the
domineering, paranoid Zdenka. . . .

" 'Quippe minuti, semper et infirmi est animi exigu-
ique voluptas ultio. Continuo sic collige, quod vindicta
nemo magis gaudet quam femina!' How's your Latin,
old bean?" Quisp glanced quickly over at Cernović as
he strode along beside him.

There had been Zora, the beautiful, husky-voiced

young widow of one of Tito's personal bodyguards, who had seen an opportunity to mitigate the loss of her husband by assuming his place just behind the Comrade Marshall's shoulder. . . . And eventually by charming her way into Tito's bed. Trading up, as it were . . .

"Not good, I see. Very well, I shall translate: 'Indeed, it is always a paltry, feeble, tiny mind that takes pleasure in revenge. You can deduce it without further evidence than this, that no one delights more in vengeance than a woman.' That quote comes from Juvenal, Cerny, my lad—d'ye see? Of course you do."

Cernović looked at Quisp briefly, having heard his nickname and little else.

And there had been Sylvia, pouting prettily at Tito like a spoiled, favored child when he'd gently chastened her away from the British and American paratroopers only two nights ago in the Soujak Mine. . . .

"I still don't see how she does that," Bristow grunted to D'Amato, looking up at the almost featureless rock face above the gap in the trail.

"Neither do I, Cole." D'Amato was punishing the gum again, cracking it between his molars.

Forty-five feet above the far side of the avalanche-ruined section of Zlostup, Sylvia Kozo, stripped once again to abbreviated black shorts, rubber-soled slippers, gray-white men's undershirt, rabbit-fur hat, and little else, was moving up the vertical cliff like a fly marching up a pane of glass. Dangling from a short line knotted beltlike around her waist was the upper block of a three-fall block and tackle, the multiple lengths of rope reeved through it snaking and twisting down behind her. Merritt stood on the trail's end at the far side of the break, tending the ropes with Weiss standing by. On the single horizontal traverse line Sylvia had secured across the gap before beginning the climb with the block and tackle, Stirling was now dangling, hooked on by carabiner and working his way across the sickening chasm hand over hand, as Merritt and Weiss had done before him.

"All right, Sergeant?" Merritt called.

"Fine, sir," Stirling puffed, kicking off the cliff face as he pulled himself along. A few shards of rock broke free under his boots and tumbled slowly into the abyss.

Throckmorton was sitting on one of the crates of high explosive that had been offloaded from the mules, watching Sylvia's progress with interest. He lit a fresh cigarette, and Vlado stepped back out of reflex.

"Captain," he said, "do you see what you're sitting on?"

Throckmorton nodded. "Yaas. Explosives."

"Er . . . the cigarette . . ."

The slender officer shrugged. "There's no danger. The stuff is completely inert unless you set off a detonator in it or hit it with a tracer round. The latest concoction, Comrade. We could even break off a chunk of it, light it with a match, and cook our dinner over it as it burns—in perfect safety."

Vlado looked dubious. "No."

"Oh yes. It needs both heat and impact to make it go off with the traditional bang. You could probably fire that rifle into it without result. Now, a tracer or incendiary round—that would be another story."

D'Amato cracked his gum again and craned his neck back, shielding his eyes from the sun with a hand to his forehead. "She's almost there. Just a few more feet and she can start runnin' line around that hunk of stone to secure the block."

"I wish she'd drive a piton or two," Bristow said. "Run a safety rope through them so we could catch her if she slips." He gestured with his Camel at the gaping void before them. "Awful damn long way to fall."

"She won't fall," Throckmorton remarked. "She's an artist immersed in her element when she's on the rock. She believes she can't fall, that the possibility

does not exist, and she certainly isn't going to under-
mine that certainty by attaching a safety rope to herself. You see?"

D'Amato grinned. "You know, Captain, in the U.S.
military there's something called a catch-22. You know
what that is?"

"No, I'm afraid I don't."

Bristow gave a snort of laughter, nodding, and drew
on his cigarette.

D'Amato grinned again and went on: "It's a clause
in army regulations that says a soldier's request to be
relieved from combat duty can only be accepted if
he's mentally unfit to fight. But it goes on to say that
any soldier with the sense to ask to be excused from
something as god-awful as war is obviously not
crazy—so he has to stay and fight. Get it?"

Throckmorton gazed at D'Amato for a few seconds,
then smiled broadly. "That's exquisite, Sergeant. Simply exquisite. And I thought only the European militaries were sufficiently evolved to come up with a
regulation that feeds off itself like a snake eating its
own tail."

"Hell, Captain," Bristow said, "the U.S. military's
evolvin' faster than a snowball meltin' in the Laredo
sun. Pretty soon them boys with the shiny brass buttons and the scrambled egg on their caps'll have us
all so locked up in regulations, the only thing we'll be
good for is marchin' around in circles."

"Anyway," D'Amato said, "it's kinda like what you
were sayin' about this little Partisan gal. Same inside-
out logic, you know? She don't believe she'll fall, so
she won't, so a safety rope ain't necessary. But if she
does the smart thing and puts a rope on, it means she
don't believe she can't fall—so she just might."

"Now I'm gettin' confused," Bristow grumbled.

Throckmorton chuckled again. "I follow you, Sergeant. You're right. It's the same thing as catch-22, as
you call it." He shook his head. "Catch-22. That's

truly beautiful. Someone ought to write a book about it."

D'Amato shrugged and looked back up at Sylvia. "Maybe someday someone will."

The lithe young woman had hung the heavy wooden block with its trailing lines on a knob of rock for the moment, and was now scrambling around the main granite knuckle like a spider, running several loops of rope around the entire outcropping. She appeared to be adhering with her fingers, toes, elbows, and knees to the smooth cliff face by magnetism or magic; there was little or nothing to hold on to. And yet there was never a slip, never a hitch in the smooth rhythm of her movements.

When she had draped a total of three loops of rope around the outcropping, she climbed up on top of it and squatted down on her heels for a moment, resting. She looked like a pale, svelte gargoyle, Throckmorton thought, crouched there on her frigid rampart of barren rock. . . . As though she might suddenly spread batlike wings, push off, and soar out into the empty air of the Zpoda Gorge.

"She sits there too long, she's gonna freeze her tits off," Bristow muttered.

As if she'd heard him, Sylvia gripped the front edge of the outcropping and swung down. Holding on by one hand, with the toes of her slippers planted against the cliff, she pulled the suspended wooden block over to the loops she'd just run and placed its supporting hook over all three ropes. Then she secured the mouth of the hook with a few wraps of twine.

"That's it," Bristow said. "She's got it. Let's get the first mule ready."

Stirling was standing beside Merritt and Weiss on the far side of the gap, removing the rope harness and carabiner he'd used to suspend himself from the traverse line. When he'd shed the climbing gear, Merritt handed him the slack block-and-tackle ropes and

together they pulled the falls tight. Up at the top
block, Sylvia deftly wrapped a leg around the ropes
and transferred her full weight to them. Then, with
Merritt, Stirling, and Weiss keeping the block-and-
tackle arrangement taut, she slid down fifty feet to
the footpath.

Merritt caught her as she reached the end of the
falls so she wouldn't break an ankle finding her footing. She couldn't have weighed much more than a
hundred pounds, and as he supported her with one
arm around her waist, he was aware that her slippered
feet barely extended past his knees. Her face was level
with his, and as she drew back and regarded him from
beneath her hooded lids, he braced himself for the
slap or blow he suddenly felt sure was coming.

Instead Sylvia crossed her arms, leaned her elbows
on his chest, and looked down her nose at him with
an expression bordering on amusement. "You may put
me down now, Major," she said.

Merritt blinked. "Of course. Ah, watch your footing
on these broken rocks." He lowered her carefully to
the ground. "We brought your clothes over while you
were setting the block and tackle. Better get into them
before you freeze." He pointed at the bundle lying on
a a flat boulder nearby.

With the upright poise of a dancer, Sylvia swiveled
toward the clothing, then looked slowly back over her
shoulder at Merritt and smiled. "Thank you," she said.

Merritt nodded, the corner of his mouth tightening
upward. "You're welcome." As Sylvia began to collect
her winter clothes, he caught Stirling's eye and indicated with a jerk of his head that the girl was still to
be watched closely.

Then he turned to face the rest of the party, waiting
with the mules and equipment on the opposite side of
the gap. "Duncan!" he called. "You come across and
help us on this side. Sergeant Bristow, Sergeant D'A-
mato! Pull this block over and hook it up to the harness of that first mule." He picked up the lower block

of the hoisting arrangement and rapidly tied it onto a secondary line that had been strung below the main traverse rope. As D'Amato pulled the block across, suspended on its three falls from the granite outcropping overhead, Merritt fed out his end of the secondary line while Stirling paid out slack to the block and tackle.

Throckmorton clipped a carabiner from his rope harness onto the traverse line, let it take his weight, and began to make his way hand over hand across the dizzying void while behind him D'Amato, Bristow, and Vlado blindfolded the first mule and maneuvered it into position. The animal was skittish, well aware of the drop and not wanting to move while deprived of its sight. Finally the three men got it to the edge of the pathway and secured the lifting block to its body harness at a point just behind the shoulders. Bristow tied a holdback line to the lifting block and coiled the slack into the snow at his feet.

Opposite them, Throckmorton clambered up beside Merritt, gasping for air. "Next time pack me a pair of wings, old fellow," he cracked.

Merritt smiled and steadied him with a hand on his shoulder. "Get your breath, Duncan. When you're ready we're going to need your weight on this block and tackle."

"I suppose we have to lift the filthy beast at least a foot or two off its hooves, eh?" Throckmorton coughed wetly, turned his head, and spat. "All right, more damnable blue-collar labor. Let's get about it, then."

He stepped in between Stirling and Weiss and seized the main hoisting line of the block and tackle with both hands. The two other men did likewise, and with Merritt at the front of the hauling contingent they took up all the remaining slack in the system. Stirling looked over his shoulder quickly as Sylvia moved up behind him and gripped the rope, as well.

"Ready?" Merritt called. Bristow, standing beside

the mule with a hand on its halter, gave the thumbs-up. "All right, then," he continued. "As we take its weight, push it off the edge!"

"And mind the beast doesn't kick your teeth in as it goes," Throckmorton added. "It has no gratitude, you know."

"All right," Merritt said, setting his feet. "One, two, three—*pull!*"

The block-and-tackle falls snapped tight and the mule was jerked a foot in the air. D'Amato and Vlado barely had time to push before the animal was off the end of the footpath and swinging along the cliff face, bucking and kicking in its harness. Its hind hooves clapped into the rock, sending shards spinning into the abyss. Bristow leaned back, attempting to control the mule's swing by putting some tension on the holdback line as it ran through his gloved fingers.

Merritt, Weiss, Throckmorton, Stirling, and Sylvia dug in their heels as the animal swung forward, scraping along the sheer granite wall. As the block and tackle went completely vertical, the mule's kicking forehooves clattered against broken rock at the far side of the gap. Merritt stepped up, seized the animal's halter, and yanked backward with all his might as the remaining four lifters threw their combined body weight against the rope. Its fore and hind legs working like pistons, the mule clawed its way up onto the trail, bucked and shied several times, and then stood still, trembling and snorting and steaming.

Sylvia stepped forward, removed the animal's blindfold, and began to talk to it in a low voice, holding its halter and rubbing its nose and jaw. Merritt disconnected the lifting block and holdback line, helped her lead the mule along the trail for a few yards, then returned to address the men on the opposite side of the gap again.

"That's one," he called. "So far, so good, gentlemen. Pull the block back and let's have another."

Bristow waved and began to haul in on the holdback line. "Damnedest thing I ever seen," he said to D'Amato. "A flyin' mule. Lead that next critter on up here, Frank, and make sure its blindfold's on real good."

"We ain't got a lotta horses in the Bronx, ya know," D'Amato told him, moving to the head of the next mule. "Used to be plenty when my folks came over from the old country back in 'oh-five, pullin' milk carts and meat wagons and the like. Nowadays it's all cars and trucks." The little sergeant cracked his gum. "Less shit to sweep up."

"You don't say," Bristow remarked, grabbing the hoisting block and pulling some slack. "That's real interestin'. And by the way, that ain't a horse you got there, city boy. It's a mule."

"I know it's a goddamn mule," D'Amato shot back, stepping carefully between the animal and the edge of the dropoff. "Who can tell the difference? Looks like a horse to me. Stinks like one, too."

"Just bring it up here, willya?"

"I ain't kiddin', Cole. Damn animal stinks worse'n—"

Vlado struck D'Amato across the face with the butt of his Mauser rifle. The American sergeant reeled back, clutching at thin air. His boot crunched on broken rock and ice at the edge of the trail and then he toppled backward off the precipice with a cry of despair. From the far side of the gap, Merritt and his companions watched stunned as D'Amato's body dropped into empty space, turning slowly over before disappearing from view.

"Frank!" Bristow yelled, dropping the block and reaching for the .45 automatic holstered at his side.

Vlado brought the Mauser down and fired from the hip at point-blank range as Bristow was twisting out of the way. The bullet tore through the breast of the big sergeant's combat jacket, cutting a furrow in his pectoral muscle. Like D'Amato, Bristow took a bad backward step. He lost his balance and fell off the end of the path, partly against the cliff face. Unlike D'Amato, his clawing hands found purchase and he managed to arrest his fall after sliding down only a couple of feet. He got the toe of one boot into a small niche, braced himself against the rock, and looked up to see Vlado just above him on the path, swinging down the barrel of his rifle. The Partisan guide's eyes were as black and hollow as the muzzle opening pointed at Bristow's head.

Stirling fired across the gap from a kneeling position, having dropped to one knee to snatch up his Enfield sniper rifle. The hurriedly aimed .303 slug smashed through the knuckles of Vlado's right hand and into the teak stock of his Mauser in a small spray of blood, bone, and wood splinters. With a howl, the Partisan dropped his rifle and staggered back from the edge of the path, bending nearly double to clutch his wounded hand to his midriff.

Stirling racked another cartridge into the breech of his Enfield and fired again. The slug missed the lurching Vlado by an inch and passed between the legs of the second mule. With a backward sneer, the turncoat Partisan began to bull his way past the shying pack animals toward the last bend in the trail.

"Kill him, Stirling!" Merritt shouted, brandishing his Sten but powerless to use it for fear of hitting Bristow or the mules. "Don't let him get around the corner!"

The British sergeant rose to his feet, working the bolt of his rifle, and took aim. At that moment Bristow, who had been trying to get his .45 out of its holster one-handed, lost his grip and slid down another five feet before catching himself. Stirling's eyes flickered onto him, and that second of distraction was enough time for Vlado to get past the last mule and stumble out of sight around the bend.

Throckmorton fired his revolver once, more out of frustration than anything else; the slug chipped the rock impotently where the Partisan's head had been two seconds earlier.

"Watch the girl!" Merritt barked to Weiss. "Keep her here!"

As Sylvia gave him a startled glare, he slung his Sten over his shoulder, grabbed the traverse line, and began to scramble hand over hand across the gap toward Bristow. The big sergeant was losing his grip, his arms and legs shaking with the strain of bracing himself in the vertical corner formed by the foundation rock of the trail and the cliff wall.

Merritt covered the ten-plus meters of empty air in as many seconds and clambered up onto the trail. Dropping to his stomach with his head over the edge, he tossed a loop of holdback line down to Bristow.

"Grab this!" he panted.

Bristow seized the rope with one hand just as his boot toe slipped out of its precarious niche. He swung for a second or two, legs bicycling, then got his other hand on the rope as Merritt gritted his teeth and bore the downward strain of his entire 250-odd pounds. Snow disturbed by Merritt's exertions fell in small clumps past Bristow, tumbling with interminable slowness into the gaping chasm beneath his dangling boots.

And then Throckmorton was there beside and slightly above Bristow, breathing hard, hanging from a six-foot length of rope knotted around his waist and clipped by carabiner onto the traverse line. Finding toeholds for his boots, he seized the American sergeant by the coat collar and hoisted.

"Come on, old fellow," he grunted, "can't have you hanging about all day long, you know."

Using their combined strength, Throckmorton and Merritt managed to help Bristow get his elbows up over the edge of the path. Then with one last effort, the sergeant heaved himself up onto the trail and rolled over on his back in the snow, gasping.

Merritt had snatched up his Sten and was just getting to his feet when a little cascade of rock flakes fell on him from above. He raised an arm to protect his head and face and peered up. Sylvia Kozo, clad in baggy fatigue pants, slippers, stained men's undershirt, and fur hat was scrambling across the vertical wall some seventy feet overhead, heading toward what looked like a long shelf of rock that led to a crevice some thirty feet above her. Her Schmeisser machine pistol was slung across her back.

Merritt swore under his breath and shot a glance back across the gap. *"Weiss!"* he yelled. Then he pulled back the bolt of his Sten and raised it high, sighting in on Sylvia Kozo's fast-moving form. With a single burst he could stop at least one potential traitor from escaping and informing the Germans of the sabotage mission; the girl was still a good five seconds from the lip of the shelf.

Throckmorton and Bristow were barging past the mules in pursuit of Vlado. As Bristow hustled along, grimacing with the pain of the flesh wound in his chest, he glanced back at Merritt.

"What are you waitin' for?" he rasped. "Shoot the bitch!"

Merritt's finger tightened on the Sten's trigger—but he didn't fire. He wasn't sure. And then Sylvia was up and over the lip of the rock shelf. Merritt saw the fur hat and pale shoulders moving laterally as she ran toward the crevice, and then she was gone.

"What the hell, Major!" Bristow shouted angrily, moving out after Throckmorton.

Merritt didn't bother answering. On the far side of the gap, Stirling was helping a dazed Weiss to his feet. Even across the forty-foot distance, Merritt could see the bloody gash on his temple where Sylvia had struck him.

"Stirling!" he yelled, "take care of Weiss and secure the mules!"

Then he tucked his Sten into the crook of his arm and ran down Zlostup after Bristow and Throckmorton.

Chapter Eleven

"I'm telling you, those shots we heard weren't that far off," Cernović said, holding his carbine at the ready as he stalked along the footpath. "I'm not denying that sound travels amazingly well in the these gorges, especially in winter, but I'm sure it wasn't hunters shooting for the pot in the forest down below."

"All I'm saying, my boy," Quisp replied, "is that we didn't hear a single machine gun. Merritt's people, according to you, are carrying Stens, Thompsons, and Schmeissers as well as rifles. The Germans have no end of Schmeissers, in addition to Mausers. If they were involved in some kind of firefight up ahead on Zlostup, wouldn't you think we'd be hearing automatic weapons? Yes, you would, old bean. Yes, indeed."

Cernović broke into a trot, his eyes searching the rocky, snow-covered terrain ahead. "I hope you're right, Professor," he panted. "I don't—"

He halted abruptly and jerked up his carbine as Vlado came stumbling at the run around the next

John McKinna

bend in the path, clutching his bloodied right hand
to his stomach. The wounded Partisan did not notice
Cernović and Quisp right away; when he did, he
balked sideways like a frightened animal and threw a
desperate glance over his shoulder.

"Vlado," Cernović called out, lowering the carbine
and raising a hand, "what's wrong?"

The lanky Partisan hesitated, looking at Cernović
and Quisp and then back up the trail again. Then he
seemed to make up his mind and ran forward, his face
deathly pale, his dark hair flopping over his forehead.

"Comrade Commander!" he gasped. "Jagdkommando patrol, coming down the path after me! They
are only minutes behind!" He staggered up to Cernović, apparently on his last legs. "I'm wounded,
sir. . . . Shot in the hand . . ."

"Take cover, Quisp!" Cernović hissed, grabbing
Vlado by the shoulders and hustling him into the lee
of a nearby boulder. The Englishman was already behind a slab of granite on the opposite side of the trail,
sighting in on the next bend with his machine pistol.

"Where's Merritt?" Cernović asked, bringing his
carbine up to the firing position on top of the boulder.
"What happened?"

"Dead, Comrade Commander," Vlado panted. His
eyes were wild as he stared from Cernović to Quisp
and back up the trail. "They . . . he . . . the Jagdkommando were coming down Zlostup from direction of
Mount Zpoda and ambushed us. I-I think all the others are dead. Either that or they . . . they may still be
fighting. I was separated from the group and shot. I
only just got away, Comrade Commander. There—
there was nothing I could do."

"How many are after you?" Quisp demanded from
across the path.

"May-maybe eight," Vlado stammered. "Maybe more."

Quisp looked at him, frowning. "An ambush, eh?
How long ago?"

Vlado threw up his good hand, wincing in pain and

196

exasperation. "How long ago? Only a few minutes . . . perhaps ten? How do I know? I've been running for my life!"

Quisp continued to stare at him. "Why haven't we heard any machine-gun fire? Or any sustained firing at all, for that matter? Eh?"

Vlado's face twisted. "You—"

"A pretty quiet ambush, my lad, if you ask me." Quisp's fierce, arching brows knitted together. "Something isn't right. . . . Rotten in Denmark . . ."

"Look out!" Vlado screamed, yanking a small pistol from his pocket with his good hand and wildly throwing his arm up over the top of the boulder. He loosed off four shots in rapid succession—*powpowpowpow!*—at the bend in the trail, the weapon jumping in his fingers.

From behind the rock formation around which the footpath curved came an immediate answering burst of machine-gun fire: *brrrrrrrrrraaaaap!* Vlado recoiled with a sharp cry, spinning back from the boulder and flopping into the snow. Cernović and Quisp ducked as slugs zipped and cracked around them, chipping up ice and granite fragments. Then, as one, they returned fire, Cernović with his Mauser carbine and Quisp with his Schmeisser.

Bristow jerked back with a curse, cordite smoke curling out of the muzzle of his Thompson, as bullets hammered into the rock at the bend in the trail. Merritt, just catching up, hunched down beside him. Throckmorton—long bypassed by the two fitter men—was several hundred yards behind on the descending footpath, still out of sight.

"He must've run into a Kraut patrol!" Bristow rasped, breathing hard. "Goddammit, Major—this mission's been snakebit right from the git-go!"

Merritt put a hand on Bristow's shoulder and peered cautiously down the path. "How many, do you think?"

The American shrugged. "Volume of fire ain't much. I dunno—maybe five or six guys. Maybe less."

Merritt thought a moment. "Alright—we're going to find out, Sergeant." He pointed left and right. "We've got broken ground on either side of the trail here to move on. I'll go this way and you go that. Stay low—we'll draw fire and see if we can spot how many shooters and where."

"Well, let's give 'em a volley to get their heads down," Bristow grunted, checking his Thompson, "before we go runnin' out into their sights like a pair of jackrabbits."

Merritt nodded, his thin smile flickering across his face. "Absolutely." He glanced over his shoulder as Throckmorton came puffing down the trail, slipping and sliding on the loose rock and snow. "Duncan! Stay low!"

Throckmorton collapsed to his haunches next to Bristow, wheezing. His face was the color of soggy newsprint. "Good . . . *Lord!*" was all he could say.

"Are you alright?" Merritt asked. Throckmorton nodded, licking spittle off his lips. "Fine. Listen: there are a handful of Germans up on that rise where the trail runs between the granite slab and the big boulder. We want to find out how many and where they are. Sergeant Bristow and I are going to flank out left and right to draw their fire. Try to spot them, will you? Maybe pop off a few shots while we're running, just to keep them from getting too ambitious." He clapped Throckmorton on the shoulder.

The badly winded captain managed a grin. "Ri-righty-o, old chap." He pulled his Webley revolver from its holster, checked the cylinder, and set it on the rock just above his head. Then he hefted his Sten and looked at Merritt. "A burst or two for luck as you leave, I take it?"

"Correct," Merritt said. "Ready, Sergeant?" Bristow nodded, turning to the right, setting his feet under him. "All right, then." Merritt crouched, preparing to sprint left. "Fire on my command. . . . And . . . *fire!*"

Together, Merritt, Throckmorton, and Bristow brought their weapons to bear over and around the rock and opened up. There was a tremendous blast of combined automatic fire from the two Stens and the Thompson—and then Merritt and Bristow were sprinting left and right, respectively, hunched low and moving fast with the peculiar skittering run of the trained soldier. Throckmorton finished the clip in his Sten, grabbed his Webley, and began to crack off individual shots at the granite slab and boulder.

There was no return fire at all.

Throckmorton cocked the pistol and rested its butt on the rock, the barrel pointing skyward. Keeping low, he glanced left and right. Thirty feet away, Merritt was lying in the snow behind a little rise, crawling for a better vantage point. Bristow was kneeling behind another large boulder, his Thompson at his shoulder and pointed down the trail. Both men were unscathed.

Throckmorton ran his eyes over the assumed enemy position. He could see nothing. On impulse, he brought the pistol level and squeezed off a shot. Chips flew off the granite slab, but again, there was no return fire or movement.

Then a voice, clear and incredulous, sang out in impeccable English:

"I say, do my eyes deceive me, or was that a ruddy *Yank* that just cavorted out on our left flank?"

Cernović leaned over cautiously and peered up the footpath from behind his boulder as Quisp's shrill voice died away. "It's Cernović!" he shouted. "Who's there?"

"What the bloody hell—" came the furious reply from across the rocks. "It's Merritt! *Merritt!*"

"What?" Cernović blinked across the trail at Quisp and stuck his head up over the boulder. Off to his

τ

right, some twenty yards away, Major Walter Merritt was just getting to his feet from behind a small rise.

With a curse, Cernović swung around to confront Vlado.

"What the hell are you playing at, you—" he began, enraged.

But Vlado was gone.

Bewildered, Cernović searched the terrain behind him. It was several seconds before he was able to pick out Vlado's fleeing form among the broken rock, scrub brush, and drifted snow. The Partisan guide was a good three hundred yards away; a dark, elusive shape moving fast over the rough ground.

"I'd say the bugger's turned," Quisp remarked, observing Vlado's headlong flight. "There's your Judas, Cerny—one of 'em, anyway."

"I don't believe it," Cernović muttered, staring. "Not Vlado."

"Believe it!" Merritt panted, rushing past him. "He killed Sergeant D'Amato and took a shot at Sergeant Bristow. Come on! We have to stop him before he reaches the Germans!"

"What about that damn girl?" Bristow shouted, charging down the path between Quisp and Cernović. "She's up in those crags somewhere to our right!"

Merritt ran onto the trail just ahead of the big American. "She has to come this way to get out of the gorge," he replied breathlessly, "according to the topo map. Otherwise she'd have to climb across an entire high-altitude snowfield, and she doesn't have the clothing to do that. No coat, remember? And if she just stays hidden up there she'll freeze. We'll see her again soon, I'm sure."

"I'm glad somebody's sure about something," Bristow growled, pounding along behind Merritt.

Vlado was fast on his feet for an undernourished man enduring the pain of a nasty hand wound. The knowledge that the comrades he had just betrayed—

and had, in fact, been betraying for many weeks—
would not hesitate to execute him on the spot if they
caught him was a powerful incentive to keep moving.
The thought of being confronted by Cernović, in particular, gave him a sick feeling in the pit of his stomach; the Partisan commander, normally a man of even
temperament and compassion despite his hardness,
had been known to shoot confirmed traitors in the
kneecaps before dispatching them.

There were few ways to get off the lower reaches
of Zlostup beyond descending near-vertical slopes on
one side or climbing truly vertical cliffs on the other—
but just ahead was one of them: a rare thicket of low,
dense evergreen trees with a single thin side trail snaking through it and up toward the high crags that lined
the gorge all the way to Mount Zpoda. The trail was
known only to a few scouts who had spent considerable time on Zlostup, and its divergence from the
main path was not obvious. A good place to hide.
Vlado glanced over his shoulder as he ran the last
fifteen feet into the trees; his pursuers, not more than
a few hundred yards behind, were out of sight for the
moment. Perfect.

After he let Cernović and the others pass by, he
could make his way on up the side trail to the base
of the crags, and then climb the long, rough route to
the Zpoda snowfields. A day to get across that high
alpine desert of snow and rock, and he would reach
the German lines. Reach SS Hauptsturmfuehrer Ulrich Haak.

The trek would be hard, but Vlado Kusić was used
to hard things. So used to them, in fact, that he had
woken up one morning—sick and exhausted from yet
another late-night running battle with the SS Division
Handschar—to find that he had forgotten how to feel
anything at all. Period. The futility of his situation had
finally come home to him.

That had been nearly two months ago, and soon
after he had made contact in the field with the Ger-

man officer Haak. After years of suffering for everyone around him—especially the little tyrants (for that is what they were) in the Communist Central Committee—Vlado Kusić had decided to do something for Vlado Kusić. Life was pitifully, brutally, *terrifyingly* short. . . . As he had seen time and time again. Even without a bullet or explosion or disease to snuff it out in its early prime.

He hunkered down in the snow behind a thick cluster of pine boughs. The main trail was icy in this area, for a stretch of a mile at least. Too icy for footprints to show up with any regularity. His pursuers would not see that he had left the trail.

They were coming. He could hear them now, moving fast with boots pounding and fabric whiffing and weapons clinking and lungs pumping like bellows. They would not think that he had gone to ground here, for the thicket was very small and looked like a dead end, and they would assume—correctly—that he would not want to risk letting them get ahead and cut off his escape route. An assumption that was correct, needless to say, only in the absence of knowledge about the existence of the alternate trail. Despite the agonizing pain of his shattered knuckles, Vlado smiled and flexed his good hand around the butt of the small-caliber Walther pistol with which he had murdered Bozidar Yagovac.

He kept low, peering out between the pine boughs—and then suddenly there was Merritt, less than ten feet away, sprinting grim-faced down the trail with his harness jangling and his Sten gun clutched loosely in front of him. On his heels was the big American sergeant, Bristow, looking twice the size of the average Partisan and moving with the feral grace of a catamount, his Thompson held one-handed to cover the path ahead.

Then, several yards behind, came Cernović, his face dark with fury. Involuntarily Vlado ducked a little lower. And behind him, Quisp, the inexplicable Englishman who seemed to make a habit out of showing up when he was least expected. Vlado had only encountered him previously on two occasions, and hadn't enjoyed either; the man made him nervous.

And then they were past him, moving out the far end of the thicket and on down Zlostup. It would be many minutes, perhaps even an hour or more, before they realized their mistake. By then he would be far over the crags to the southwest and moving across the snowfields toward Mount Zpoda.

Idiots. Vlado smiled again, got to his feet, and turned to walk up the hidden trail.

There was a harsh metallic clack-*clack* as Sylvia pulled back the bolt of her Schmeisser.

"Stay where you are," she said, her voice low and very steady.

Vlado stayed.

She was sitting cross-legged on a large boulder about ten feet farther up the trail, very erect, with her spine straight and shoulders back. Her head was back, as well, small chin in the air, and her mouth was set, unsmiling. The eyes beneath the mottled gray rabbit fur of her winter hat were so heavy lidded as to appear almost closed. Almost. And once again, despite the fact that her arms, shoulders, and throat—all as pale as ivory—were bare and her torso was covered only by her worn-out men's undershirt, she appeared not to feel the bitter cold. The barrel of the machine pistol she held with easy familiarity wavered not a fraction of an inch.

"Drop the pistol in the snow, Vlado," Sylvia said.

Vlado obeyed, then swallowed and licked his lips. "Syl. How long have you been there?"

"Ten minutes. A long time." Sylvia's flat expression did not change. "Long enough to see you run into Commander Černović and that Quisp fellow. Long enough to see you fire at the British major and the American sergeant to fool everyone into shooting at each other while you sneaked away. Long enough to see you duck off the trail onto this little side path and hide—as I knew you would."

Vlado's mouth twisted into a pained grin. "No one ever accused you of being dim, Syl. I didn't know you knew about this hidden trail." He glanced anxiously over his shoulder at the far end of the thicket.

"They'll be back soon enough," Sylvia said. She paused, then added, "Tell me what you did, Vlado."

"I . . . what do you mean?" Vlado reached inside the lapel of his coat with his good hand, but froze as Sylvia jerked up the machine pistol and squinted at him through its ring sight. "Wait, wait . . . just getting a cigarette." He withdrew a tarnished brass 20-millimeter shell casing with a small wooden plug in the end—many Partisans used such shell casings to keep their little hoards of tobacco dry—removed the plug, and shook out a black-and-gold Richterhaus. Clamping the filter between his lips, which were trembling slightly, he smiled, shook another cigarette partway out of the casing, and held it out to Sylvia. "You like these, Syl. Have one."

Sylvia lowered the Schmeisser and stared at him in silence.

Vlado took a step forward, continuing to smile. "Oh, come on, now. You weren't so particular about taking my cigarettes the night we slept together in the mine. Remember?"

Sylvia nodded. "I remember. That was a month ago. I was cold and lonely that night. And I also remember asking you how you suddenly acquired such fine cigarettes when everyone else was smoking dried weeds wrapped in old newspaper." She blinked slowly. "Where *did* you get them, Vlado?"

Vlado took another step forward, fumbling for his lighter with his good hand. "I told you: I took them off the body of an SS officer we killed during an ambush."

"Yes. One cigarette case full. Maybe a dozen cigarettes. They're lasting you a long time."

"Well, these are the last of them. I gave you five

or six, Syl. Remember?" Vlado smiled again, edging closer as he lit his own cigarette. "That was a good night, wasn't it? Worth a half-dozen fine cigarettes."

Sylvia's eyes widened a fraction of an inch. "Are you suggesting that you bought me for the night for six cigarettes?"

Vlado shook his head quickly. "No, of course not. I . . . but it was a good night, don't you think?"

"I told you," Sylvia said, "I was cold and lonely. I needed someone. You happened to be there."

"And you haven't let me near you since then—for nearly a month, as you said."

"I haven't been cold and lonely since then," Sylvia told him, "which is nothing to do with you, incidentally, so don't flatter yourself. As for your cigarettes, I smoked my last one this morning, after saving it for the past two weeks." She raised the Schmeisser again slightly. "That's close enough. Stop sidling toward me."

Vlado kept his feet still, looking hurt. "Syl—"

"Move toward me again and I'll kill you where you stand. On the other hand"—a flicker of a smile lifted the corners of her mouth—"tell me what I want to know and perhaps I'll let you go, for old times' sake." The smile ebbed away as quickly as it had come. "That's more than Cernović will do for you when he returns, I'll guarantee."

Vlado paled at the thought. "What . . . what do you want to know, Syl?"

"I want to know what you did. All of it. And you'd better hurry up, because when Cernović and Merritt get back, I won't be able to stop them from killing you."

Vlado plucked the cigarette from his mouth and exhaled shakily, looking trapped. "Syl—"

"Talk," Sylvia said. "That's the only way you're getting by me and on up this trail before the others return."

"All right!" Vlado jammed the cigarette back into

his mouth. "All right. I made contact about seven weeks ago with an SS officer named Haak. Hauptsturm-fuehrer Ulrich Haak. I agreed to give him information about the Second Proletaran Brigade's operations in the Majevica Mountains until early summer."

Sylvia's eyes were almost closed again. "For what? Cigarettes?"

Vlado shook his head. "No, no. The cigarettes are his, naturally—he's from a rich family and has them custom made in Germany—but they're just a tidbit from our meetings. I've been contacting him during my solo patrols, feeding him information about Partisan movements. . . ." Vlado's voice faltered, and he looked at Sylvia with a sickly expression.

"And what do you get for this betrayal?" Sylvia asked quietly.

Vlado drew a breath. "By spring, the Germans expect to have driven us out of the Majevicas. That's their schedule, anyway. All Germans are fanatical about schedules, like human machines. Haak wants me to continue to provide him with information until June. Then, at that time, I will be given safe passage through German lines and transported to Berlin, where I will be decorated in secret as a hero of the Third Reich, commissioned as an officer in the Wehrmacht, and given a permanent state pension in addition to my army salary. I will spend the rest of the war out of the line of fire, building a new life as a military bureaucrat in the regime that is going to control all of Europe for the next thousand years."

He paused, put his cigarette to his lips, and gazed at Sylvia with empty eyes. And then, like many a man who has sold his soul irredeemably to the devil only to realize in hindsight, to his utter horror, what he has lost, he surrendered to an overwhelming compulsion to keep talking. "I killed Bozi Yagovac, you know. Shot him in the back during the Storch attack a few days ago. It was all prearranged. I was having trouble getting away on solo patrols to contact Haak—people were becoming very paranoid and suspicious, what with all the successful Jagdkommando ambushes and rumors of an SOE team jumping into the Majevicas to join us for some undisclosed operation. So I encouraged Yagovac to harass the retreating Jagdkommado unit that had nearly grabbed Merritt and his men off the drop zone all the way back to the Zpoda Gorge area, where the Storches would attack them at dawn. I would make sure that Yagovac—a combat leader very troublesome to the Nazis—was killed in the assault, and then place a map on his body pinpointing the exact location of the Soujak Mine. Haak would have no trouble finding it; all he had to do was return to the site of the Storch ambush with an adequate force for protection and locate the biggest corpse there. The map would be inside Bozi's shirt, and there was also a statement confirming Tito's presence inside the mine. No one would suspect me, because I would be long gone—still with the Second Brigade. I could continue to provide information to Haak for the foreseeable future, as long as we were creative and cautious about communicating with each other." Vlado paused again to draw on his cigarette. His hand was shaking. "Aren't you wondering why I'm telling you all this, Syl?"

Sylvia's expression did not change. "Confession."

"Eh?"

"Confession. You want me to forgive you."

Vlado looked at Sylvia uncertainly. Then his dark, furtive eyes filled, and he looked away. "I think you may be right."

"I'm no priest," Sylvia said, "and the dead comrades you betrayed are the ones whose forgiveness you need."

Vlado said nothing, but drew on his cigarette.

"You killed Sergeant D'Amato and tried to kill Sergeant Bristow," Sylvia went on. "You knew in advance that a landslide had carried away part of Zlostup and that Merritt's team would be held up trying to get around it. You waited for just the right moment."

"I was going for the German lines," Vlado said hollowly. "I couldn't very well let Merritt blow up the Zpoda Skyway Bridge. Haak would never trust me again if I let that happen right under his nose."

"Of course."

Vlado glanced fearfully over his shoulder at the main trail again. "Syl. I've answered your questions. Merritt and Cernović may be back at any moment. Now I have a question for you."

Sylvia tilted her head back, listening.

"Why don't you come with me?" Vlado suggested. "You know I have feelings for you. Come with me and let's get out of this hellish war together. You know what it is to live well in a great European city. Come with me and leave Yugoslavia to the damned Partisans and Chetniks and Ustashe and Muslims and Nazis and British and Americans and all the rest of them. There's nothing for you here but bitter memories and death."

Sylvia slid off the rock to a standing postion and smiled openly for the first time. "I thought you'd never ask," she said.

The cigarette slipped from between Vlado's fingers and dropped into the snow. "So you'll . . . you'll come with me?"

"I didn't say that."

Vlado's hopeful smile faltered, and he spread his arms in a gesture of confusion. "Wha-what? But you just said—"

Sylvia's eyes narrowed. "I said I thought you'd never ask. And that's all I said."

"But . . . but . . . you're coming with me, aren't you?"

"No," Sylvia declared.

Vlado's arms dropped to his sides, and his expression became ugly. His dark eyes flickered to the Walther pistol lying in the snow at his feet.

"What are you doing?" he growled.

"Giving you my answer, traitor," Sylvia said. "And my answer is no." She turned her head slightly to the side, keeping her hooded eyes on Vlado. "Did you hear that, Captain Throckmorton?"

There was a gentle rustle of pine needles, and Throckmorton stepped out from behind a nearby tree, looking at Vlado over the sights of his Webley revolver. "Yaas, my dear," he drawled, "I heard it. In fact, I've heard it all."

Vlado stared at the British captain in shock, his mouth falling open. Then he turned back to Sylvia. "You . . . you knew he was there. . . ."

"I saw him as he came down the trail five minutes ago," Sylvia said. "And he saw me see him." She looked over at Throckmorton, and a hint of a real smile appeared on her lips. "Captain Throckmorton, as it turns out, is a highly intelligent man—despite his being an English aristocrat. He realized right away that I wanted him to hear what you had to say to me."

Vlado was beginning to shake. "But . . . if you were never going to . . . to come with me, why this long, drawn-out—"

"Because Major Merritt and his men suspect that I may be a traitor just like you," Sylvia told him. "I've known it since we reached the avalanche this morning. I don't know exactly why, but I could feel it, and it was obvious. The major had everyone watching me. He *ordered* Sergeant Weiss to hold me on the far side of the gap in Zlostup when you made your break." She paused and looked at Throckmorton again. "How *is* the sergeant's head, by the way?"

Throckmorton, his gun arm fully extended, didn't take his eyes off Vlado. "A bit bloody, I'm afraid, but I saw him on his feet soon after you whacked him. He's a strapping young lad; I imagine he'll shake it off."

Sylvia returned her gaze to Vlado. "And are you satisfied, then, Captain, that I am not disloyal like this . . . creature?"

Throckmorton nodded. "More than satisfied, my dear."

"Then will you excuse us for a moment?" Sylvia hefted the Schmeisser, the sinewy muscles in her strong, pale arms flexing.

Throckmorton paused before answering, then lowered his Webley and stepped back. "Certainly. If you're sure . . ."

"I'll be fine," Sylvia said. She half turned and motioned with the machine pistol up the little side trail. "Walk up there, Vlado, ahead of me."

"Syl—" Vlado pleaded, his voice cracking.

"Walk."

Merritt was moving at a fast trot back along Zlostup when he caught sight of Throckmorton sitting on a boulder at the edge of the trail in the little copse of evergreens, smoking a cigarette.

"Duncan!" he called out, raising his Sten gun in greeting. Immediately behind him, looking flushed, tired, and angry, were Bristow, Cernović, and Quisp. Throckmorton waved a hand and got to his feet.

"Gotten enough exercise for the day, gentlemen?" he inquired.

Merritt jogged up to him and halted, breathing hard. "This is no time for humor, Duncan," he panted. "Vlado's escaped, and we haven't seen Sylvia, either. We have a major problem."

A sudden burst of machine-gun fire shattered the stillness of the little copse. Merritt, Bristow, Cernović, and Quisp all dropped instinctively onto their bellies in the snow and jerked up their weapons. Throckmorton alone remained standing, unperturbed.

"No, we don't," he said, looking calmly off into the trees and drawing on his cigarette.

Bristow rolled onto his side and glared up at him. "You got a death wish, Captain?" he growled.

The slender Englishman glanced down and cocked

an omniscient eyebrow. "You don't know the half of it."

Merritt rose to one knee with his Sten leveled at his hip, searching the trees behind Throckmorton. "What's going on, Duncan?" he demanded.

Throckmorton flicked the butt of his cigarette into the snow and turned around. "You don't have to concern yourself with Vlado anymore," he said. "Or Sylvia, for that matter."

Cernović exchanged glances with Merritt and got to his feet. The expression on his face would have sent a wild boar running for cover. "Where is Vlado?" he asked Throckmorton, his voice hoarse with suppressed rage.

"Why don't you ask Sylvia when she comes back?" the slender captain replied. "She'll just be a minute."

Cernović stared at him, then abruptly turned aside and walked into the trees in the approximate direction of the little side trail. In a moment he had found the path and was beginning to stride up it when Sylvia appeared, heading down into the copse. She was carrying her Schmeisser slung over her shoulder and a bundle under one arm.

"Comrade Commander," she said, nodding as she went by him.

Cernović eyed her as she passed, then turned and ran up the side trail, disappearing behind the trees.

Sylvia walked into the small knot of men and sat down on the boulder Throckmorton had just vacated. Then she set the olive drab bundle she carried on the ground and began to unlace the black ballet-style slippers she favored for rock climbing, ignoring the tall soldiers hovering over her. Bristow examined her briefly, a scowl of distrust on his face. She was so pale that in the shade of the copse, her skin appeared almost blue.

Throckmorton pointed up the side trail. "Vlado ducked in here," he told Merritt and the others. "Apparently this little path leads up to the crags, and from there on up toward Mount Zpoda. You ran right by him—which is understandable since you can't really see the second trail. I'd have missed it myself if my wind was as good as yours. He thought he had us snookered, old boy, and he would have, too, if not for Sylvia."

Throckmorton glanced down at the pale girl, who was unlacing her second ballet slipper. "She wasn't fooled. Back at the avalanche site, we thought she was scrambling up the cliff to get away from us, like Vlado, but all she was doing was taking a fast route across the top of the crags to cut him off here. She knew about this little trail, you see."

Merritt looked down at her. "I nearly shot you off that cliff," he said.

Sylvia looked coolly up at him and batted her heavy lids. "But you didn't."

The corner of Merritt's mouth twitched upward, and Throckmorton went on. "By the time I got to this little thicket, you and the others were long gone ahead and I could hear voices through the trees. So I cocked the old Webley and sneaked along the trail like a proper footpad, keeping low. There was Vlado with his back to me, and Sylvia holding him at gunpoint. He was talking a blue streak. Sylvia caught my eye but didn't react, so I put two and two together and managed to skulk on up to where I could hear what was being said." He glanced down at Sylvia again. "What I heard explained everything. Vlado was the traitor, no doubt about it. And the only reason he didn't give us the slip is this petite Amazon sitting here." He let out the English blueblood's short, dry laugh. "By God, she's a cool one, I can tell you."

There was a crunching of snow as Cernović came back down the side trail. His livid expression had eased into mere grimness. He was carrying Vlado's Mauser rifle as well as his own carbine.

"Are you satisfied?" Throckmorton asked him as he stepped back onto the main trail.

Cernović's mouth worked for a second or two in silence. Then he suddenly dropped his carbine, seized Vlado's rifle by the barrel with both hands, and swung it like an ax into the trunk of the nearest tree. The wooden stock of the Mauser splintered at the hand grip. Cernović smashed it twice more into the tree, pieces flying, and then flung the ruined weapon through the snow-laden branches and down the slope. He stood there for a moment, arms by his sides and shoulders heaving, exhaling clouds of condensation into the frigid air, and then turned to face Merritt.

"I am sorry one of my men failed you," he said. "If not for his treachery, Sergeant D'Amato would not be dead."

"And quite possibly not Sergeant Hurst," Throckmorton added, "from what I've just heard. Not to mention Bozidar Yagovac and probably quite a few others."

Cernović looked at him briefly, then nodded. "I want to hear everything Vlado Kusić said," he muttered, "but for now, it is sufficient that he has been found out and executed." He looked down at Sylvia. "You shot him in the face," he said. "Good. It warms my heart to know he saw it coming."

Sylvia picked up the olive drab bundle at her feet and shook it out. It was Vlado's combat jacket. She glanced up at Cernović as she slid one pale arm into a sleeve. "Why ruin a perfectly good coat?" she commented. "Or waste a good pair of boots?" She slid her feet, now covered by heavy wool socks, into Vlado's rag-wrapped size-eleven shoepacks. "They're too big, but they'll get me back to my own. I'm not walking through snow and ice along Zlostup for a kilometer or more in climbing slippers."

She got to her feet and picked up her machine pistol. "Shall we go, Comrade Commander?"

Cernović looked at Merritt. "You have, regrettably, taken casualties, Major, but your mission is still secure. And I have new information that makes its success even more vital—that is why I have been trying to catch up to you for the past day. But I will leave it to you to answer Comrade Kozo's question. Shall we go on, or shall we abort?"

Merritt's eyes roved over the men, and came to settle on Bristow. "I can speak for the British, Commander Cernović: myself, Captain Throckmorton, Sergeants Stirling and Weiss—we will carry on. But Sergeant Bristow is an American—under my command, but still an American. He has just lost a comrade in Sergeant D'Amato. I feel I should let him speak for himself." He paused and met Bristow's eyes. "What about it, Sergeant? This mission has been, as you put it, 'snakebit from the git-go.' I don't want a man at my side or watching my back who'd rather be somewhere else. Do you want to see it through?"

The big Texan held Merritt's gaze unwaveringly for a several seconds, then grunted and looked off into the trees. "Hell, yeah, Major—I'll take the whole ride. I'll do it for Frank, like Stirling's doin' it for Hurst. That ain't the only reason—I'll do it 'cause I was sent here to do it, too, and I follow orders when they're given to me—but I'll play the game through the bottom of the ninth for Frank D'Amato." Bristow paused as his throat constricted slightly, and he swallowed to clear it. "He was a professional. He wouldn't want it any other way."

Merritt nodded. "Thank you, Sergeant." He turned back to Cernović. "There you have it, Commander. It's still on, and we're all going."

"Good," Cernović said. "Good. Then I have much to tell you as we walk. And time is of the essence. . . ."

He and Merritt moved off along the main trail in the direction of the avalanche gap, the Partisan commander speaking rapidly in low tones. One by one, the others followed.

" 'O God of battles!' " Quisp recited abruptly, " 'steel thy soldiers' hearts; possess them not with fear; take from them now the sense of reckoning, if the opposed numbers pluck their hearts from them.' "

Bristow blinked and looked sideways at him, practically for the first time. "Who the hell is that?" he growled to Sylvia, meaning Quisp himself.

"Shakespeare," Quisp said, before she could reply.

Part Two

*"History will be kind to me,
for I intend to write it."*

—Winston Churchill

Chapter Twelve

The exiled Grand Mufti of Jerusalem was not a happy man. The lecture to which Hauptsturmfuehrers Juttner and Neurath were being subjected, in a gaseous bubble of affronted dignity, had been dragging on for more than an hour. And Haj Amin al-Husseini, true to form as both fundamentalist cleric and reactionary politician, was showing no signs of tiring. Both Juttner and Neurath were reaching the end of their capacity to nod sympathetically and look interested as the mufti paced up and down the length of his private rail car—rocket-shattered windows now boarded over and glass fragments swept up—and holding forth on the negligent criminality of the indignities he was being forced to endure. As usual, Mustapha Snagi loitered silently off to one side as the car, its undercarriage slightly damaged in the Typhoon attack, chattered and shook down the track ahead of the King Tiger train's lead locomotive. The constant vibration was enough to rattle one's fillings and generate a throbbing headache.

"Never before have I been treated with such blatant

disrespect by a senior military officer!" al-Husseini fumed, prowling along the carpet with one hand behind his back and the other upraised, index finger waving. "This SS colonel—Kronstadt—has exhibited a total lack of consideration for both my personal safety and the crucial mission I have agreed to undertake as a special favor to the Fuehrer!"

Neurath remained as animated as a death mask, but Juttner couldn't help drawing a silent sigh and rolling his eyes as the mufti stalked past. The circumstances under which Haj Amin al-Husseini had agreed to tour the SS Division Handschar in Yugoslavia were well known to him. "Special favor" indeed . . . more like bartering one's thumb out of the screw before the bone was crushed.

However, one man's discomfiture was another man's opportunity—particularly, in this case, if Neurath happened to be out of earshot. Juttner rose casually to his feet and walked over to the dining table where a broad-bottomed carafe of good red wine had been placed. There were also three crystal goblets wrapped in white linen napkins and laid on their sides. Juttner picked up one of them, poured it a third full, and swirled the wine against the sides of the glass. Then he turned smoothly on the heel of his jackboot, inhaled the wine's bouquet, and took a sip.

"Whatever the Italians' shortcomings as combatants in this particular war," he said, rolling the wine on his tongue, "they haven't lost their knack for turning out an excellent Chianti."

"And that's about all they're good for," Neurath declared. He was desperate to forestall the mufti's interminable rant, or he would never have deigned to engage Juttner in conversation. "Digging in the dirt and stomping grapes with their bare feet. Just another race of mud people, barely higher on the evolutionary scale than Slavs or Africans." He gave a snort of disgust through his thin nose. "I mean, really—look at the stubby, pithecanthropoid physiology of most of them, how low to the ground . . . and the coarseness of their skull structure . . ."

"How very phrenological of you to note that," Juttner said, beaming down at Neurath with his most engaging smile. "The party scientists would be proud."

Neurath blinked up at him, unsure whether he was being complimented or insulted. That was the trouble with this damned Juttner, with his easy charm and razor wit—you never knew. *He* didn't, anyway.

But at least the cursed Grand Mufti had shut his trap, however temporarily. *Keep the conversation going,* Neurath thought; the subject changed.

"Yes," he said, regaining steam, "a race of mud farmers, grape stompers, and common laborers. But soldiers? Don't make me laugh. Look at the hash they made in Ethiopia, Libya, and on their own ground in Sicily. We even had to bail them out of their predicament right here in Croatia when they were about to lose control of the situation, the damned incompetents!" Neurath snorted again. "Believe me, it was a big mistake for us to ally ourselves with Mussolini. He may be a great leader, but his people are racially unfit to be soldiers. The blood of the warrior does not flow through their veins."

"Oh, I'm sure you're right, undoubtedly," Juttner said, sipping wine, "although I can think of a few people who just might—perhaps—take exception to your assertions."

Neurath, of course, was too belligerent, too indoctrinated, too self-absorbed, and too stupid to avoid the trap.

"Who?" he demanded.

"Well . . . Julius Caesar, Scipio Africanus, Pompey the Great, Marcus Vipsanius Agrippa, and every legionary, prefect, centurion, and tribune in the armies of the Roman Empire, for example . . ."

Neurath paled and clamped his lips together.

"You *have* heard of the Roman Empire?" Juttner went on. "Yes? No?"

Neurath got to his feet. His expression was not pleasant. "I was referring to the present-day Italian soldier," he said tightly. "You know that."

Juttner blinked innocently. "Were you, Hauptsturm-fuehrer? I thought we were discussing the blood of the warrior and through whose veins it flows." He sipped his wine. "I was merely playing devil's advocate—offering an alternative point of view."

Neurath opened his mouth to retort, but in his suppressed rage only a choking sound came out.

Juttner leaned in, lowering his voice so that the mufti could not hear, although the cleric was now seated at the far end of the car and appeared to be lost in thought. "But supermen of the Reich like yourself—you're not really very interested in alternative points of view, are you?" He smiled pleasantly in Neurath's face.

The Gestapo man's left cheek developed a persistent tic, but still he managed to keep himself in check—barely. "Your choice of words is disturbing, Hauptsturmfuehrer Juttner," he snarled through clenched teeth, "to the point of being treasonous. I find your random disrespect for the sacred philosophies of National Socialism both offensive and subversive—all the more so because you are an officer in the SS."

"Oh, come now," Juttner replied, pulling back with a guileless grin. "Loosen up a bit, Julius, before you burst a seam."

A blue vein was now throbbing in Neurath's temple. Juttner noted it with satisfaction; he had been working on both tic and vein since the beginning of the trip.

"Once again, I have had enough of you, Hauptsturm-fuehrer," Neurath said. "I will retire to my berth, and I warn you: provoke me any further and you will find out that I am quite capable of dealing with insolent peers on a one-to-one basis."

Juttner sipped his wine. "How terrifying."

The vein in Neurath's temple squirmed like a fat

blue worm, and the tic in his cheek doubled in frequency. "I will file a full report on your conduct with both the Gestapo and SS at my earliest convenience," he said, brushing past Juttner and heading for his quarters, "and I will make sure that a copy reaches Reichsfuehrer Himmler, as well."

"That's one of the most annoying things about the glorious Third Reich," Juttner muttered, half under his breath. "Everyone's always *telling on* everyone else—like nasty little schoolchildren competing for the best spot in a barbed-wire sandbox."

Neurath stopped halfway across the car and whirled. "What did you say?" he hissed.

"I said, I like this tasty little wine and that it's the best of an otherwise bad lot," Juttner replied. He lifted the glass and smiled. "*Prosit*, Hauptsturmfuehrer."

Neurath snarled unintelligibly and stalked past Mustapha Snagi to the door of his quarters, which he opened and, upon entering, shut with a subdued bang.

Juttner felt warm inside. A tic, a blue vein in the temple, and yet another indignant exit complete with slammed quarters door. Things were going well.

He refilled his wine glass, extracted one of his thin black cigars from its case, and strolled toward the front of the luxury car. The Grand Mufti of Jerusalem, seated in a velvet-upholstered chair near the forward door to the exterior end platform, looked up as he approached.

"Your colleague seems disagreeable," al-Husseini said. "He is a competent enough security officer, but I find his sour demeanor quite wearing in these close quarters we must share."

Juttner smiled. "An irritant **you should not have to** put up with, Your Excellency, along with all these other inconveniences. I will speak to him about it."

"Another thing," the mufti said. "According to the schedule provided by that reptile Kronstadt, this train will stop once more to take on water for the locomotive boilers, at a town called Bljak. I want you to speak to him for me. I insist on being transported to Belgrade in the company of my armed escort by over-land vehicle. I have been consulting the map, and there is a serviceable road from Bljak to Belgrade. Since the train must stop, anyway, Kronstadt has no grounds to refuse me. You will convey this demand to him on my behalf."

Juttner had been expecting this. He dipped his head and clicked his heels together. "Of course, Your Excellency. I will do my utmost to make him realize that he must honor your insistence on this matter." He paused. "However, I do see one problem that may be insoluble." He paused again as the mufti looked up sharply. "Vehicles, Your Excellency. With respect, we do not have vehicles available that are adequate for the task of transporting you and an armed contingent of forty SS troopers from this rail line to Belgrade, and we are unlikely to find them by chance in Bljak."

"That is why you must radio ahead and comman-deer the necessary vehicles from the nearest German military ground force," al-Husseini told him. "You see, I have thought it out. You have been using the radio room in this car to provide security updates on our progress periodically throughout this journey. Now you will use it to see that the vehicles required to conduct me safely to Belgrade are waiting at the station in Bljak when this train arrives."

Juttner hesitated, opening his mouth to speak. "You may go," the mufti said, waving a hand.

Juttner closed his mouth, bowed his head, and clicked his heels again. "At once, Your Excellency."

He turned and walked down the car toward the nar-row passage that led to the berths and staterooms. The tiny radio room was at the very rear of the car, the last door before the exit to the back-end platform. There was a yellow glow as Juttner entered and switched on the light, then a dimming in the passage-way and a quiet click as he shut the door behind him.

The Grand Mufti had picked up a book and begun to read when the radio room door opened again after only a few minutes and Juttner reemerged. He made his way forward through the luxury compartment, past the dozing Snagi, and halted in front of al-Husseini with the requisite nod of the head and click of the heels.

"My apologies, Your Excellency," he said. "Some unfortunate news: the radio has been damaged beyond repair. It occurred during the Typhoon attack, apparently; a small piece of rocket shrapnel penetrated the back of the set. The internal workings are completely smashed. It was an oversight on my part not to have checked it sooner."

Al-Husseini's mouth began to work, the color rising to his cheeks.

"However," Juttner continued smoothly, "I intend to walk back past the locomotives and coal cars, using the external catwalks, and locate Standartenfuehrer Kronstadt. I will request that he permit me to use the tank train's communications room for a routine security transmission. He has no reason to refuse me this courtesy. After I have made contact with the local occupation forces and have the necessary vehicles on their way to Bljak, I will inform the Standartenfuehrer of our intent to leave the train and proceed to Belgrade by road. With the logistics of our transportation to Belgrade already in place, he will have no objection to our departure, since he cannot then be accused of simply abandoning you in a potentially hazardous area."

The mufti sniffed. "I have the distinct impression that not only will he not object," he said, "he will be nothing less than overjoyed."

"That may well be the case, Your Excellency," Juttner affirmed, "but the essential point is, we will be off the train and on our way to the relative safety of Belgrade. And in all fairness to Standartenfuehrer Kronstadt, he has his own problems and priorities. I know the type well: he is a front-line soldier, rather bullish and mechanistic in his thinking, and is ill prepared to handle the complex and sophisticated needs of a person of your eminence." The handsome SS officer flashed his irresistible grin. "We will leave him to his Tiger tanks, where he is happy."

The mufti nodded, looking more pleased. "This course of action will be satisfactory."

"Very good, Your Excellency," Juttner said. "Now, with your permission, I must go and make arrangements with Standartenfuehrer Kronstadt to use his radio room. It may take some time to establish communications with the nearest motorized German ground force, and I must get started."

Al-Husseini waved a dismissive hand. "On your way, Hauptsturmfuehrer."

"Thank you, Your Excellency." Juttner bowed, clicked his heels, and strode toward the rear of the luxury compartment, collecting his knee-length black leather coat and SS officer's peaked cap as he went.

A blast of frigid air greeted him as he exited the mufti's private car and stepped out onto the metal grating of the rear-end platform. He shrugged on his leather coat and, turning the collar up and tugging his cap down over his brows, crossed the shaking, swaying catwalk between the private car and the following caboose.

The caboose was empty but for a lone civilian railwayman snoring in one of the side bunks. A bottle of cheap schnapps, nearly empty, was tucked under his arm. A pot of coffee, still steaming, sat on the kerosene stove of the small galley. Juttner located a mug, wiped the grime out of it with a dish towel, and poured coffee into it. The brew was as black as crankcase oil and about as tasty, but the night was bitterly cold and it was a long walk back—a dozen cars at least—to Kronstadt's quarters and the radio room.

He went out onto the rear-end platform of the caboose and paused, looking at the huge front end of the Tiger train's lead locomotive. The noise was deafening—a cacophony of clattering ties, screeching wheels, pounding pistons, and hissing pipes. The vibration of the immense steam-driven power plant rattled the chassis of the caboose under Juttner's feet, giving him the uneasy sense that he could be shaken off the metal grating at any moment. From beneath the driving wheels of the locomotive, a cascade of sparks crackled out into the night as the train began to negotiate a long, gradual turn to the left.

There was a five-foot gap between the narrow service catwalk that ran around the locomotive and the end platform of the caboose. Juttner considered for a moment, then gulped his coffee and pitched the mug out into the darkness. Taking a careful stance, he waited for the train's motion to subside for a second or two, then leapt across the gap.

The metal grating of the catwalk was icy; his jackboots slipped and he nearly fell, but managed to catch himself by the catwalk railing and avoid tumbling down onto the tracks. He looked down at the dark blur of rushing cross ties and breathed a short sigh of relief. Too close. That would be a stupid way to die in a shooting war—fall off a moving train and get cut in half by its wheels.

He made his way back along the side of the locomotive's massive iron boiler to the engineer's cab. There were two Waffen-SS troopers armed with machine pistols inside it, along with the engineer and his stoker. The steel floor of the cab was scattered with coal fragments and dust, and the door of the boiler-furnace had been left open, white-orange flames roaring inside, to offset the brutal chill of the winter windblast.

Juttner tapped the engineer on the shoulder. The jowly, unshaven civilian, dressed in greasy work coveralls and swathed in scarves, turned and looked at him in annoyance, the stub of a dead cigar jammed into the corner of his mouth. Juttner leaned in close.

"How many engines on the front of the train?" he

yelled into the engineer's ear. "Was it four or five? And how far back to the commander's car?"

"Five engines on the front," the heavyset engineer yelled back. "Three more spread out over the length of the train. You only have to walk the outer catwalks on these four back here, though, because there aren't any more between the last engine and Kronstadt's car."

"How many cars back from the last engine?"

"Seven, I think, Herr Hauptsturmfuehrer. Four ammunition cars, two bunk cars for troops, and one anti-aircraft gun car. The next one should be Kronstadt's. Nothing but flatcars full of Tiger tanks behind that."

"*Standartenfuehrer* Kronstadt to you!" Juttner shouted, hardening his expression. The engineer's eyes widened and he straightened out of his slouch. The two SS troopers glanced at each other and stiffened their own posture. Juttner turned on his heel, regarded them with cold approval, and proceeded onto the service catwalk around the lead locomotive's coal car.

Damned Nazis, the engineer thought, slouching over the locomotive's controls again and breathing a sigh of relief.

Ten feet along the catwalk Juttner smiled to himself. It never hurt to play the diehard SS fanatic with the lower orders when the opportunity presented itself. It reinforced his reputation on the brewhouse-and-barracks grapevine as an officer not to be trifled with—and favorable gossip was good security in the Third Reich. Someone was always sneaking around behind your back, looking for scurrilous rumors with which to discredit you.

By the time he reached the fifth locomotive, after ten fairly nerve-wracking minutes of clambering along icy, swaying steel catwalks in a bone-chilling wind-blast, his leather-gloved fingers were numb and he was all but certain he would lose his ears and tip of his nose to frostbite. After taking an extra minute to put a scare into the engineer, who had been dozing on the floor of the cab near the open boiler-furnace door, he walked around the last coal car and entered the first of the four ammunition cars. It was packed from floor to ceiling with ordnance for the King Tigers: 88-millimeter cannon shells and heavy machine-gun ammunition, primarily. A narrow walkway had been left down its center. Juttner wasted little time moving through it and the other three cars; with the train's constant swaying, the possibility of having an ammunition crate shift and drop on one's head seemed imminent.

The bunk cars housing the Waffen-SS support troops for the King Tigers were jam-packed with sleeping men, the bunks themselves closely spaced and stacked five high in four rows down the length of each car. No one was awake. Multiple snorers competed with the clattering rhythms of the train, and here and there a man noisily passed gas in his sleep. Despite the cold draftiness of the cars, the atmosphere within them was redolent of human wind. Juttner exited the second bunk car with his eyes tearing and his gloved hand over his mouth and nose. Then he remembered: the soldiers' last meal had been pork sausage and cabbage soup. Horrors.

He bundled up once more to walk the length of the open antiaircraft gun car, casually returning the straight-arm salutes of the unfortunate troopers manning the two sandbagged 40-millimeter pedestal cannon that were mounted at either end. Then he crossed the last catwalk and entered the warm vestibule of Kronstadt's car, closing the door behind him.

Kronstadt was sitting behind a plain steel desk, going over some papers, lamplight glinting off his steel-rimmed glasses and a cigarette in a slim black holder between his fingers trickling smoke up toward the ceiling. He looked up as Juttner approached; the latter whipped his cap off and under his arm in one motion and gave a smart Nazi salute with a click of his heels.

"So?" Kronstadt said, flipping up his cigarette hand to return the salute.

"Pardon me for disturbing you at this late hour, Herr Standartenfuehrer," Juttner said. "I have a request."

Kronstadt looked back down at his papers wearily. "What?"

"As one of two personal security officers assigned to His Excellency the Grand Mufti of Jerusalem," Juttner went on, "my duties include the periodic transmission of security checks and progress reports back to SS central headquarters, for the attention of Reichsfuehrer Himmler himself."

At the mention of Himmler's name, Kronstadt's eyes flicked up. "I'm hearing a lot about reports to the Reichsfuehrer these past few hours," he remarked, "first from that odious partner of yours, Neurath, and now from you."

Juttner smiled. "A different issue in my case, sir, I assure you. Merely routine—a cautionary procedure to track the mufti's safe progress through Yugoslavia. I fully understand and appreciate your military priorities and responsibilities, and have no wish to interfere with them now or later."

Kronstadt relaxed slightly. "What is it you need?" he asked, drawing on his cigarette.

"Simply the use of your radio room, Herr Standartenfuehrer," Juttner replied. "A staggered series of coded transmissions, for which I must then wait for reception confirmation. It can take an hour or two, sometimes, to send and receive the proper sequences."

"What's wrong with your own radio? You must have one in the mufti's private car, eh?"

"Destroyed by a piece of shrapnel, sir," Juttner explained. "I only just discovered it."

"Well," Kronstadt said, waving his cigarette like a man who wanted to get back to his reading, "the radio room is at the back of this car. My communications officer has retired for the night, and no one's using it. Take what time you need."

"Thank you, Herr Standartenfuehrer," Juttner said. "I will try to get it done as quickly as possible." He got his heels together and snapped off another straight-arm salute. *"Seig heil!"*

"Ja, ja," Kronstadt muttered without enthusiasm, cocking his cigarette hand. *"Seig heil."*

Juttner executed a sharp parade turn to the left and strode toward the rear of the car. The door to the radio room was latched open and the overhead light was on. Juttner entered, shut the door, and switched on a desk lamp near the radio set before turning off the overhead light.

The radio was on, the tubes already warm. Juttner draped his coat over the end of the room's small day cot and put his black SS cap with its death's-head insignia down on the radio desk. Then he sat down in front of the radio set, donned a pair of headphones, and began to dial in a high-frequency wavelength.

Pushing aside the microphone in front of him, he checked the connections on the Morse key next to the set. Then, very rapidly, he began to transmit a complex Morse signal, the locked fingers of his right hand vibrating on the sending key with machinelike precision, in one of the most closely guarded codes in Europe: the top-secret cipher used solely for internal memoranda by the Abwehr.

He was done in less than three minutes. Slipping off the headphones and replacing the key next to the set, he spun the frequency dial off the wavelength he'd selected and pushed his chair back. Propping his jackboots up on the desk and crossing his legs, he settled back and took the thin black cigar he hadn't smoked in the mufti's presence from his breast pocket. He lit it, inhaled luxuriously, and blew a long stream of smoke across the room, a smile playing on his lips.

After smoking half the cigar, he butted it out in a metal ashtray and turned off the desk lamp. Then he crossed his hands over his stomach, tipped his head forward, closed his eyes, and went to sleep.

Chapter Thirteen

Merritt's small team of commandos and Partisans had walked all day after returning to the avalanche site and lifting the remaining two mules and all the equipment across the gap in the trail. They had continued along Zlostup until two hours before dusk, winding their way up the southern wall of a gorge that became ever more breathtaking in its depth and overall scale, as well as increasingly difficult to traverse; the trail was badly snowed in and extremely narrow—less than three feet wide in some places. The mules balked as they lumbered forward through snowdrifts deeper than the trail was wide, pack loads scraping against the cliff to the left, and wide, frightened eyes on the dizzying drop mere inches to the right.

Periodically Merritt had halted the group, concealing them temporarily behind a convenient outcropping of rock, and gone on ahead to scan the next section of trail with binoculars, as well as the ridges on the far side of the Zpoda Gorge. As they approached the head of the gorge, the antiaircraft gun emplacements positioned at regular intervals on the northern ridge-tops were markedly closer. The chance of being spotted was very real.

Finally, with the sun about to drop behind the mountains to the west and plunge the eastern Majevicas into shadow, Merritt and Černović, leading the team, had rounded a sharp turn in the trail and found themselves staring at a spectacular, panoramic view of the head wall of the Zpoda Gorge.

It was truly an awesome sight. The head of the gorge widened into a steep-sided geologic bowl perhaps two miles in diameter from rim to rim and thirty-five hundred feet deep to the bottom of the heavily forested valley floor. The head wall itself was a massive sheer cliff of gray granite—an anomaly in the primarily limestone Majevicas—that plummeted nearly two thousand feet from the top of its thick overhanging cap to the broken rock and gravel of the talus slope at its foot. A natural fault in the otherwise featureless granite bisected the cliff horizontally just above midpoint along its entire quarter-mile width.

It was along this precarious route that the ancient hunter's trail Zlostup ran, on a rocky pathway barely wide enough for a man to walk on without constantly bumping one shoulder on the head wall. Mules had to be side loaded—a highly dangerous practice—and shepherded along; there was no room for them to pass otherwise. On many previous occasions, a hunter's pack animal had panicked on the terrifyingly narrow head wall section of Zlostup, shied and bucked, only to be toppled off its hooves by the uneven weight of its load and pulled into the yawning maw of the gorge. The talus slope far below was littered with the bones of men and animals that had lost their footing.

Zlostup followed the horizontal crack all the way to the northern side of the gorge, eventually switchbacking its way up and over the rim. Four hundred feet above the crack, embedded in the vertical granite, were the mortar-and-steel footings of the Zpoda Skyway Bridge's main support girders. The bridge itself curved around the width of the head wall, tucked in beneath the impregnable overhanging layer of cap rock. The tunnels at opposing ends of the bridge gaped across the chasm at each other like small, dark mouths.

Merritt had declared a halt and backed the team and animals up to a natural alcove in the rock, concealed from view by the turn in the trail and the dying light. The final approach and assault on the Zpoda Skyway Bridge would be a night operation; during daylight hours anyone on the head wall section of Zlostup was clearly visible to the enemy troops manning the antiaircraft gun emplacements on the upper north rim, and to the garrison in the old stone chalet near the far end of the north tunnel.

The team members had waited in the chill shadow of the the alcove until a half hour after sunset, then slowly and cautiously worked their way around the southern wall of the gorge and onto the head wall.

Now, in the small hours just after midnight, Merritt and his comrades were halted two-thirds of the way across the great cliff, unloading ordnance and equipment from nervous mules on a pathway less than a yard wide. Directly overhead were two of the girder footings for the bridge's support members. Four hundred feet of vertical granite gleamed in the moonlight between the footings and the little knot of soldiers working silently and feverishly on Zlostup.

"Put the first six crates of explosive into these niches," Merritt said in loud whisper. "We're not going to get all four footings rigged and wired before dawn, and we don't want the boxes seen when daylight comes. We're going to have to lie low for one more day, then rig the last one or two footings after dark. And keep your voices down; even quiet sounds travel a long way when they bounce off this cliff face."

"Why four, Major?" Cernović puffed, maneuvering a crate into a shallow crack in the head wall. "It seems risky, chancing a second night of climbing. If you get two footings mined, would that not be adequate to bring down the bridge and whatever train may be on it?"

"Our SOE engineers say no, Commander," Merritt replied. He pulled a heavy coil of climbing rope off the back of the lead mule and laid it on the pathway against the cliff. "They tell us that with the quality of construction in the Zpoda Skyway Bridge, a minimum of four consecutive support girders have to be displaced in order to ensure that a span of sufficient size falls away. Otherwise, the bridge may not drop at all—even with a train passing over it—or if it does, lose only a small section that would be too easy to repair."

Cernović looked at him in the darkness. "We need this bridge down and as many of those King Tigers as possible at the bottom of the gorge."

"That," Merritt said, smiling grimly as he unloaded more equipment, "is the general idea." He looked over his shoulder. "Stirling."

"Sir." The British sergeant was manhandling a crate of explosives into a niche in the rock, and didn't pause.

"When we get done with the equipment, string up the mules with breakaway cord and lead them along the rest of the trail to the northern rim. Find some place to hide them—and us—for the next fifteen hours. Captain Throckmorton will accompany you."

"Sir," Stirling said, finishing with his crate. He back-tracked along the ledge to the third mule, carefully sidestepping the other team members, and grasped its halter.

"Watch them ornery critters don't nudge you off into thin air," Bristow muttered to him as he led the mule forward. "They got a bad attitude for some reason."

Stirling grinned as he passed. "Thanks, mate."

"Don't mention it."

Stirling tied the third mule to the second with a six-foot length of thin manila twine, then did the same with the second and the first. Throckmorton pushed a spool of detonator cord into a rock niche already full of explosives and straightened up, his face slick with sweat despite the cold.

"What's the idea of the thin cord?" he asked. "Why not just use their regular lead ropes?"

"Hedging our bets, sir," Stirling replied. "We need to string the mules up to lead them down the trail together. If one animal slips and falls with the other two tied to it with heavy ropes, we lose all three. This way, if one falls, the cord breaks and we only lose the one."

"I really should read up on this mule-skinning business," Throckmorton mused. "Perhaps in another life."

Merritt sidled along the cliff wall toward Stirling and Throckmorton. "All right, Duncan," he said. "Have you got everything you need?"

Throckmorton slapped a large weatherproof suitcase that was one of the few items the lead mule still carried. "Kit and kaboodle right here, old man," he replied. He smiled at Merritt. Merritt returned it and the two men locked eyes and stood for a long moment in silence. Stirling saw something pass between them that was more than the expected "good luck" or "good hunting." It looked very much like "good-bye."

Merritt held out his hand. "Fair winds, old friend," he said.

Throckmorton took the hand and shook it. "And the same to you, Walter. Until we meet again."

"Aye. Maybe I'll see you in an hour or two over on the gorge rim."

"Maybe," Throckmorton replied. "I might go in later rather than sooner."

Stirling saw Merritt's jaw tighten and then Throckmorton turned, let out a deep breath, and clapped his hands to his chest. "Ahhh! Lovely night, what?" he declared, beaming at Stirling. "Well, then, shall we go, Sergeant?"

"Yes, sir."

Stirling let Throckmorton move ahead, then tugged the first mule's lead and set off after him. As he did, he sent a puzzled look over his shoulder at Merritt. The tall major was standing very still, leaning against the cliff and watching Throckmorton depart, an expression on his face that could only be described as haunted. Then he noticed Stirling looking at him, smiled quickly and nodded, and turned away.

"What was that about?" Cernović asked him. "What does that mean, 'fair winds'?"

Merritt pulled a climbing harness from a duffel bag. "It's something sailors say to each other," he said. "It means something like 'good luck,' I suppose."

"Captain Throckmorton is a sailor?" Cernović inquired.

"Yes. A very good one. A racing yachtsman who's sailed all over the Mediterranean and Atlantic. All over the Adriatic, too, before the war—from Trieste to Dubrovnik to the heel of Italy."

"You sound as if you know him well."

"I do. We go back to the early 'thirties, and the 1936 British Olympic team. We've been friends for many years."

Cernović grunted, helping pull out a heavy coil of climbing rope. "Not much salt water in the Majevica Mountains. He's a long way from the sea here."

Merritt glanced once more at the little mule train moving off into the darkness along Zlostup. "Yes," he said. "He is."

Cernović was silent for a moment, then changed the subject: "This message I was asked to give you through Professor Quisp, along with the update on the King Tiger train's schedule . . . it's obviously some kind of code, eh?"

Merritt finished knotting two ropes together. "You mean the reference to gamecock?"

"I believe the exact phrasing was 'gamecock in the field.'" Cernović's eyes searched Merritt's face. "If that message has anything to do with the interests of the Partisan Army of Yugoslavia, I'd like to know about it."

"I understand, Commander," Merritt said, stepping into a webbed climbing harness and tugging it up around his hips. "The fact is, it doesn't concern you or your people at all. It has to do with extraction options for my team once this job is done."

Cernović spread his hands. "Say no more, Major. I was just inquiring."

"There's never any harm in asking," Merritt replied, cinching up his harness.

"All right. I'm at your disposal. What do you need?"

The British major began to shed his heavy outer coat, revealing a tight-fitting black turtleneck sweater underneath. "Well," he said, "I need *her*." He pointed at Sylvia.

"Hssst!" Cernović caught the girl's attention and beckoned. "Sylvia! Come here."

"I say," Quisp declared, stepping past Cernović and Merritt on the narrow ledge, "will you be needing my assistance in whatever deviltry you have planned for the next four hours, Major?"

Merritt looked at him. "Not especially, Professor Quisp. Three of us will be climbing the rock face, and Commander Cernović and Sergeant Weiss will be down here on the trail, rigging explosives for us to haul up. You're not under my command, though I appreciate your assistance thus far. Perhaps you should go after Captain Throckmorton and Sergeant Stirling and help them locate a convenient place to hide somewhere on that forested rim."

"Capital!" Quisp enthused at low volume. "Simply

super! I never was particularly fond of playing the baby roc in the eyrie, anyway. Off I go, then! Ta-ta!"

He executed a little jig step and trotted off northward along the unnervingly narrow path, humming to himself.

"That's one strange sonofabitch," Bristow muttered, watching him go.

"A common enough type of Englishman," Merritt said, "as Miss Kozo will no doubt confirm." He glanced at her, and the corner of his mouth twitched upward.

She gave him a slow smile. "I'm beginning to change my opinion of eccentric English aristocrats," she said. "Some of them, like Captain Throckmorton and Professor Quisp, are surprisingly effective."

"They're the reason the map of the world is three-quarters red," Merritt said. "Eccentric wanderers like those two built the British Empire. They're the reason you can pull into a port in the South Pacific and order a gin and tonic in English from an aboriginal bartender who used to be a headhunter."

"Did anyone ever ask the headhunter how he felt about it?" Sylvia commented.

"Touché," Merritt said. "But this ledge isn't the place to have a philosophy discussion. Sergeant Bristow, are we rigged and ready?"

"Ready, Major," Bristow answered, tugging on his own hip harness. "I don't know a quiet way to bang in pitons, though."

"That's where our secret weapon comes in." Merritt rested his steady eyes on Sylvia. "Have you got another long climb in you? If you establish a line to that first footing, we won't need to hammer in a single piton. We can just ascend the rope."

Sylvia looked up. "It's a long way, but I can climb it. What I can't do is pull the weight of four hundred feet of dangling rope with me. Two hundred, yes. Not four."

"We'll use manila twine instead," Merritt said.

"Once you're at the footing you can pull the main rope up after you."

"Fine." Sylvia began to shrug off her coat. "Tie it on when I yank twice on the manila."

"I want you to do something else for me this time, though," Merritt told her.

Sylvia blinked her hooded eyes at him.

"I want you to keep your trousers and a sweater on, or at least pull them up after you. We'll be up there for hours and you'll freeze without them."

"No, I won't. I don't get cold when I climb."

Merritt shook his head. "I insist."

Sylvia stuck out her lower lip and glanced at Cernović. The Partisan commander shrugged. She looked back at Merritt. "Alright. I'll pull them up after me. I don't wear heavy clothing when I have to do a long ascent."

Merritt nodded. "Good enough." He tipped his head back and peered upward. The vertical expanse of the cliff face soared upward for what seemed to be a mile, disappearing into the night sky. The footings of the first two bridge supports were tiny, indistinct bumps in the pale moonlight. "Try for this one directly overhead first," he said to Sylvia, pointing. "It looks like there are a couple of small surface cracks running toward it. That may help you."

Sylvia stepped up beside him and put her hands flat on the rock face. "They will. I saw them."

"Frankly, I don't see how you're going to use them without pitons—they get so thin after about fifty feet that I don't think even you can get a fingertip into them."

"You let me worry about that, Major."

Merritt glanced down at her. She was clad in her familiar white undershirt, black shorts, black slippers, and fur hat. This time, however, she wore a climbing harness around her hips and upper thighs. It was much lighter and more minimal in design than Merritt's and Bristow's, consisting of only a few straps of canvas

241

webbing. There was a large carabiner hooked into a reinforced loop on the hip belt, and from it swung a curious selection of round objects ranging in size from a cue ball to a pea. Each was suspended by its own twelve-inch loop of thin, strong wire and small individual carabiner.

Merritt's brow furrowed. "What are those?" he asked.

Sylvia blinked her hooded eyes at him and smiled. "My nuts, Major," she said, and hoisted herself up the cliff by her fingertips and toes. In ten seconds she was twenty feet overhead, trailing the thin manila transfer cord behind her.

Bristow edged over beside Merritt. "What the hell'd she just say?" he asked in a gravelly whisper.

Merritt shook his head. "You wouldn't believe me if I told you, Sergeant." He squinted upward and blew out a slow breath. "Stand by. If she makes it, we're next."

"Yessir," Bristow muttered, watching the girl's uncanny, spiderlike progress. "Crazy broad . . ."

The hunting chalet at the north end of the Zpoda Skyway Bridge's two-hundred-yard-long northern approach tunnel had been in existence far longer than the bridge itself, and was much more than a simple mountain cabin. Built in the early 1800s by the despotic Serbian ruler Milos Obrenović as a gift to his border ally, the despotic Bulgarian baron Janos Barbo, the chalet was, in fact, a small stone fortress—a great house built in the shape of a U with attached guest quarters, staff barracks, and supply buildings. The entire structure was enclosed by a rectangular stone wall twenty feet in height and ten thick, with a two-man guardhouse at each of its four corners.

Both Milos Obrenović and Janos Barbo had not lacked for enemies who would have delighted in the opportunity to flay them alive, and dared not even go hunting in their own lands—separately or together—without a full contingent of escort troops and a secure stronghold to which they could retreat at night. Hence the creation of Barbo House—110 years before the laying of the railway line up the forbidding Majevica foothills toward Mount Zpoda, and the subsequent construction of the Skyway Bridge across the Zpoda Gorge head wall.

Barbo House was currently the forward headquarters for the SS Division Handschar, under the command of Standartenfuehrer Egon Zweig, and was garrisoned by a full company of battle-hardened Bosnian Muslim troops. These same troops also provided security for the northern and southern ends of the Zpoda Skyway Bridge, constantly patrolling the associated tracks, sidings, tunnels, and approaches. From Barbo House, the balance of the division was spread out east and west in a thin line of advance along the northern rim of the Zpoda Gorge and the western shoulder of Mount Zpoda, respectively.

And there the SS Division Handschar had been stalled—much to the disgust and frustration of Standartenfuehrer Zweig—for going on eight weeks now. Oh, there had been assaults and ambushes, probes and penetrations, mostly by Jagdkommando units under hard-charging officers like Ulrich Haak, but on the whole the division's formerly impressive progress across the flat river plain approaches to the Majevica Mountains had been lost to nearly impassable alpine terrain, overstretched and inadequate supply lines, persistent harrassing attacks by Partisan guerillas, and absolutely brutal winter weather. It was like Stalingrad in 1943 all over again, when the icy breath of Mother Russia had frozen General Paulus's proud Sixth Army in place to die by inches. Zweig could see a similar fate threatening the SS Division Handschar now: lack of forward momentum was killing morale, and some of his less-than-enthusiastic Muslim troops were beginning to desert. The trend both outraged and unnerved him. But at least he wasn't an indecisive ditherer like Paulus. At least he knew what he was doing.

Zweig looked up from his huge oaken desk in the middle of Barbo House's spacious common room. The Serbian state railway had formerly maintained the old hunting chalet as staff accommodation for personnel servicing the Zpoda Skyway Bridge, but since the Nazi-assisted establishment of the greatly enlarged puppet state of Croatia,[1] which had swallowed nearly all of Serbia, the remote structure had fallen into neglect. The deterioration was not too far advanced as yet, but there was a general shabbiness—a smell of mold and dry rot—that permeated the great wooden beams and once elegant furnishings of the place.

A fire burned in the massive stone hearth at one end of the room, sending shadows dancing over the three tiers of mounted game heads that lined all four walls. Zweig gazed at them—red stag, European elk, brown bear, wild boar, black alpine goat—the orange firelight dancing in their mad glass eyes. Barbaric trophies of a distant, long-forgotten glory, dark and ratty with age, moldering away the years in anonymous isolation on a remote mountaintop. There was something about the eyes when the firelight was in them—a staring, accusatory quality—that Zweig found vaguely chilling. He'd always disliked the killing of animals.

Abruptly he looked back down at the papers stacked in front of him and took a cigarette from a silver box on one corner of his desk. If those dozens of eyes continued to watch him as he worked, follow him as he walked through the room, he'd have to have the heads removed. Particularly if the SS Divison Handschar was going to continue to be held up here for any length of time. He lit the cigarette with a gold lighter, took off his glasses, and rubbed the bridge of his nose between his thumb and forefinger.

And now, with everything else he had to worry about, there was this damned mufti showing up—right *here*, for pity's sake. More bloody nonsense. He had the solution for declining morale among the Muslim rank and file: decimation. Line them up and shoot one out of every ten, then see how quickly the remaining nine could rediscover their loyalty and motivation. The Romans had had the right idea two thousand years ago when they invented the practice.

Distractions, distractions. Between the unreliable supply lines, the miserable winter weather, and now the pending arrival of Haj Amin al-Husseini—who would undoubtedly require much fussing over—it would be a miracle if he could plan a way to jump-start Handschar's advance and get it back on schedule before spring. SS and Wehrmacht commanders had been relieved, and some of them shot, for less.

The loud click of a side door opening startled him, and he glanced across the room in annoyance. The Muslim staff sergeant who had drawn night watch at his aide's desk was standing there, gray SS field fez cocked on his head.

"Excuse me, Herr Standartenfuehrer."

"What is it?" Zweig snapped. His persistent insomnia was making him permanently bad tempered.

"Haupsturmfuehrer Haak has returned from the field with most of his men," the substitute aide said. "He wishes to report, since the Standartenfuehrer is awake and in his office."

Zweig scowled at the floor and drew on his cigarette. Might as well. Sleeping was out of the question. "Send him in, Scharfuehrer."

"*Jawohl*, Herr Standartenfuehrer."

The aide disappeared, and a few seconds later Ulrich Haak entered the room through the same door, wearing Fallschirmjager winter white camouflage and a scruffy four-day growth of beard. He pushed the door shut with a snow-encrusted jump boot, removed his battered death's-head fez, and came to attention, knocking his heels together in a pool of meltwater.

"*Heil Hitler*," he said, extending his arm in the Nazi salute.

Zweig returned it casually and looked him up and down. "Stand at ease, Haak," he said, gesturing with his cigarette. "Well . . . what do you have for me? I take it your much-ballyhooed Jagdkommando parachutists were able to achieve some tangible successes in the past hundred hours or so? Particularly since I stuck my neck out in authorizing this pet operation of yours and convinced Luftwaffe command to provide the transport aircraft you requested."

Haak's tired eyes flickered off to the side. "Definitely, Herr Standartenfuehrer. We took the Partisans by surprise at the Soujak Mine, as per my informant's information, and harassed them all the way out of the valley."

Zweig walked slowly around his desk and ashed his cigarette in a carved stone tray. "I see. Why did you not destroy them in said valley?"

Once again Haak's eyes shifted. "It was not possible to cut off their escape, Herr Standartenfuehrer—they were too quick. But we killed a great many as they fled, shooting from both sides of the gorge, and then linked up with our ground Jagdkommando forces and harassed them all the way to the Ugljevik Pass, where they finally retreated up into the high plateau country."

"So you flushed them from one stronghold to another, but did not destroy this sizeable contingent of the Second Proletarian Brigade."

"As I said," Haak replied, "we killed a great many."

"How many? Give me a number."

"Impossible, Herr Standartenfuehrer," the grimy officer said. "It was a running battle, through snowfall and rough, heavily treed terrain. It stretched out over twenty miles and nearly three days by the time we were done. There are bodies strewn from Soujak to Ugljevik; bodies covered by snow, bodies down ravines and in frozen streams. I can't give you even a close guess as to how many there are."

"Then give me a percentage, man. A battlefield estimate of their percentage losses."

THE WAR MOUNTAINS

Haak sighed, his jaw flexing. "Maybe . . . ten percent," he said.

Zweig sat down and looked up at him. "Ten percent? Not exactly a decimation, is it?"

"Actually that's exactly what it is, sir." Haak replied, his tone just short of retort.

Zweig's face reddened. He'd just been thinking of decimation and the word had popped back into his head. Unfortunately his mouth had been running a little faster than his brain and he'd used the term descriptively instead of literally. But, of course, a 10 percent death rate was precisely the definition of decimation, and Haak—damn his impudence—was smart enough to have caught the mistake. And if there was one thing Standartenfuehrer Egon Zweig's Prussian temperament couldn't tolerate, it was being caught with his foot in his mouth by a subordinate.

"Hold your tongue, Hauptsturmfuehrer!" he barked. Haak didn't come to attention, but did fix his eyes straight ahead. Zweig let his blood settle, then went on with what he hoped was some semblance of his former composure: "What about Tito? He was supposed to be in the mine, wasn't he? That was the juicy carrot that sold your operation to the Luftwaffe."

Haak cleared his throat. "I myself led an assault team into the mine, Herr Standartenfuehrer," he said. "We pursued a small group of Partisan officers and soldiers deep into its inner passages, engaging in an ongoing firefight as we went. I am sure I spotted Tito at one point. When the Partisans saw that we had them trapped, they set off pre-laid explosives and brought a large section of the mine down on themselves and some of my men, unfortunately. The rest of us got out and sealed up the mine entrance with demolition charges, just to make certain no one who might be left alive could escape."

"So Tito is dead?" Zweig inquired, leaning forward with genuine interest.

"I am sure I saw him in the mine, sir," Haak replied.

Zweig's eyes narrowed and he settled back. "How sure are you?"

Haak looked down at him. "Would you like it expressed as a percentage, sir?"

Zweig, just beginning to inhale from his cigarette, emitted a short strangling sound.

"Ninety-nine percent sure, Herr Standartenfuehrer," Haak followed up smoothly, before his superior could speak. "I am ninety-nine percent sure that Tito is dead inside the Soujak Mine."

"That—that is news of . . . extreme importance," Zweig said, dismissing Haak's sarcasm in favor of trying to suppress a cough. "Why did you not radio it in, Haak? The loss of Tito will change the nature of the entire Balkan campaign."

"Because ninety-nine percent is not one hundred percent, sir," Haak told him, "and before I could make an irrefutable claim to have killed Yugoslavia's premier Communist insurgent, I would have to see his body—or at least observe his army undeniably without his leadership for several months."

Zweig wiped his lips with his fingers and butted his cigarette in the stone ashtray. "Where is the Second Proletarian Brigade now?"

"Somewhere southeast of here in the Ugljevik Plateau region," Haak said. "At least forty miles away, I estimate."

"Where *exactly*?"

Haak let out a long breath. "Again, it is impossible to say, Herr Standartenfuehrer," he replied. "They are maneuvering in the high country, and bad weather is setting in again. We will have heavy snowfall for the next seventy-two hours. Reconnaissance flights will be grounded. We will not be able to track their movements from the air."

Zweig chewed his thin lower lip. "The bad weather

should limit Partisan mobility as well as our own," he mused.

"I wouldn't count on it, sir," Haak said. "Their ability to execute forced marches in the worst conditions is becoming legendary."

"I am thinking of sending a large-scale penetration to the southwest," Zweig declared, spreading his fingers on a small map on his desk. "Perhaps engage the Partisans after they have been starving in the higher altitudes for a day or two more."

Haak had gotten used to Zweig's limited capacity for making sound tactical decisions under less-than-perfect circumstances. The man, despite his rank, simply wasn't that gifted a planner—a rather major flaw in a division commander. He tended to forget things.

"Herr Standartenfuehrer," Haak said, "there are other Partisan battalions and regiments opposing our forces to the southwest and beyond. We cannot just chase blindly after this one part of the Second Proletarian Brigade and leave a large gap in our line. We create two unprotected flanks that way."

This was something Haak had not gotten used to: finding himself—a mere captain—in the position of having to correct his division commander, a full colonel in the Waffen-SS, and having that commander quite obviously fish for further input, as if he really had no idea of how to proceed himself.

Not exactly confidence inspiring, this Standartenfuehrer Zweig. A competent staff officer who should never have been made a field commander. Exactly like the mediocre Paulus, whose lack of imagination and aggression had killed the Sixth Army at Stalingrad in early '43 . . .

If there was one thing Ulrich Haak did not lack, it was aggression. He was a hands-on combat leader—someone who put himself repeatedly at the broken end of the bottle—and the first to suffer, along with his men, if the decisions that sent him into harm's way were unsound. And he was getting tired of propping up Zweig, offering good idea after good idea only to have the inexpert division commander reserve all the credit for these ideas for himself, as if they'd been his alone. Why, the man had even shot off the tip of his own left little finger a month ago, cleaning his service pistol. Idiotic. Haak had been watching the slow-healing stub with its crusty brown scab waver uncertainly over topographic maps for the past two weeks. . . . Rather disgusting . . . why couldn't the damned fellow wear a glove or a bandage or something? . . .

"Haak, have you heard a thing I've just said?" Zweig was looking at him impatiently, his glasses back on his face.

"*Jawohl*, Herr Standartenfuehrer," Haak declared. "Every word."

"Good. Then you agree that we should delay any further attempts to pursue the Second Proletarian Brigade or advance our main line until after the next bout of inclement weather has passed."

Haak smiled slightly. "That would be my recommendation, sir. We should hold the line and let the Partisans exhaust themselves running around in blizzards if they so choose." Bismarck's Beard—hadn't he just said as much two minutes ago? How he hated having to repeat the obvious.

"Herr Standartenfuehrer," he said, "my men and I have just completed nearly four days in the field with no hot food and next to no sleep. If there is nothing more I can do for you at this time, I would like to see to them and get cleaned up myself."

Zweig, looking down at his desk, didn't answer right away. Rather distractedly he ran his right hand through his limp blond hair and continued to float his left, with its revolting partially amputated little finger, over the topo map. Haak's eyes flickered over the man's gaunt, weedy face, and he wondered for the umpteenth time how such an unimpressive creature

had attained the rank of full colonel in the SS by—
what?—his midthirties. Certainly not more.

Well, he was ten years younger than Zweig, and
intended to be a general in the same time frame. So
be damned to him.

"Herr Standartenfuehrer," he said again.

Zweig looked up suddenly as if startled and cleared
his throat. "*Ahem.* Yes, well, Haak—I've made my
decision. We'll hold our current position and suspend
any further offensive operations until the bad weather
clears."

Haak closed his eyes for a moment. By Lucifer, one
could almost hear the rusty gears grinding in the
fool's head.

"There is one good thing about this weather,"
Zweig remarked, reaching for another cigarette.
"There is a large shipment of King Tigers arriving by
train approximately twenty hours from now. If the
rails don't become blocked by snowslides, the blizzards should keep the Partisans from attempting to
sabotage it between Bljak and here."

"King Tigers?" Haak echoed, blinking. "Up in
these mountains?"

• "Yes," Zweig said, sitting down and lighting his cigarette. "Apparently they are a new variant specially
designed for use in mountainous regions. Their deployment here is highly classified, which is why you
haven't heard about it until just now."

Haak blinked again, his mind racing. "How many
King Tigers?" he asked.

"Oh, fifty or so, I think."

Haak felt his heart leap in his chest. "*Fifty* Tiger
tanks?" he said. "Here at Mount Zpoda?"

"That's right, Haak. To be deployed in concert with
Handschar, at some point."

At some point? The myriad tactical possibilities
came to Haak in a flood. The things that could be
achieved with the support of that many specialized
battle tanks—it boggled the mind! And on the eve of

their arrival, here was Zweig, chewing his cud over some ill-conceived notion to send troops hither and thither without a comprehensive strategy that included the use of this deadly new asset. It was enough to make one weep.

Suddenly Haak was very tired. There would be much to do in only a few hours, and he needed rest to clear his mind for the task of making sure that Zweig did not end up concocting some ridiculous new plan that was doomed to disaster. He mustered his strength and drew himself stiffly to attention.

"This is welcome news, Herr Standartenfuehrer," he said. "The arrival of these tanks will give us a decisive advantage in our next thrust against the Partisans."

"Yes, it will," Zweig agreed. "And that's not all that's arriving. The Grand Mufti of Jerusalem is on that train. He is coming to tour the division and boost morale. So we will have a visiting dignitary to deal with, as well. I expect you to help out with security, Haak."

The Grand Mufti of Jerusalem? Good God, why not the Archbishop of Canterbury? Things were moving from the unexpected to the absurd. Who had time to nursemaid some unctuous caliph in a war zone— least of all combat specialist Ulrich Haak?

It was all too exhausting. He would deal with it in the morning.

"Will that be all, Herr Standartenfuehrer?" Haak declared.

"For the time being," Zweig said. "You're dismissed."

Haak knocked his heels and raised his arm. *"Heil Hitler."*

Zweig tipped back his cigarette hand. *"Ja.* Good night."

"Good night, sir."

Haak executed a right turn and made for the door, exhaling one long, weary breath the entire way.

Chapter Fourteen

They really were nuts. Standard, high-quality, forged-steel, octagonal nuts meant for securing machine bolts or any other type of threaded bar. But Sylvia Kozo had invented an ingenious new use for them.

Merritt, an extra coil of heavy rope slung diagonally across his chest, was hanging from a sliding prusik[1] hitch two hundred feet above Zlostup, at the midpoint of the rope Sylvia had secured to the closest support footing of the Zpoda Skyway Bridge. This was where the girl, climbing freely without pitons and trailing the thin manila transfer line behind her, had first paused in her remarkable solo ascent.

Far below on the trail, Merritt and Bristow and the others had been unable to see what she was clinging to. It looked like nothing at all, and as it turned out, that was almost exactly what it was. Without any apparent support, Sylvia had used the transfer line to pull up four hundred feet of stout rope, tied it to her harness, then continued to climb the sheer cliff to the bridge footing, dragging half the rope after her in one great drooping bight.

Now dangling at the spot where Sylvia had paused, Merritt took a moment to rest and inspect the minuscule rigging that had secured her to the nearly featureless head wall. A single nut, not more than a half inch in diameter and with a short length of ultrathin aircraft cable looped through it, had been inserted into a thin crack in the rock and carefully seated until the nut itself was lodged behind a portion of the crack that was only a quarter inch wide, with the wire loop and its attached carabiner protruding. This tiny, fragile-looking arrangement, carabiner clipped into the front of Sylvia's harness, had been the only thing supporting her as she hauled up the climbing rope. Merritt grasped the wire and pulled. To haul a half-inch steel nut through a quarter-inch crack in solid granite was a physical impossibility, and the wire itself was extremely strong and unlikely to fail. Merritt was astounded by the simple ingenuity of it: a reuseable anchor, noiselessly and instantaneously installed, that would not give way unless actively dislodged, and which could be used to attach oneself to even the smallest crack.

Sylvia had knotted the middle of the rope into the carabiner. Above his head, at intervals of perhaps twenty feet, Merritt could see where she had inserted other nut-and-wire combinations into the crack and then run the rope through the carabiners. More ingenuity: if she lost her hold on the cliff, the rope attached to her harness would snap tight after she'd dropped past the highest carabiner, and arrest her fall. An involuntary smile crossed Merritt's face. So the invincible Sylvia the Great took a few precautions now and again after all.

Smart. Smart to think of it, and smart to actually do it. There were plenty of ways to get killed in a world war without taking a preventable nosedive off a sheer cliff. With another short length of line, Merritt tied a second prusik hitch around the main ascent rope above the carabiner knot, let it take his weight, untied the first prusik, and then released the main rope from the carabiner. The initial crack anchor wasn't needed now, but they might be able to use Sylvia's device again higher up, moving between bridge footings. He wiggled the nut free, pulled it out of the rock, and clipped its carabiner to his own harness. Then once again he began to climb, hoisting himself up the main rope and sliding the prusik hitch as he went.

It began to snow very lightly, the tiny flakes floating in the moonlight. Merritt looked up at the bridge and the dark sky above it. It was difficult to tell what kind of weather was moving in, but the stars were no longer visible to the north so there had to be cloud cover in that direction. He hoped that heavy snowfall would hold off until they got the bridge mined—twenty-four hours or so. After that, a blizzard might well help their escape.

As he climbed, Merritt removed each successive nut he came to, clipping it onto his harness. By the time he reached the massive concrete footing with its equally massive steel support girder, he'd collected six nuts of varying diameters. Sylvia, sitting cross-legged at the very edge of the footing with her forearms resting on her knees, looked down heavy lidded at Merritt as he hauled himself up the last few feet of rope.

"Are you quite comfortable?" he panted, grasping the edge of the footing.

"Yes, quite," she replied.

Merritt heaved himself up another foot. "Don't waste energy lending me a hand," he grunted.

"I climbed up here by myself," Sylvia told him. "So can you."

"Huh!" Merritt grimaced, shaking his head, and with one more effort heaved himself over the back of the footing where it joined the cliff. He lay there for a moment, trying to catch his breath.

"You may be stronger than I am," Sylvia commented, looking off into the dark vastness of the Zpoda Gorge, "but you've also got to haul all that heavy muscle up the cliff, big man." She turned her head and regarded him over one shoulder. "Everything is relative in climbing, Major. Pound for pound, I'm actually stronger than you."

"I believe it," Merritt panted, still lying on his back with his chest heaving in and out. "By the way, I have your nuts." He patted the collection of wires and carabiners on his hip.

"I see. I was wondering if you were going to figure out that you should bring them with you. Thank you."

Merritt sat up, his breathing returning to normal, and pulled over his head the coil of rope he'd been carrying. "It's an ingenious way to secure yourself to the cliff. How did you come up with it?"

Sylvia shrugged her bare shoulders. "Just common sense. If you climb enough and look at all the different kinds of cracks and crevices in cliffs, rock faces, and even buildings, it becomes obvious that something much lighter and easier to use than a piton can usually be placed in them as a kind of support. I thought about it for a while—the materials were already available. We'd used sailboat carabiners and airplane control-cable wire as rigging accessories in the family trapeze act. The nuts were my idea—it just came to me in a flash one day. I put the wires and carabiners on the nuts and tried climbing with them.

"They worked like a charm. You can pull yourself past an otherwise unclimbable spot with one of them. You can leave them in the rock behind you and run a belayer's rope through them if you think you might fall on a difficult stretch ahead. You may think me reckless, Major, but I know what I can climb and what I cannot. I don't have a death wish. I'll protect myself with a belay rope if I think it's necessary." She smiled and went on. "If you have a consistently thin crack that you can't get a finger in, you can even sling one unit to each wrist and climb by alternately placing and pulling each nut in succession." She turned her head and pointed toward the next footing over, some sixty feet away. "Which is what we may have to do to move to the next support girder. The rock is really smooth here—nothing to hang on to. All there is is that very thin horizontal crack. My smallest nuts should work in it."

"If they don't, we'll have to risk quietly tapping in a few pitons," Merritt said. "We have to get over to that footing and eventually the two beyond it." He got up on one knee. "By the way, Miss Kozo, I'm impressed. You are one very sharp woman."

"Yes, I know, " Sylvia replied. "And you may call me Sylvia, Major, if you think it wouldn't rupture your English propriety."

Merritt smiled. "All right then, Sylvia." He moved to the edge of the concrete pad and peered down. Bristow was ninety feet below, working his way up the primary rope with another large coil of line looped diagonally over his shoulder and across his chest. He paused and looked up, his barely visible face shiny with sweat, his lips moving in what Merritt supposed was a characteristic string of muttered curses.

"Come on," Merritt called, as loudly as he dared, waving him on. The big American sergeant put his head down and resumed his dogged hand-over-hand ascent. Merritt watched him for a few seconds, rueing the time it was taking Bristow—and had taken him—to reach the footing. But four hundred vertical feet was a long way.

He turned and surveyed the second footing. Like the one on which he was kneeling, it was a massive block of steel-reinforced concrete embedded in the rock face with a hundred-foot steel girder extending up and out from it at an angle perhaps five degrees off dead vertical and tying into the bridge spans overhead. There was indeed a thin split in the rock that seemed to run the entire distance between the footings.

"Sylvia," Merritt said, "can you take this other rope

over to that second upright while we're waiting for Sergeant Bristow? We need to pick up the pace."

The lithe Partisan uncoiled to her feet from her cross-legged position and rubbed her upper arms with her hands. "About time," she said. "I was almost starting to feel a chill." She stepped behind the support girder and picked up one end of the rope Merritt had laid on the concrete pad.

"I tied your clothes to the first crate of explosives," Merritt said, "since you apparently forgot about them. We'll pull them up for you." He glanced down at Bristow again—still with sixty feet to go—and grasped the second rope, as well. "You don't have any objection to me belaying you across that gap, do you?"

"Sylvia," Sylvia said.

Merritt smiled briefly. "Sylvia."

"Not in the slightest, Major." She held out her hand. "My nuts, please."

"Oh—right you are." Merritt unclipped and handed them to her one by one.

"Thank you."

Turning toward the second footing, Sylvia flexed her fingers, shook out her arms, and stepped off the concrete pad onto the cliff. She worked her way along the crack for no more than ten feet, with Merritt paying out rope, before stopping.

"I can't even get a fingertip into this crack for the next twenty feet," she called back softly, "and there are no toeholds, either. I'll have to alternate with my two smallest nuts."

"Be careful," Merritt said, because what else was there to say? He checked the short safety tether he'd looped around the girder and tied into his harness, and firmed his grip on the rope that was wrapped around his shoulder blades in a body belay. A gust of tiny snowflakes whirled up into his face; he shook his head and blinked them away.

"Jeezus . . . *Christ*," Bristow gasped, getting one

arm over the edge of the concrete pad. "Felt like . . . I was . . . climbin' to the . . . goddamn moon . . ."

Merritt stooped to help him, taking one hand off his belay rope. "Here. Grab hold."

As his hand closed over Bristow's, there was a sudden sharp popping sound. The belay rope snapped taut around Merritt's upper back, yanking him sideways. If not for Bristow's weight counterbalancing him, he would have been snatched right off his feet to the limits of his safety tether. He staggered, let go of Bristow as the big sergeant was pulled onto the top of the pad, and seized the belay rope with both hands. The safety tether came up tight as his feet skidded to the very edge of the concrete and he teetered there, caught between the tether and the tension of the rope around his shoulder blades.

He willed his rope-burned hands to stay closed and glanced at the horizontal crack. Sylvia was gone. But there was a single nut in place approximately fifteen feet out. The belay rope was as tight as a guitar string through its carabiner, quivering, and ran straight down from there. Merritt looked down as Bristow scrambled to his feet and grabbed the rope to assist him.

Twenty feet down, Sylvia was sitting calmly in her harness, her slippered feet planted against the cliff, looking up at him.

"The nut I had my weight on ripped out," she said, holding up a tiny wire unit by its carabiner. "I thought that might happen, so I put a solid one in behind me and clipped the rope to it." She half smiled. "See how it works? If you fall, you don't fall as far, and you don't swing. It's easier on the belayer, too."

"Thank God for that," Merritt breathed.

"Easier, she says," Bristow muttered, leaning back on the rope. "She should be on this end." He coughed and spat. "You okay, Major?"

"Barely, but yes," Merritt replied. "Really took me off guard."

"You should have been watching," Sylvia said, overhearing him. "You're the belayer. And you should have had both hands on my rope."

"I'll try to improve," Merritt retorted.

"Are you two going to pull me up so I can try again, or leave me here to die of boredom?"

"God*damn*," Bristow growled, incredulous. "Let's just cut the sonofabitchin' rope."

"Ready, Sergeant?" Merritt said. "Together, now . . ."

The two men hauled, hoisting Sylvia until she was back at the nut that supported her.

"Stop," she said, and began to work her way along the crack again, going hand over hand with a pair of small nuts and her toes smeared against the vertical rock.

Merritt stepped around behind the support girder and braced himself against it, watching Sylvia and feeding her slack from a secure belaying position. "I've got her now, Sergeant," he said. "Go ahead and drop your third line to Cernović and Weiss. Start hauling the explosives up here."

"Yessir," Bristow replied. He pulled the coil of rope he'd brought with him off his shoulder and began to tie one end of it to the base of the girder.

Merritt turned his wrist up and looked at his watch. "Zero three hundred hours," he said. "Maybe an hour and a half of true darkness left. We have to have at least two of these supports mined and be off Zlostup by zero four thirty hours at the latest." He glanced at Bristow before returning his attention to Sylvia, who was now approaching the halfway point of her traverse to the second footing.

"I hear you, Major," the big sergeant said, lifting the heavy coil of rope. "Pedal to the metal all the way. We'll make it." He swung the coil once and heaved it out into space. The loops separated cleanly as it fell. Two seconds later the rope snapped taut alongside the concrete pad.

Bristow peered over the edge, squinting. "Kinda

dark to see all the way down there," he muttered, "and this little bit of snow fallin' don't help, but they've got it. It didn't get hung up nowheres."

"Good," Merritt said. "We need at least two crates per girder, Sergeant. Haul until you're tired and then we'll switch out."

"Yessir," Bristow replied.

"Hsst!" The sound came from the trail behind.

Stirling whirled, dropping to one knee and bringing his rifle up to his shoulder. Throckmorton, pistol in hand, sidestepped quickly behind one of the stunted, snow-laden evergreen trees in the dense thicket they had been penetrating since leading the mules off Zlostup below the northern bridge tunnel. The pack animals nickered uneasily and shied, reacting to the two British commandos' sudden movements.

"God save the king," came the loud whisper a second time. "It is I—Quisp."

Stirling and Throckmorton exhaled and lowered their weapons as the professor emerged from the dark gloom behind the little mule train, his Schmeisser at the ready. He raised a finger to his lips as he approached, the whites of his manic eyes gleaming, and the three men knelt together in the snow, heads close.

"There is a two-man patrol moving parallel to us on a larger path just thirty yards through those trees," Quisp whispered, his voice barely audible. "Handschar SS. Watching the side approach to the tunnel, I daresay."

Stirling glanced at Throckmorton and nodded. "We've already seen a single sentry walking the top of the tunnel and another two-man patrol at the gorge rim. It's a bloody miracle they didn't spot us." He licked his dry lips. "I think we should get off even this secondary trail, head down around these steep rock formations"—he indicated a series of ten- and twenty-foot miniature crags that stepped down through the trees and drifts to their right—"and try to find some kind of overhang or cave to shelter in. One of us can go back later to lead Major Merritt and the others in before dawn."

"What-ho—I'll do that!" Quisp whispered instantly. "A Zulu leopard soldier can't hold a candle to me when it comes to stalking, d'ye see? I'm a ghost, I tell you—a veritable will-o'-the-wisp! Quisp the Wisp, as it were . . ."

"Fine, fine—we've got it, old man," Throckmorton cut in, patting the air impatiently. "Right, now, let's find cover, as the sergeant says."

"Spot on, old boot! And Quisp shall lead the way, my merry men, whilst you deal with the beasties, what? 'Hark! The shrill trumpet sounds, to horse, away! My soul's in arms, and eager for the fray!' Cibber, that one, don't you know? 'Course you do . . ."

Despite his lunatic persiflage, Quisp's voice never rose above the same low whisper. He was up and striding ahead through the deep snow before Throckmorton could say another word. Stirling caught his captain's eye and they exchanged an exasperated shake of the head before getting to their feet and leading the mules on, watching and listening for signs of the enemy, with senses heightened by tension almost to the point of pain. A generous dusting of snowflakes whirled around them as they left the tiny trail and began to descend the short, steep slope alongside the nearest rock outcropping. It was beginning to snow in earnest.

"The snowfall should help mask our tracks, sir," Stirling muttered quietly. "Make them harder for a patrol to see. And we'll make sure we keep to the trees and off the trails when we have to move." He stepped down around a large section of fractured rock and coaxed the lead mule down with tugs on its halter. "Watch the footing right here—it's a bit treacherous."

"Right," Throckmorton replied, stepping down and to the side. "Lead on. I'll make sure the other two mules follow properly." He paused. "By the way, I suppose if we turned the beastly creatures loose, since we don't need them anymore, they'd just head for the nearest human noises in search of food and shelter, eh? Meaning that German garrison over there."

Stirling nodded. "Almost certainly, sir. Especially in this weather. And I can't think of a better signal that something's afoot than three Partisan pack mules suddenly showing up at the SS Division Handschar's front gate. The animals have to be secured, out of sight."

"I thought as much," Throckmorton grumbled, pushing on the third mule's mangy flank as it stepped down past him. "Hello—here's the mad professor again. . . ."

Quisp had backtracked into view at the very bottom of the forty-five-foot combination crag. He gestured emphatically as Stirling and Throckmorton worked their way down the last third of the broken incline.

"Eureka! I have it!" he hissed. "Come, gentlemen, come. An accommodation worthy of the most discerning Neanderthal, and not a mountain troll in sight to contest our residency! 'Seek, and ye shall find!'—Saint Matthew, by the Gay Lord Grimsby!"

"Bloody hell," Stirling muttered to Throckmorton under his breath. "His nonsense is getting to me, sir. Does he think we're walking through the bloody Globe Theatre?"

"I really don't quite know what he thinks, Sergeant," Throckmorton replied, "but let's see what he's found."

They followed Quisp for a hundred yards through deep snow around the base of the crag, finally coming to a narrow split in the rock behind several scrubby evergreens. It was half drifted in and just barely wide enough for a mule to get through. Quisp turned, hand on hip, and gestured with the barrel of his Schmeisser.

"Behold the gates of the underworld!" he declared. "I've been inside. A damned cozy place, if you ask me—demons and gremlins and hobgoblins notwithstanding."

John McKinna

"Christ," Stirling growled, stalking past him. He bulldozed through the snow and into the narrow entrance.

The crevice widened rapidly, until Stirling could no longer feel both walls with his outstretched arms. It was absolutely dead black fifteen paces in, and he fumbled inside his coat for his Zippo. There was a metallic *clink* as he opened and fired the lighter.

He was standing in a rectangular cave some twelve by twenty by ten feet high, apparently formed by natural fracturing and slippage of the parent rock; there was no evidence of erosion by water, nor was there any dampness present—frozen or otherwise. The cave floor was flat, dry stone and quite devoid of dirt or rubble.

Cautiously Stirling walked forward, holding the Zippo up in front of him. At the far end of the cave, there was evidence of fire building—black soot on the rear wall and a crumbled pile of charred wood, as well as what looked like broken fragments of animal bone—but it did not appear to be recent. Most likely a hunter, someone who knew the terrain well, stopping in to shelter for the night. And how long ago? Ten, twenty, a hundred years? Stirling walked to the rear of the cave and squatted on his haunches, poking through the ash and char with his index finger. No German wrappers or cans, no cigarette butts, no wine or beer-bottle shards—none of the evidence that soldiers from time immemorial have always left in the wake of their passing.

Stirling rose to his feet. No, this cave had not been used in a very long time.

And it would do.

"Come on, boy, hurry," Cernović said, dragging another crate of explosives along Zlostup's narrow ledge toward Weiss. The young sergeant was lashing Bristow's dangling haul rope around the crate already at his feet, working feverishly. The snow, which had been

264

light and dustlike all night, was now coming down in heavy flakes and starting to drive into the Zpoda Gorge head wall as the wind picked up. Weiss's black wool balaclava, folded back off his flushed face, was caked with snow, as were his eyebrows and sparse, five-day growth of beard.

"I'm hurrying, Commander," he panted. "This is number seven. That one you have there makes eight—two crates per support." He wiped snow out of his eyes, stood up, and squinted up into the darkness. "Damned snow . . . can you see them up there?"

Cernović, peering up, as well, with his hands shielding his eyes, shook his head. "No. But if things don't start moving faster we're all going to see them at those bridge footings very soon—all of us including the SS. It will be light in less than forty minutes."

Weiss yanked three times on the rope. It went tight immediately and the crate was lifted into the air, bumping along the cliff as it rose. "Maybe the snow will keep it dark a bit longer," he said, looking out at the black skies to the north. "Buy us another half hour."

"Possibly," Cernović replied. "At any rate, we're not staying here to get shot off this ledge in broad daylight, if those three don't come down in time."

Weiss frowned at him through the falling snow. "You'd leave them out here?"

The Partisan commander shrugged. "Don't look at me like that, boy. I wouldn't be abandoning them—they'd be doing it to themselves. I'm not throwing my life away, or yours, for that matter, for no reason. Major Merritt has a choice: get down here while it's still dark so we can all get to cover together, or don't. He knows that."

Weiss looked back up at the swirling gloom overhead. "I just don't like the thought of having to leave without them."

Cernović shrugged again. "Like I said, it's out of our hands. . . . And I don't intend to die before I have to." He was quiet for a moment. "Dying is a terribly easy thing to do in Yugoslavia right now, Sergeant Weiss. You'd do well to remember that."

Weiss opened his mouth and then shut it again. Cernović was only telling the truth.

"Rope!" the Partisan commander hissed, stepping quickly to one side. Bristow's haul line came slapping down the rock face again and hung there, vibrating.

Weiss picked up the slack as Cernović hoisted one end of the last crate and dragged it over to the rope.

"All right, boy," he said, and his gravelly voice was not unkind, "tie."

Sylvia Kozo had put on all the clothing Merritt had passed her—pants and heavy British army sweater—and was working her way along a convenient series of two-inch horizontal ridges in the cliff face toward the bridge's third support footing. The snow was coming thick and fast now, and before every placement of her bare fingers on a new hold she was forced to scoop the buildup off the rock to avoid slipping. Her toes only occasionally found purchase, and skidded off the snow slick granite more often than not.

With all her weight continually supported by her arms, she was getting very tired, and her fingers were running with blood from torn nails and rock cuts. And there was no crack on this route in which to place a safety nut; the belay rope hung down in a large loop from her waist back up to Bristow at the second footing. He dared not keep any lateral tension on the rope for fear of hindering her forward progress, or worse, pulling her off the cliff.

She looked ahead. Only another fifteen feet to go forward. Forty-five feet to go back. Easy decision. Despite her trembling arms and numb, bleeding fingers, she was confident. She'd made short work of ledges only a quarter the width of these many times before—although admittedly not at four in the morning in a snowstorm. But there was no doubt that she would make it . . . that she would not fall . . . none whatsoever . . .

She fell. There was no reason for it, no justifiable excuse. No granite flaking away under her fingers or icy patch sabotaging her grip. Her strength, for the first time in her life, simply failed her. One second she was clinging to the rock, her arms shaking and her fingers hooked onto the little ledge like claws, and the next her fingers had opened and she was tumbling backward into a rushing, snowflake-filled blackness. Incomprehensible. The breath came out of her in a silent scream—and then the belay rope went taut and snatched at the waist belt of her harness.

What little air was still in her lungs was forced out in a gasp as she bounced on the end of the line and swung in a great arc under the second footing, frigid air whistling past her ears and snow whipping horizontally into her face. She tried to breathe, but her wind was gone, her solar plexus paralyzed. She twisted helplessly at the end of the rope as she reached the top of the arc . . . dropped back . . .

She hit the wall on the backswing, slamming into it with her left shoulder and hip. A glancing blow, but a painful one. Still trying to get a breath, she seized the rope with one hand and pulled herself upright.

The rock face loomed again, and this time her instincts took over. She flipped around to a sitting position and hit the granite with the soles of her feet, absorbing the shock with her legs. Two more swings and she managed to halt herself seventy-five feet below the second footing. She sat in her harness, feet against the cliff, clinging to the rope with both hands and sobbing in partial breaths of air.

On top of the second footing, Merritt was now beside Bristow, helping him take the strain of the taut belay. He grasped the upright girder with one gloved hand and leaned out, trying to see.

"At least she's still on the end of the rope," he said. "What happened?"

Bristow shook his head, grimacing as he held his share of Sylvia's weight. "I dunno, Major. I was lookin' right at her. She just came off the rock—boom—like that. Fell so damn far I almost couldn't hold her." He glanced at Merritt. "Good thing she don't weigh no more'n a plucked chicken."

"I didn't see it. I was still bringing that last crate across from the first footing on the transfer line."

"Goddamn, Major—I think she hit pretty hard down there."

"All right. Let's pull her up. One, two, three . . ."

The two big men heaved, getting about three feet at a time. It was nearly four minutes before the snow-caked top of Sylvia's rabbit-fur hat appeared at the bottom of the footing.

Merritt dropped to one knee. "Sylvia," he called softly. "Are you all right?"

She tipped her head back and looked up at him, hugging the rope. Her eyes were quite wide and she was shaking uncontrollably. She did not speak.

"Get her up here," Merritt said to Bristow. "She's frozen, and I don't mean from the cold."

"Shit," the big sergeant said. "Just what we need. Okay, Major . . . heave."

They hauled the girl up the final ten feet and lifted her onto the top of the concrete pad. She kicked back from the edge and sat huddled against the steel girder, still hugging the rope with both bloodied hands. She was staring out into the darkness, shivering.

Merritt and Bristow glanced at each other. Merritt moved forward, knelt, and put his hands on her trembling shoulders.

"Sylvia," he said gently. "You're alright now. You're alright."

Without warning, she leaned into him and buried her face in his chest. A single wracking sob escaped her, and she let go of the belay rope to clutch the sleeve of his sweater.

"I'm cold," she whispered, pulling herself closer. "I'm . . . so . . . cold."

Perplexed, Merritt drew her in and rubbed her shoulders and back. "Sylvia. It's alright. You just slipped. The rope caught you." He glanced at Bristow again. The big sergeant was grim faced, and tapped his wristwatch. "Sylvia," Merritt said again. "Sylvia. Come on. We have to finish and get down before daylight."

Her response was to shake even harder and press her face into his sternum.

"We've got to get her off of here," Merritt said. He locked eyes with Bristow. "Cole. You have to finish running detonator cord to the two sets of charges we've placed while I try to lower her down to Cernović and Weiss. Pile snow on the set charges to camouflage them—the snowfall should do the rest. These other four crates . . . they're too small to see from the antiaircraft gun emplacements on the north rim of the gorge, but if some sentry happens to look down off the bridge—"

"I was thinkin' about that, Major," Bristow interrupted, "and I had an idea: I thought I'd tie two crates together with about twenty feet of line between 'em and lower 'em on opposite sides of this big concrete block. They'll hang down under it, close to the cliff, and be hard to spot. Snow'll cover 'em a bit, too. I'll do the same with the last two crates, 'cept make the connectin' line a little shorter. They'll lie flat alongside the cliff, like the other ones. We can pull 'em up when we come back tonight to finish the job."

"Do it," Merritt said. "Then finish running the det cord, and let's get out of here."

"Yessir." Bristow turned and began to peel off arm lengths of rope from one of the spare coils.

Merritt put a hand on the back of Sylvia's neck and squeezed gently. "Sylvia. Sylvia. You have to move. I have to lower you down to the trail. Now, Sylvia . . . there's no more time. . . . Come on. . . ."

*   *   *

Cernović stamped his feet, hands in the pockets of his greatcoat. "We'll wait five more minutes," he said. "Then we're leaving."

"I wish we could see through this blasted snow," Weiss grumbled, looking up. "I wonder if they're in some kind of trouble."

"Well, they're not in the worst kind of trouble they can get into on a sheer cliff," Cernović remarked, "because we haven't seen any of them come plummeting past us."

"Gallows humor, Commander," Weiss said. "They—" He frowned, shifting his gaze slightly to the left. "Wait a minute. . . . What's that?"

He slid past Cernović and began to work his way quickly southward along the snow-choked trail, staring up with both hands on the head wall.

Cernović followed, squinting up into the snowflakes.

"It's the girl!" Weiss said. "She's being lowered from the second footing! Come on!"

Cernović's expression hardened as he caught sight of her, a small, huddled form bumping slowly down the rock face. "Get a hand on her, Weiss," he rasped. "There's something wrong. . . ."

Chapter Fifteen

"Inexcusable! Inconceivable!" the Grand Mufti of Jerusalem ranted. "You guaranteed me, Juttner, that I would be off this train at the town of Bljak and heading for Belgrade in a land convoy!"

Al-Husseini grabbed the back of an armchair to steady himself as the private car continued to rattle up the rails on a steep incline, swaying. Outside the boarded-up windows, the blizzard buffeted the train with increasing force.

"With all due respect, Your Excellency," Juttner replied, "I guaranteed no such thing. I merely stated that I would do my best to accommodate Your Excellency's wishes. It cannot be helped that there were no Wehrmacht or SS units near Bljak that could spare vehicles adequate for your journey to Belgrade, nor can it be helped that I was unable to make contact with any German units at all until just before the train pulled into Bljak to take on water. You must understand, Your Excellency, that there is a war on, and military forces may not always be exactly where we *expect* them to be—nor able to render spur-of-the-moment assistance."

"Do not lecture me, Hauptsturmfuehrer!" al-Husseini raged. "You will not lecture *me* on life's realities!"

Juttner waved a languid hand. "Perish the thought, Your Exellency," he said mildly. "I certainly did not mean to give offense—"

"Well, you have! You have given offense! I am *offended*!"

"Your Excellency—"

"I am offended by your inappropriate manner of speaking *and* I am offended that my simple request for safe conduct to Belgrade has been disregarded!" The mufti was now a deep shade of purple. "I am offended by the callous attitude of Standartenfuehrer Kronstadt! I am offended by Hauptsturmfuehrer Neurath's peristent surliness and the transparent acrimony between the two of you! *I am offended, Hauptsturmfuehrer Juttner!*"

"A veritable bounty of offenses," Juttner muttered casually, looking off to one side.

"What?"

"A regrettable sequence of events, I said, Your Excellency," the elegant SS officer replied, raising his voice again. "I can only hope to make amends once we reach the field headquarters of the SS Division Handschar at the Zpoda Skyway Bridge." He smiled ruefully, with a sympathetic cast to his eyes. "For that is surely where we are going to end up now."

"But it is not what I wanted!" the Grand Mufti opined, throwing a hand up into the air in disbelief. "I specifically stated that I do not want to be exposed to the hazards of a front-line position! I was to conduct lectures for visiting imams from a safe zone—such as Belgrade!"

"That is what you told the Fuehrer?" Juttner inquired, knowing full well it wasn't.

"Yes, of course," al-Husseini snapped indignantly. "And who are you to question me?"

Juttner raised a palm. "Your pardon, Your Excellency. I was merely inquiring into the original details of your plan to tour Handschar, to which I was not privy."

"Where is Neurath?" the mufti demanded. "I have not seen him since discovering your turpitude at Bljak. He must account for his part in this deluge of bungling."

"In his room, I believe," Juttner said, extracting a cigar from its case.

"Snagi!" al-Husseini declared, clasping his hands behind his back and pacing hunchbacked up the carpet. "Get Hauptsturmfuehrer Neurath out of his room. And bring me a tonic at once!"

The silent Macedonian, who had been standing at the end of the dining table with his arms folded, immediately walked across the car, entered the room-access passageway, and rapped on Neurath's door.

The door clicked open an inch. Neurath's blue eye stared out.

"His Excellency wishes to see you," Mustapha Snagi muttered. He turned and left.

Neurath closed the door. His trousers, which he had just pulled on, were still open at the front. He buttoned them up. A trickle of sweat ran down the center of his bare chest, and as he reached for his shirt, he fixed the naked girl lying on the tangled sheets of his bunk with a cold stare.

"No noise," he said in Serbo-Croatian. "I will keep you for a few days, and if you cooperate, I may send you back to Bljak with some money in your pocket. Perhaps some vouchers for food, yes?" His pale face twisted. "But if you do not obey me, you will be given to the regular soldiers—or worse. I am Gestapo. . . . And you know what that means, don't you?"

The girl, her long, dark hair matted around her

shoulders, pulled up a rumpled sheet to cover herself. She appeared to be in shock.

"Don't you, little one?" Neurath hissed suddenly, leaning forward.

The girl's eyes darted to his and she let out a weak yelp, hugging the sheet. "Ye . . . yes, sir," she whispered.

Neurath straightened and began to put on his uniform shirt. "Good. Very good. Now wash yourself at the sink and keep absolutely quiet until I return. Do not open the door for anyone who knocks, and do not speak if they call. Do you understand me?"

"Yes . . . yes. I-I understand, sir. . . ."

"Wish we could make a goddamn fire," Bristow grumbled, squatting down and prying the lid off a small tin of bully beef. He gestured at the half-dozen guttering candle stubs that had been set up on the cave floor in a two-foot circle. "Them little bastards don't throw much heat."

Stirling passed him another olive green tin. "Here, mate. Warm that bully up with this. It goes down easier if you melt the grease and soften the bone chips." He grinned.

"Hey, thanks," Bristow said, taking it. "What is it?"

"Jellied fuel. Our version of what you Yanks call canned heat or Sterno."

Bristow nodded and set the bully beef down to open the second can. "Thanks, Colin."

"Let's be careful with food smells," Merritt said, pulling a steel cup and spoon from a packsack. He was sitting against a boulder on the opposite side of the candle circle. "Don't burn anything or boil anything but water. It's not very likely to attract attention, but we're close to the garrison and some of those patrols may have dogs."

Bristow flicked open his Zippo and lit the purple gel inside the can. "Don't worry, Major. I'm just gonna take the frost off this dog food before I eat it." He shivered momentarily inside his combat jacket. "Brrr! It's goddamn cold in here. Good thing we brought them three mules in, too. They'll warm the place up some."

"It's colder out there," Weiss remarked, chewing on a K-ration bar. "And it sounds like the wind's picking up."

"It definitely is," Cernović said. He was seated between Weiss and Merritt on a canvas groundsheet. "And it's snowing hard. But that's a good thing. It will cover our tracks and hopefully the explosives on the bridge footings."

"Sentries aren't as observant and patrols aren't as active in blizzards," Merritt said. "If we didn't have to climb back up that head wall to place those other two sets of charges and finish stringing the detonator cord, the snowstorm would be nothing but a good thing for us." He glanced over at Bristow. "It's going to be tough, whether it stops snowing by nightfall or not."

Stirling cleared his throat. "Sir, do you want me to come along this time? I haven't climbed yet."

Merritt shook his head. "No, Sergeant. Bristow and I will handle it. I have something else in mind for you." He looked around the cave at his companions. "In fact, this is the point at which some of us split off and concentrate on tasks other than blowing up the Zpoda Skyway Bridge."

Everyone seated within the flickering candlelight paused and looked up. "How's that?" Weiss inquired.

"I'm dividing the team," Merritt said. "Most notably, Captain Throckmorton and Sergeant Stirling will be leaving later this morning, after they get a few hours' sleep. The rest of us will concentrate on the mining of the bridge. Our latest information, provided by Commander Cernović"—Merritt nodded in the Partisan's direction—"indicates that a military train loaded with King Tiger tanks will arrive at the fortified chalet near the north tunnel sometime around midnight, and attempt to cross the bridge to Mount Zpoda soon after."

"King Tigers?" Bristow said. "That what you and the commander here were whisperin' about all the way along Zlostup?"

"Yes," Merritt said. "Intelligence update. Instead of just blowing the bridge, we now want to blow the bridge with the train on it. So timing suddenly becomes a factor."

"And a variable," Cernović added.

Merritt nodded again. "And a variable. We have to be ready to set off the charges whenever the train moves out onto that bridge."

"I don't like Tiger tanks," Bristow muttered. "A person can get seriously killed messin' with Tiger tanks."

"That's why they're going to the bottom of the gorge along with the bridge," Merritt said, "where they can't do any harm. If we have our way, that is." He paused. "Which brings me to Professor Quisp."

The wild-eyed Englishman was squatting quietly on a little shelf of rock behind Weiss and Cernović. "What-ho?" he declared.

"I have a job for you, if you'd like to continue helping us," Merritt said. "I want to know exactly when that train arrives, especially if we happen to be up on the cliff when it does. It shouldn't be here that early, but we'll chance blowing just the two supports we've already got mined if we're caught short of time. Anyway, I need a train lookout."

"Capital! Splendid!" Quisp enthused, leaping to his feet. "I'm your man. Approach with stealth and monitor the buggers, eh? Well, let me tell you, Major—a Zulu leopard soldier—"

"—can't hold a candle to Professor Quisp when it comes to stalking," Stirling cut in, looking sideways at the demonstrative academic. "He gets around pretty quietly, Major. I can vouch for it."

"So I've noticed," Merritt said. "Anyway, I don't

want to count on the chance that the train may sound its whistle as it reaches the chalet. A lot of military trains don't use their whistles. I want to know when it's coming, preferably while it's still down below the last ridgeline, about half an hour away."

"I know the very thing, old fellow," Quisp declared. "A gamekeeper's cabin on that ridge, some distance from the tracks. It's abandoned, with the roof partly caved in, and I doubt if the Huns use it for anything or have anyone stationed near it. It's about two miles north of here and a quarter mile east of the rail line. Nothing around it but scrub forest. From there I can spot the train while it's still a long way down the grade."

"How will you signal us if you see it?" Merritt asked.

"There's the rub," Quisp said. "Can't chance a flare, can't fire a series of shots without arousing suspicion. I'll just have to hoof it back to the gorge rim if the train manifests itself, what? Tell you myself, won't I? Yes, I will."

"You can cover two miles through heavy snow that fast? Without getting caught?"

Quisp rolled his crazed eyes. "You haven't been listening, dear boy. A Zulu leopard soldier has nothing on—"

"Of course, Professor," Merritt interrupted, smiling. "I forgot. Very well. I'll leave the spotting of the train to you."

"Marvelous!" Quisp pronounced, hopping down off the ledge and slinging his Schmeisser over his shoulder. "Well, I'm off!" He strode across the cave toward the narrow entrance passage, pulling his hood up over his head. Two seconds later he was gone.

"No quotations this time," Stirling commented. "Thank the Lord for small blessings."

"Here," Bristow said, holding out a steaming tin. "Have some hot bully beef. Warm you up."

"Appreciate it, mate."

A sound halfway between a sigh and a moan came from the darkness at the rear of the cave, followed by a rustling of cloth.

"I'd better have a look at her before we continue," Merritt said, starting to rise.

"Don't bother," Sylvia said, her voice quiet but steady. She walked into the flickering candlelight between Bristow and Stirling, her hands in the pockets of the baggy greatcoat she was wearing. There was a slight hitch in her usual gliding step.

She squatted down on her haunches and gazed at the candles from beneath her hooded lids, her small mouth fixed in a frown.

"How are you feeling?" Merritt asked.

"Foolish," Sylvia replied.

Bristow scraped the bottom of his bully-beef tin with his spoon. "What for?" he asked. "Not getting killed?"

The small frown turned into a small smile. "Partly," she said. "But mostly for overextending myself, falling, and then losing my nerve on the head wall."

Merritt waved a hand. "Understandable. You were exhausted, trying to climb in impossible conditions. It could have happened to anyone."

Sylvia looked at him. "But it happened to *me*," she said. She looked back at the candles. "A thing like that does not happen to me."

"Well, it won't again," Merritt said, putting a tea bag into a cup of hot water. "Sergeant Bristow and I will finish setting the charges tonight. You'll stay on lookout with Commander Cernović and Sergeant Weiss at the Zlostup trailhead, below the tunnel."

She kept looking into the candle flame. "You don't trust me on the rock anymore."

"I didn't say that," Merritt countered. "You did the hardest part: you made that free-climbing ascent from Zlostup to the first footing and established the main rope. You got us across to the second footing using that tiny horizontal crack, which looks to be the most difficult of the three traverses between bridge supports. Sergeant Bristow and I can handle the rest. We transferred the main ascent rope to the second footing and left it hanging there, so we can climb back up without any trouble."

"How will you get across to the third and fourth footings?"

"If we can't free-climb the traverses like you, we'll use a few pitons," Merritt said.

"The Nazis might hear you," Sylvia pointed out. "I can do it without a sound."

Merritt looked at her for a long moment.

"No," he said finally.

"Why?"

"Because you've done enough. Bristow and I will finish mining the bridge supports."

"You're afraid I'll freeze," Sylvia said. "Lose my nerve on the rock again."

Merritt pulled the tea bag out of the cup of hot water and tossed it into the corner of the cave. "I don't think that would happen," he replied quietly, "but I can't take the chance."

Sylvia drew a deep breath. "I won't freeze. I won't. What happened to me has passed, Major. And I can climb that rock better than either you or Sergeant Bristow."

Merritt shook his head and sipped carefully at the rim of his steaming cup. "No."

Sylvia grimaced and turned to look directly at him once more. "If you start pounding pitons into that cliff, you and Sergeant Bristow run the risk of alerting the Germans," she said. "You may be shot off the head wall, and the explosives discovered. The entire mission, all this effort, would be a waste—along with the lives of your Sergeant Hurst and Sergeant D'Amato." Her eyes shifted to Stirling and Bristow and back to Merritt again. "And besides, no Englishman tells me what to do and when to do it! I—"

"You are wrong, Miss Kozo," Merritt cut in, setting

his cup down. "In this case, an Englishman—me—*is* telling you what to do. . . . And you will do exactly that. You will not climb that head wall again. Period."

"You are—"

"In command here!" Merritt's voice was steely. "And I have a mission to accomplish. That mission takes precedence over your desire to indulge in some kind of dramatic atonement for your paralysis on the cliff. This operation is not a stage upon which you can flog your immaturity and self-absorption, Miss Kozo. You can engineer your personal catharsis on your own time. Right now, you will do as you're told. You will obey orders like any other soldier—if that is truly what you consider yourself to be."

Sylvia blinked at him, then looked at Cernović. The swarthy Partisan commander was lying back on one elbow, chewing slowly on a ration bar. He returned Sylvia's glance without expression, then looked off across the cave and continued to eat.

Abruptly she got to her feet and stomped off into the darkness. The action was very much like that of a spoiled child—a fact that was not lost on any of the men sitting around the circle of candles. Sylvia Kozo could not have proven Merritt's curt assessment of her any better if she'd done it on paper. There was a light thump as she threw herself down on her makeshift pallet of tarpaulins at the rear of the cave.

"I say, gentlemen—how do I look?"

Throckmorton emerged from a dark corner where he'd been rummaging for the past forty minutes. Bristow, Stirling, Weiss, and Cernović stared. He was dressed in the field uniform of an officer of the SS Division Handschar, complete with swastika-and-scimitar emblem on the collar and death's-head insignia on the gray fez cocked on top of his head.

Merritt smiled over his tea. "You look like a right old goose-stepper," he said. "Handschar style."

Throckmorton adjusted the fez slightly. "Thanks awfully, old bean," he drawled. "I wouldn't want to have come all this way and not pass muster." He coughed suddenly, turned his head, and spat into the darkness. "Ugh."

Bristow was cleaning his fingernails with his jump knife. "So, Major . . . since we've waded this far up the creek together, what is it with that cough of yours? You've been spittin' up like a lunger since we first met in Scotland. If I was any kind of a sawbones, I'd say you had yourself a whoppin' case of the consumption."

Throckmorton wiped his lips on the back of his hand. "And you'd be wrong, Sergeant," he said. He locked eyes with Merritt for a moment. "I do not have tuberculosis. I have wet pneumonia that has been slow to go away, that's all."

Bristow looked up at him and slid his jump knife back into its boot scabbard. "If you say so, Captain." He refrained from asking why a sick man would have been sent on a dangerous, physically demanding mission in an occupied country at all.

Merritt got to his feet. "I'm glad you were still here when we got off the cliff, Duncan. But it really is going to be good-bye this time, isn't it?"

" 'Fraid so, old man." Throckmorton grinned suddenly. "The game's on now, and no mistake." He glanced down. "Sergeant Stirling."

"Sir."

"Over in that suitcase you'll find the field uniform of an SS private first class, coincidentally just your size. Please put it on, and make sure you keep your shirt and stripes on underneath it. That way, if you're captured, there's at least a small chance you won't be executed on the spot for not wearing your own uniform."

Stirling hesitated for only a second. "That's a cold comfort, sir," he said, "but I'll take a small chance over no chance at all." As he headed for the rear of the cave, unbuttoning his combat jacket, he let out a dry chuckle. "This mission's getting more interesting all the time. From British sergeant to Nazi Sturmman in one fell swoop—complete with uniform switch.''

"I'll fill you in as we make our way toward the garrison," Throckmorton said. "In the meantime, you need to collect your complete kit, and wrap that Enfield in strip cloth from muzzle to butt plate so it doesn't look like anything but a Mauser. We'll be leaving in about two hours."

"Yes, sir."

Merritt put a hand on Throckmorton's shoulder. "Get that two hours' sleep, Duncan. I'll wake you when it's time to leave."

"All right, old man."

Merritt returned to his boulder and sat down with his back to it. Pulling his collar up and his black balaclava down over his ears and neck, he crossed his arms and stretched-out legs, settled back, and closed his eyes. Bristow and Cernović, taking their cue from him like the experienced hands they were, rolled over on their backs and likewise tried for some sleep. Throckmorton and Stirling were rustling quietly through clothing and equipment. Sylvia was dead silent in the darkness at the rear of the cave, and Quisp was gone. The mules nickered softly, herding together for warmth. Outside the wind whined and moaned past the cliff—a lonely, primordial sound. A few stray snowflakes floated into the cave through the entrance passage.

Weiss spoke: "Major."

"Mmf . . . what is it?"

"What's going on, sir? What are we doing?"

There was a pause before Merritt answered. "What you're doing, Sergeant, is supporting the demolition of the Zpoda Skyway Bridge, hopefully with the King Tiger train on it. You're with me—as are Commander Cernović, Sergeant Bristow, and Miss Kozo. Captain Throckmorton has a separate task to accomplish, for which he can use the assistance of Sergeant Stirling. The original mission always had two parts—one of which was my priority, and the other Captain Throck-morton's. None of you needed to know that until now, so you weren't told."

Weiss's voice was very quiet. "What exactly *is* Captain Throckmorton's objective, sir?"

Merritt sighed, and settled himself more comfortably against the boulder. "You still don't need to know that, Sergeant Weiss," he said.

It was snowing hard in London, too, the wet, heavy flakes of southern England drifting down to accumulate six inches deep on the windowsills of the Prime Minister's residence. Seated at the great desk in his study, Churchill poured more sherry into a cut-crystal glass and pushed it across the polished walnut top.

"Have another, Martin," he said in his rumble of a voice. "I think the present circumstances justify it."

The elegant, white-haired industrialist seated opposite Churchill ceded a slight smile. "Well, I don't often indulge in refills, Winston. You know that. Even during strictly social engagements I usually end up watering the potted plants on the sly with them."

"No wonder my ficus trees are looking sickly," Churchill remarked. "And I thought it was the weather." The two men exchanged a brief laugh. "Come now, Martin," the Prime Minister said, tapping the glass. "On occasion it's good for the nerves."

The white-haired man picked up the glass and tipped it forward. "Your health, Winston," he said.

"And yours."

The two old friends drank. Martin Judson held his glass thoughtfully in his lap as Churchill selected a cigar from the box on his desk and proceeded to clip the end of it with a sterling silver cutter.

"Stop worrying," he growled, without looking up.

Judson shifted in his chair. "When was the last communication?"

"Twelve hours ago. Nothing since."

"The train must be well up into the Majevicas by

now." He took a small sip of sherry. "When do you think we might hear something?"

"Menzies' people have received no further messages from Berlin as yet," Churchill said. "Unfortunately, it's just a wait-and-see proposition, Martin. That's all I can say, and you know it."

"Yes, I do," Judson replied. "That's the trouble."

Churchill lit the cigar and drew on it until the end was glowing like a miniature furnace. A great pall of aromatic smoke began to collect in the air above the desk.

"It's going to be fine," he said. "With him it always is, because he's always smarter than everyone around him."

Judson looked at the Prime Minister, then out the frost-etched windows at the falling snow. "How many incredibly smart people have we lost in the past several years because the infinitely more stupid people surrounding them finally managed to put two and two together and not get five, Winston?"

Churchill harrumphed and drew on his cigar, frowning. "Have some more sherry, Martin," he said.

Chapter Sixteen

"Ready, Sergeant?" Throckmorton muttered through the scarf covering most of his face.

"As ready as I'll ever be, sir," Stirling answered.

"Then let's go."

Throckmorton stepped out from the behind the scrub trees at the edge of the rail bed and made his way quickly—but not too quickly—up onto the train tracks. Stirling followed, a bulky figure in white hooded anorak, German helmet, and scarved face, rucksack on his back and cloth-wrapped rifle slung over one shoulder. Throckmorton, too, wore the German winter camouflage parka, but with his head almost completely wrapped in scarves, leaving only a slit for his eyes. Under the coat's white hood, he also wore an officer's Bergmütze mountain cap.

The snow was still falling very heavily, and although it was now close to noon, the dense overcast of the blizzard kept the daylight muted almost to a twilight level. Up ahead, perhaps two hundred yards away, Throckmorton could just make out the looming gray mass of the fortified chalet, and below it to the left, the dark arched entrance of the northern bridge tunnel. Coming up on the right side of the main line was a switching signal for the small siding that paralleled the primary tracks and dead-ended in front of the chalet. The dim figures of at least a dozen soldiers, singly and in pairs, were moving in the area between the chalet and tunnel entrance.

Throckmorton and Stirling walked together down the tracks, keeping to the cross ties between the rails, Stirling staying a pace or two behind his captain. They moved purposefully but unhurriedly, like soldiers following routine. There was a pair of what seemed to be sentries hanging on the left bank of the primary rail line, across from the walled chalet's main gate. To avoid them, Throckmorton veered unobtrusively to the right, following the siding tracks.

He saw the sentries' body language change as they noticed him, saw them stiffen and orient toward the two new arrivals. He did not alter his stride as he approached, and trusted that Stirling would do the same. Indifferent confidence was the key. However, if they were challenged, asked for a password, things could get a bit sticky. . . .

As he drew near, the two sentries came to attention and gave him the Nazi salute. He returned it casually and strode on past without giving them a second look. He could hear Stirling's boots crunching in the dry snow behind him. Two seconds went by. Five seconds. Ten. But no verbal challenge came. Throckmorton let out a long breath through his scarf and started up the short incline between the siding tracks and the chalet gate.

The gate was a twelve-foot-high archway in the twenty-foot stone wall. Its massive wooden doors were pulled back, and a sentry stood to one side of the entrance. Both Throckmorton and Stirling noted the sandbagged machine-gun positions next to each of the two corner guardhouses in view atop the wall, and the paired guards manning them.

The sentry at the gate seemed, unfortunately, to be attentive to his duties, despite being obviously very cold. He stepped forward, shivering, as Throckmorton and Stirling approached, his Schmeisser slung across the front of his snow-powdered greatcoat, his free hand moving up in a halt gesture. . . .

"My God, man," Throckmorton said in perfect German, "haven't you had the hot soup ration yet? You look half frozen."

The Muslim trooper, who had learned the command language of the SS only in the past year during division training in France, and then only partly, lowered his hand. "Your pardon, Herr—?" His eyes roved quickly over Throckmorton's clothing, searching for an insignia of rank.

"Sturmbannfuehrer," Throckmorton filled in for him. "Sturmbannfuehrer Mendel. Carrying intelligence updates from the western flank to Standartenfuehrer Zweig."

The Muslim private licked his lips. Throckmorton could see him thinking: *An SS major—and an SS major entrusted with intelligence reports for the division commander.*

"Answer me, Schütze," Throckmorton demanded, in a tone that was neither hostile nor friendly. "Have you or have you not had the hot soup ration today?"

"Er . . . *nein*, Herr Sturmbannfuehrer . . ."

Throckmorton shook his head in disgust. "Ridiculous," he said. He turned and looked at Stirling. "Even the first pair of sentries who challenged us this morning had their ration, didn't they, Suljak?"

Stirling nodded. "*Jawohl*, Herr Sturmbannfuehrer," he grunted through his scarf.

"And the second pair and the pair after that," Throckmorton went on, turning back to the sentry. "And yet the cooks forget the man at their very gate."

He eyed the Muslim private sympathetically. "Well, this won't do. Suljak: I want a double ration of hot soup and a half ration of bread—hot bread, with butter—brought to this man immediately after we report to Standartenfuehrer Zweig's office. See to it."

"*Jawohl,* Herr Sturmbannfuehrer," Stirling grunted again.

"Um—" the sentry began.

Throckmorton clapped a gloved hand onto the private's shoulder and squeezed good-naturedly. "Damned inefficiency. The fools in their warm kitchens keep forgetting that an army marches on its stomach. Well, if that doesn't include the good soldier faithfully standing guard in a blizzard, who does it include? Eh?" He clapped the shoulder again, making the sentry stagger sideways a step.

"Er—" the soldier said.

"Your name, trooper, so I can mention your good conduct to Standartenfuehrer Zweig."

"Ah—Fikret Pandža, Herr Sturmbannfuehrer. Schütze Fikret Pandža."

Throckmorton stepped back and regarded the sentry approvingly. "Very good, Schütze Pandža," he declared. "Very good indeed. Carry on!" He stood there, plainly waiting for a salute.

The sentry got his heels together and snapped his arm out. "*Jawohl,* Herr Sturmbannfuehrer!"

Throckmorton flipped his hand back, turned briskly, and stalked through the gate toward the chalet greathouse, with Stirling close behind.

"Sergeant Weiss," Merritt said. "Wake up."

Weiss pushed himself up to a sitting position, yawning. He rubbed his eyes and looked around him. The candles had burned down to stubs; only four of the original six were still alight. The cave was as dark and cold as ever, except that now it also stank of mule dung. Cernović was still sleeping nearby, flat on his back in his heavy winter coat with his arms folded across his chest, as was Bristow. The big American sergeant was snoring gently in a rumbling baritone.

The young commando looked over his shoulder toward the rear of the cave. Sylvia, wrapped in layers of winter clothing and a canvas groundsheet, was an indistinct lump in the meager glow of the candles. Closer to the mules were several rucksacks of gear and the suitcase that had contained the German uniforms worn by Throckmorton and Stirling.

Merritt was sitting on his boulder, waiting, a weatherproof document folder in one hand. He was looking into the darkness without expression.

Weiss eased onto one knee, stiff from lying on the cold stone of the cave floor. "You want me, Major?" he whispered.

"I do," Merritt replied. "Come here."

Weiss did so, squatting in front of Merritt and stretching his aching back. "Yes, sir." He glanced around the cave again. "Captain Throckmorton and Sergeant Stirling—they've left already?"

"An hour ago," Merritt said. "They're no longer your concern."

Weiss looked at him. Merritt's voice held the same steely edge that earlier had stopped Sylvia Kozo in her tracks.

"Yes, sir," he said quietly.

There was a pause. Merritt gazed down at the document folder in his hand. For a brief second, Weiss had the impression that the man was gathering himself. Then Merritt spoke:

"You're familiar with the Grand Mufti of Jerusalem, Haj Amin al-Husseini?"

Weiss's eyes widened. The name was anathema to a member of the Jewish Brigade.

Merritt waited.

"I know who he is," Weiss said.

"Good. Do you know what he looks like?"

"I have a vague idea."

Merritt opened the document folder and extracted

a five-by-seven-inch black-and-white photograph. "He looks like this," he said, holding out the picture.

Weiss took it, leaned down, and picked up the stub of one of the candles. He examined the photo by the light of the guttering flame. Merritt watched him closely. The young sergeant's face seemed to contort as he surveyed the mufti's neatly barbered features, Muslim cleric's headdress, and robe.

Weiss lowered the photograph. "Why are you showing me this?" he asked tightly.

"That individual," Merritt said, "is one of the worst enemies the Jewish people have got. He is a Nazi collaborator who advocates the extermination of the Jews in Europe so that they cannot emigrate or be transported to Palestine. He is responsible for the recruiting of thousands of Muslims into Heinrich Himmler's SS Division Handschar."

Weiss looked down at the photograph again, then handed it back. "I know this," he muttered. "What does it have to do with—"

"Sometime tonight," Merritt said, "the train we have come to destroy along with the Zpoda Skyway Bridge will arrive at that chalet over there. The Grand Mufti of Jerusalem will be on it."

Weiss was dead silent.

"He was to give a series of inspirational lectures to the imams in charge of the spiritual welfare and morale of the Muslim soldiers in Handschar. He hoped to do this from the safety of Belgrade—or at least some point well behind the front lines." Merritt paused. "Chance and circumstance have redirected him here."

Merritt did not look at Weiss as he extracted a second photograph from the document folder. Then he raised his eyes and fixed the young sergeant with a penetrating gaze.

"Just a few weeks ago," he said, "the mufti was the target of an assassination attempt in Berlin. It was very nearly successful. His bodyguards, however, were able to intervene and kill the assassin."

Weiss swallowed as Merritt went on:

"The assassin was a young Jew, a member of the Jewish Agency out of Cairo and, at the time, an active SOE cooperative. He had been deeply under cover in the heart of Berlin, in disguise, for nearly four months. Waiting for a chance to kill the Grand Mufti of Jerusalem. He gave his life trying to accomplish this.

"His name was Aaron Weiss. He was your brother."

Merritt held out the second photograph.

"This is what they did to him."

The stark image of the young man who had tried to assassinate Haj Amin al-Husseini outside the Hotel Jürgenplatz was truly horrible. He was pictured from head to midthigh, naked, on some kind of metal slab. His well-muscled body was black with numerous bullet holes, slash wounds, and contusions. His dark hair was a frayed mat, his once handsome face bloated and distorted in death, the jaw broken. His eyes appeared to have been punctured by a knife blade or spike. His abdomen had been laid open, the intestines visible. His genitals were half gone, mutilated and partly torn away.

Merritt got up and walked slowly toward the rucksacks at the rear of the cave.

From Sergeant David Weiss, hunched over the photograph holding the stub of a flickering candle, there came a muffled choking sound.

Merritt picked up Throckmorton's suitcase and, taking his time, carried it back to the boulder on which he'd been sitting. He set it down in front of Weiss.

"In here you'll find one more SS field uniform," he said, "complete with full white winter camouflage anorak and trousers. You will also find one .45 caliber De Lisle fully silenced short carbine, painted white, with sixty rounds of ammunition. There is a cloth carrying sheath for it, as well, which makes it look a common German artillery spotting scope.

"You speak fluent German and adequate Serbo-Croatian. You are a crack shot. Before the King Tiger train crosses the bridge, the mufti's private car will almost certainly be moved onto a short siding in front of the chalet and uncoupled, as it is his mobile base of operations and there is no reason to expose it—or him—to the fighting front. He will be received by the division commander, which means that at some point he will have to leave the car." Merritt let a beat pass. "A man with your abilities should be able to find a way to get close enough."

Through the hot tears stinging his eyes, through the grief that threatened to close his throat, and through the fierce rage rising in him like a flood, Weiss could hear, echoing in his head with haunting clarity, the words of General Sir Colin McVean Gubbins:

Anyone in our business can find himself in the position of having to use lies or manipulation, even with respect to allies, to achieve an immediate goal. Could you respect the higher motive, even if it was done to you?

"This was . . . all set up . . . in advance," Weiss croaked. "You must have had this picture of . . . my brother . . . before we left Bari." He let the photograph slip from his hand. "Where's . . . where's his body?"

Merritt shook his head. "It was in Berlin when this picture was taken. By now it will have been disposed of."

"How did you get hold of that . . . that photograph?"

Merritt suddenly became aware that Cernović and Bristow were both wide awake and watching the exchange intently. He ignored Weiss's last question.

"You have an opportunity to finish your brother's mission and avenge him at the same time," he said, "by killing the man most responsible for his death. You also have an opportunity to rid the Jewish people of one of their worst enemies."

Weiss hung his head. "You set me up," he repeated.

"You . . . Gubbins . . . whoever provided you with that picture from Berlin . . . all of you."

"The mufti was going to be in Yugoslavia at the time of Operation Handschar," Merritt said. "His presence in the country was a bonus that couldn't be ignored. The only thing we didn't know was exactly where he'd be—Belgrade, Zagreb, or closer to the front."

"So you attached a Jewish commando who didn't know he had a dead brother to your team," Weiss filled in, regaining partial control of himself, "knowing that if you unleashed him somewhere near the mufti after telling him about his brother, there wouldn't be any chance he wouldn't take—anything he wouldn't risk—in order to hunt him down. Like cutting a cannon loose on a rolling deck to see what it hits."

Merritt's face was impassive. "You don't have to go," he said simply.

Weiss looked at the suitcase. Then he got to his feet, picked it up by the handle, and carried it over to his groundsheet.

"Of course I do," he said, setting the suitcase down. "And you know it. You've always known it—even when I didn't."

He knelt in front of the suitcase and opened it, and said nothing more.

Standartenfuehrer Egon Zweig had just pulled on his black leather gloves and was reaching for his winter coat when he sensed the door opening behind him. Irritated, he took the coat from its hanger and began to brush the lint off, without bothering to turn around. Feder, his regular aide, hadn't announced any visitors, and he was about to take his daily constitutional: a walk down the north tunnel and back.

"Who are you and what do you want?" he demanded snappishly. "You don't enter my office without first identifying yourself to my aide and being announced."

"Your pardon, Herr Standartenfuehrer," a muffled voice said. "Your aide is not at his desk. Perhaps he has stepped out."

Zweig's irritability flared. "What? Impossible." He turned on his heel. "He had better be at his . . . desk . . . " His voice trailed off. Standing in the middle of the chalet common room were two tall men in winter camouflage—one obviously an officer, since he wore the Bergmütze under his anorak hood. Their faces were completely obscured by scarves, and both were caked with snow from head to foot.

There was something intimidating about them, something predatory in their poise, that had made Zweig lapse into involuntary silence. They were Jagdkommando, he decided. Most of them had that unsettling, latent lethality.

"I'm busy," Zweig said, walking forward and standing behind his desk. He folded his coat over his arm. "I also don't like to repeat myself: who are you and what do you want?"

The officer pushed back his hood and began to unwrap the first of the two scarves that covered his face. "My name is Zwilling," he said, "and I have a question for you."

Zweig was appalled by the man's effrontery. He could feel the the flush rising to his cheeks. "Rank, damn you!" he barked.

The officer continued to unwrap his scarves. "Standartenfuehrer," he said.

Zweig gaped. "Wh-what?"

"Standartenfuehrer, Herr Standartenfuehrer."

The other soldier moved slowly off to one side.

Zweig came around the desk. "What is this nonsense?" he exclaimed, clenching a fist. "You are insubordinate! You—"

He stopped in his tracks as the last scarf fell away from the officer's face. His eyes widened and his jaw went slack.

Throckmorton grinned at him. "My question is, Standartenfuehrer Zweig: would you like to retire?"

"It—it can't . . . *be!*" Zweig whispered, staring. "You . . . you're . . ." His eyes remained fixed on Throckmorton as the British captain began to circle him.

"Unbelievably handsome?" Throckmorton drawled in English.

Zweig sucked in breath for a yell—and in one lightning motion, Stirling snapped a wire garotte down over his head and around his neck. The German commander's eyes popped and his tongue bulged from his mouth. Stirling crossed his powerful forearms, cinching the garotte, spun 180 degrees, and leaned forward. Zweig's booted feet came off the floor. Stirling carried him, back to back, across the room to a small walk-in closet. Throckmorton opened the door. Stirling stepped inside, with Zweig still thrashing energetically. The only sound was a low, horrific gurgling.

Throckmorton was about to follow when a knock at the main entrance of the office stopped him. He nodded to Stirling and hurriedly shut the closet door. Crossing the room, he began to shed his winter clothing.

"Yes?" he called out. "Speak, but do not enter. I am busy."

There was silence outside the door, then a voice:

"It is Hauptsturmfuehrer Haak, sir. I—"

"Can you not announce yourself through Feder, Hauptsturmfuehrer?" Five minutes earlier, in the process of eliminating Zweig's aide, Throckmorton had noted the nameplate on the outer desk. "These sudden interruptions are most distracting." He bundled the winter camouflage anorak and tucked it behind a filing cabinet. His gloves and undercoat he threw onto a corner armchair.

"Untersturmfuehrer Feder is not here, Herr Standartenfuehrer," Haak said.

There was a rattling thump and the closet door jumped on its hinges as something—probably a kicking boot—walloped it from the inside. Throckmorton cast an anxious glance that way as he hurried across the common room to Zweig's desk, smoothing his blond hair into place with the palm of his hand. He dropped into the commander's oak swivel chair and picked up a sheaf of reports just as Haak's voice came again:

"Is there something wrong, Herr Standartenfuehrer?" The main office door unlatched and swung open a couple of inches. "Herr Standartenfuehrer?"

"Come in if you must, Haak," Throckmorton called, swiveling the chair so that his back was to the door. He pulled a small Walther pistol from his uniform pocket, tucked it between his legs, and began sorting through the reports.

There was a creak of hinges and a clicking of jackboots as Haak entered and proceeded across the common room. Throckmorton gave him time to come within what sounded like ten feet of the desk and then swung around to face him.

Haak looked at his commanding officer, came to attention with a curt smile and a click of his heels, and snapped off a Nazi salute.

"Heil Hitler!" he said.

Throckmorton nodded and flipped his hand back. *"Heil Hitler,"* he echoed. He glanced back down at his reports. "Where is Feder, Haak?"

The SS Hauptsturmfuehrer stood easy and shot Throckmorton a puzzled look. "I have no idea where your aide is, sir."

"Don't be impertinent, Haak," Throckmorton said idly. "I was merely wondering if you happened to know." He peered up at the combat officer. Haak was a big man, rangy and tough looking, with a truly Aryan hawk face.

Haak was looking back at him. "Do you feel all

right, sir? You seem rather pale, and your voice—well—it sounds odd."

"Another damned cold," Throckmorton said, coughing for effect. "It started coming on last night. I'll survive, I suppose." Noticing the carved box on the corner of the desk, he reached over, opened it, and extracted a cigarette. "Cigarette, Haak? Help yourself."

Haak was taken aback. It was the first time in their entire two-year association that Standartenfuehrer Egon Zweig had offered him anything. His brow furrowing, he stepped forward and selected a cigarette. "Thank you, sir. I've run out of my own."

"Don't mention it," Throckmorton said, sliding a box of wooden matches across the desktop at the same time as he transferred the Walther to an open desk drawer and pushed it shut. "Now, what can I do for you?"

What in the name of Odin has infected Zweig's brain this morning, Haak wondered as he lit the cigarette. The commander was positively amiable—not to mention relaxed. Even if he did look a little unwell.

"Er . . . I thought we would discuss possible scenarios for utilizing the King Tigers in conjunction with Handschar, Herr Standartenfuehrer," Haak said, "since their arrival is imminent."

"Ah, yes. Well, why don't we?" Throckmorton stood up, still holding the sheaf of reports in his left hand. He dropped them on the desk, put that hand in his pocket, and cleared a space on the desktop with his right. "Damned mess. Here we are—a decent topographic map of Mount Zpoda, with our positions drawn on it." He pointed at the markings clearly representing Handschar's deployment, his unlit cigarette cleated between his second and third fingers. "Any suggestions you have would be welcome."

Baffled but pleased, Haak stepped around to the side of the desk and perused the map. "Well, sir," he said, "I'm concerned primarily about our right flank, since the Second Proletarian Brigade has repositioned itself somewhere west of the Ugljevik Pass. The potential exists for it to continue to move west across the alpine plateau south of Mount Zpoda, then north to link up with other Partisan battalions and regiments currently opposing us here"—Haak tapped his index finger on the map—"here, and here. It's possible that their combined forces could drive forward and split us in half at the mountain, with the Zpoda Gorge making it impossible for our left flank to sweep around the Partisan salient and attack it from the side and behind."

Throckmorton nodded. "I see," he mused, getting into the spirit of the thing. "We should reinforce our right quadrant by advancing south along the western shoulder of Mount Zpoda, and deploying perhaps a quarter of the Tiger tanks to hold positions there—mobile artillery, if you will—while the bulk of the tanks and infantry assault units from, say, the Twenty-eighth SS Regiment push forward in an arc that follows the mid-level elevations. Oh, and I would suggest that elements of the Twenty-nineth—perhaps Battalions Three and Four—be moved into the slot and held in reserve in case the Partisans launch a serious counterattack from the northwest."

Haak blinked in astonishment. What had happened to Zweig? Not only had the Standartenfuehrer developed a personality overnight, he had also apparently turned from a dull-minded tin soldier who could barely read a map into a shrewd military tactician with an appreciation of terrain. Security of the position currently held by the Twenty-eighth SS Regiment was critical, the lynchpin of the Mount Zpoda defensive strategy. If the Twenty-eighth SS was ordered to advance, other forces would have to be shifted to take its place. . . . And Zweig had understood that instinctively. Absolutely stupefying.

"That is a very good point, Herr Standartenfuehrer," Haak followed up, checking the map again. "We should indeed have reserves available to protect the neck of our own salient." There was a scratching sound as the division commander fired a match to light his cigarette.

"I'm glad you agree, Haak," Throckmorton said, shaking out the match and exhaling smoke. "And I think the majority of the tanks should be deployed like the tines of a fork along these three descending ridges." He leaned forward slightly and pointed. "Here, here, and here. They will give fire support to the infantry units sweeping the valleys in between. Do you concur with that assessment?"

There was no answer.

"Haak?"

Throckmorton looked up and straight into the muzzle of a Luger pistol. On the other side of the weapon, Hauptsturmfuehrer Ulrich Haak's face, completely drained of color, was working in confusion.

"Don't move," he blurted, taking a step backward with his gun arm fully extended. "Whoever you are."

Chapter Seventeen

Throckmorton brought his cigarette to his lips and drew on it, one eyebrow raised. "What do you think you're doing, Hauptsturmfuehrer?" he demanded, turning to face Haak.

"I told you not to move," Haak hissed. His prominent Adam's apple moved up and down as he swallowed. Throckmorton's split-second assessment was that the man's reactions were generated by alarm rather than fear—he was obviously too seasoned a combat soldier to be unnerved for very long.

"Now see here, Haak," he said, stepping forward, "this has gone far enough."

The German officer moved back. "One more step," he snarled, "and you're dead."

Throckmorton spread his open hands, palms forward. "Alright, alright."

"You are not Standartenfuehrer Zweig," Haak declared.

Throckmorton smiled and raised his cigarette to his

lips again. "You're delusional, Hauptsturmfuehrer Haak," he said. "The strain of too much combat, perhaps. Of course I am Egon Zweig."

Haak wagged the Luger. "Then explain to me," he retorted, "how it is that the little finger of your left hand, which was accidentally shot off a month ago, has somehow grown back overnight."

Throckmorton's expression remained a pleasant blank as he blew out a long stream of smoke.

"No answer, Standartenfuehrer?" Haak said. He was breathing hard, focused on Throckmorton. "Incredible. Subtle differences in appearance, but nothing to speak of. Noticeable differences in personality, ability, and intellect, but in the context of the astounding physical resemblance—dismissable. I would have been completely fooled if not for the finger." He paused, shaking his head. "Unless you are an unknown twin brother, you are a true doppelganger. An unrelated near-perfect double of Egon Zweig."

"Well, old man," Throckmorton said in English, calculating that the well-spoken German would likely understand it and several other languages, "not so near perfect as you might imagine. My natural hair color is brown, not blond, and my nose was once not as thin as Herr Zweig's. Fortunately, however, I had access to such things as peroxide and surgery."

"You're British," Haak replied. "I might have known. SOE, I expect."

"A captain, actually. Like you."

"Remarkable," Haak said. "Congratulations. Your German is excellent."

"Why, thanks awfully, old fellow," Throckmorton acknowledged. He thought fleetingly of the Walther in the lower desk drawer.

"But, Captain," Haak went on, making the mistake of starting to enjoy his own cleverness, "you are very seriously in the wrong uniform. You are impersonating an SS division commander. That makes you a spy.

And spies are shot." He smiled. "After they are questioned by our intelligence services . . . rather extensively."

Throckmorton drew on his cigarette again. "You don't say."

Haak's eyes narrowed, and the smile left his face. "I would hardly be flippant if I were in your position," he growled. "Now, then, before I march you out of here: where is Standartenfuehrer Zweig? What have you done with him?"

Too arrogant, Throckmorton thought. *Too self-absorbed. You should have called in a squad of soldiers three minutes ago.*

"He's around," he said.

Haak stepped forward and placed the muzzle of the Luger against Throckmorton's forehead. *"Where?"*

Throckmorton cleared his throat. "The closet. The one over there underneath the Russian boar."

Haak stepped back and glanced up quickly at the huge black trophy head with its curling tusks and insane glass eyes. He gestured with the pistol. "Walk over to the closet—carefully."

Throckmorton eyed him, took one last draw on his cigarette, and butted it in the desk ashtray. Then he began to saunter slowly across the room. Haak followed, keeping his gun arm at full extension with the Luger aimed at the back of Throckmorton's head.

"Stop," the German ordered.

Throckmorton strolled to a halt in front of the closet and began to turn around, habitually putting his left hand into his pants pocket.

"Keep facing the closet door," Haak said, "and keep your hands out of your pockets."

Throckmorton shrugged, removed his hand, and turned the other way.

"Open that door," Haak told him, moving up until he was less than six feet behind the British captain. "And stay in the doorway until I tell you to move."

Throckmorton put his hand on the latch and opened the door, pulling it outward. Haak cocked his head to one side, then the other, trying to see past him. As instructed, Throckmorton remained in place.

"Step aside," Haak growled.

Throckmorton took one long step to the left, revealing the interior of the closet. Egon Zweig was sitting up against the back wall, legs outstretched and hands in his lap, head lolling onto one shoulder. His face was the color of a boiled beet, his tongue protruding from his mouth. His bulging eyes, bright but lifeless, stared out through the doorway in mute shock.

Haak's own eyes fastened onto Zweig's in an uncontrollable reflex.

In that moment of distraction, Stirling dodged out from behind the right-hand doorjamb and shot Hauptsturmfuehrer Ulrich Haak through the left eye with a silenced .22 caliber Hi-Standard automatic pistol.

Chuff.

Haak's gun arm sagged, his knees buckled, and he collapsed onto his back on the floor without a uttering a sound. Blood pooled in his left eye socket; the other stared straight up at the ceiling, as inanimate as the dozens of glass eyes staring down from the walls.

"Excellent marksmanship, Sergeant," Throckmorton commented. "A very clean kill."

"Thank you, sir," Stirling breathed, tucking the automatic with its long silencer back inside his jacket. "Into the closet with him?"

"Most definitely." Throckmorton took one of Haak's boots, Stirling the other, and together they dragged the dead German through the closet doorway.

"We're getting a bit of a body count in the vicinity of this office," Throckmorton said. "That aide, Feder—we'll need to move him in here, as well. Other personnel have too much access to the outer closet, even if it is locked."

"We'll see to it, sir," Stirling replied. "But no rush,

I think. We can make sure the coast is clear. Herr Feder's nicely tucked away in that trash can for the moment."

Throckmorton nodded. "Agreed. Now, I want to look at my dear departed doppelganger here. I wasn't quite doppelganger enough, apparently." He stooped, lifted Zweig's left hand, and pulled the glove off it. "Damnation. He *is* missing half the little finger. A fresh wound. Certainly a dead bloody giveaway if you happened to be in daily contact with the man, eh?" He dropped the hand back into the corpse's lap, collected Zweig's left and right gloves, and stood up. "No way we could have known about this back in England so soon after it happened. We're lucky, Stirling, but we won't press our luck. Strip the fellow down and let's check him for any more unknown anomalies. Who knows? Maybe he's recently had a toe shot off, as well."

"Yes, sir."

As Stirling began to undo the buttons of Zweig's coat, Throckmorton pulled on the dead Standarten-fuehrer's fine black leather gloves. "Mmm. Kid leather," he muttered. "Very nice—and a perfect fit, too. Good thing, because I guess I'll be wearing the left one pretty continuously from now on."

"You could always wrap the finger with a bandage, sir," Stirling said, peeling Zweig's coat off. "Claim it's slow to heal."

"True," Throckmorton returned, "but I rather like the affectation of black leather." He held up his left hand and flexed the fingers inside the glove. "There's something so fundamentally . . . *German* about it. Don't you think, Stirling?"

"Whatever you say, Captain," the commando sergeant replied. "Whatever you say."

Throckmorton exited the closet and walked over to the commander's desk, taking a good look out the windows as he did. Everything seemed normal outside; there was no indication that anyone had noticed anything amiss. There were a few soldiers moving here and there through the continous snowfall, but that was it.

On top of Zweig's desk was an appointment ledger. Throckmorton took another cigarette from the box, lit it, and began to browse through the last few pages of the book, stopping at the current date. There were no entries.

"Huh," Throckmorton grunted. "Lazy bastard."

When he returned to the closet, Stirling had Zweig's body stripped to its underwear. "Nothing else, sir," he reported. "No scars, no abnormalities—everything where it should be, right down to his wedding tackle."

"Fine, Sergeant,'" Throckmorton said. "Tuck the bugger into a corner along with Haak and let's lock them up."

Stirling dragged the bodies into one end of the closet, shoved a large trunk in front of them, and stepped out into the common room. Throckmorton locked the door with the old-style key that protruded from the latch and put it into his pocket.

"Alright, Sergeant," he said, "except for moving Feder, we're done. I can handle my end now. Are you clear on your part in this thing from here on out?"

Stirling nodded. "You've explained it perfectly, sir. Filled in all the blanks."

"I'm sorry about Hurst," Throckmorton said, meeting his eyes.

"Yes, sir," Stirling replied. "I appreciate that, sir."

Throckmorton looked out the window at the falling snow. "You've picked your spot?"

"Yes, sir. That tall pine on the rise just above the north tunnel. I get a clear view over to the German positions on the gorge rim where the tunnel connects to the bridge."

"And you have all your gear? White camouflage shroud, rifle silencer, and such?"

Stirling nodded again. "Yes, sir. If it all goes to hell, I'll be up there doing as much damage to the SS as I can, for as long as I can."

"Very good, then. But remember: only in support of the team blowing the bridge, if they're discovered. Otherwise, sit tight and then slip away once the bridge is gone. If you can link up with some of the others, fine, but try to get back to the Partisans." Throckmorton turned away suddenly, put his fist to his mouth, and coughed violently for several seconds. He stepped to the desk, leaned down, and spat red into the wastepaper basket beside it.

Stirling waited for him to collect himself before speaking. "Well, sir, I think maybe we'd better transfer Feder's body, if there's no one around. I should get moving."

"Fine," Throckmorton said, looking flushed. "Let's see to it, shall we?"

"But first, sir, I'd like to shake your hand."

"Eh?" Throckmorton finished wiping his lips on the back of his glove and raised a skeptical eyebrow.

"I said I'd like to shake your hand, Captain Throckmorton," Stirling said quietly. "That's all."

"Why . . . certainly, Sergeant," Throckmorton replied.

He put his hand out and the two men shook solemnly.

"You're a brave man, sir," Stirling said. "I just wanted to tell you that."

Throckmorton looked at him and smiled his cynical half-smile. "It's easy to be brave when you have no choice, Sergeant. But thank you. Thank you indeed."

"Yes, sir," Stirling said. "You're welcome." He looked down at the floor for a moment, then over at the office door. "Well, then—time to move this Feder bloke."

Quisp had been running for twenty minutes through thigh-deep snow when he finally reached the small series of granite inclines that concealed the cave. He rolled and tumbled the forty-five feet down to the cliff base, mindless of the snow-covered rocks he crashed into, and floundered through the drifts toward the entrance crevice. His lungs were all but frozen solid from sucking in frigid air by the time he staggered into the cave and collapsed to the floor in a spent heap.

"*The train!*" he gasped. "*The train . . . . it's coming . . . maybe ten minutes . . . from the chalet . . . now . . .*"

Merritt leapt to his feet and looked at his watch. "Bloody hell!" he exclaimed. "The damned thing's not supposed to be here until after midnight!" He cut his eyes at Cernović. "How did it make up so much time?"

The Partisan commander shrugged as he scrambled up and collected his small packsack and Mauser carbine. "I don't know, Major," he said. "Maybe your intelligence services underestimated the train's speed—or overestimated the delay caused by the Typhoon attack."

"That's pretty goddamn obvious," Bristow growled, slinging up his Thompson.

Cernović shot him a hard look. "I reported the last information we received from British intelligence to you word for word, Major."

"I believe you, Commander," Merritt said. "I believe you. But it's only thirteen hundred hours right now—the middle of the day. We can't climb that cliff from Zlostup without the cover of night—we'll be spotted from that first antiaircraft battery along the rim. Unless the train stays on this side of the gorge until after dark, we're going to have to try blowing the bridge with just the two supports mined as it goes across."

"But *you* said SOE's *own engineers* said that would not be enough to guarantee the collapse of the spans!" Cernović exclaimed in frustration. "*Žplūgk!* To have come so far and risk complete failure . . . ." He gnashed his teeth and spat. "Major. Those King Tigers must not make it across the bridge to be deployed against my people on the slopes of Mount Zpoda. The

Majevicas are the Partisans' last stronghold in central Yugoslavia. We cannot allow ourselves to be pushed back into Montenegro and Albania."

"Then you'd better hope we planted enough plastic explosive on those first two supports, Commander Cernović," Merritt retorted, starting for the cave entrance, carrying his Sten and demolition rucksack. "Sergeant Bristow! Bring the detonators and the rest of the det cord! Professor Quisp"—he glanced down at the prostrate eccentric as he passed by—"I assume you're going to come back to life at some point. When you do, feel free to rouse Miss Kozo, who is apparently either indisposed or uninterested, and lend us what reinforcement you can at the gorge rim."

"Wh-where is . . . that young sergeant . . . Weiss?" Quisp gasped.

"Gone," Merritt called over his shoulder. "Forget him." He began to run as he entered the cave's entrance passage. "Come on, Bristow!"

The American sergeant hurried out of the cave, swinging two half-empty rucksacks over the same shoulder, with Cernović right behind him. Merritt was already churning up the steep slope beside the crag, digging into the snow with his free hand and driving with his legs. Through the dense curtain of falling snow—from very far off, it seemed—came the faint, drawn-out scream of a train whistle.

By the time Bristow and Cernović reached the top of the crag, gasping for breath, Merritt was already a hundred yards through the trees, following the little footpath that descended gradually to the gorge rim below the northern tunnel and just above the short climb down to Zlostup. He paused in the deep snow and turned, beckoning urgently. Bristow and Cernović steeled themselves and plowed toward him, trying to recover their wind as they went.

Merritt had started down the trail again before he noticed that he had been running along in another set of relatively fresh tracks; they were only partly filled by falling snow. He twisted around as Bristow and Cernović caught up, patting the air with his hand.

"Keep a sharp-eye out!" he whispered. "And no noise. There are new tracks on this trail—probably a German patrol. Maybe only one man, maybe two."

They continued on down the path in a tight, single-file group, no one speaking, dark gray phantom figures moving rapidly through the stunted trees and whirling snow. They were traveling too fast to be truly careful, and each man knew it. At any moment they expected to encounter the enemy in some form—a lone scout, a two-man patrol, or even a full Jagdkommando squad conducting a precautionary sweep of the area prior to the arrival of the approaching train.

Merritt plunged on through the drifts as the vast gray emptiness of the Zpoda Gorge appeared through the trees. The snowfall had lightened somewhat; he could just make out the entire head wall through the blizzard's gray veil, the Zpoda Skyway Bridge curving in a dark arc across the top of the granite face beneath the huge, overhanging rock cap.

The throaty scream of the train whistle pierced the air again, reverberating off the cliffs and crags. It was much closer this time. Merritt willed his aching legs to carry him even faster. Up ahead, through the snow-laden evergreens, he caught a glimpse of the stone-work that formed the foundation of the north tunnel. . . . The horizontal steel girders of the bridge itself where it joined the tunnel's southern exit . . . the sheer drop down the granite face beneath it . . . and a sandbagged machine-gun nest—

Merritt dove to his left, toward the very rim of the gorge, and belly-flopped into deep snow. He could feel some part of Bristow's body strike his boot and hear the sergeant grunt as he duplicated the maneuver immediately behind him. A third light thump in the snow and Cernović was down, too.

Merritt kept his head low as Bristow wormed up beside him on his left. A few seconds later Cernović's swarthy Gypsy face appeared to his right.

"Machine-gun nest," Merritt whispered, pointing a gloved finger. "Right above the climb down to Zlostup. It's level with the train tracks, just to the side of the tunnel. About a hundred yards ahead. See it?"

"Goddammit," Bristow muttered. "That wasn't there yesterday."

"They must have just put it there this morning," Merritt replied, pulling a small set of powerful binoculars from his rucksack. He focused through the trees. "Probably a precaution to defend the approaches to the bridge as the train goes across."

"Do you think they know about Zlostup?" Cernović asked. "Maybe they've set up to sweep it clear if they see anyone on it."

"I don't think so," Merritt said. "They could fire down the four hundred vertical feet to Zlostup, but they're not oriented in that direction. They've got that gun angled more toward the woods, as if they think any attack might come from the trees." He passed the binoculars to Bristow. "I imagine they want to stop sappers with charges from getting to the southern mouth of the tunnel and the first bridge span. I don't think they're worried too much about the main supports and footings way down the cliff. They probably don't consider them accessible."

"MG-42 with a two-man team," Bristow growled, squinting through the binoculars at the nest. "Nobody's runnin' into that chopper and livin' to tell the tale."

"Nobody's going to, Sergeant," Merritt whispered. He glanced at Cernović. "We can crawl over the rim about twenty yards ahead, climb down below the edge where we can't be seen, and traverse through the broken rock to the head of Zlostup where we left the end of the detonator cord we laid out along the trail."

Merritt was interrupted by a series of thumping and

clanking sounds from the direction of the chalet, accompanied by blasts of what was obviously high-pressure steam being vented.

"They're uncoupling the mufti's private car, I expect," he muttered. "Leaving it on the siding." He looked back at Cernović. "Anyway, we put a short time-delay fuse on the end of the det cord and activate it once we see the train moving onto the bridge. Then we get the hell out of here."

Cernović grimaced. "But, Major, again—we do not have enough supports mined! What if the bridge doesn't fall? What if only one span collapses and three-quarters of the Tiger tanks make it to Mount Zpoda? We have to set more charges!"

"You tell me how," Merritt shot back in frustration. "I'd take any chance if I thought we might succeed, but in broad daylight there's no way to backtrack along Zlostup without being—"

"Holy shit, Major," Bristow grunted, focusing the binoculars on the head wall. "You're not going to believe this. . . ."

Theobald Quisp had lain on the stone floor of the cave for nearly twenty minutes, praying that his lungs would eventually defrost and permit him to breathe properly once more. Finally, when the raw, burning pains had stopped lancing through his chest with every inhalation, when his heart had slowed from a crazed paradiddle to a brisk, steady thump, he got laboriously to his feet and began to stagger toward the rear of the cave. *From a purely physical standpoint,* he thought, *it's bloody terrible to get old.*

He dropped to one knee beside Sylvia Kozo's groundsheet-swaddled form and tapped her gently on the shoulder. "Wake up, my dear," he sighed. "There's work to be done, don't you know? 'Course you do!"

When the young woman didn't move, he tapped again, a little harder.

"Come now, little one," he coaxed. " 'Stiffen the sinews, summon up the blood . . . and once more unto the breech'—to play fast and loose with the inviolate verse of the Bard, damn me! We have companions who need support, do we not? Yes, we do!"

There was still no sign of movement. Tired and exasperated, Quisp clapped a hand down and shook hard.

"Miss Kozo!" he barked. "Arise, I say!"

The carefully arranged bundle of coats and tarpaulins fell apart beneath the groundsheet that covered them. Quisp swept the canvas to one side, probed the loose pile for a second or two, then sat back on his heels and peered quickly around the cave.

But Sylvia Kozo was gone.

"Jeezus H. Christ," Bristow muttered, squinting through the binoculars. "It's her. It's that crazy Partisan broad."

"What?" The same astonished exclamation escaped Merritt and Cernović in unison. "Where?" Merritt added quickly.

"On the goddamn bridge," Bristow said. "Or rather . . . *under it.*" He handed the binoculars back to the British major. "About halfway between the first and second vertical support members."

Merritt focused, searching. Then he saw her. "Jesus bloody Christ," he muttered.

"That's about what I said," Bristow grunted.

"I can't make her out," Cernović said. "Still too much snow falling, I think."

"That's good," Merritt returned. "Maybe the Germans in that antiaircraft battery back behind us won't be able to see her, either. Or in this machine-gun nest up ahead."

"I don't think anybody's gonna be able to see her from the tracks or the tunnel area," Bristow put in, "as long as she stays up under those girders."

"What exactly is she doing?" Cernović pressed.

Merritt passed him the binoculars. "You have to see it to believe it, Commander. Look carefully: right up underneath the second span."

Cernović raised the glasses to his eyes. At first, through a thin gauze of falling snow, he could see only the massive gray-black girders, rivets, gussets, and doubler plates that made up the steel skeleton of the bridge. He focused and concentrated. Then a movement caught his eye.

Sylvia Kozo, clad in her familiar black shorts, old undershirt, black slippers, and rabbit-fur hat, was making her way steadily along the span—hanging upside down from the outermost horizontal support girder. She was clinging to the lower flange of the huge steel I beam with hands and heels. Her only concession to the freezing climate and her own torn fingers, apparently, had been a pair of dark gloves. She was wearing her small, light climbing harness, and from it swung her collection of wired nuts and carabiners. A large coil of rope was draped over her shoulder and across her chest like a bandolier.

"What the hell's she thinkin'?" Bristow rumbled. "What's she gonna do up there—start takin' apart nuts and bolts? She ain't got no charges with her."

"I'll tell you what she's going to do," Merritt said. "She's going to tie off that rope at the third vertical support and rappel down to the footing. Then she's going to try to finish mining the third and fourth bridge footings before the train starts to cross."

Bristow looked at him. "But how's she gonna do that?" he exclaimed in a hoarse whisper. "I left the last two sets of charges tied together in pairs and draped over the number two footin'. That little gal can't tote them four boxes across a hundred and twenty feet of cliff by herself. Then she's gotta place 'em right and run the det cord to string 'em all together! How many trips back and forth is that, even if she can carry the charges? Six? Eight? She's gonna get spotted, Major!"

Merritt chewed his lower lip for a moment in silence. Then he made up his mind. "She's got something figured out," he said, "or she wouldn't be there. As far as her being spotted, we might be able to prevent that." He turned onto his side and looked back the way they had come. "The only SS with a good view of the cliff and bridge supports are manning that first antiaircraft gun emplacement." He caught Bristow's eye. "Sergeant, do you think you can clean house up there without attracting any attention?"

Bristow nodded with a hard smile. "That's what I do, Major. It's what Frank D'Amato did, too. Betcha he'll be watchin' my back."

"Do you have the necessary tools?"

The big sergeant patted his chest. "Silenced Hi-Standard right here, sir," he growled. "Stiletto in my boot. That's all I need."

"Right," Merritt said. "Go. Be careful, but hurry. Commander Cernović and I will work our way down to where we can monitor the girl's progress and put the fuse on this end of the det cord. Work your way back as soon as you can. . . . If you can."

Bristow nodded once more and began to squirm backward through the snow, keeping low. "Remember," Merritt called softly, "it's about not raising the alarm. No noise, Sergeant."

"Yessir." Bristow worked his way over a little rise, out of sight of the machine-gun nest, then got to his feet and hustled back up the rim trail.

"All right," Merritt breathed. "We've got to move, too, Commander. Are you ready?"

"Yes," Cernović replied. He was silent for a moment. "I'd hate to see anything happen to Sylvia."

"So would I," Merritt told him. "But she's taken matters into her own hands. All we can do is try our best to give her support. And Commander"—Merritt turned and looked at him directly—"just so you know: if that train pulls out onto that bridge, I'm waiting until the last possible moment and then I'm firing those charges—no matter where Sylvia Kozo is."

He crawled forward through the snow and low evergreens, leaving Cernović staring darkly after him, his jaw muscles working.

"*Žplagk!*" the Partisan commander swore, and began crawling along in Merritt's track.

Chapter Eighteen

Sergeant David Weiss had crossed the tracks several hundred yards north of the tunnel and siding, under cover of the incessant snowfall, and worked his way around to the northwest corner of the chalet compound, keeping to the trees. There he had found a perfect spot: a thirty-foot-high granite crag with a shallow ledge just beneath its overhanging crest. The ledge was concealed by drifted snow and just large enough to accommodate a man lying at full length.

The ledge was about ten feet higher than the stone wall enclosing the compound, and offered a clear view down into the inner quadrangle. The linear distance from the ledge to the sentry box on the northwest corner of the wall was approximately 100 feet—quite close—and another 250 feet to the front door of the chalet great house, for a total of 350 feet. The view from the great house door to the arched main gate was unrestricted. By a stroke of good luck, the two sandbagged machine-gun positions on the wall were located beside the southeast and southwest corner sentry boxes—oriented, understandably enough, toward the Partisan forces to the south. Single sentries paced slowly back and forth on the north wall—one for each of the two remaining corner boxes—trying to keep warm.

In the dense trees immediately below and to the left of the ledge, there was an old wooden shack— perhaps once used for the hanging of game meat— that was on the verge of collapse from the weight of the snow that had accumulated on its roof. The windows were broken out of it, and through one of them Weiss could see the shack's dark, dirty interior. It was less than fifty feet away, looking down at a forty-five-degree angle. There was no evidence that it was currently being used for anything.

He settled back into the deepest recess of the rock cavity, taking care not to disturb the drifted snow in front of him. Well shielded from the wind and insulated by the high-quality German white-camouflage anorak and pants he had put on over his regular winter combat clothing, he felt almost warm. That was good, because he had no idea how long he would have to lie within the confines of the ledge without moving. Waiting.

The .45-caliber De Lisle silenced carbine was an unusual weapon, specifically designed by the SOE for the covert removal of sentries. It was basically a standard-issue Lee Enfield infantry rifle, cut down until virtually only the stock remained. It had been rechambered for the subsonic .45-caliber pistol round, and its new nine-inch barrel was encased along its entire abbreviated length by a two-inch-diameter silencer. It made for a strange, clumsy-looking weapon—like a rifle stock with a foot-long section of thick black pipe grafted to it—but in the hands of expert commando marksmen like David Weiss, the De Lisle had proven to be deadly accurate at up to 250 yards and, as a result of its below-the-speed-of-sound ammunition and huge silencer, completely noiseless.

Using the utmost care, Weiss cut a deep, narrow groove with the edge of his hand through the wave-shaped snowdrift that concealed his vantage point—just enough to accept the long, fat silencer of the De Lisle and allow him an unhindered view of the area between the compound's main entrance and the great house. Then he settled the odd rifle into position, ensuring that its muzzle did not protrude beyond the front of the drift, and got himself as comfortable as possible.

With typical efficiency, the Germans had placed high-powered lights around the compound, Weiss noted; some on poles, others mounted on the compound wall and the eaves of the chalet buildings. That was good. He had no doubt that they'd be lit after dark, and if the gamecock didn't make the trek between his private rail car and what was clearly the division headquarters office in the great house before then, he'd nevertheless be easy to see in the glare of the floodlights.

These had been Merritt's final words to him as he'd departed the cave:

"The gamecock you're hunting now has the white turban of a Muslim cleric, Weiss. Remember that . . . a white turban. He won't be seen without it. It's his badge of office."

Gamecock. The same bird General Gubbins had so casually referred to during the interview at SOE headquarters in London.

Weiss stared grimly over the sights of the De Lisle. He'd been waltzed into position like a puppet on strings. And *oh* how the puppet masters loved their game.

Hauptsturmfuehrer Matthias Juttner tucked the wool scarf a little tighter around his neck and turned up the collar of his black leather greatcoat. His ears stung from the cold, but his peaked SS cap looked less elegant when it was combined with earmuffs or the like, and it was important to make a solid first impression on the Handschar rank and file. Latent intimidation always made doors easier to open—and easier to walk through.

He stepped down from the forward-end platform of the mufti's private car and backed away from it a few paces, his jackboots crunching in the snow. The rolling stock that made up al-Husseini's original train—SS escort bunk car, antiaircraft flatcar, private coach, and caboose—was now parked on the siding directly in front of the main chalet compound gate and had just been uncoupled from the lead locomotive of the King Tiger train. The big engine was now some two hundred yards away, backing the train up onto the main line again in preparation to cross the Zpoda Skyway Bridge. True to his word, Standartenfuehrer Kronstadt was wasting no time in dispensing with the inconvenient Grand Mufti of Jerusalem and his entourage and proceeding to his priority destination on the slopes of Mount Zpoda.

Snowflakes were catching on Juttner's eyelashes; he blinked them away, then pulled his coat cuff back and glanced at his watch. Midafternoon. Both the Tiger train and the Grand Mufti were at Barbo House at least ten hours earlier than anticipated. The hard-driving Kronstadt had let no grass grow under his feet in Bljak and spared no coal in getting the train up the Majevica foothills.

Well . . . time to announce al-Husseini to the commander of the Muslim SS Division Handschar. The mufti might as well start moving about in the fresh air instead of hibernating in his private car. Juttner smacked his leather-gloved hands together, turned, and began to stride purposefully up the short, snow-packed incline toward the chalet compound gate.

Pushing the raggedly dressed girl ahead of him with a hand clamped on the back of her neck, Hauptsturmfuehrer Julius Neurath descended the steps of the private car's rear-end platform, his long coat flapping around his jackboots, and began to march up the siding next to the caboose. A couple of Muslim troopers loitering nearby took notice, but quickly turned away. What a well-connected Aryan dressed in what looked ominously like Gestapo plainclothes did was his business, and his alone.

With a few surreptitious glances over his shoulder, Neurath hurried the girl past the caboose and up the tracks about seventy-five yards. Then he redirected her toward the wooded area just north of the chalet compound. Very soon they were off the rail bed and moving into the trees, all but hidden by the falling snow.

Neurath was in his usual foul mood, made even worse by the incessant carping of the mufti and Juttner's relentless sly mockery. He needed release. True release. And at the same time, he needed to take out the trash. It wouldn't do to be caught with this little Jewess—for that is what he had decided she was—in his quarters, and besides, she whimpered too much. Like right now. Her terrified sniveling was getting on his nerves. One more day, he knew, and he would be thoroughly bored with her.

Better to do it now while he was still interested enough to draw some pleasure from the act.

"Do my eyes deceive me," Handschar antiaircraft gunner Muhammed Korkut said to the Scharfuehrer beside him, "or is that something swinging from the bridge?"

"What?" The Scharfuehrer, whose name was Turku, stepped past the 40-millimeter automatic cannon and squinted across the gun emplacement's top row of sandbags. "How, by the Beard of the Great Bey, can you see all the way to the cliff through this cursed snow?"

"I'm telling you, Scharfuehrer Turku, I caught a glimpse of something. Something swinging like a pen-

dulum around the base of the . . . one, two . . . the
third upright support from the north. Look! There it
is again! It swung to the base of the fourth support
and stopped there!"

. "Korkut," the Scharfuehrer said, his dark face twist-
ing into a scowl, "I warned you several days ago that
I would no longer tolerate you sneaking that putrid
Lebanese hashish into your cigarette tobacco."

The Bosnian Muslim gunner whirled. "Let's get this
straight between us, Turku," he snarled. "Now that
you've been promoted to Scharfuehrer, you can come
and go as you please—spend as much time as you
like hanging around the soup wagon near the officer's
outpost down behind the ridge. But we're stuck up
here in this isolated shit hole, freezing our balls off,
day in and day out." The other two enlisted men in
the emplacement, seated on planks next to the sandbag walls, giggled. "What's it to you if we share a
little something to take the edge off the cold? Eh?"

"If I catch you again," Turku said, "it's punishment
detail for you."

"Bah!" Korkut jerked his head around and squinted
at the head wall again. "There's something there, I
tell you. . . . Something strange . . ."

The Scharfuehrer sighed. He liked his new noncom-
missioned rank, but didn't like the dissention—the
resentment—it had caused in the two weeks since his
promotion. "Very well, Korkut," he said. "Let's have
another look. Mahmet! Glasses!"

One of the enlisted men got slowly to his feet and
picked up a set of Zeiss binoculars. "Here you are,
Scharfuehrer," he said, bringing them over. Turku
took the glasses; the soldier moved back against the
sandbags to join his friend in a standing stretch,
yawning.

"There, see?" Korkut said, leaning forward and
pointing. "A line of some kind hanging down from
the bridge. I can just barely see it."

"By Shaitan, you're right!" Turku exclaimed. "And

321

there's somebody moving around on the base of the fourth upright. Mahmet," he said without turning around, "ring up division headquarters. Find out if there is some kind of work being done on ropes underneath the north spans of the Zpoda Skyway Bridge."

"Do you see any workers on the bridge itself?" Korkut demanded.

"No," the Scharfuehrer replied, "just the one person." He stared a few seconds longer, then lowered the binoculars. "Mahmet! Are you going to ring headquarters or not?"

He looked behind him in irritation. Mahmet and his friend were crumpled on top of each other in the frozen mud at the base of the sandbag wall.

"Korkut!" Scharfuehrer Turku blurted, reaching for his sidearm. The Muslim gunner spun around, alarmed by the urgency in the sergeant's voice.

Chuff.

Turku's chin snapped down onto his chest and he pitched forward on his face.

Muhammed Korkut's final yell was cut off before it left his throat by the fourth .22-caliber slug from the silenced automatic, which tore through his larynx from behind, just to the left of his spinal column. He gurgled once, half turning and reaching for his collar, and Bristow, who'd been lurking on the outside of the sandbag wall, finished him off with a fifth shot to his left temple. The gunner dropped like a stone on top of Turku.

Glancing around quickly, Bristow scrambled over the sandbags and crouched down inside the emplacement, out of sight. After checking that all four SS men were truly dead, he picked up the Zeiss glasses the Scharfuehrer had dropped and cautiously focused them on the head wall, keeping low.

He was just in time to see, through the veil of falling snow, a tiny figure in black shorts and a white undershirt swing on the end of a long thread from the fourth to the third bridge support footing.

Once again, Sylvia Kozo was working too hard to feel the bitter cold that enveloped her partly clad body. Having secured the rope to the underside of the bridge span just behind the third vertical support girder, she'd rappelled down the one hundred feet to the footing, concealed from view by the girder itself. She hadn't lingered long; in a great, looping arc, running across the rock face on the end of the rope, she'd swung over to the second footing.

Then the manual labor had begun. One by one, she'd hauled the four dangling boxes of explosives up onto the concrete pad and taken them—tied to her harness two at a time—back to the third footing. Then she'd planted two of the boxes on the base of the third support girder as she'd seen Bristow and Merritt do on the first and second, and carried the remaining two boxes over to the fourth footing.

By the time all the charges were placed, her arms and legs were trembling and she was gasping for breath. It had taken a total of five great swings, fully exposed to any watching eyes on the gorge rim, to transfer the explosives from the second to the third and fourth footings. The falling snow provided some cover, no doubt, reducing long-distance visibility, but it was still broad daylight. That she hadn't been spotted, she concluded, was nothing short of a miracle.

The only thing left to do was swing back to the second footing once more and collect the long coil of detonator cord Bristow had left there. Run it across the cliff to the third and fourth supports, tie it into the charges, and the task was done. The far end of the detonator cord was lying on the Zlostup trail head just below the rim of the gorge. All Merritt or one of his men had to do was attach a short fuse and detonator to it and wait for the train to cross.

Sylvia took a deep breath, tensed, and lunged out yet again into empty space on the end of the rope, swinging toward the third footing.

"Standartenfuehrer Zweig insists that you come to the chalet great house immediately," Juttner told the Grand Mufti. "Word of your arrival has spread, and the imams and Muslim troops are anxious to see you. The Standartenfuehrer also wishes me to convey to you that he cannot ensure your security while you remain aboard your private car, and that you should enter the compound without delay."

Al-Husseini remained hunched in his favorite armchair. "No," he said, his eyes furtive, nervous. "I shall remain here until the locomotives return to take me back down to the flatlands. Zweig can no more guarantee that there are no Partisan sharpshooters nearby in this front-line area than I can turn lead into gold." He fluttered his fingers in a cranky, dismissive gesture. "That is my final word on it."

Mustapha Snagi, leaning against the wall with legs crossed and arms folded, stirred and crossed his legs the other way.

"Your Excellency," Juttner said, "the very purpose for which you have come to Yugoslavia, as per the Fuehrer's wishes, is right outside this door. The men of the SS Division Handschar know you are here and long to catch even a glimpse of you. What it would mean to their morale . . ."

"I will conduct a rotating series of lectures for visiting Handschar imams from the safety of Belgrade," the mufti declared, "which was always my intent. I will not expose myself to these front-line conditions." Then his frightened eyes narrowed and Juttner could see his mind working. "But you are correct. Perhaps the men stationed here should at least see their spiritual leader firsthand as he visits the division commander's office. . . ."

It had just occurred to al-Husseini that it was in his

best interest to ensure that at least some of the Muslim troops in Handschar be able to corroborate the fact that he had been at the front in person. . . . In case his movements became an issue with Hitler at some later date.

"Yes," he mused, stroking his beard with two fingers. "I think that the good Muslim soldiers of Handschar's headquarters garrison deserve to see the Grand Mufti of Jerusalem in their midst, even from a distance. . . ."

The long, loud scream of a steam whistle jolted everyone's nerves. The King Tiger train was on the move. Out of idle exasperation with the mufti and his own natural interest, Juttner stepped over to one of the private car's boarded-up windows and peered out through a crack between planks, looking toward the main tracks and the wooded area beyond. Through the whirling snow, something caught his attention on the far side of the rail bed, just at the edge of the trees.

Abruptly he backed away and headed for the front door of the car.

"Your pardon, Your Excellency," he said quickly. "I must attend to something."

And then, to the Grand Mufti's considerable pleasure, he strode through the forward exit and disappeared.

"Snagi," al-Husseini commanded, "come here."

Sylvia made one final outward swing to the fourth footing, the blue-and-red detonator cord tied into her harness and trailing behind her. Once on top of the concrete pad, she pulled the slack out of it, wrapped it three times around the plastic explosive inside the first crate, then did the same with the second, making certain in both cases that the cord was well buried in the waxy compound.

A last swing back and she was on the third footing, the rope hanging straight down from the bridge span overhead. As she summoned her remaining strength and prepared to climb, the muted blast of the train whistle sounded again, echoing through the gray emptiness of the Zpoda Gorge.

She had considered rappelling down to Zlostup and rejoining Merritt's team that way, but the newly placed German machine-gun nest above the trailhead made using the trail impossible. Anyone approaching on Zlostup from the south, coming off the head wall, would be spotted. It was climb up to the bridge and crawl along its underside back the way she had come, or nothing. And there was no time to waste, because from the sound of the steam whistle, the train could emerge from the tunnel and move out onto the bridge at any moment. Sylvia had not the slightest doubt that Merritt or any one of his men would blow the bridge at the crucial moment, regardless of whether or not she was in the clear. So, for that matter, would Comrade Cernović.

And so would she, if their positions were reversed. The destruction of not just the Zpoda Skyway Bridge, but the Zpoda Skyway Bridge *and* the King Tiger train, was that vital. It was worth however many lives it took to do it.

But, truth admitted, one did not stop trying to live. Not even if, with failing hands and trembling arms, a simple hundred-foot climb up a rope looked more like a thousand.

Sylvia wiped the palms of her blood-soaked gloves on her black shorts, flexed her fingers around the rope, gritted her teeth, and began to climb.

Juttner bounded over the main tracks ahead of the oncoming locomotive and trotted toward the three gray figures he'd spotted emerging from the trees. The King Tiger train was still some distance away, moving slowly forward. There were constant intermittent blasts of steam as the engineers on each of the eight locomotives checked boiler pressures for the upcoming run across the bridge and up the shoulder of Mount Zpoda.

The SS Hauptsturmfuehrer glanced left and right as he hurried along, his black leather greatcoat flapping against his jackboots. There were few other soldiers around, and most of them had congregated in the vicinity of the tunnel entrance and the approach to the chalet compound. As had been the case all day, the falling snow was a ubiquitous gray shroud that obscured both detail and motion.

He held up a hand as he approached the three men. Two were helmeted Handschar SS troopers, bundled up for patrol. The third man, who was stumbling along between them, wore a British military issue olive drab jacket and battle harness. His head was bare and he appeared to be half dazed, disoriented. A trickle of blood ran down the side of his face from an ugly gash in his temple.

"Halt!" Juttner ordered, moving in close. "What do we have here?"

Seeing the immaculate SS uniform with its peaked death's-head cap and captain's insignia, the two Muslim troopers drew themselves up straight but did not salute, opting instead to keep their machine pistols trained on the man between them. "A prisoner, Herr Hauptsturmfuehrer," one of them said. "He was moving through the trees near the gorge rim, only a few hundred yards from the tunnel. Sturmmann Ibrahimović"—he indicated the other trooper— "stepped out from behind a tree and struck him on the head with his weapon when he walked past." The first man unslung a Sten gun from his shoulder and held it up. "He was carrying this."

"Does he say who he is?" Juttner asked, peering at the man's unshaven face.

"He claims to be a Muslim deserter from the Partisan Army," the trooper said. "He claims his name is Sulejman Hafiz and that he wishes to join the SS Division Handschar." The soldier scowled. "But he is well

John McKinna

equipped for a deserter, do you not think? This is a British weapon."

"The British and Americans drop their weapons and equipment to the Partisans all the time," Juttner remarked. "His clothing and gear tell us only that he is not in the German military. More likely he is a Partisan scout, lurking around to see if there is an easy way to disrupt operations at the bridge. You!" he demanded in Serbo-Croatian, addressing the prisoner. "You do not look like a Muslim to me. And you do not have the look of a deserter. You are a Partisan spy, aren't you?"

"Ugh—" the man grunted, his eyelids fluttering.

Juttner slapped him hard across the mouth with his gloved hand. The prisoner's head jerked up and back, but he did not cry out. "Silence!" Juttner barked. "Don't even attempt to lie to me!" He looked at each of the SS troopers in turn. "We want information from this fellow. We will escort him to Standartenfuehrer Zweig's office immediately. Bring him along quickly, and say nothing to anyone as we go. I do not wish to raise an unnecessary alarm while the Grand Mufti is present. Do both of you understand me?"

The two SS troopers stiffened again and nodded. "*Jawohl,* Herr Hauptsturmfuehrer," they chorused.

"Very well. Bring him."

Juttner spun on his heel and stalked back the way he had come, eyeing the soldiers around the tunnel entrance and compound gate. Behind him, the two troopers thumped their fists into the prisoner's back, driving him forward, and followed.

The four men marched briskly down the siding tracks, the prisoner stumbling occasionally between the two SS troopers, and past the Grand Mufti's private car. Juttner led them up the incline to the compound gate, pushing a bow wave of Nazi officiousness that parted the Muslim troopers, loitering in his path, like the Red Sea before Moses. He did not even deign to look at Schütze Fikret Pandža, who was still on guard duty at the gate, wondering when his double ration of hot soup and buttered bread would arrive.

The prisoner was hustled through the archway and across the compound to the front of the chalet great house. Juttner mounted the stone steps to the large vestibule and opened the front door.

"Inside with him!" he ordered, drawing his Luger. He waited as the two troopers shoved the weaving captive through the doorway, then followed, closing the door behind him.

They were in the deserted outer office of Zweig's aide, Feder. Juttner walked past the aide's desk and knocked on the door to the division commander's inner sanctum, the greathouse trophy-and-common room.

"Who is it?" a voice shouted.

"Your pardon, Standartenfuehrer Zweig," Juttner called. "It is Hauptsturmfuehrer Juttner again. I only just spoke to you about receiving the Grand Mufti."

"Juttner?" the voice said. "Enter."

The SS Hauptsturmfuehrer pushed open the door and grunted over his shoulder, "Bring the prisoner."

He marched across the spacious common room and stopped three paces from Zweig's desk with a sharp click of his heels and a Nazi salute. *"Heil Hitler!"* he rapped out. Behind him, the two Muslim troopers came to a halt, jostling the prisoner between them.

Throckmorton rose out of his chair, removing the reading glasses with which he had been perusing daily reports, and flipped his hand back. *"Heil Hitler."* His eyes roved over the two troopers and their captive. "What's the meaning of this intrusion, Juttner?" he demanded.

"This man claims to be a Partisan deserter, Herr Standartenfuehrer," Juttner explained. "A Muslim—or so he says. He was captured by these two excellent troopers while they were on patrol near the gorge rim. He states that he wishes to join the SS Division Handschar."

"Indeed?" Throckmorton peered at the wobbling captive. "What is your name, Partisan?"

"Sulejman Hafiz," Major Walter Merritt said.

"Huh!" Throckmorton drew back and examined Merritt from head to toe. "He doesn't look like much of a Muslim to me," he said. "Take him out and shoot him."

As the two SS troopers grinned and seized Merritt by the upper arms, Juttner raised a gloved finger. "Excuse me, sir, but shouldn't we interrogate him first? I'm sure that with a little . . . motivation . . . he could be convinced to tell us everything he knows about the lastest Partisan troop movements. That is, unless he truly *is* a deserter who wishes to join Handschar—in which case he should be only too happy to bring us up to date."

Throckmorton scratched his chin and nodded. "You have a point, Juttner, you have a point." He regarded each of the two troopers in turn. "An excellent job of picking up this specimen, for which you will both be commended," he said. "Hauptsturmfuehrer Juttner and I will have a word with him. You are dismissed. Oh, and in light of the Grand Mufti's presence here, you will not speak of this capture to anyone for the time being, not even your fellow soldiers. That is a direct order. Do you understand?"

"*Jawohl,* Herr Standartenfuehrer."

"*Jawohl,* Herr Standartenfuehrer."

"Good," Throckmorton said. "You may go."

The Muslim troopers saluted and departed, closing the door behind them. Merritt was left standing in a puddle of melting snow, his left eye swollen partly shut from the bloody smash on his temple and brow.

Throckmorton sat back down behind his desk as Juttner turned to face the British major. Merritt locked eyes with the SS Hauptsturmfuehrer. Then his mouth twisted into a pained smile.

"Well, Matthew," he said in English, "do you think

it's safe for me to sit down for a moment now—before I fall down?"

"It's fine with me, Walter," Juttner replied in kind, "but perhaps you'd better ask Duncan. After all, it's his office."

Chapter Nineteen

"The train," Merritt said to Throckmorton. "It's here early. We've only got the bridge supports partly mined." He winced, stiffening in the armchair as Juttner dabbed at the open wound on his temple with a disinfectant swab. "It's building steam to move onto the bridge as we speak, isn't it? Can you stop it? Buy us some more time?"

Throckmorton shrugged helplessly. "On what pretext? That train's movements are the responsibility of the tank unit commander charged with getting his King Tigers to Mount Zpoda. I have no plausible excuse for stopping it."

"Kronstadt," Juttner said. "His name is Kronstadt. SS Standartenfuehrer. And he's not the type to hold up for anyone without an ironclad reason."

"The only way I could delay the train," Throckmorton said, "would be to declare the bridge unsafe—which would result in an inspection and the discovery of the explosives. It would defeat the whole bloody purpose. . . ." His voice trailed off in frustration. "And we all have our separate missions, Walter. You know that. You know we're bound by the Prime Minister's Priority Directives. We daren't jeopardize my position here, or Matthew's vital placement. There is only so much we can do right now, or all our plans for the future—and all the unforseen opportunities that may come our way—will be lost."

"You have to get me out of here now," Merritt said, rising unsteadily to his feet. "The bridge is partly rigged to blow. It may be completely rigged by now, for all I know. I have Cernović positioned at the Zlostup trailhead, ready to ignite the fuse on the main cord detonator when the train's lead engines pass the fourth vertical support."

"How could it be completely rigged?" Throckmorton asked. "Who did it in broad daylight?"

"Sylvia," Merritt replied. "She must have slipped out of the cave when I was dozing. Took it on·herself. She climbed out on the underside of the bridge spans and rappelled down to the footings to place the·rest of the explosives. She may or not have finished. I didn't see. I had to try to divert those two damned sentries when they suddenly came through the trees near the rim where Cernović and I were hiding. We were too close to a new machine-gun nest—any commotion would have alerted the crew manning it. So I had to draw the sentries back into the woods, away from Cernović and the machine gun."

"So you diverted their attention by allowing one of them to bash you in the head with a machine pistol?" Juttner remarked, taping gauze over Merritt's temple.

Merritt sent him a dry glance. "That wasn't my original idea," he said, "but that's the way it worked out. And incidentally, you didn't have to cuff me so hard across the mouth out there on the railroad tracks."

"For benefit of those two SS troopers, old boy," Juttner replied, clapping him on the upper arm. "Realism counts in this business, as you know perfectly well."

"Of course." Merritt looked from Throckmorton to Juttner and back again. "I have to get out of here," he reiterated. "I know you can't help me without jeopardizing your own separate missions, but I have to get to the bridge and do what I can."

"There is a conveniently dead Jagdkommando Hauptsturmfuehrer dressed in SS winter combat clothing in that closet over there," Throckmorton said, pointing. "He's behind the chest at the far end, along with Zweig and his aide. He's about your size. Why don't you try on his things, wrap your face up, slip out the back window like Stirling did, and stroll out through the front gate. You should be able to duck into the trees again without too much trouble and get down to Zlostup."

"What choice do I have?" Merritt muttered, hurrying toward the closet door.

"I'll help him," Juttner said to Throckmorton. "You'd better stay at your desk, eh?"

"Yes." Throckmorton let out a short sigh as Juttner moved after Merritt. "Do you know what just occurred to me?"

"I haven't the foggiest," Juttner said over his shoulder.

"I was just thinking," Throckmorton went on, "that it's been an awfully long time since we three had ales and bangers and mash in Picadilly together. A long time since school days at Oxford."

Juttner managed a smile before he ducked into the closet after Merritt. "A long time, Duncan," he said. "And awfully far away."

Quisp watched from the trees as a stocky man of middle height, wearing a fine winter overcoat, thick scarf over his nose and mouth, and a strange, wedge-shaped white turban on his head descended the forward steps of the luxury passenger railcar on the siding and hurried, in the company of several uniformed SS bodyguards, toward the chalet gate. To most Europeans, the turban would have been an anonymous curiosity; nothing more. But the culturally astute Quisp recognized it for what it was: the headgear of a senior Muslim cleric.

Interesting . . . but not more interesting than the fact that the luxury car that had just disgorged the cleric was sitting on slightly inclined rails—rails that inclined to the south and declined to the north. The car's manual brakes and those of the caboose, bunk car, and antiaircraft flatcar to which it was coupled were all that prevented it from rolling back down the siding the way it had come.

Again . . . interesting. A possibility with potential. Quisp just adored possibilities with potential. Galileo and Leonardo would have been lost without them.

And here was something else interesting: the massive, oncoming bulk of the King Tiger train, five great black locomotives huffing and screeching and steaming, tank-laden flatcars stretching down the track behind them as far as the eye could see. Quisp could feel the ground vibrate through the snow as the train rumbled up abreast of him at five miles per hour. Heading for the tunnel to the bridge.

The snowfall, which had lightened but never ceased throughout the day, was becoming heavier again, further reducing visibility and obscuring detail. Soldiers would soon be only vague gray shapes at more than fifty yards.

Slowly Quisp rose to his full height behind a convenient evergreen, watching the King Tiger train rumble and clank by at its snail's pace. He shifted his Schmeisser to the crook of his elbow and dug into his pocket for a piece of dried beef he'd been saving.

A little snack, a little more train watching, and then it would be time for a stroll.

Weiss had first caught the movement out of the corner of his eye.

A pinch-faced Aryan type with the plainclothes look

of a Gestapo officer had come through the trees near the dilapidated little shack below and to his left. Stumbling along in front of him through knee-deep snow, her long black hair flyaway and her ragged coat clutched around her, was a teenaged girl. She was being driven forward by the scruff of her neck, and she was absolutely terrified.

Weiss had been unable to look away as the German, noticing the shack, had dragged the girl inside it and thrown her down on the filthy floor. She'd tried to crawl away, but he'd kicked her to a wall and hovered over her, opening his coat and unbuckling the belt of his trousers.

Weiss had little doubt what was about to happen next. He could hear the German snarling at the girl above her quiet sobbing.

He refocused his attention down the barrel of the De Lisle. The fate of one more refugee was none of his business. He would not give away his position, not risk missing a clear shot at the Grand Mufti of Jerusalem, for the sake of one Yugoslav girl. Thousands if not millions of rapes had already occurred in Europe throughout the course of the war and there would be thousands if not millions more before it was done.

His people needed deliverance from a mortal enemy, and his brother needed to be avenged. That was all that mattered.

He flinched as the girl let out a little shriek.

Then, through the veil of falling snow, he saw what he had been waiting for. Coming through the compound gate at a brisk walk, waving and nodding to the sentries and soldiers of the SS Division Handschar—some of whom bowed their heads and clasped their hands in deference—was the Grand Mufti of Jerusalem, Haj Amin al-Husseini, his white turban distinctive even in the deteriorating visibility. He slowed his pace as he passed a knot of troopers between the great house and the gateway arch, his SS guards shadowing him.

Weiss rested his right cheekbone on the De Lisle's wooden stock and sighted in on the white-turbaned figure. The snow was an irritant, but he could still see just well enough to make the shot, and the light wind was not a factor.

Below and to his left, the girl shrieked again. The sound was so despairing that Weiss lifted his cheek from the stock and turned his head to look.

The girl was on her back and the German was on top of her, still clad in his heavy trench coat. His pants were loose around his ankles, and his hips were moving in a frantic rhythm. His hands were locked around her thin throat.

He was strangling her.

Weiss's eyes darted back to his target and he resettled his cheekbone on the carbine's stock. The mufti was in front of the great house now, moving toward the vestibule. Some of the Handschar troopers were walking beside him, bowing their heads repeatedly.

Weiss's finger tightened on the trigger. He would not try for a head shot at this distance, in this visibility. Instead he would aim at the center of body mass, concentrating on the chest region, and the massive .45-caliber slug would do the rest. Few people survived. the tremendous impact of the round originally designed for the American Colt 1911 automatic pistol, if they were hit in the thorax or abdomen.

The girl was trying to scream, but only a thin, gurgling sound reached Weiss's ears. The German was wheezing and grunting like a pig.

The Grand Mufti of Jerusalem mounted the steps of the great house vestibule, waving to the soldiers on the compound wall.

Weiss focused every shred of his concentration on the center point of the black coat below the white turban, and began to squeeze the De Lisle's trigger.

The German's frenzied grunting was reaching a crescendo. From the girl there was no sound.

The Grand Mufti faced the north and spread his

arms to the watching soldiers. Behind the scarf that protected his face from the bitter cold, he was almost certainly smiling. The thick snowflakes whirled this way and that, pushed by random puffs of wind.

The piercing scream of a steam whistle cut the air. Weiss fired.

The train was coming.

Sylvia could hear it. Its rumbling and clanking and squealing reverberated out of the tunnel mouth. Under her bloody hands, the outer girder from which she was hanging began to vibrate. On impulse, she swung over to the inside of the span next to the rock face, stood up cautiously on the inner girder's lower flange, and peered over the steel-grating catwalk that ran alongside the rails.

She was hoping to see the train coming through the tunnel. Instead she saw multiple flashlights swinging back and forth in the tunnel's dark mouth. It was quite apparent what was happening: SS troopers were walking the rails ahead of the train, checking them for any indications of structural failure or sabotage. Someone—probably the tank group's commander—was taking no chances.

Sylvia had little doubt that the SS would inspect the bridge, too—its spans, supports, and footings—before waving the train on. Unless they could be distracted.

The lead flashlights were almost out of the tunnel. She pulled herself up onto the catwalk and began to run back toward the center of the bridge, partially concealed by the interlocking steel beams that formed the upper strength members of the individual spans.

Bristow, still in the antiaircraft gun emplacement high up along the gorge rim, refocused his Zeiss binoculars, tracking the girl as she ran back to the south.

"What the hell's she doin'?" he muttered under his breath. "Crazy broad . . ."

The clanking and squealing of the train, interspersed

by steam blasts, echoed off the head wall and through the gorge. Bristow shifted the binoculars to the right. He could just make out the north end of the tunnel through the falling snow and treetops, and the tank-carrying flatcars of the King Tiger train filing slowly into it. Any moment now the lead locomotive would emerge from the tunnel's south end and move onto the bridge.

He trained the binoculars lower, below the rim of the gorge to the Zlostup trailhead. Cernović was still crouched there, a dim shape in the snow behind a stunted evergreen, staying below the line of sight of the men in the new machine-gun nest. Of Merritt there was no sign, and had not been for nearly half an hour. Bristow had no idea where he'd gotten to. He shifted the binoculars to the bridge's support footings.

The explosives were in place, thanks to the girl. Bristow chewed the unlit Camel in his mouth. You had to give her credit: that was one tough little broad.

He glanced over his shoulder as the shifting wind moaned through the trees near the gun emplacement for a few seconds. Still no sign of anyone. There was some kind of temporary field outpost about a quarter-mile down a shallow ravine behind his position, but no one seemed to be in a big hurry to leave it.

Good, he thought. *Everybody stay right where they're at for another five or ten minutes.*

He lit the Camel with his Zippo and squinted through the glasses toward the south end of the tunnel again, looking for the train.

Two small columns of SS troopers, one on either side of the tracks, were emerging from the tunnel mouth and proceeding onto the bridge. The men were well spaced, perhaps ten feet apart, and were walking with weapons loosely at the ready, looking this way and that. The lead SS trooper in each column began to glance down over his side of the bridge, as well.

"*Shit,*" Bristow breathed. He jerked the binoculars to the left, searching.

Sylvia Kozo was in the middle of the bridge between the third and fourth vertical supports. She was walking back toward the SS men in plain sight, down the center of the tracks.

Back at the tunnel mouth, the massive front end of the lead locomotive nosed into view, keeping pace with the flanking infantry columns.

For a moment, the lead SS man on the outermost side of the bridge, a veteran Scharfuehrer named Vogel, thought he was seeing things. Through the flurrying snow up ahead, in the center of the rail line, there appeared to be a scantily clad girl. A scantily clad girl in very abbreviated shorts, an undershirt, a bulky fur hat, and gloves . . . standing at rigid attention, giving the Nazi straight-arm salute. Vogel blinked and looked again—but the appartition was still there.

He was so surprised that he didn't think to stop the train. Rather, he stepped over to the edge of the left-hand rail and began to trot forward, sending a curt order across the tracks to his counterpart at the head of the second column:

"Bauer! With me!"

The other SS man picked up the pace, falling in beside him along the opposite rail, and the two of them jogged down the track toward the lone figure standing in the middle of the bridge. Several other troopers, catching sight of the girl, began to hustle along behind them.

The train kept moving forward, slowly gathering speed.

Cernović had lost sight of Sylvia when she'd climbed out of the bridge's underpinning girders and up onto the rail bed. All he could see now from his position several hundred feet below on the Zlostup trailhead was Tiger tank after Tiger tank sliding out of the tunnel and onto the bridge, with a thin column of capable-looking SS troops moving alongside it. The

Partisan commander hunched closer to his evergreen tree, fingering the igniter of the fuse he'd attached to the end of the main detonator cord. If one of those SS men on the bridge took a good look down . . .

But they weren't looking down. Most of them seemed to be looking forward. . . . And a few were beginning to trot, as if something ahead on the bridge had caught their attention.

Černović put Sylvia out of his mind and began to count the seconds until the lead locomotive would reach the fourth vertical bridge support.

Sylvia backed slowly off the center of the track, still holding the Nazi salute, as the SS men approached at the run. Behind them, the huge black shape of the King Tiger train's lead locomotive loomed larger with each passing second, gaining speed. She backed between the upright girders of the bridge's superstructure, until she was against the catwalk railing next to the bare granite of the Zpoda Gorge head wall.

The SS Scharfuehrer in the lead slowed to a walk and ran his eyes up and down her, taking in the pale, slender figure with its youthful shapeliness, the completely inadequate garb covering—or rather, not covering—it, and the stiffly held Nazi salute. Then he began to laugh, and stepped through the girders to confront what appeared to be a very attractive young Yugoslav mental patient.

"Where have you sprung from, pretty one?" he demanded in Serbo-Croatian, eyeing the firm breasts beneath the filthy undershirt. A knot of SS troops began to gather behind him, most of them grinning in bewildered amusement. The lead locomotive of the train drew near, then clanked on past.

"Seig Heil, mein Fuehrer!" Sylvia shouted at the top of her lungs, stiffening her straight-arm salute and snapping her shoulders back until her breasts strained at her undershirt.

Scharfuehrer Vogel raised an eyebrow, still chuckling. "What the devil do you make of this, Bauer?" he said out of the side of his mouth.

"I couldn't tell you," Bauer responded, "but she's not supposed to be on this bridge."

From the soldiers gathered behind, the comments began to flow thick and fast over the metallic clamor of the passing King Tiger train:

"Is she crazy?"

"Why isn't she cold? She should be freezing."

"She is cold. Look at them pointing."

"I don't like it. What's she doing here? Where did she come from?"

"Maybe she likes schnapps. Would you like a drink to warm you, fraulein?"

"Herr Scharfuehrer, don't you think we should get her to shelter? I volunteer to be in charge of getting her to shelter."

"No, I volunteer for that duty. . . ."

"No, I do!"

The fifth locomotive of the front five chugged past. The bridge shook with the weight of the tons of steel passing over it.

Come on, Sylvia prayed silently, staring out into space as if demented. *Come on . . .*

"Forgive me, girl," Cernović whispered, and pulled the igniter.

He clambered away over the steep, snow-covered rocks below the gorge rim, trying to traverse beneath the sight line of the soldiers manning the machine-gun nest just above him. He managed to cover about fifty feet before the fuse burned down and the detonator went off.

SNAP.

The detonator fired the det cord that led to the bridge charges. A fraction of a second later, the cord— nothing more than an elongated version of the same material that made up the bulk explosives—vaporized along thirty feet of Zlostup.

CRACK!

And there it stopped.

Cernović whirled, staring at the trail in confusion. Then he saw it: the reason the entire cord had not detonated all the way back to the charges on the bridge supports. A small rockfall—an unlikely, chance occurrence—had, by the worst luck imaginable, cut the cord at some point during the day.

Cernović stared up at the bridge. The King Tiger train was more than halfway across now, its five lead locomotives on the far side of the fourth vertical support. Everything was perfect—except for the faulty det cord.

Voices were coming from above the gorge rim, alerted by the explosion of the detonator and the short length of cord. Cernović didn't even stop to think. There was no time.

He leaped down toward the trailhead, bounding from rock to rock. In his coat pocket were two more fused detonators. The little rockfall that hid the cut end of the det cord was less than ten running strides away. To find the end and attach another detonator would take no time at all. And this time, it would work. It had to.

They could not fail when they had come so far and were so close.

He dashed down Zlostup, vaulted over the little rock pile, and dug frantically in the snow with both hands. Where was it? Where—

There.

Yanking the cord out of the rocks, he pulled a detonator from his pocket and began to affix it to the cut end, fumbling in his hurry. His fingers felt like rubber balls. . . . *Žplŭgk!* . . . *clumsy oaf* . . .

Done, by God.

The rogue-Gypsy grin creased Cernović's swarthy face once more as his fingers touched the igniter.

Brrraaaaaaaaaaaaaaaaaaaaaap!

The savage hail of bullets from the MG-42 in the

machine-gun nest on the gorge rim hammered into Cernović's chest, driving him back off the rock pile. The unignited detonator dropped into the snow as his body spasmed and shook in a frenzied final dance on the edge of Zlostup.

And then Anton Cernović fell, tumbling like a dark, ragged sacrifice into the empty gloom of the Zpoda Gorge.

Merritt broke into a run as he heard the buzz saw chatter of the MG-42. So did every soldier in the vicinity of the siding and the chalet gate. The last flatcar of King Tigers was just disappearing into the north end of the tunnel, followed by the inevitable caboose. As the tail-end car entered the tunnel, several dozen SS troopers swarmed across the main rail line and down toward the machine-gun nest overlooking the gorge.

Merritt, bundled up in Ulrich Haak's Hauptsturmfuehrer's uniform, slowed and hung back when the machine gun did not fire again. He'd heard the crack of the misfiring det cord, but hadn't been sure what it was. Now, with a dozen SS clustering around the machine-gun nest and pointing down toward Zlostup, he knew with dreadful certainty that the courageous Partisan commander Anton Cernović was gone.

Equally dreadful was the knowledge that the Zpoda Skyway Bridge had not been blown, the King Tiger train was well on its way across the head wall, and there was absolutely nothing he could do about it. He did not even know what had gone wrong—whether the detonators or the det cord or the charges themselves had malfunctioned. Something had exploded, but what? Whatever it was, it had not taken the footings out from under the bridge.

He could only watch in helpless desperation as the King Tiger train chugged around the long curve beneath the overhanging rock cap, heading for the safety of the southern tunnel.

* * *

"Did you hear something?" one of the SS troopers behind Scharfuehrer Vogel shouted to a comrade. Standing as they were in the narrow gap between the passing train and the solid rock face of the head wall, the clanking and screeching of metal on metal was almost deafening. "Something like firing."

The other trooper was still gazing hungrily at Sylvia Kozo's breasts. "What? No. Who can hear a damn thing with all that racket going on?"

"Listen to me, girl," Vogel called, leaning in toward Sylvia. "You're going to have to come with us."

Sylvia responded with a pirouette into a ballerina's stance. *"Jawohl, mein Fuehrer!"* she shouted. "But only after we dance!"

How long can I keep this up? she thought.

"The woman's a lunatic," Bauer said into Vogel's ear. "We're going to have to drag her off the bridge."

Vogel nodded, then noticed the carabiners and wired nuts swinging at Sylvia's hip. Curious, he pointed at them. "What are those, pretty one?"

At a loss for anything better to do, Sylvia pirouetted again. "My nuts, *mein Fuehrer!*" she shouted at the top of her lungs.

"Your what?"

"Nuts!" Sylvia yelled. *"Nuts, nuts, nuts!"*

"Truly unhinged," Bauer growled to Vogel. "I've had about enough of this."

"Wait," Vogel said. He didn't often encounter distractions this entertaining. "What are your . . . nuts . . . for, girl?"

"For climbing!" Sylvia bellowed. "Watch me! Watch me!"

She turned, hopped up on the catwalk railing, and leapt across the four-foot gap onto the nearly featureless granite of the head wall. There was a collective gasp from the soldiers, followed by a series of exclamations.

Sylvia unclipped a tiny nut and inserted it into a

small crack. "See?" she shouted, swinging from it like a monkey. "See what my nuts are for?"

Vogel started to smile, then realized that he couldn't lay a hand on the girl while she was clinging to the cliff. His expression reorganized into a frown. "Get down from there," he ordered over the rumbling of the train. "Right now."

At that instant, nearly a mile away on the upper north rim of the Zpoda Gorge, Sergeant Cole Bristow depressed the firing triggers of the 40-millimeter anti-aircraft cannon he'd aimed at the gorge head wall and walked a long burst of incendiary shells across the rock and into the explosive charges on the bridge's second vertical support footing.

Chapter Twenty

The first white-hot incendiary shell from Bristow's volley to hit the paired charges on the second bridge footing detonated them. They exploded as one with a thunderous *CRACK* that caromed through the gorge from head wall to peak to precipice. A fraction of a second later, the long runs of det cord connecting the other three sets of charges on footings one, three, and four vaporized simultaneously, detonating the remaining explosives. The rapid-fire blasts sounded like a triplet rolling off a titanic snare drum:

CRACKCRACKCRACK!

The powerful explosions shattered the concrete bridge footings and sheared through the thick steel of the vertical support girders as if it was so much tinfoil. Their primary bracing gone, the bridge spans beneath the overhanging rock cap sagged.

Vogel and his men were still looking up at Sÿlvia when the bridge suddenly tilted twenty degrees away from the head wall in a screeching of metal and a popping of rivets. The violent vibrations shook Sylvia's slippered feet off their tenuous purchase on the granite and she swung free, suspended by one hand and the tiny nut she'd jammed into the thin crack. There were shrieks of alarm as some of the SS troopers fell back through the superstructure girders toward the rumbling wheels on the train tracks.

For a few brief seconds, the bridge held. Then, with a horrible grating screech of tearing metal and the *CLANG-BANG-CRACK* of buckling joints and snapping gussets and failing rock anchors, the entire northern two-thirds of the Zpoda Skyway Bridge broke off the head wall and dropped into the yawning depths of its namesake gorge—carrying with it the last twenty cars of the King Tiger train.

Sylvia twisted in the air on the single wire and stared down goggle-eyed as the steel superstructure surrounding her . . . and the great tank-laden train caged within it . . . simply fell away. It dropped slowly at first, then faster and faster, the huge interlocking spans twisting and undulating as they shrank into something resembling a child's toy. . . .

And then it struck the talus slope at the foot of the head wall, tons of iron and steel crashing into boulders and gravel and snow in a great boiling eruption of white and gray and black and smoke and flame. The shattered girders tumbled down the steep incline into the dense trees at the bottom of the gorge; in the same avalanche of broken metal rolled the battered black carcasses of dozens of King Tiger tanks, most with their turrets and long guns wrenched off, some with ruptured fuel tanks spewing fire.

Bristow was watching openmouthed from the gunner's seat of the 40-millimeter antiaircraft cannon that had literally triggered the whole sequence of destruction. And it was not over yet. The weight of the falling flatcars had yanked the front third of the train backward, the steel wheels of its five lead locomotives screaming and throwing sparks. The coupling at the rear of the fifth locomotive's coal car then failed, leaving the engines to drive forward again, suddenly relieved of tons of load. As Bristow continued to watch, all the detached cars—ammunition boxcars, SS barracks cars, Kronstadt's headquarters car—were pulled in succession off the remaining section of bridge like the links of a chain dropping off the edge of a table. The last of the forty-eight King Tigers tumbled into the mangled forest at the bottom of the Zpoda Gorge in billowing clouds of kicked-up snow.

"Damn!" Bristow muttered, as the booming echoes of the cataclysm died away.

He slid off the gunner's seat of the 40-millimeter, seized his Thompson and the Zeiss binoculars, vaulted over the sandbag wall of the emplacement, and ran for the trees. But before he lost sight of the head wall, he stopped to focus on the spot beneath the rock cap overhang where, just before he'd fired at the explosives, he'd seen Sylvia Kozo climb into view above the passing train. He searched and squinted. . . . And then grinned.

She was still there.

Merritt, in the company of a dozen other soldiers who'd run up the rim trail to get a better look at the wreckage of the Zpoda Skyway Bridge and the King Tiger train, could also see Sylvia clinging to the head wall under the rock cap. She was inconspicuous, high up in the deepening shadow beneath the overhang, and the late-afternoon light was waning quickly. No one else appeared to have noticed her; they were all staring down.

Merritt turned and walked, then ran, back down the rim trail. At the dead end of the rail siding onto which the four cars of the Grand Mufti's private train had been shunted there was a lineman's utility shack. Merritt kicked open the door and found what he was looking for: rope. Hundreds of feet of heavy-duty manila used for block-and-tackle rigging in various types of bridge service.

It would be dark in an hour. Merritt glanced hurriedly around. Most of the SS had run to the gorge rim, but there were still a few near the tunnel entrance.

"*Achtung!*" he shouted in German, pointing a rigid finger. "You and you! Get over here right now!"

The two Handschar troopers glanced at each other, then jogged back through the falling snow toward Merritt.

"*Jawohl,* Herr Hauptsturmfuehrer!" the first man panted. "The bridge . . . it—"

"I know all about the bridge, idiot!" Merritt snapped. "We have a man trapped on the cliff beneath the overhang, several hundred yards out. Pick up this rope—that coil and that coil—and follow me. We're going out on the rock cap ridge to save him!"

Once again the soldiers glanced at each other. The top of the rock cap was a broken, knife-edged arête, barely safe for a mountain goat to walk on, which was why the Zpoda Skyway Bridge had been constructed *beneath* it in the first place. It was hazardous in the best of conditions, never mind a snowstorm in the dark.

"Get moving, curse you!" Merritt barked. "That is a direct order!"

They moved. Between the two of them, they hoisted the big coils of rope over their shoulders and, working together, waddled clumsily after Merritt as he led them up the steep, broken incline above the tunnel. Two hundred backbreaking vertical feet later, they were trudging out onto the rock cap, gasping for breath, urged on by their clearly sadistic Hauptsturmfuehrer.

The Hauptsturmfuehrer was over the edge of the rock cap the instant the first rope was secured and flung off the edge, rappelling downward with the second coil lashed to his back, mountaineer style, then somehow swinging under the overhang and working his way in to the head wall. He hadn't even bothered to take off his gun belt and sidearm, but the two SS troopers weren't about to argue the point with him. The man was clearly one of those overzealous Nazi diehards—a person with whom it was a good idea not to get into conflict.

It was more than an hour later, and well into dusk, when the two troopers finally became impatient enough to pull the rappelling rope back up from beneath the overhang—only to realize that the hard-driving Hauptsturmfuehrer was no longer attached to it.

David Weiss was running through the trees, plowing through the deep snow as fast as his tired legs would carry him. He was heading northeast, away from the chalet compound, on a diagonal course that would eventually intersect the main rail line. Behind him, being virtually dragged along by one hand, was the girl who'd been assaulted and nearly murdered in the dilapidated shack. She was in a state of shock, and only Weiss's constant admonitions to keep moving kept her staggering forward in his tracks.

Gestapo Hauptsturmfuehrer Julius Neurath was lying on his back on the dirt floor of the shack with his trench coat open and his trousers bunched around his ankles. He was staring up at the musty, sagging rafters of the derelict structure's collapsing roof. The .45-caliber slug meant for the Grand Mufti of Jerusalem had punched a large hole in the center of his forehead and turned the back of his skull into a crimson mush.

Weiss had swung the De Lisle back toward the mufti after the girl's final pitiable moans and her murderer's obscene grunting had stung him, at the last second, into shifting his aim. But al-Husseini had already turned and started through the door of the great house. And then the sentry on the northwest corner of the compound wall had spotted him. Weiss had shot him off the wall as he'd yelled a challenge, then bolted out from beneath the ledge and down the rocky slope to the shack.

The girl had been nearly catatonic, trembling and staring with her mass of tangled dark hair falling over her tear-stained face, but somehow Weiss had gotten her to her feet and out the door as German and Serbo-Croatian shouts echoed down from the compound walls. He'd been running for his life and hers when a series of what could have been either thunder-claps or explosions had boomed through the gaunt black trees and undulating snowdrifts. The bridge? One could only hope.

He had no idea where he was going—only that if they could get onto the rail bed far enough away from the chalet garrison, they could travel more quickly on its shoulder. The snow was not as deep beside the tracks.

"Come on, girl!" he panted in Serbo-Croatian. "You have to keep moving! Quickly, now!"

"I . . . can't," the girl sobbed. She sank to her knees in the snow and tilted her head back, tears streaming down her young face. "I . . . want . . . to . . . die . . ."

Weiss looked back through the trees in desperation, then dropped to one knee in front of the girl and took her head in his hands. "Look at me," he said.

Her flooding eyes opened and fixed on his.

"What is your name?" Weiss asked.

"M-Magda," the girl replied.

Weiss nodded. "Listen to me, Magda. My name is David. And I want you to live. I want you to keep going."

The girl's dark, lovely eyes remained fastened on his, full of pain.

"Will you do that for me?" he prompted. "We don't have much time."

She nodded. "I'll . . . I'll try."

"Good. That's all a person can do." He got to his feet, helping the girl up at the same time. "Now let's go."

They ran on through the snowbound forest, until at

last the trees thinned and an open corridor appeared to their right.

"The main rail line," Weiss panted. "It's starting to get dark. We'll follow the tracks for a while. It'll be easier to walk along the . . ."

His voice trailed off as the rumbling of steel wheels caught his ear. He ducked low, pulling the girl down with him, and swung up the De Lisle. Through the trees to the south, movement caught his eye. The rumbling grew louder.

The caboose and private car of the Grand Mufti's train slid into view, rolling northward down the slightly declining tracks, powered by nothing but gravity and momentum. Sitting on the roof of the private car with a Schmeisser across his knees, atop the flywheel that controlled the brakes, was Professor Theobald Quisp.

On the private car's rearward-end platform, looking back up the tracks toward the chalet, was Sergeant Colin Stirling, his long Enfield sniper rifle resting on the platform's handrail. Beside him was Sergeant Cole Bristow, his Thompson submachine gun cradled in his arms. A cigarette dangled from his mouth.

Magda let out a terrified whimper, but Weiss jerked her to her feet and began to run toward the free-rolling cars, pulling her along at his heels.

"Run, Magda!" he blurted over his shoulder. "Run just once more! If we can catch those cars, we're free and clear!" He raised the De Lisle above his head as they floundered out of the trees. *"Hey!"* he yelled in English. "Stirling! Bristow! Quisp! Don't shoot! It's me, Weiss!" He plowed forward through the snow, dragging the girl along with all his remaining strength.

The two sergeants started at the sound of his voice, bringing their weapons around, then lowered them as they identified him. Stirling stepped down on the platform boarding stairs, holding out a hand. Bristow climbed the roof ladder and yelled to Quisp: "Put a little brake on, Professor! That's Weiss over there!"

Quisp got up and spun the braking flywheel as Weiss and Magda cleared the deep snow and dashed down the edge of the rail bed through the flurrying snow in pursuit of the caboose and private car. There was a squeal as the brake linings tightened on the wheel drums, slowing the cars just enough to allow them to catch up.

As Sergeant David Weiss lifted the exhausted girl into Colin Stirling's strong arms, he was struck out of the blue by a sudden pang of regret. It was a regret he would carry with him the rest of his life.

To the end of his days he would never be able to forgive himself for failing to kill the man most responsible for the death and mutilation of his brother.

There was chaos in the aide's office adjoining Standartenfuehrer Egon Zweig's inner chambers. Handschar SS officers and noncoms of every rank between Scharfuehrer and Sturmbannfuehrer were crowded into the small space, spilling through the doorway into the common room, pushing and jostling and shouting reports and requests at the slender blond division commander who was standing calmly in front of his desk, smoking. He was nodding at everyone at the same time, his brow furrowed in apparent concern, as the information came thick and fast.

"Sabotage, Herr Standartenfuehrer! The Zpoda Skyway Bridge has been completely destroyed! A Partisan was shot and killed below the gorge rim just before the explosions! There may be more saboteurs still about!"

"Sir! The north-ridge outpost reports that all members of the gun crew assigned to antiaircraft emplacement number four—that was the position seen firing at the bridge just prior to the detonations—have been found dead! Executed with single shots to the head!"

"The Grand Mufti's private coach, Herr Standartenfuehrer! Someone has uncoupled it and its caboose from the escorting gun car and allowed it to roll back down the main track! It is not in sight, sir!"

Throckmorton homed in on that one. "And why wasn't someone watching it? Why do I post sentries and run patrols if not to secure the immediate area?"

The youthful lieutenant who'd spoken shrank visibly at being singled out. "Everyone was . . . distracted by the collapse of the bridge, sir."

"Bah!" Throckmorton declared. "Dereliction of duty. Put yourself on report, Untersturmfuehrer."

As the cacophony continued Hauptsturmfuehrer Matthias Juttner unobtrusively slid along the wall of the common room and out the connecting doorway into the aide's office. The Grand Mufti of Jerusalem was sitting quietly in a chair at one end of the room, letting the frenetic activity rage around him. He was still wearing his winter coat, the collar turned up, and still had his thick wool scarf wrapped around his mouth and nose. Only his keen eyes showed in the slit between the top of the scarf and the bottom edge of his white turban.

Juttner was on the verge of making the decision, since the assassin attached to Merritt's team had been unable to get the mufti in his sights, to talk al-Husseini into a back room where he could quickly and quietly slit his throat. It violated his Priority Directive from Churchill, but he had come to the conclusion that the benefit was worth the risk of discovery. The free world would be much better off without the Grand Mufti of Jerusalem constantly plotting against it and abetting the Nazi regime.

He put a hand on the mufti's shoulder and leaned down. "Your Excellency," he called over the noise.

Al-Husseini looked up at him.

"Your Excellency," Juttner said, removing his hand and giving a little bow. "Perhaps we should get out of here. Go to one of the back rooms until the commotion dies down. You should stay inside where it is safe until the situation has been properly analyzed and the area secured, but there is no need for you to be subjected to this uproar."

The mufti blinked at him, reached up, and pulled down his scarf.

Juttner stared.

"I think I stay here," Mustapha Snagi growled in his broken German.

Back in the common room Throckmorton was still standing against the front of his desk, gazing up at the mad glass eyes of the mounted game heads as they in turn gazed down at the madness seething beneath them.

"Standartenfuehrer Zweig! We estimate that the destruction of the bridge and train has just cost us in excess of four hundred men—tank crews, SS supporting infantry, and various Handschar personnel!"

"Herr Standartenfuehrer—the commander of the King Tiger tank group, Standartenfuehrer Kronstadt, has been killed along with all his men! His tanks have all been completely destroyed! Not one is left!"

"Herr Standartenfuehrer! There is enemy activity at the north wall of the chalet compound. One sentry has already been killed—others claim that Partisan infiltrators are active in the trees as close as fifty yards!"

Throckmorton almost smiled as he finished his cigarette. It was music to the ears. As sweet as a Brahms lullabye.

"Sir! This is critical! A report has just come in of a coordinated series of Partisan attacks against the Twenty-eighth SS Regiment on the northeastern shoulder of Mount Zpoda! The attacking forces appear to be made up primarily of elements of the Second Proletarian Brigade! Fighting is intensifying, sir!"

Again Throckmorton almost smiled. *Tito.* He'd made it across the Ugljevik Plateau and linked up with other Partisan units for a diversionary attack against the Handschar main line of advance, as Cernović had promised.

Well, they didn't need a diversion anymore—the bridge was down and the Tiger train with it. But there was certainly another opportunity here. . . .

You're on, Duncan, he thought. *Time to tread the boards and chew the scenery.*

He looked at the anxious Hauptsturmfuehrer who'd stammered out the last report. "Communicate this order at once to the commander of the Twenty-eighth SS Regiment," he said. "Pull back to the northwest without delay. Take no further casualties. Disengage the enemy and retreat into the Bulvar Valley immediately to regroup."

The Hauptsturmfuehrer looked aghast. "But . . . but—Herr Standartenfuehrer," he protested. "That will allow the Partisans to break through—"

"Do not second-guess my direct orders!" Throckmorton shouted, purpling nicely. "The Twenty-eighth SS will withdraw, regroup, and counterattack at my discretion!"

"But, sir," the Hauptsturmfuehrer soldiered on bravely, "should I at least . . . relay your *additional* orders to move the third and fourth battalions of the Twenty-ninth SS Regiment into the gap? Sir?"

Triumph was spreading through Captain Duncan Throckmorton like warm wine. He lit another cigarette, gazed beneficently down at the stupefied young officer, and cleared his throat.

"No," he said.

Chapter Twenty-One

By the time word of a pair of runaway train cars—a caboose followed by a passenger coach—reached each successive repair station and gunnery unit along the Zpoda Gorge main line, the cars had already rumbled past. . . . A result of some kind of inexplicable inefficiency in communications from the Barbo House field headquarters of the SS Division Handschar, which had lost the rolling stock in the first place. It was well after dawn when the coach and caboose, which had been rolling backward down the line all night with brakes tightened just enough to prevent the wheels from jumping the track, finally slid out between the lowest foothills of the Majevica Mountains and onto the frozen, marshy flatlands beyond.

The coach and caboose squealed slowly to a halt as gravity finally relinquished its grip. The cars sat on the rails in the middle of an empty winter landscape, burnt brake linings smoking, for ten minutes before the two self-powered jitterbugs that had been chasing the runaways down the slopes for nearly fifteen miles finally caught up. Each small service trolley contained, in addition to a railroad lineman, half a squad of SS troops, armed to the teeth.

The Obersturmfuehrer in charge of the squad leapt out of the lead jitterbug as the lineman braked it twenty feet behind the passenger coach. Luger drawn, he ran along the snow-covered rail bed, waving his men on.

"Take the right side, Scharfuehrer!" he shouted. "And I want men up at the front of the caboose! We'll enter and clear the cars from both ends at the same time!"

"*Jawohl*, Herr Obersturmfuehrer!" the sergeant barked. "Kruger! Buschhagen! At the other end of the caboose. *Schnell!*"

The fifteen SS troops fanned out around the cars, machine pistols pointing up at the board-covered windows of the coach and caboose.

"Careful, careful!" the lieutenant instructed, bracing himself at the boarding stairs of the coach's end platform. He glanced down the sides of the cars, checking the positions of his men, then nodded to the Schmeisser-bearing trooper opposite him. "Ready? . . . *now!*"

At both ends of the caboose and coach, SS troopers lunged up the platforms and through the doors. There were shouts—but no shooting—as the assault personnel communicated with each other and then linked up inside the cars.

The coach and caboose were empty. If there had ever been anyone riding in them during their lengthy roll down from Mount Zpoda, they were long gone now.

The Obersturmfuehrer holstered his pistol and walked slowly through the luxurious interior of the private car, taking in the velvet armchairs, polished mahogany, and lush carpets. He paused beside the dining table, pulled the stopper from a cut-glass decanter that sat in a specially made nook, and sniffed it.

"Chianti," he muttered. "Good, too." He lifted the decanter. There wasn't much left. Pity.

He passed the decanter to his Scharfuehrer. "Here, Emil. Have a drink."

The noncom smiled as he took it. "Thank you, Obersturmfuehrer Dietrich."

Dietrich's roving gaze settled on a teacup jammed into a crumpled cloth napkin in the center of the table. It had been used as an ashtray. There were two crushed cigarette butts in it. On a whim he picked them out and examined them. Then his eyes widened: the tiny logos both read CAMEL.

The muted clang of a cooking pot sounded through the open door of the luxury car's small, narrow galley. Every man in the compartment flinched and swung up his weapon. Obersturmfuehrer Dietrich yanked his Luger from its holster again and dodged behind the the jamb of the galley doorway. Cautiously he peered around the corner, pistol brandished.

Empty.

"Nobody there," he whispered, turning his head. "Maybe just something shifting—"

There was another dull clang, followed by a sustained rattling.

The SS troopers crowded up behind their lieutenant, machine pistols ready. Dietrich crouched low to allow them to fire over his head if need be, then sprang into the galley onto one knee, searching down the barrel of his Luger for a target.

The elongated little kitchen was truly empty. But the sliding metal door of the storage cabinet beneath the food-preparation countertop was vibrating. It had been jammed shut by a heavy crate of canned ham that had fallen over and become wedged against it.

"Emil," Dietrich said to his sergeant again, this time waving him forward with his pistol. He took up a position just to one side of the cabinet door as the Scharfuehrer stepped past him and gripped the crate with one big hand.

"Ready?" Dietrich mouthed, aiming carefully. "Pull."

The Scharfuehrer jerked the crate loose. The door slid back with a bang.

Dietrich stared.

The man in the sights of his Luger was curled up in a fetal position, his long robes bunched around his torso. He was covered in baking flour, apparently from a sack that had burst next to him. His reddish-blond beard and thinning gray hair were caked with it, and his eyes, blinking painfully in the sudden light, were sticky and red. He focused on the SS Obersturm-fuehrer, then asked in a cracked, plaintive voice:

"Are they . . . are they gone yet?"

Dietrich glanced up at his sergeant, then back down at the cramped figure jammed in with the cooking pots and dry goods. "Who the hell are you?" he demanded.

"Who am I? *Who am I?*" the well-floured cabinet inhabitant responded, his energy if not his dignity apparently returning. "I am Haj Amin al-Husseini—*the Grand Mufti of Jerusalem!*"

Dietrich looked at his sergeant again, then pursed his lips in irritation and glared down at the stowaway.

"Of course you are," he growled. "And I'm the man in the moon." He waved the Luger. "Now get out of there."

Chapter Twenty-Two

London, three weeks later

"A remarkable achievement," Wild Bill Donovan said, swirling the cognac in his glass. "Really quite unbelieveable that it went as well as it did." He raised the snifter toward Winston Churchill and Stewart Menzies, who sat opposite him in the Prime Minister's 10 Downing Street study. "Here's to Operation Handschar."

"Here's to the men who pulled it off, General," Martin Judson appended, lifting his small glass of sherry, "and the woman."

Donovan, ever the American gentleman, turned and nodded courteously in Judson's direction. "Of course. To them. To all of them."

The four power brokers drank, and afterward sat in silence for a long moment. With practiced ritual, Churchill cut and lit one of his trademark cigars.

"So that's your boy, Martin," Donovan said to Judson. "SS Hauptsturmfuehrer Matthias Juttner is actually . . ."

THE WAR MOUNTAINS

"Matthew Judson," the elegant industrialist filled in. "My only son."

Donovan shook his head, smiling. "How the Sam Hill did you get him into the SS," he asked, "much less placed so highly? He's right in the wolves' den, for God's sake—rubbing shoulders with Kaltenbrunner and Schellenberg and even Himmler himself. I hear he even sat in on piano at a few dinner parties when that animal Heydrich—may he rot in hell—got an uncontrollable urge to show off his violin skills to a captive audience."

"According to Canaris, he did indeed," Judson replied. "Matthew always had a nice touch for both Bach and American jazz. In his teens he used to sit for hours, trying to replicate the phrasings of a rather disreputable New Orleans bordello musician by the name of Jelly Roll Morton—much to my dismay, I'm now sorry to say. I felt he should be spending more time studying business management fundamentals, since he was going to work for me at my offices in Munich after completing his studies at Oxford."

"And that's where he first met Merritt and Throckmorton?"

"Yes. They were together at Oxford from 1928 to 1931. Inseparable. Young and handsome and smart and athletic and . . . rich, of course. The cream of the English upper class, denied nothing by their proud parents. Perhaps, I remember fearing at the time, overindulgently so." Judson smiled a bit sadly. "Their peers used to refer to them, with considerable lack of originality, as the Three Musketeers."

Donovan, his instincts flawless as usual, promptly came up with the perfect comment: "I would say your fears have proven groundless, Martin—with regard not just to your son, but all three of these exceptional men."

Judson inclined his impeccable head. "Thank you, General."

"Bill, please," Donovan said.

John McKinna

"Of course—Bill." Judson sipped sherry and crossed his legs. "You asked how Matthew came to be a member of the SS. It's quite simple. He had been working for me since 1932 in a rather anonymous capacity as an industrial salesman, learning the business he would one day inherit from the ground up. He was based in Munich, but traveled extensively through Germany and the rest of Europe, servicing and setting up new accounts. His language skills—particularly his German—became first-rate. After Hitler and his Nazi gang pulled off what was effectively a coup in 1933, a group of us—Winston, Stewart, myself, and a few others—were quite certain we could see the writing on the wall, though we could never convince that prevaricating milksop Chamberlain[1] to hold a hard line against the so-called Fuehrer and his political thugs." For a moment the perpetually composed English gentleman looked almost angry.

"Matthew was approached with the idea of infiltrating the SS in its formative stages by becoming a willing recruit—a long-term commitment, though no one had any idea exactly *how* long. I suppose I should have realized that he would jump at the chance to take part in some kind of cloak-and-dagger adventure; he was only twenty-four at the time and quite bored with the life of an industrial salesman–cum–privileged heir. It was a simple matter for MI-6 to create a new identity for him and provide forged documents of the highest quality—birth certificate and such—that identified him irrefutably as one Matthias Juttner, scion of a well-established family of German brewers from southern Bavaria. My long-standing business connections in and around Munich helped in this regard."

"So he's been a bona fide member of the SS since 1934?" Donovan said. "That's *ten years.*" He paused. "And in that time he's attained the rank of captain and positioned himself next to the most powerful people in the SS hierarchy. Amazing. That would make him—"

364

"One of the most important Allied agents in Europe," Churchill grunted, puffing on his cigar. "He's situated himself perfectly, right on the periphery of the Nazi inner circle, remaining inconspicuous by keeping his head low and turning down promotion after promotion. A high-ranking officer—a lieutenant colonel, full colonel, or general, for example—has duties and responsibilities that limit his movements; a lowly captain can go anywhere . . . particularly if that captain has the social and political skills—the intellectual *dexterity*—of Matthew Judson."

"You wouldn't want a man like this compromised by allowing him to take unnecessary risks," Donovan remarked. "He's far too valuable right where he is, feeding information out and disinformation back in."

"Exactly," Menzies said, "which is where the Prime Minister's concept of Priority Directives comes in. A Priority Directive is a standing order to an operative who occupies a covert position of extreme importance. He is not to risk discovery under any circumstances. He is to limit the chances he takes in order to preserve his position. This means, for example, that even though Matthew Judson, as Matthias Juttner, passes within arms' reach of many notables in the Nazi regime on a regular basis, he cannot actually reach out and assassinate any of them—not even Hitler himself. The damage he is able to do by orchestrating events and passing information far exceeds the value of removing a single man, regardless of who he is."

"So he's still well placed," Donovan said, "despite the debacle with the Grand Mufti."

Menzies and Churchill and Judson exchanged amused glances. "An embarassing episode from which Haj Amin al-Husseini's prestige within the Third Reich may never recover," Menzies commented. "But the redoubtable Hauptsturmfuehrer Matthias Juttner has managed to deflect all blame for the fiasco onto a degenerate, and *dead*, Gestapo agent named Julius Neurath, and a belligerent, and also dead, SS Standartenfuehrer named Wilhelm Kronstadt, the commander of the King Tiger tank group."

"It's too bad Weiss wasn't able to take the Grand Mufti out," Donovan said. He looked at Churchill and Menzies. "You didn't tell Joe Haskell and me about that part of the operation during our meeting a month or so ago."

"Well, that was something we threw in at the last minute," Menzies explained, "once we heard through Juttner and Canaris that the mufti was heading for Yugoslavia after the failed assassination attempt by Aaron Weiss in Berlin. The main objective of Operation Handschar was to get the bridge blown and Throckmorton positioned. Merritt was instructed to turn Weiss loose against the mufti with the appropriate amount of—shall we say, *motivation*?—at the most opportune moment. It almost worked. The assassination of al-Husseini would have been a nice bonus."

"One can't have everything," Churchill growled, exhaling smoke, "although one can try."

"I suppose," Donovan said. "But now—the personnel involved. I know we have Bristow and Stirling back. They made their way to Slovenia in the north and managed to make contact with the OSS mission working with Partisan groups up there. They were flown out by Blenheim bomber to Sicily. But what about Weiss?"

"No word," Menzies told him. "According to Bristow and Stirling, he and the girl, Magda, left the rolling cars in the lower foothills of the Majevicas without explanation, only shaking hands and saying good-bye. They jumped on a slow corner just before dawn and disappeared into the trees."

Donovan was silent for a moment. "Do you think Weiss was annoyed that you used his brother's death to manipulate him into taking a shot at the Grand Mufti of Jerusalem?" he asked.

Menzies's face was a pleasant mask. "He may have been a touch put out."

Churchill filled in the slightly charged void that followed by changing the subject: "Merritt and that extraordinary young Yugoslav woman Sylvia Kozo made it down off the head wall of the Zpoda Gorge. They waited until dark, then used the rope Merritt had brought, Sylvia's climbing nuts, and their own incredible mountaineering skills to descend to Zlostup. Then they retraced their steps along that ancient hunter's path all the way back to the grove where Sylvia had executed the traitor Vlado. They scavenged the remaining clothes from his body—Merritt had been sharing his with Sylvia, and they were both close to freezing—then took the ascending side path to the Zpoda snowfields. Two days later they rendezvoused with rear-guard elements of Tito's Second Proletarian Brigade.

"Major Merritt was flown out to Bari five days later, and Sylvia Kozo elected to go with him, with Tito's blessing. They're in London at this very moment, having a late dinner, I expect." Churchill beamed around his cigar, the broad grin creasing his bulldog face. "By George," he declared, his shrewd eyes twinkling, "if there's one thing I like as well as a fine adventure story, it's a fine romance."

"I suppose MI-6 and SOE aren't done with them yet," Donovan surmised. "They're valuable assets. So is Stirling."

"So is Bristow," Menzies pointed out.

"You can't have him," Donovan retorted good-humoredly. "He now belongs exclusively to me, as a full-time member of OSS."

Menzies chuckled. "Touché, General," he said. "And you're right: we'll find a use for Major Merritt and Miss Kozo again soon enough. But for the time being, we'll leave them alone."

"It's a shame about Cernović," Judson said quietly. "Not to mention Hurst and your other man, Bill— Sergeant D'Amato."

Donovan nodded. "A shame. But they helped get the job done."

" 'Favored are the warriors who fall in the just fight,' " Churchill recited, " 'for they shall dwell forever in the undying glow of their own glory.' " He drew on his cigar. "A quote from my favorite poet."

"I like that," Donovan said. "Who is it?"

Churchill blew out smoke and smiled. "Me."

Donovan returned the smile and sipped cognac. "Speaking of quotes," he said. "What about this Quisp fellow? He seems more than a little useful, if odd. Where is he?"

"Still in Yugoslavia," Menzies replied. He waved his fingers. "We don't know exactly where. He got Bristow and Stirling moving in the right direction, traveled with them for a day and a half, then said adieu and split off. He's back in his beloved Majevicas, making trouble for the Germans and their allies, I expect. I imagine we'll hear from him in some form or another eventually. . . . We always do."

Donovan drained his snifter, savored the cognac, and held up his glass. "Do you mind, Mr. Prime Minister?" he said to Churchill. "I really feel that by the time I've heard the full story of Captain Duncan Throckmorton, I'll need a fully charged glass."

Churchill, always delighted to accommodate a fellow drinker, got out of his chair to proffer the cognac decanter. "Allow me, General Donovan."

"Thank you, sir," Donovan said. Churchill poured a generous splash of the premium brandy into his snifter, and both men reseated themselves.

Martin Judson began, "Duncan Throckmorton is from one of the great landowning families in northwestern England, a dynasty with holdings on both sides of the Scottish border. He's the second son of his generation. He was a tremendous sportsman in his teens and early twenties—a sailor, skier, and crack shot with rifle and especially pistol. He was on the 'thirty-six British Olympic team with Walt Merritt, and won a silver medal in pistol shooting.

"But his great love was acting. He understudied

Olivier at the Royal Shakespeare Company and performed in productions all over Britain. His Hamlet was one of the best I've ever seen. A true natural, and with such a genuine interest in portraying *character* that he did not become particularly famous: he was so chameleonlike that you couldn't put your finger on him. He had no desire to be a star, per se.

"Like many young men of his age and class, he was recruited into MI-6, and from there into SOE. His skills as an actor, as well as his education and ability to handle a pistol, made him an ideal covert agent."

"Not unlike his old friend Matthew Judson," Churchill rumbled. "They both share the same poise, the same damn-your-eyes confidence that enables them to function convincingly in the company of some of the most dangerous villains in Europe."

Judson smiled appreciatively at Churchill before continuing: "Duncan Throckmorton had already been on half a dozen missions into occupied Europe—two with Walt Merritt—when we received an intelligence report on the composition of Reichsfuehrer Himmler's latest creation, the all-Muslim SS Division Handschar, which was just completing its formative training in France. In that report were photographs of Handschar's commanding officer and his staff. It was General Gubbins, I believe, who was first struck by the uncanny resemblance between Egon Zweig and Duncan Throckmorton.

"We dug up everything we could on Herr Zweig—family photos, school pictures, military portraits and field shots. We even obtained some invaluable film footage of him reviewing the newly trained Muslim troops of Handschar—courtesy of SS Hauptsturmfuehrer Matthias Juttner and his Berlin connections."

"Useful, that Juttner, isn't he?" Donovan remarked.

Judson smiled his appreciation. "It became clear to us that Duncan Throckmorton was indeed a virtual double of Egon Zweig—what is referred to in German as a doppelganger. Oh, there were a few subtle differences in hair color and the bone structure of the face—particularly the nose—but those were easily corrected by surgery."

"Throckmorton had no problem with that?" Donovan inquired. "Having his face surgically altered to resemble another man?"

Judson glanced over at Churchill and Menzies. The silent exchange between the three Englishmen was noticeably sober.

"No," Judson said. "Duncan didn't mind."

Donovan shrugged. "I mean, having to spend the rest of your life with a face other than your own—surgically modified so that you can eliminate and then impersonate someone you don't particularly admire. Not many people would do it."

"The rest of his life," Menzies echoed. "He knew that when he agreed to go under the knife."

"He's a tremendously dedicated soldier," Donovan said, raising his snifter to his lips. "I admire him."

"Yes," Menzies commented. "Quite."

"The idea to actually replace Zweig was Duncan's," Judson said. "We'd been trying to think of some way to exploit the resemblance, perhaps by having him impersonate Zweig here and there, temporarily, to obtain certain kinds of intelligence or use his authority as a Standartenfuehrer to enable saboteurs to access this or that target. Duncan volunteered to have surgery so that the resemblance would be perfect, and then take Zweig's place at the head of the SS Division Handschar."

"Amazing," Donovan said. "For how long?"

"Indefinitely," Menzies said.

Donovan looked at him. "What do you mean, indefinitely? How and when are you going to pull him out?"

"We're not going to pull him out," Menzies said.

"I don't understand," Donovan persisted. "What he's doing right now, effectively mismanaging Handschar on purpose, is very dangerous. Sooner or later he's going to be called to account for it—for getting one of Himmler's pet SS divisions raked over the coals. And when he does he'll probably either be hanged or shot."

"It's Duncan Throckmorton's decision," Menzies declared. "He can request an extraction any time he chooses." He paused. "But none of us think he will."

Donovan was about to ask why not when Churchill harrumphed and exhaled a long cloud of cigar smoke. "Damn fine work he's been doing, too, these past several weeks," he growled. "The day after the Zpoda Skyway Bridge and the King Tiger train were destroyed, Tito's Partisans broke through a gap in the Handschar lines on the western shoulder of Mount Zpoda. They trapped the Twenty-eighth SS Regiment in the Bulvar Valley—which is something of a box canyon, to use one of your American Old West metaphors, General Donovan—and shot it to pieces. The Twenty-ninth SS Regiment lost its third and fourth battalions due to poor tactical deployment. Essentially the SS Division Handschar took two black eyes, a broken nose, and a bloody lip at the hands of Captain Duncan Throckmorton, alias Standartenfuehrer Egon Zweig."

"The Handschar advance across the Majevica Mountains has been stalled decisively," Menzies said, "and the division's ability to prosecute further campaigns in Yugoslavia severely curtailed." His smile was hard. "If the SS leadership thought they had a morale problem with the Muslim rank and file before, it was nothing compared to the one they're having now. There are more Bosnian Muslim troopers shedding their uniforms and heading for home in the dead of night these days than there ever were."

"Incredible," Donovan said. "But that's our business, isn't it? Engineering the incredible."

"Oh yes," Churchill remarked dryly, "we're incredible, all right." He raised his cognac glass. "Here's to us, damn it."

John McKinna

Everyone toasted and drank.

"Who," Donovan inquired mildly, setting his snifter down, "is the Black Lyre?"

Churchill's sharp eyes flicked over to Menzies and Judson.

"Let me guess," the OSS general continued. "Juttner?"

The three Englishmen were silent.

"Canaris?"

No answer.

"Someone I'm not aware of, then," Donovan said, shrugging. "I thought all of us in OSS, SOE, and MI-6 trusted each other. We're in this fight together. . . . Aren't we?"

Churchill harrumphed again, then began to cut the end of another cigar. "Point well taken, General Donovan," he said. He stuck the cigar between his lips, fired it up, and settled back with his cognac glass. "Admiral Wilhelm Canaris, as you well know, is the head of Abwehr. He is also an old-school German patriot who despises the Nazis—in particular Hitler and Himmler. For years now he has been trying to effect political change in Germany while retaining his position of power within the regime—not an easy trick when you're dealing with Nazis. But he has managed this delicate balancing act successfully so far

"Canaris is also the head of the Schwarze Kappel. Do you know the translation?"

" 'Black Orchestra,' " Donovan replied without hesitation.

Churchill nodded through a fog of cigar smoke. "Correct, General. The Black Orchestra. It is a code name for the high-level German opposition to Hitler and the Nazi regime. The Black Orchestra includes in its membership some of the most important men in Germany. Under Canaris's leadership, they have been trying and continue to try to destabilize the Nazi regime without having the country they love collapse with it into a smoking ruin."

372

"They'd better hurry up," Donovan remarked.

"Yes, they had," Churchill went on. "But with respect to the Black Lyre: that is a code name we came up with to identify specific communications between Juttner, Canaris, and the men in this office. A conspiracy ring within a larger conspiracy ring, if you like. The Black Lyre is an instrument that plays in the Black Orchestra—and we are all part of it."

"Evocative," Donovan said. "I like the name."

"It's apropos, isn't it?" Churchill replied. "Look at it, General Donovan. What do we do? We deceive, we manipulate, we mislead, we connive. We prowl like thieves and strike without warning out of the darkness. We endeavor to create confusion and misdirection at every turn. We set up puppets and dance them across the stage, and for this we use friend and foe alike, if it will further our aims.

"In wartime, Truth is so precious that She should always be attended by a bodyguard of lies. With that as our premise, every last one of us, out of necessity, is a black liar."

Donovan smiled slowly. "A black liar. By God, Mr. Prime Minister, I do believe I am. *Mea culpa*, and no excuse submitted." He raised his snifter. "And your remark about Truth needing to be attended by a bodyguard of lies—a memorable turn of phrase. You should use it in one of your speeches."

Churchill raised his own glass. "Why, thank you, General," he said in his bulldog growl of a voice. "I do believe I shall."

Epilogue

You could smell summer in the air, even in the grim inner courtyard of a gray-walled prison. And overhead, feathery white clouds were scudding across a clear blue sky. . . . The kind of fast-moving clouds that were harbingers of fair winds and fine sailing on the Adriatic Sea south of Trieste.

It had been nearly a month since the Allied invasion of Normandy. The Americans, British, and Canadians had secured their beachheads, moved inland, and were battling their way through France with multiple supply lines pumping munitions, machinery, and fuel to their spearhead units in a ceaseless flow. Not even Rommel could stop them now.

The SS Hauptsturmfuehrer was reading something. Something to do with charges. Throckmorton caught fragments of it, though he wasn't really paying attention.

". . . Treasonous incompetence . . . criminal irresponsibility . . ."

He coughed wetly—it was truly painful now—turned his head, and spat on the gray flagstones of the courtyard.

". . . Betrayal of trust . . . failure to follow established tactical doctrines . . ."

Throckmorton put a cigarette into his mouth and

calmly lit it with a wooden match. His prized jeweled Dunhill he'd given to Walter Merritt months earlier.

". . . Resulting in the virtual nullification of the SS Division Handschar as an effective fighting force . . ."

He inhaled the cigarette smoke deeply. Funny that it didn't hurt his chest the way coughing or panting did. It was still a pleasant enough diversion, even if it had probably contributed to the terminal lung cancer he'd been diagnosed with a year earlier. Thank God he hadn't had to walk over any more mountains during his four-month tenure as division commander of Handschar. A Standartenfuehrer always got to ride, even when he was retreating.

There was a loud CLACK-*CLACK* of Mauser rifle bolts.

Throckmorton drew on his cigarette again, looking up at the clouds riding the wind far overhead. It had been a good life, if a short one. And he was lucky: not many men were given the opportunity to choose their own exit, and accomplish something meaningful in the process.

He coughed again, grimaced, and spat, tasting blood. Yes, it had been a good life. But now it was time to go.

Captain Duncan Throckmorton flicked his cigarette away, clasped his hands behind his back, and picked one perfect cloud to watch sail across the sky.

He was thinking again of the sea off Trieste.

"What's that?"

Magda jumped down off the sun-warmed rock of the little outcropping, ducked behind a stunted olive tree, and dropped to her haunches with coltish energy in front of David Weiss, who was sitting in the grass, dashing water from a canteen on his sun-bronzed face.

"The Bosporus," he said. "It's a narrow strait that's part of the waterway connecting the Mediterranean and Black Seas. Istanbul is at the southwestern end of it." He held out the canteen. "Here. Drink some."

Magda shook her head, her mane of dark hair flailing around her shoulders. "I'm not thirsty."

"You soon will be. Drink."

The girl stuck out her lower lip, then took the canteen and tipped it up. *She is nearly as brown as the bark of the tree I'm sitting beside,* Weiss thought. Months of moving slowly through mountainous country, living off the land and avoiding settlements and soldiers of every kind—for in Nazi-controlled Macedonia and Greece and Bulgaria they were invariably hostile—had made both of them lean and fit, and almost feral in their survival instincts.

"Do we have to cross it?" Magda asked, her dark eyes flashing. She tossed him the canteen and shifted the strap of the Schmeisser machine pistol she carried over one shoulder. She'd flourished on the long journey despite its many privations, turned from frightened child into confident, capable young woman. Weiss had noticed this happening and felt justified in taking some credit for it.

"Yes, Magda," he said. "We have to cross it. Then we have to get through the rest of Turkey—past Ankara, Tarsus, and Antioch—to reach Syria."

"Are there Germans in Turkey?" Magda inquired, looking deeply into his eyes, as she always did.

"There are Germans everywhere," Weiss grunted, leaning back on one elbow. "Including Turkey."

"Mmm. Well, we'll have to be careful." *She doesn't sound too concerned,* Weiss thought.

She moved up beside him and rolled onto her back in the grass. "Do you know what day it is today?"

Weiss put a hand over his eyes to block the sun. "No idea. How about Wednesday?"

Magda dug her elbow into his ribs, giggling. "Stupid man. It's my birthday."

Weiss removed his hand from his eyes and looked at her. "Really?"

"Really."

"How old are you?"

She propped herself up on one arm, letting the machine pistol slide to the ground. "You have to guess," she said mischievously, tickling his jaw with a piece of grass.

He slapped the grass away and scratched his face. "Seven," he said.

She pulled his hair. "No! Guess again."

"Umm . . . eight, then."

Magda lunged onto his chest, forcing him back into the grass and pinning him there. He let her, laughing.

"I'm sixteen today," she said, smiling down at him.

He smiled back. "Happy birthday, Magda," he replied.

She looked at him for a long moment, then sat back and looked out toward the strait of blue water in the hazy distance.

"What do we do after we get to Syria?" she asked.

"We go through it," Weiss told her, sitting up and brushing loose grass off his collar.

"Is it far? Through Turkey, I mean."

"Yes. Very far."

"That's all right," Magda said. She thought for a moment. "And Syria? Is it far, too?"

David Weiss looked at her and nodded. "Very far, Magda. A long way."

"But then we're in Palestine?"

He nodded again, this time with an encouraging smile. "Then we're in Palestine."

She smiled back, her strong white teeth gleaming in her tanned face. Then she rocked onto one knee, picked up her Schmeisser, and got to her feet.

"We'll make it, won't we, David?" she said. It wasn't really a question.

David Weiss picked up his own machine pistol, the canteen, and the small rucksack he always carried, and hoisted himself to his feet beside her.

"Yes, Magda," he said. "We will."

Postscript

"The bomb did not go off, Colonel. The triggering mechanism failed."

"Thank God for sloppy workmanship." The Israeli Defense Force colonel adjusted the Glock automatic in its holster on her hip and looked again at the scared Palestinian boy sitting on the steel bench in the holding cell of the Tel Aviv police substation. "What's that he's got on under his shirt?" she demanded.

"Some kind of medieval chain-mail vest, believe it or not," the young IDF sergeant said. "A museum piece, really." He patted the homemade bomb belt laid out on the table next to him. "We noticed it after we stripped the explosives off him. I thought I'd leave it on so you could have a look."

The colonel walked over to the boy and gently tugged down his shirt. "It's chain mail, all right. And very old." Her eyes narrowed as she looked at the boy's back. "This is interesting: there are three holes in the back of it. Like bullet holes. See where the links are torn?"

The sergeant moved up on the boy's opposite side and examined the holes. "You're right, Colonel. Maybe bullets—although I suppose, from the age of the thing, they could just as easily have been made by spears or lances."

"Mmm." The stern, handsome woman stood back,

folded her arms, and gazed into the child's eyes. "Palestinian ID card?"

"Yes," the sergeant said, holding up the little rectangle of plastic. "This is Jamal Amin Snagi, resident of Ramallah."

"How old?"

"Eleven."

The colonel shook her head. "God."

She sighed, pulled up a chair, reversed it, and sat down facing the boy. "Jamal."

The boy glanced fearfully at her, taking in the olive drab military fatigues, the hard lines of the face beneath the gray-streaked black hair, and the strong brown forearms that were folded on the back of the chair.

"Who sent you to blow yourself up on the bus?"

The boy was too young and frightened not to answer. "G-grandfather Mustapha," he stammered.

The young sergeant scribbled in his notebook.

"Did he give you the bomb?" the woman went on. "Did he help you put it on?"

"Y-yes," the boy said. "Grandfather Mustapha and . . . some other men . . ."

"Who were they?" the IDF sergeant barked, stepping forward.

The boy cowered back on the table, clamping his lips together. The colonel shot the sergeant a quick glare and raised a hand to make him back off. Then she waited until the boy had stopped trembling before speaking to him again.

"Jamal. Do you know why your grandfather and his . . . friends . . . told you to blow up the bus full of innocent Israelis?"

The boy nodded, his wide dark eyes flicking from side to side. "Y-yes."

"Why?"

"Be-because!" the child blurted. "Grandfather Mustapha says that all Jews hate all Muslims, and we are Muslims, and we should not allow . . . allow people who hate us to—to tell us where . . . and how . . .

we can live in—in our own land. . . ." His outburst trailed off.

The IDF colonel sighed quietly again, then leaned toward the boy. "Jamal. Do you want to know something interesting?" The boy looked at her without answering, but nodded. "My name is Magda Weiss. My father, David, was a Jew. But my mother, Magda, for whom I was named, was a Muslim orphan girl from Yugoslavia. Her full name was Magda Noor Mahmutović. She was adopted and raised by an old Serbian couple who took her in out of kindness after her parents died. The old couple were Christians."

The IDF colonel paused. It was a lot of information for a frightened eleven-year-old to absorb.

But the Palestinian boy was intelligent, and surprised her with his comment: "So . . . you are . . . both a Muslim and a Jew?"

Colonel Magda Weiss nodded. "Yes, I am. Half and half."

Jamal's smooth young brow furrowed. "But you wear the uniform of a soldier of Israel."

"I live with my father's people," she explained. "But inside, I am still half Jewish and half Muslim."

Jamal considered this, chewing his lip, then said, "I think that would be very confusing."

Magda Weiss brushed a hank of salt-and-pepper hair off her forehead and smiled. "Sometimes it is."

She sat in silence, gazing at Jamal Amin Snagi. He, in turn, gazed back at her, reexamining her tanned face, hard but kind, and sinewy forearms and military fatigues and the big automatic pistol holstered on her hip. After a few minutes he spoke again:

"We can talk some more, if you'd like."

Magda lifted an eyebrow. "Oh? You don't mind?"

Jamal shook his head. "No. I like talking to you."

Magda drew a deep breath, resettled herself on the chair, and smiled once more at the Palestinian boy.

"I think that's a good idea, Jamal," she said. "Let's talk."

*"In wartime, Truth is so precious
that She should always be attended
by a bodyguard of lies."*

—Winston Churchill
Teheran Conference, World War II

Notes

Chapter 1

1. This is a short extract, slightly modified for clarity, from an actual letter written by Palestinian Arab leader Haj Amin al-Husseini, the Grand Mufti of Jerusalem, to Adolph Hitler, leader of Nazi Germany, on January 20, 1941. For the complete, unaltered text of this historical document, see appendix B of Zvi Elpeleg's *The Grand Mufti: Haj Amin Al-Hussaini, Founder of the Palestinian National Movement* (London: Frank Cass & Co. Ltd., 1993).

2. Italy surrendered to the Allies in September 1943, barely six weeks after dictator Benito Mussolini had been removed from power by his own Fascist party. Under the new premier, Marshall Pietro Badoglio, Italy declared war on Germany—its former Axis partner—in October 1943. In response, German military forces proceeded to occupy the country, seizing Rome and other key cities.

3. Abwehr was the military intelligence branch of the regular German army, the Wehrmacht. Although controlled by Germany's political leadership, Hitler and his Nazi Party, the Wehrmacht was not a Nazi entity. The SS and its constituent intelligence and security branches, the SD and Gestapo, on the other hand, were entirely Nazi creations, devoted to the Fuehrer and the party rather than to the German nation as a whole.

4. This is a direct quote attributed to al-Husseini. *(Elpeleg.)*

Chapter 2

1. The Special Operations Executive, or SOE, was the British espionage and sabotage organization authorized by Churchill and given by him the famous directive, "Set Europe ablaze." It was headed by General Sir Colin McVean Gubbins. Its American counterpart was the Office of Strategic Services, or OSS—the WWII precursor to the CIA—headed by General William "Wild Bill" Donovan.

2. The Jedburgh teams were joint American-British-French commando units trained in clandestine warfare and intended for insertion by parachute into occupied France in advance of the D-day invasion, where their mission would be to link up with the French Resistance and disrupt the German military infrastructure in every way possible.

Chapter 3

1. A static line is a length of heavy webbing used to automatically deploy a parachute. One end is attached to the top end of the packed parachute canopy, the other to an anchor point inside the aircraft. As the jumper or cargo package falls away from the aircraft, the static line pulls the canopy out of the pack tray, then breaks free as the parachute begins to fill with air.

Chapter 6

1. German paratrooper.

2. The German invasion of the British-held island of Crete in the eastern Mediterranean Sea, in May 1941, was the first large airborne operation of World War II. Deployed and supplied entirely by air, a force of nearly twenty thousand Fallschirmjager and glider troops were able to wrest control of Crete from twenty-seven thousand British troops, mostly tough Australians and New Zealanders, who initially fought the invaders to a standstill. Lack of effective resupply eventually handicapped the British, and they were forced to withdraw from the island. But the

victory cost the Germans dearly: sixteen thousand men were killed or wounded, and two hundred out of five hundred transport aircraft were lost. Hitler was so appalled by the casualty figures that he prohibited all such operations in the future. It was the last major use of airborne troops by Germany during World War II.

3. Literally, "assault rifle." The Sturmgewehr was the world's first true assault rifle, and the source of the term. All well-known assault rifles of the last half of the twentieth century—the AK-47, the M-16, the Galil—are line descendants of the Sturmgewehr.

Chapter 9

1. Dr. Ivan Ribar was a distinguished Yugoslav intellectual and politician who became a key member of the Communist Partisans during World War II. Both his sons, Ivo-Lola Ribar and Jurica Ribar, were Partisan commanders who were killed while fighting the Nazi invaders. All are revered as heroes of the long and successful Yugoslav Communist resistance to the Third Reich and its allies.

Chapter 10

1. A Tyrolean traverse is a horizontal rope stretched tightly over a gap, to which climbers and equipment can then be secured by carabiner or block and pulled across.

Chapter 13

1. The enlarged Kingdom of Croatia, originally formed with the help of the invading Axis Italians under Mussolini, was ruled by one of the most murderous racists in European history, Ante Pavelić. Pavelić was the leader of the Ustashe—a band of Croatian fascists whose goal was to eliminate the Serbian minority in Croatia, along with all its Jews and Gypsies. Perversely, the Ustashe had no qualms about murdering Muslims as well, even though both Croatian Catholics and Muslims served in various (racially and ethnically separate) German combat units.

Chapter 14

1. A prusik hitch is a method of securing a thin line to a thicker one with a knot that binds when tightened and slides when loosened, enabling a climber to ascend a vertical rope without supporting his/her weight by main strength alone.

Chapter 22

1. Pre-WWII British Prime Minister Neville Chamberlain has gone down in history, perhaps not quite fairly, as the man who was soft on Hitler during Germany's ever increasing aggression in the late 1930s. Famously, he favored a policy of appeasement rather than confrontation, which enabled the Nazi dictator to retain newly annexed territories such as the Sudetenland and Czechoslovakia and to continue to build the Third Reich's war machine. The then-unpopular Winston Churchill's trenchant comment was that it was utter folly to try to appease a ruthless dictator. He was right.

Waffen-SS/U.S. Army
Rank Conversion Chart

Schütze	Private
Sturmmann	Private First Class
Rottenfuehrer	Corporal
Unterscharfuehrer	Sergeant
Scharfuehrer	Staff Sergeant
Hauptscharfuehrer	Master Sergeant
Stabsscharfuehrer	Sergeant Major
Untersturmfuehrer	Second Lieutenant
Obersturmfuehrer	First Lieutenant
Hauptsturmfuehrer	Captain
Sturmbannfuehrer	Major
Obersturmbannfuehrer	Lieutenant Colonel
Standartenfuehrer	Colonel
Brigadefuehrer	Brigadier General
Gruppenfuehrer	Major General
Obergruppenfuehrer	Lieutenant General
Oberst-Gruppenfuehrer	General
Reichsfuehrer-SS	(No equivalent; title reserved for SS head Heinrich Himmler)

About the Author

Before his untimely death in 2016 **John McKinna** was an Underwater Technical Supervisor and Operations Manager, responsible for overseeing upkeep of the main structure and support systems of the Key Largo Undersea Park home of Jules' Undersea Lodge. A former offshore commercial diver of twenty years' experience, he came on the Jules'/KLUP team as an adjunct to his primary line of work, that of internationally-known novelist and local musician. Like his wife Teresa, he was an avid free-diver, spearfisherman, lobster hunter, and cruising sailor. RIP John McKinna.

Coming Soon!

CHAINS OF GOLD
John McKinna

**Greed, drug trafficking,
kidnapping and murder...**

The Spanish Galleon Arista sank in 1539 due to
a storm and the heavy weight of its cargo. The
ship had been carrying Aztec golden treasure...

When the treasure proved to be illusive, the job
became treacherous with twists and turns...

**For more information
visit:** www.SpeakingVolumes.us

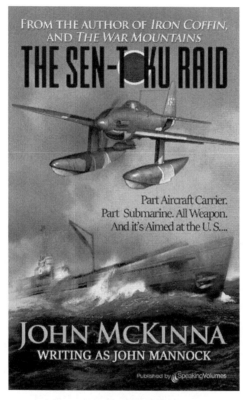

On Sale Now!

IN THE JAWS OF LIFE . . .
AND DEATH

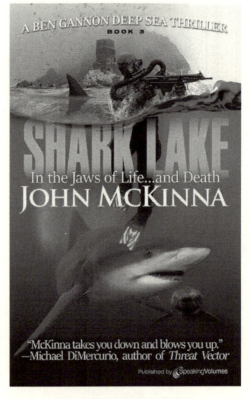

For more information
visit: www.SpeakingVolumes.us

On Sale Now!

WHERE DANGER LURKS...

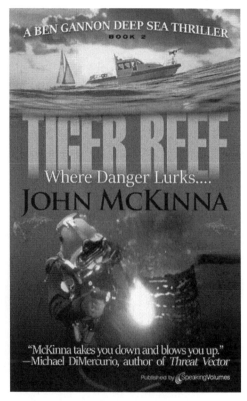

For more information
visit: www.SpeakingVolumes.us

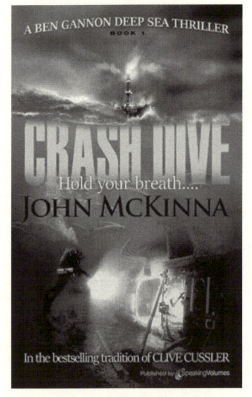

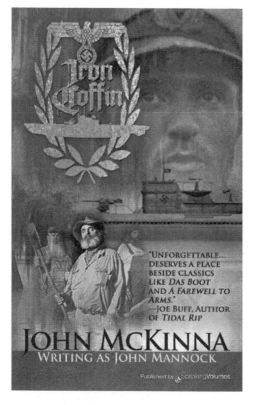

On Sale Now!

"A one-of-a-kind underwater thriller.
The sinister beauty of the underwater world
is painted in hues that only an avid diver and
inspired novelist could capture."
—Dr. John Clarke,
Navy experimental dive researcher

**For more information
visit:** <u>www.SpeakingVolumes.us</u>

On Sale Now!

EDGAR AWARD WINNING AUTHOR

JOHN BALL

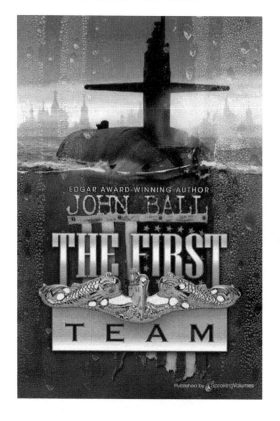

**For more information
visit:**

Sign up for free and bargain books

Join the Speaking Volumes mailing list

Text

ILOVEBOOKS

to 22828 **to get started.**

Made in the USA
Middletown, DE
17 May 2024

54501938R00241